WASP'S NEST

WASP'S NEST

❖ A JELF ACADEMY NOVEL ❖

JENNA E. FAAS

SPARKS AND CINDERS PUBLISHING
PITTSBURGH

Jenna E. Faas asserts the moral right to be identified as the author of this work.
First U.S. Edition
Cover art and formatting by Damonza

ISBN 978-1-956207-11-8 (hardback)
ISBN 978-1-956207-10-1 (paperback)
ISBN 978-1-956207-09-5 (ebook)

WASP'S NEST

*Kayla, my best friend and chosen sister,
you've been one of my biggest supporters despite
the fact that you don't read. LOL
LYLAS forever!*

OTHER BOOKS BY JENNA E. FAAS

Pixie Dust
Dragon Scales
Secret Siren
Unicorn Blessed (coming 2025)

1

A Slow, Hot Summer

TIME WAS MY enemy. It was either moving too fast or too slow. Time never cared whether you were happy or sad. The sad moments seemed to last forever, and the happy ones were always too short. Time was a malevolent keeper that never doled out enough of itself to the people who meant the most to me. I had been robbed of time with my mother, father, and Robert. Time had cackled like an evil witch when it had taken all three of them from me. Now, all I could do was hope, be patient, and allow time to continue to plod along, although my patience was running thin.

I'd been at the manor for almost three months. I spent the sweltering summer days doing everything Marie and her family asked of me. Breaking my back was nothing new, but I'd been hoping there would be a short refrain. At the end of my third year at the Jelf Academy, I discovered a clue about the location of Robert's family. Mr. Withermyer promised he would take me to investigate, but he also asked me to be patient. Every day, I was beginning to lose hope. Soon, Dr. Tweedle would arrive to take me back to the Jelf Academy. Perhaps Mr. Withermyer decided not to come at all.

If Mr. Withermyer didn't arrive soon, it wouldn't be the first time I was disappointed, and I was sure it wouldn't be the last either. I was no stranger to heartbreak. My life had been a series of calamities since I'd been a baby.

My hand subconsciously went to Robert's ring, which I always wore beneath my blouse. Before Robert passed, he'd given me his family ring, the only token from his past. Stamped into the metal was Robert's family crest: a lion in the center of the design. It was by chance that Lena saw the crest, which may have triggered a memory. Now, it seemed the answers to finding Robert's family might lie in a village called Peach Glen.

I sighed as I changed the sheets on Marie's bed. It was silly of me to hope so much. Lena Rodriguez wasn't the most reliable person when it came to recalling things from her memory. Her past had been as tragic as mine. The W.A.S.P. had captured Lena, and somehow she had managed to escape. Unfortunately, she couldn't remember anything about her past. Lena didn't know how she had gotten away, had no memory of what had happened to her, and didn't recognize anyone she'd known. Strangely enough, she only managed to remember the lessons she had learned at the Jelf Academy.

I fluffed the pillows on Marie's four-poster bed and ensured the green comforter was straight. I had spent all morning washing clothes and bedding, and they had finally air-dried by late after-noon. I had to remake all the beds. Now that Marie's room was finished, I could move on to Emily's room. With a bit of help from my magic, I lifted the heavy basket. Slowly, I made my way down the hallway since I couldn't see over the mounds of linens. When I reached Emily's door, I put the basket down to open the door. Emily and her mother were in the sitting room having tea, so I didn't have to worry about knocking. Mr. Doyle and Preston were out hunting, and I was glad I wouldn't have to run into them either.

I carried the laundry into the room and began sorting through it to find Emily's sheet set. Her sheets were white, but they had red roses stitched in the corners of the pillowcases and the top of the sheets. When I found them, I laid them on a chair while I looked for the sheet that covered the mattress. After finding it, I pulled it from the basket and fanned it over the bed. The tiny breeze from the motion passed over my hot face, and I sighed. The manor was always unbearably hot at this time of year. There was never a good way to escape the oppressive heat.

I was almost finished in Emily's room when Emily herself strolled in, brandishing her hand-held fan and holding a cool glass of water in the other hand.

"What are you doing here?" she snapped, her eyes taking me in.

I tried to keep the expression off my face as I continued to stuff one of her pillows into the pillowcase. Over the years, I discovered Emily wasn't the most intelligent person. What could she possibly think I was doing when she'd caught me with her pillows in my hands? I cleared my throat and stated what I had thought was obvious.

"Your linens have finished drying, and I'm putting them back on your bed," I replied, pulling the sheet up to the pillows.

"Are these Drake's linens?" Emily questioned, indicating the laundry basket at her feet.

"Yes, ma'am,' I answered, coming around the bed to finish straightening the sheets.

Suddenly, Emily upended her water glass onto the freshly dried linens. "Now Drake will have to sleep in here tonight," she said with a shrug.

"Your brother's bed sheets were in that basket, too," I replied, scooping the basket off the floor. "I hope you were anticipating him sleeping in here as well," I said before quickly leaving the room. I needed to get the sheets back on the clothesline, and hopefully, they would dry before nightfall.

Luckily, Emily didn't follow me to reprimand me for my

comment. Mr. Doyle's room was across the hall from Emily's, and it didn't seem like they shared a bed often. Most of the time, Mr. Doyle was in the city for his job or running off to meetings. His job kept him away, and I knew it bothered Emily. The Doyle mansion wasn't finished being rebuilt yet, so the happy couple still lived at the manor. Even though Emily complained about how long it was taking to rebuild, the wait was mostly her fault. She always demanded the best, and Mr. Doyle requested that most of the materials be shipped from Europe. He also hired the best architects he could find. In his free time, he was either discussing blueprints or hunting.

Carefully, I walked down the slope toward the barn. The clothesline was on the left side, and I watched my step as I made my way toward it. I didn't need to fall, spill the sheets onto the lawn, and then have to wash out grass stains. My body felt drenched in sweat by the time I put the basket down. I was grateful for the slight breeze as the sun bore down on my back. I shifted my blonde braid to my shoulder and grabbed the clothes pins. For the second time today, I hung the sheets on the line and prayed they wouldn't take too long to dry.

Leaving the laundry basket next to the clothesline post, I hiked back to the house. I had a few rooms I needed to clean before it would be time to help prepare dinner. As soon as I entered the house, I walked toward the kitchen closet. All the brooms, mops, and cleaning supplies were organized inside, and I collected what I needed. Then, I shuddered as I walked down the hallway in the direction of Preston's trophy room.

A few months ago, Marie had allotted the room next to the library to become Preston's hunting room. Whenever Preston killed an animal, he had the animal preserved and stuffed so he could display his accomplishments. I hated cleaning in there. Even though I had tried to hide my revulsion, Preston must have sensed it. Since the room had been furnished, he requested it to be cleaned at least once a week, specifically by me.

With a deep breath, I pushed open the door to the trophy room. The same chill crept up my spine, and it was hard to believe this room used to be my playroom when my father was alive. I could still remember some of the stories he'd tell while we were in here. Most of them were about my mother and how alike we were. I treasured those memories the most. My father loved my mother, and I was sure he had mourned her loss daily. This playroom had been one of our special places. Now, it felt like the glass eyes of the animals were staring right at me.

Another shiver passed through me as I continued into the room. The windows let in the sunlight, but the room had a dark and eerie aura. I placed the bucket of soapy water down and held onto my dust rag. On one shelf, Preston had put the smaller animals. The lifeless eyes of rabbits, groundhogs, and foxes stared blankly at me as I dusted off their stands. Preston had even added engraved plaques with the dates he made the kill. His interest and excitement in death sickened me.

Quickly, I wiped off the dust that was barely there. I never wanted to linger in this room and wished I could use a *quick complete charm* to clean it. Unfortunately, using magic during the day would be impossible, and even at night, I refrained. Since Mr. Doyle had brought some of his servants to live with us, I never knew who could be watching. The W.A.S.P. was gaining information about pixies, and I didn't want to risk my life.

Once the smaller animals had been thoroughly dusted, I moved on to the bigger ones. There weren't many of those, and the room had a lot of empty space, but I was sure Preston had plans for filling it with his morbid obsession. Carefully, I ran my rag over the body of a doe. I shuddered, touching the rag to the marble eyes and the plaque at its base. Preston had also killed a stag, but he only kept the head. It was mounted on the wall behind the doe.

There were only two other larger animals in the room: a small mountain lion and a coyote. I hurriedly brushed over those and went to get the mop.

I began in the furthest corner, mopping my way toward the door. Sweat dripped down my brow, and I wiped my forehead with the back of my hand. The air was stifling, and I couldn't wait to escape this oppressive room. I paused for a moment and lifted my braid off my neck. Then, with my other hand, I fanned the air and conjured a tiny bit of movement that brought me a few seconds of relief. As a pixie, I could increase or lower my temperature, but that took a lot of my energy. I was sure Marie still had a long list of things for me to do, and I didn't want to drain my body more than necessary.

I was almost finished in the trophy room when I heard the gong of the doorbell echoing through the house. Slowly, I leaned the mop against the wall. Who could possibly be coming to visit? Marie hadn't informed me anyone would be stopping by. I was just about to enter the hallway when I heard the sound of the front door opening. I paused, listening as I heard Marie's voice addressing whoever was on the doorstep. Her voice sounded muffled, and I couldn't understand what she was saying. What sounded like a man's voice answered whatever she had asked. I was about to pick up the mop again when Marie's voice sounded louder in the hallway.

"Jane, where are you?" she screamed. "Jane!"

My skin crawled at the sound of her voice, and I quickly opened the door. The hallway seemed dim, and I could only make out two silhouetted figures at the end of the hall. I picked up my pace, and Marie turned toward the sound of my footfalls. Her body slightly blocked the visitor as she stepped toward me.

"Jane, there is a gentleman here who claims he knows you. Do you care to explain?" Marie asked in a clipped voice.

Finally, she moved enough to the side so I could see the man standing just inside the door. My breath caught in my throat, and my heartbeat sped up momentarily as I stepped closer. His bright green eyes found my face, and a slight trace of a smile grazed his lips.

After another breath, I was able to find my voice. "Good afternoon, Mr. Withermyer."

2

MR. WITHERMYER'S ARRIVAL

"GOOD AFTERNOON, MISS Fitzgerald," Mr. Withermyer replied.

He wore a light gray suit with polished silver buttons and a white button-down shirt. His black tie matched his shiny black shoes. Mr. Withermyer's dark hair was neatly trimmed, and I noticed he had grown a short beard and mustache. He looked so polished and clean that I was instantly aware of how dirty I must look. I was sure my clothes were disheveled, and my hair was probably wildly coming out of my braid. I could feel my already colored cheeks turning even redder.

"Jane, do you care to explain?" Marie asked again in an annoyed voice, which pulled me from my daze of seeing Mr. Withermyer standing in my childhood home.

"Mr. Withermyer is a teacher at my school," I replied.

"Okay. What is he doing here? I didn't think you started back to that school for another week or so. Besides, where is the old gentleman, Dr. Twaddle, or whatever he calls himself?" Marie snapped at me.

Emily, hearing the commotion, came out of the sitting room. She took one look at Mr. Withermyer and put on the sweetest smile.

"Mother, who is this gentleman?" Emily asked in her fake voice as she crossed the front entry hall. She fanned herself with her paper fan, and her smile stretched across her face. I knew why she was behaving in such a way. It wasn't hard to notice how handsome Mr. Withermyer was.

I tried to keep my face neutral as Mr. Withermyer glanced at Emily. His gaze quickly passed over her before he turned back to Marie. "As I was saying, ma'am, I came to retrieve Miss Fitzgerald. Unfortunately, Dr. Tweedle," he said, emphasizing the name pronunciation, "was detained and sent me instead."

When Emily realized Mr. Withermyer was here for me, her face fell slightly.

"Aren't you here too early? Jane doesn't leave until the end of the month," Marie questioned. Her hard-gray eyes were full of suspicion.

"I was just getting to that. Miss Fitzgerald is one of our brightest students. At the Jelf Academy, we like to expand on the experiences of our more qualified students by allowing them to excel in other types of lessons. We have an event coming up this week and the next where our top students gain even more experience by putting their etiquette lessons to use. Dr. Tweedle has many dignified associates coming to the school, and we wouldn't want to miss the opportunity to show off one of our star pupils," Mr. Withermyer finished.

"So, Jane would be gone for two weeks?" Marie asked.

"Yes, ma'am, and then she'll begin regular lessons the week after. As always, we would need the weekend to collect her school supplies. She'll return to her regular schedule in two weeks." Mr. Withermyer explained.

"Two weeks for an event seems excessive. So, she will begin

regular classes?" Marie responded. I could almost see her calculating how many days it would be without having me at the manor.

"Yes, ma'am. We wouldn't take Miss Fitzgerald away from you if it wasn't absolutely necessary for her education. We wouldn't want you to be disappointed by Miss Fitzgerald when she serves your guests. It would be best for her to learn as much as possible while at our academy."

I could almost see the cogs in Marie's head turning. I knew she was wondering if letting me go would benefit her or not. Mr. Withermyer's glance strayed to me for a moment, and I tried patting down my unruly hair. It was a moment before Marie finally answered.

"I suppose Jane can go, though I'm not happy about the loss of her time here," Marie replied, turning to look at me. "Just know your time away will cost you, so be aware that when you return in three weeks, you'll have a long list of tasks to complete."

"Thank you, ma'am," Mr. Withermyer said with a slight bow. "I promise you won't regret having Miss Fitzgerald attend our event."

"How many years does she have left? Her training seems to be taking a long time," Marie huffed.

"Miss Fitzgerald has two more years. I know it seems like a while, but I'm sure you'll be pleased with the results," Mr. Withermyer stated, and he even allowed a small smile in Marie's direction. "Well, if we have your permission, Miss Fitzgerald should probably collect her belongings."

Marie and Emily gave me a nasty glare. "I suppose. Run along, Jane. You heard the gentleman's request," Marie bit out, gesturing toward the stairs.

I bowed to Marie, making my way past her toward the stairs. I couldn't believe she was allowing me to leave. I was sure she was going to put up a fight. Trying not to look too eager, I climbed the stairs at an average pace and walked down the hall toward the attic stairs. With no one around to witness, I rushed up the stairs two at a time and flung open the door to the attic. The heat of the day seemed even more oppressive up here, and I took a moment to catch my breath. My school supplies were hidden on a sheet-covered vanity set. I collected my books and pixie dust case and then stuffed them into the bag Dr. Tweedle had bought for me at the beginning of my first year. When I'd finished, I pulled out my other hidden suitcase containing my school uniforms and all the fantastic pixie clothes I'd been given. If Marie ever found out my small bag was filled with beautiful possessions, she would take it away from me.

When I packed everything, I paused to look into a handheld mirror. I was embarrassed by my reflection. Dirt and sweat streaked my face, just as I'd assumed, and my hair looked frizzy and wild. My brown servant's dress also looked filthy, and I blushed, knowing Mr. Withermyer had seen me like this. No one besides Dr. Tweedle really understood what my life was like here. I hadn't thought about Mr. Withermyer finding me in this condition when he promised to come for me. It was foolish not to realize the state I'd be in when all I could think about was his arrival. Now, I felt slightly ashamed another person had to discover what I was subjected to when I came back to live at the manor. Would he pity me now?

Quickly, I splashed water on my face to remove some of the dirt and sweat. Again, I smoothed down fly-away hair that had escaped my braid. It would take too long to fix it properly, and I didn't want to keep Mr. Withermyer waiting. Marie had agreed to my leaving, and I didn't need her to change her mind. I gripped both bags, one in each hand, and left the attic without another glance.

I heard Emily's voice as I headed to the entrance hall.

"So, what did you say you taught at Jane's school?" Emily cooed. She followed her question with a demur giggle that made me sick. I couldn't believe she was talking to Mr. Withermyer in such a way.

"I didn't," he replied, not impolitely.

From the top of the stairs, I could see Mr. Withermyer standing with his arms across his chest. Emily was leaning toward him, and he was trying not to make eye contact with her. Marie stood facing the door. I could tell by her stance that she was annoyed. I quickened my step. Once I escaped from this house, Marie wouldn't be able to pull me back until I returned. We really needed to be on our way.

Mr. Withermyer gazed up at me, and I thought I saw a hint of relief cross his expression. It seemed he wanted to be on our way as much as I did.

"Let me help with your bags," Mr. Withermyer declared, brushing past Emily and Marie to meet me halfway on the staircase.

He effortlessly lifted both bags, and I mumbled my thanks as we continued down the stairs. Emily rolled her eyes and stalked back to the sitting room. Her attempt to capture Mr. Withermyer's attention hadn't gone as planned. I could tell she was irritated that he had moved away from her to help me with my suitcases.

"Good day, madam,' Mr. Withermyer said, addressing Marie as he managed to open the front door.

Marie just nodded in his direction, and then her steel gray eyes glowered at me.

"Enjoy this little event, whatever it is, because I can guarantee you'll have many sleepless nights when you return. You had better show improvement in your manners and serving techniques. If you don't, I might see to it that you'll never see your precious academy again," Marie muttered.

Her stare sent icy chills down my spine. I had gotten away with the guise of an etiquette school for three years, but was Marie becoming suspicious?

I bowed to her as I stepped out the door of the manor. Her eyes stayed on me in warning even as I reached to pull the door closed. I followed Mr. Withermyer down the steps to his simple carriage. I didn't want to look too excited in case Marie was watching out the window. Mr. Withermyer placed my bags in the back of the carriage, which wasn't covered like the one Dr. Tweedle usually brought. Instead, it was wide open.

Carefully, Mr. Withermyer took my hand to help me climb onboard. His hand felt warm and slightly dampened with sweat. Instead of sitting in the back with the bags, I sat in the front. Mr. Withermyer came around and climbed up beside me. His knee bumped mine, and I scooted over to allow more room. Only a large brown Clydesdale was hitched to the carriage, and when Mr. Withermyer flicked the reigns, the horse began moving. Neither of us spoke as the horse trotted down the manor's drive.

It wasn't until we passed beyond the manor's front gates that I allowed myself a sigh of relief. Mr. Withermyer steered the Clydesdale onto the road, and a few minutes passed until he finally spoke.

"I was afraid I wouldn't be able to get you out of there," he said, tugging at the collar of his shirt.

"I have that fear every time Dr. Tweedle comes to retrieve me," I admitted.

"I don't know what I would've done if she had said no. My backup plan wouldn't have been too promising."

"What did the plan consist of?" I asked.

"I don't know. Grabbing you and running, I suppose," Mr. Withermyer said with a chuckle, his green eyes glancing in my direction mischievously.

I couldn't help but laugh at his ridiculous plan B. I couldn't help but imagine it for a moment. What would Marie have done if it had happened? Mr. Withermyer smiled at my laughter, but after a few moments, he looked serious again.

"Miss Fitzgerald, I had no idea your family," he began, but I held my hand up to stop him.

"Please, I don't think I could bear it if you pitied me," I said.

"I don't pity you. If anything, I admire you and believe you're a strong woman," he said, his words making me blush. "I'm just stating I didn't understand what your life was like until now."

He released the reigns from his right hand and gently touched my left hand.

"Oh, you couldn't see how wonderful Marie and Emily were? People don't notice how pleasant they can be in your first meeting with them. Usually, it takes a couple of times in their company," I sighed, attempting to be humorous. "I'm sure they kept you entertained while I collected my belongings."

"I wouldn't call it entertaining, but they didn't leave me to stand in silence. Your stepmother didn't believe you'd be bright enough to be a star pupil, and your stepsister kept inching closer to me. They both lacked manners, which I find ironic since they're both so concerned about you having them," Mr. Withermyer said, placing both hands back on the reigns.

"If you believe that of them, then you should've met Preston. He makes Marie and Emily look cultured. He turned sixteen this summer, and he'll still have his childish fits every now and again," I replied.

Mr. Withermyer shook his head in disapproval. Slowly, he steered the horse around a bend in the road and then began leading the horse off on a path into the woods.

"Where are we going? Will we be using a teleportation charm soon?" I asked anxiously. Now that Mr. Withermyer had come for me, I wondered what his plans were.

The horse plodded deeper into the forest before Mr. Withermyer pulled it to a stop. Then he turned to face me.

"I have arranged for us to stay at an inn in Gettysburg. That town isn't far from Peach Glen, maybe an hour or so. I wanted to ask around about the Lyon family before we knocked on their doorstep. I wasn't sure how long our endeavor would take, so I told your stepmother the event was two weeks long," Mr. Withermyer explained.

I nodded in understanding. "I'm very grateful you came," I replied.

"I made a promise, didn't I?" he said, quickly jumping from the carriage. Then, he came around and extended his hand to me.

"Why are we getting down? Aren't we taking the horse and carriage with us?" I asked, puzzled.

"Yes, we are, but I can't allow you to arrive in this state," Mr. Withermyer said, taking my hand.

I blushed again. "I apologize for my appearance. I must confess, I had given up hope of you coming. I figured the next friendly face I'd see would belong to Dr. Tweedle."

"It is I who must apologize, then. I was detained by my other obligations and had no way of sending word to you."

"I understand," I replied, glad he was with me now. "I just didn't anticipate you would find me so disheveled."

"It's nothing a charm can't fix," Mr. Withermyer replied, leading me a few steps away from the carriage. He pulled his pixie dust case from his pocket and riffled through it. Finally, he extracted a vial containing purplish-blue dust layered with orange. "This is a *transfiguring charm*. Now close your eyes and stand still."

I did as Mr. Withermyer said. I could feel the dust settling over me, and it was tempting to open my eyes, but I resisted. A breeze blew around my body, cooling me from the stifling summer air. When the breeze finally subsided, Mr. Withermyer told me I could open my eyes. Glancing down, I was amazed to see my brown servant dress had become a beautiful purple gown that matched my eyes. The sleeves came down to my elbows, and a dark purple sash was tied around my waist. Ruffles cascaded down the length of the skirt, and instead of my beat-up boots, my feet were encased in soft suede slippers. My hands reached up to touch my hair, and I could feel that my braid was back in place. It had been twirled and pinned atop my head. Holding my skirt, I spun around in amazement at the transformation. A laugh escaped my lips in wonderment. Mr. Withermyer grinned at my reaction.

"I assume you find the dress suitable," he asked, standing back to admire his work.

"Yes, it's very lovely. Thank you," I replied, walking back toward the carriage. I reached for the suitcase where I'd packed my handheld mirror. My face was no longer smudged with dirt. It looked freshly cleaned, and my cheeks had a hint of color. My hair looked beautiful. It was braided like a crown around my head, and the loose hairs curled around my face in a flattering way.

"I hope you find my charm satisfactory," Mr. Withermyer said, watching me appraise my reflection.

"Yes, the transfiguration is wonderful! I don't believe I could have styled my hair this way on my own. I assume the *transfiguration charm* works the same way as the *transfiguring objects charm*. How did you ever manage to have such a grasp on women's fashions?" I teased.

"Younger sisters," he replied with a smirk as I replaced the mirror in my bag.

"Oh, I was unaware you had siblings," I responded.

"You never asked," he replied.

In all those months of our private lessons, I'd never thought to inquire about Mr. Withermyer's personal life. It probably would have seemed meddlesome since we hadn't always been on the best terms. Besides, our time together was spent focusing on the topics of my lessons, lessons that could potentially save my life if I were ever confronted with members of the W.A.S.P.

I was about to close my suitcase when a shiny object caught my eye. I reached into the case and pulled out my purple hair clip. Mr. Withermyer had gifted it to me on my birthday to make amends for how horrible he treated me in the past. Carefully, I reached up and pinned the amethyst clip into the braid. From Mr. Withermyer's expression, I could tell he recognized it.

"Now my transformation is perfect," I said with a smile as I closed the suitcase.

Mr. Withermyer climbed back up onto the carriage and reached his hand down to pull me up. I took his hand, and his firm grip pulled me aboard. I sat down beside him and straightened my skirt. When I was situated, Mr. Withermyer searched through his pixie dust case again and pulled out a charm that I was very familiar with. I gripped the side of the carriage in preparation for him to perform the teleportation.

"Are you ready, Miss Fitzgerald?" Mr. Withermyer asked.

I nodded, and when Mr. Withermyer tossed the pixie dust into the air, my world turned black.

3

GETTYSBURG

WHEN THE DARKNESS cleared, I could see we were in a different-looking forest. Mr. Withermyer snapped at the reigns, and our horse began trotting forward. We followed a trail past large boulders haphazardly sticking out of the ground. I had never seen anything like it, and Mr. Withermyer noticed my expression.

"Battles in the American Civil War were fought here. Monuments commemorating the fallen soldiers are around the town. There is a lot of history here; some even say ghosts reside in this area."

I shivered even though the sun was hot against my skin. "Mr. Collyworth lectured about the American Civil War during my first year, though he failed to mention any ghosts," I replied.

"I'm sorry. I didn't mean to frighten you. Ghosts are more of Ms. Crescent's expertise, anyway. I'm sure you'll be learning about contacting the spirit world this year," Mr. Withermyer stated.

"No, you haven't frightened me at all. What harm can the dead do when most of the living appear to be far more dangerous?" I replied bravely.

Robert already haunted my dreams. So what could be more frightening than reliving his death every time I drifted off to sleep at night?

We rode into the small town of Gettysburg, and Mr. Withermyer stopped the carriage outside an inn. Slowly, he lowered himself to the road and came around to help me. I smoothed down my skirt as Mr. Withermyer held the hotel door open. My feet stepped over the threshold, and my eyes took a moment to adjust to the change in lighting. The floor was brown hardwood, and the walls had a light cream wallpaper. The windows were open to let light in and to allow a subtle breeze to blow through the room. A staircase with a polished balustrade was to the left, and behind the front counter, a woman was waiting. Mr. Withermyer walked up to the woman, flashing a charming smile.

"Good afternoon. My name is Mr. Withermyer, and I've made arrangements for my sister and me to stay here," he said, giving me a quick glance.

I tried not to look so surprised at being referred to as his sister. Instead, I managed to smile, looking at the woman behind the counter. Her brown eyes briefly looked me over before scanning the list on the counter in front of her.

"Yes, there you are," the woman replied, and when she spoke, I could see she had a few missing teeth. "My name is Mrs. Hansen. If you need anything during your stay here." She turned toward the rack of keys behind her and found the one she was looking for. "You are in room 110. It's just up the stairs and down the hall on the right." Mrs. Hansen passed the key to Mr. Withermyer.

"Here, dear sister, why don't you head up to the room, and I'll retrieve our baggage from the carriage," Mr. Withermyer said, turning toward me. He pressed the key into my hand and quickly headed for the door. Baffled, I began up the stairs to the second floor.

At the last room on the right, I slipped the key into the lock and turned the knob. The room looked clean, with two twin beds separated by an end table. I walked to the end table and set down the key. Then, I claimed the bed furthest from the door and sat down. The comforter was soft under my fingers, and I ran my hands over it as I waited for Mr. Withermyer.

It wasn't long before he was knocking, and I crossed the room to let him in. His arms were weighed down with suitcases, and I grabbed my smallest bag to help him. Mr. Withermyer set the suitcases down and closed the door behind him.

"Sorry, I should've told you earlier. I hope you don't mind. I know it's not proper for us to share a room, but I didn't want you to be unprotected. We are surrounded by humans here, and if anything were to happen to you, I couldn't live with myself. The only proper thing I could think of would be to pass you off as my sister," Mr. Withermyer explained while I took a seat on the bed.

"Not all humans belong to the W.A.S.P., you know," I replied. "Every pixie I ever met seems to think so, and it's not true."

"Yes, I understand, but there could be humans who don't belong to the W.A.S.P. who have equally poor intentions. If you are uncomfortable, I can see if another room is available. I apologize, Miss Fitzgerald."

He turned toward the door, and my heart clenched. I realized I didn't want to be left alone in this strange place. Mr. Withermyer was a gentleman, and it wasn't as if we were sharing a bed. Since he had been training me in self-defense and defensive charms, we'd become closer, and I felt comfortable around him.

"Please, don't leave," I uttered as he placed his hand on the doorknob. "I don't want to be alone."

Staying at this inn wasn't the same as Irene's at the Jewel Caverns. At the *Leaf and Lily*, I felt safe and protected. I was more comfortable there than I had ever been at the manor. *The Leaf and Lily* felt like my home, and I didn't feel the same about this inn. Mr. Withermyer retreated into the room and sat on the bed across from me.

"I promise to be nothing but a gentleman, Miss Fitzgerald," Mr. Withermyer replied.

"I expected as much, but you'll have to stop calling me Miss Fitzgerald. If we are here under the guise of siblings, people will wonder why you're being so formal toward me and why we have different last names. Calling me Jane should be just fine," I told him.

"Jane," he repeated, my name sounding strange on his tongue. He had never called me anything but Miss Fitzgerald. "Well, in that case, I must insist that you call me Phillip," Mr. Withermyer responded.

"So, Phillip," I said, testing his first name out. "Why don't you tell me about your family so I'll know how to behave like your sister?"

Mr. Withermyer leaned forward and rested his elbows on top of his knees. His green eyes gazed at me intently, and then he began speaking.

"I have two younger sisters. Bridgette is six years younger than I am, and Charlette is ten years my junior. Charlette, we call her Lettie, has such a passion for life, and she's as wild as the wind. She doesn't want to settle down as much as my father wants her to. I think you would get along with her quite nicely, actually," he said with a chuckle. "Bridgette is my serious sister. She's always been responsible, but she had to be. My mother died in childbirth with Charlette, and Bridgette practically raised her."

"I'm so sorry. I didn't know your mother had passed when you were so young," I replied, reaching out to touch the top of his hands.

"Yes, we have more in common than you'd think. Not long after her passing, I started at the Jelf Academy. My father was distraught with my mother's death, and I believe he was relieved when Dr. Tweedle declared me a child prodigy and whisked me away. I was one less child he had to be responsible for," Mr. Withermyer said, sounding slightly bitter.

"I'm sure your father had much on his mind. He probably didn't think of it like that when you were accepted. People don't think clearly, and their actions can be misinterpreted when they lose someone very dear to them. My father grieved my mother's death for several years, and he eventually decided the best thing for me would be to marry Marie. Obviously, it didn't turn out how he had hoped," I replied.

Mr. Withermyer nodded his head. "You never cease to amaze me with how mature and knowledgeable you are for having grown up trapped at that manor," he said with a look of astonishment on his face.

"Sometimes life doesn't allow children to be children. I had to grow up rather quickly after my father died," I stated.

"Yes, I could say the same about Bridgette and me. After my mother died, I was thrust into school, and Bridgette became responsible for Lettie. My father was there, so we weren't entirely alone, but he became a different man after my mother's passing. Charlette seems to be the only one untouched by her death. As I said, she has a zest for life and a recklessness about her. Part of it is because my father spoils her and indulges her whims. At least he isn't resentful of her."

"She probably isn't as untouched by it as you'd like to believe. I know what it's like to long for and wonder about a mother you can never know," I said sadly.

Mr. Withermyer was silent for a moment, and then he spoke. "You are a lot like her, you know."

I knew he was talking about my mother. Since he had started school at the Jelf Academy at an early age, he had known her. They had been friends, and Mr. Withermyer admitted he had loved her, but she hadn't shared his feelings.

"I know you've been told many times you look like her," he continued, "but you're also similar in your actions and thoughts. Each time I'm in your company, I see more of your mother in you."

"Can you tell me more about her? I know so little," I asked.

"Rachel was such a kind and caring person. I've told you before how she accepted me even though I was so young. Though she had known loss, she hadn't allowed it to break her. Her brother, Charles, died of consumption when he was only seven. Her father seemed to be a rigorous man. All she wanted was to please him, but it always seemed impossible. He had favored Charles. I think it broke Rachel's heart, but she rarely talked about it. Your mother was strong and brilliant. She was always cheerful, no matter what she felt inside, and I sensed some turmoil in her life she never showed. I thought I might be able to fix it for her." He shook his head.

"I'm sure you were a good friend to her. I can see how much you cared about her," I replied.

"Yes, and sharing my true feelings with her seems to have cost me her friendship. After she left the Jelf Academy, I never heard from her again."

"I don't think you were alone in her abandonment. I recall Irene telling me a similar story. My mother disappeared from everyone, so I don't think she meant to offend you personally."

"I know that's probably true. Rachel was never spiteful or cruel."

Mr. Withermyer stood up and stretched his arms above his head. He looked a little weary from the day's events and stifled a yawn behind his hand.

"I'm feeling famished. Would you like to accompany me to dinner? I'm sure there are places to eat not far from here," he said, extending his hand to me.

I nodded and placed my hand in his. He pulled me from the bed and grabbed the key from the end table. We walked to the door, and he held it open for me.

"After you, Jane," he said with a smile.

"Thank you, Phillip," I replied, returning a smile of my own.

᎗

Mr. Withermyer laced my hand through his arm as we walked down the street. The sun was just beginning to set, and its rays cast beautiful reds, oranges, and yellows. It was a quaint and quiet little town, and we almost didn't pass anyone on the streets. It wasn't long before we arrived at a restaurant, and Mr. Withermyer held the door open again. The atmosphere of the place was pleasant, and each table was lit with a candle in the center. We were seated relatively quickly at a table with seats across from each other. The waiter handed us each a menu, and I glanced over the selection.

"What were you thinking about having?" Mr. Withermyer asked after a few moments. "You can pick anything you want. I was thinking about the potato soup followed by the roast filet of beef. Have you ever tried Neapolitan ice cream? It's delicious."

"No, I've never tried it," I replied.

"I'll have to order us both a cup after we've finished dinner," he stated.

"I was thinking of having the potato soup as well and then the chicken croquettes," I said, placing the menu on the table.

The waiter returned and took our orders along with the menus. The candle in the middle of the table didn't cast off much light, so I pulled my chair closer to see Mr. Withermyer better. The soft glow illuminated his strong jawline, currently covered with dark stubble. His piercing green eyes were slightly muted by the darkness of the room. The way the room was laid out made each table an intimate setting.

"I believe you were asking me about your mother," Mr. Withermyer stated, pulling my attention back to his eyes. "I remember the other students hadn't been kind to me during my first year. They were all probably wondering what a scrawny eleven-year-old was doing in the same classes as them. I spent most of my time hiding in the library to escape the taunting. Then, one day, my tormentors followed me. They taunted me and made threats. Your mother stood up for me that day. She was in her second year and already had a reputation for being a gifted pixie. She was quite fearsome to behold when she was angry. Ever since then, we quickly became friends. Rachel had noticed how alone I'd been and vowed never to let me be abused again. I never told her that being defended by a girl never helped my situation. If anything, I just had to become more creative at dodging my tormentors. I couldn't be upset about what Rachel had done because, for the first time, I finally had someone to sit with for meals and friends to study with."

We paused our conversation when our soup was delivered to the table. I stirred it with my spoon to cool it off.

"You had to have been a genius to enter the Jelf Academy at eleven," I responded before bringing my spoon to my lips.

Mr. Withermyer chuckled. "I don't think I'm that smart. I never understood what Dr. Tweedle saw in me," he said modestly.

"He must have seen something extraordinary. You don't seem like you had trouble with classes. If anything, Irene mentioned how you would help her with classwork, and she was a few years ahead of you."

Mr. Withermyer just shrugged. "I guess it's true that I wasn't a typical eleven-year-old."

"Dr. Tweedle bragged about my mother's internship with Waldrick the Great, and everyone talks about how brilliant she was, but you must've been even more so to begin school so young. Did you have an internship as well?" I asked.

Mr. Withermyer shook his head. "No, they all agreed I was intelligent, but I wasn't offered any positions like your mother. They said I was too young, and it would've been too dangerous. Besides, I wanted a career in teaching, not politics."

"What do you mean by dangerous?" I asked in between a spoonful of soup.

"Waldrick the Great was a pixie government official whose job entailed keeping the pixie world secret from humans, especially the W.A.S.P. Some of his work included spies and investigations of the human world. There would have been liabilities in sending someone younger to do that type of work."

I finished my soup and pushed the bowl to the side. "You're telling me that my mother did spy work?" I asked in astonishment.

"Yes, I suppose so. Rachel wasn't allowed to discuss the work she did with Waldrick. It was very secretive," Mr. Withermyer commented.

I was silent for a moment. What did that job entail, and how had she gotten involved in the first place? Finally, our waiter returned with our entrees and took our soup bowls from the table.

"Jane, how are you enjoying the dinner?" Mr. Withermyer said after a while, and I could tell he had deliberately used my first name, probably in an attempt to get comfortable with calling me by it.

"It's delicious," I replied. "How's yours?"

He smiled at me and assured me it was to his liking. "I enjoy the opportunity to try food in new places. However, I won't have the luxury of traveling once the school year begins. Sometimes, the academy's menu can become a tad boring."

"I've always enjoyed meals at the Jelf Academy. They're better than what I get at the manor. I guess I shouldn't complain. I should be grateful for what I get," I replied. "Speaking of the Jelf Academy, what will happen when Dr. Tweedle appears at the manor to retrieve me and discovers I'm not there?"

Mr. Withermyer touched his napkin to his mouth and then took a sip of water. "I wasn't lying when I told your stepmother Dr. Tweedle was detained. When he realized he had conflicting plans for the weekend before classes, he asked me. Though he doesn't know I came for you earlier. I have your school letters in my trunk at the hotel."

"Thank you, Mr., ... Phillip," I replied, almost forgetting to call him by his first name. He smiled, and we both resumed eating.

We finished our entrees, and Mr. Withermyer ordered the

Neapolitan ice cream for the both of us. I thoroughly enjoyed the combination of flavors. Mr. Withermyer talked of his plans to find the Lyons family. We would spend the next few days asking around town about the name to discover where their home was located. Even when we found them, there was no guarantee they were connected with Robert.

We left the restaurant when we finished our dessert, and Mr. Withermyer had paid the bill. He took my hand and placed it on his arm as we strolled up the street. Night had fallen, and the road was lit only by a few gas lamps and the stars above. A slight chill brushed my neck in the humid summer air, causing me to glance around. The street was empty. I tried to ignore the odd feeling. Perhaps it was because night had fallen in this strange town.

As we rounded the corner, a panicked feeling prickled the hair on the back of my neck. It felt as if I was being watched, but that seemed impossible. The streets were deserted at this hour. I glanced around again and subconsciously walked closer to Mr. Withermyer.

"Jane, what's wrong?" he asked, noticing my proximity.

"Nothing, just having irrational feelings. I feel like someone is watching us. I'm being ridiculous. It must be my imagination and our talk of ghosts earlier," I said lightly.

We arrived at the hotel safely, and Mr. Withermyer opened the door to our room. He stayed in the hallway to give me privacy to get ready for bed. When I was decent, I called out for him to enter. There was an air of awkwardness at first, but it passed quickly. Mr. Withermyer was a gentleman, and I realized I trusted him with my life. We didn't stay up much longer, both of us agreeing to get an early start. Mr. Withermyer turned down the bedside lamp, and soon, I drifted off to sleep.

⌘

My heart pounded in my chest as I raced through the woods. Everything around me was dark, and my feet slipped on a forest floor blanketed with leaves. Somehow, I knew I was lost in my nightmare again. I raced toward a gap in the trees, knowing I would burst into the meadow that haunted my dreams. My stomach roiled with nausea at the thought of seeing Robert dying again, but my feet continued onward. The trees thinned, and it wasn't long before I burst from the woods.

My footsteps faltered. What lay before me was not the meadow but a town. Fear filled my body as I ran up the empty streets. My footsteps echoed on the cobblestones as I darted between deserted buildings. This setting was utterly unfamiliar, and I wasn't sure which way to turn. I kept checking over my shoulder, positive I would find some kind of evil pursuing me. A cry of desperation escaped my lips as I turned down another street. My lungs burned as I gasped for air. Large black gates leaned wide open at the end of the road, and I rushed through them. I paused for a moment to catch my breath.

Suddenly, a creaking noise caught my attention, and I turned with horror, watching the black gates slam shut. Another defeated cry rose in my throat, and I rushed back to the gates. I shook them, trying to force them open, but they wouldn't budge. I sobbed, turning to face what lay on this side of the gates. I was in a garden courtyard where all the plants and shrubs were dead. The flowers were wilted and shriveled. All that remained were thorns. I started down the garden path, carefully avoiding the harsh foliage that grew into the walkway.

The dead garden seemed to stretch out in all directions. The sound of a crow cawing startled me, and I picked up my pace. I hurried along until the path widened, and a marble fountain stood before me. The water wasn't running; instead, a still brackish puddle formed in the bottom basin. The statue at the top of the fountain was an enormous lion, its mouth wide open, marble teeth glistening. I stepped back from its savage face and was prepared to skirt around it when movement on the other side caught my eye.

From the shadows stepped a young girl. Her hair was a frizzy mess, and it partially shadowed her face. Her skin was a shade of gray. Horrible marks covered her arms, and on her throat were two hand-shaped bruises. She glided toward me, and I could've sworn I saw the dead foliage behind her as if she were made of a thick mist. The sight of the girl chilled me to my bones, and I stepped backward. I stumbled over a bench I hadn't noticed and fell onto it as the figure of the girl came closer.

A scream tore from my throat as she stopped only a few paces before me. Her mouth appeared black, and she opened it as if to speak. Her lips moved, and I heard her wispy, haunted voice.

"Be careful, Jane."

&

"Jane, Jane, Jane."

I awoke to rough shaking, and Mr. Withermyer's green eyes hovered above me.

"Miss Fitzgerald, are you alright?" he asked, kneeling at my bedside. "I was awakened when I heard you screaming."

His dark hair was in disarray, and his clothes were wrinkled from sleep. I was so relieved by the sight of him that I threw my arms around his neck. Tears sprang to my eyes, and my body still shook with fear.

"Oh, Phillip, it was so awful," I uttered as he slowly embraced me. His hands calmly brushed through my hair.

"Hush, you're okay. It was just a dream," he whispered softly in my ear.

"It was a nightmare," I sobbed. "It was different from my usual nightmares."

"Nothing will hurt you," he promised as my shaking subsided.

Slowly, I released my arms from his neck and leaned back on my pillows. Mr. Withermyer took my hands in his and stared at me with concern.

"There was a girl. I think she was dead," I mumbled.

I recalled the ghastly gray skin marked with bruises and cuts and how she had glided toward me. Did she have intentions to hurt me? Her strange voice echoed in my ears. She told me to be careful, but I wasn't sure why.

4

THE LYONS' ESTATE

THE NEXT FEW days passed uneventfully. I hadn't dreamt about the girl again, but I had the eerie feeling of being watched. Finally, Mr. Withermyer and I discovered the location of the Lyons family home, which was about an hour's carriage ride away in Peach Glen. Apparently, the family name was known and respected in the surrounding area, and from the details we gathered, they seemed to be well off. Could this be the family Robert had come from?

I arose slightly rested and quietly walked to the communal bathroom at the end of the hall to avoid disturbing Mr. Withermyer. We had agreed last night to take a ride up to Peach Glen. My stomach fluttered, and I felt so nervous. I had put all my hope into today. Would my hopes be crushed? I splashed water on my face and gazed at myself in the mirror. My violet eyes looked tired, and I pinched my cheeks. By the time I returned to the room, Mr. Withermyer was already awake.

"Good morning," I said, crossing the room to my suitcase.

"Good morning. I hope you slept better last night. I didn't hear you screaming in your sleep," he replied.

I was glad I hadn't woken him again. I had been quite embarrassed about my reaction and hoped it wouldn't happen again. I searched through my suitcase for something presentable. Today could be the day I'd meet Robert's family. Mr. Withermyer and I discussed what I would tell them if they did prove to be Robert's relations. The whole truth would be horrible and unnecessary, plus it would pose too many questions about why Mr. Wicker had been trying to kill me. It would also cause them more pain to know their son had lived like a slave and that he'd been murdered by the man who had essentially kept him prisoner for most of his life. On the other hand, Mr. Wicker had died in the fire, so I felt justice had already been served.

Mr. Withermyer had decided we should continue to pass me off as his sister for my safety. I would explain that I was a maid in Marie's household, and Robert was employed there as well. When describing how Robert had passed away, I could only explain that he had died in the fire at Emily's wedding.

Mr. Withermyer headed to the bathroom, and I quickly changed into a plain white blouse and a pink skirt. I needed to braid my hair, so I approached the tiny washstand in the corner with a small mirror above it.

Mr. Withermyer returned dressed in a white button-up shirt, gray suspenders, and light gray trousers. His dark hair was neatly combed, and he hadn't yet shaved the stubble from his jaw. He strode toward his bed and sat on the end of it.

"How are you feeling?" Mr. Withermyer asked as I walked past him.

"I'm okay. Just a little nervous," I responded, glancing at him through the mirror.

"Jane, promise me you won't be upset if these people are not related to Robert. Don't get discouraged. I promised to help you, and I'll continue searching if today doesn't go as expected."

"Thank you. I really appreciate your time and effort, Phillip.

You don't have to do those things for me. If today is a failure, I should either accept it or continue on my own. I don't want to inconvenience you," I replied, pining my hair into a neat, braided bun.

"I'm not inconvenienced. I've enjoyed my time on this wild goose chase, and I do intend to keep my promise. Are you almost ready to leave?" he inquired.

"Yes, almost finished," I responded, slipping one of my last pins into my hair.

"I'm going to go downstairs and prepare the carriage. Once you're ready, meet me in the lobby."

Mr. Withermyer left the room, and I stared at my reflection. My cheeks looked paler than usual. Everything had been leading up to today, and I wasn't sure if I was ready for the outcome. Taking a deep breath, I paused momentarily, and my hand found Robert's ring on the chain around my neck. My finger traced over the upraised family crest before I tucked it under my blouse. I grabbed the key off the nightstand and walked to the door. As I exited into the hallway, I couldn't help but notice the sudden cool air that brushed the back of my neck.

The carriage ride to Peach Glen was over an hour, and Mr. Withermyer and I discussed our private lessons for when we would return to the Jelf Academy.

"I'm sure Dr. Tweedle wants us to continue with our lessons. The threat of the W.A.S.P. hasn't subsided, and there is much for you to learn. I know you combined pixie magic once with self-defense, but it was because you were angry, and your emotions took over. You'll need to learn how to control and focus your magic. Plus, there are some charms I want to teach you before you learn them in class," Mr. Withermyer stated as the horse trotted up the road.

"We'll have to review the self-defense as well. I'm sure I remember everything, but I haven't had much time to practice this summer," I replied.

"Don't worry. We'll review everything, though I doubt it will be difficult for you to remember once we start."

The day was beginning to feel hot already, even though the sun hadn't risen that long ago. Every now and then, a light breeze would blow through the trees, giving me a few seconds of bliss. The hour ride to Peach Glen went surprisingly fast, and my heart started to thrum wildly in my chest when we reached the small town. There weren't many buildings, and the main ones were on one stretch of road. Mr. Withermyer pulled the carriage over so he could ask about the location of the Lyons' estate.

"If you head to the end of this road and make the first right, it will take you in the right direction. Their drive is marked by a set of black gates," the gentleman on the road said.

"Thank you, sir," Mr. Withermyer replied, flicking the reigns, and our horse moved back onto the road.

With each step of the horse's hooves, my heart constricted. The air around me felt heavy, and it wasn't because of the humidity. Finally, we turned onto a lane shaded by giant oak trees, and I felt a little better since we briefly escaped the harsh sunlight. Whatever lay at the end of this road would determine a potential answer to the question of Robert's family.

It wasn't long before the black gates loomed in front of us. Both gates were wide open, and beyond them was a large garden, expanding on both sides of the path up to the house. Again, a strange chill caused me to shudder, and I looked around both sides of the carriage. Something had struck me as familiar, but I couldn't put my finger on what it was.

The fragrance of all the flowers surrounded us, and I tried to push away my unreasonable feelings. The garden was beautiful, with dozens of large rose bushes, sculpted hedges, and flowers of every color. The bright tulips were everywhere, and I could also see a few Japanese maple trees in the distance. The horse followed the curving path, and eventually, the trail widened and forked off in two directions. The left one led straight to the house, but my heart stopped when I looked to the right. Suddenly, I realized why this place seemed so familiar.

On my right was a fountain, and in the middle was a marble statue of an open-mouthed lion. Water flowed out of the lion's mouth and into the basin below. Though, when I'd seen it, the water had been stagnant. It was the same fountain from my nightmare, and my heart raced as I scanned the garden for the apparition of the girl with gray skin and dead eyes.

My entire body seized. Why had I dreamt about this place, and why had everything in the dream been dead? I shuddered as the horse turned away from the fountain. Mr. Withermyer touched my hand, and I lifted my head to meet his face. He was looking at me with concern clouding his green eyes.

"Jane, are you alright? Your face has lost all color, and you seem troubled by something."

"No, I'm alright. I'm just really nervous," I replied, brushing off the chill. I didn't want Mr. Withermyer to think I was crazy.

We continued up the path, and Mr. Withermyer stopped the carriage in front of the house. The house was large, and it rose several stories. There was no question the people who lived here were wealthy. The front porch was more expansive than the manor's, and the wooden doors had to be over ten feet tall. On both sides of the entrance were two long windows, and I could've sworn I saw a pair of eyes peering out at me.

Mr. Withermyer climbed down from the carriage and came around to help me. I accepted his hand gratefully and lifted my skirt slightly so I wouldn't trip. My knees felt like they were shaking, and I was glad to have Mr. Withermyer's strong presence beside me. At least I didn't have to do this alone.

We mounted the stairs and crossed to the large wooden door. The eyes I had seen earlier appeared to have vanished, and I wondered for a moment if I'd invented them. On the right side of the door was the doorbell, and Mr. Withermyer looked at me as he raised his hand toward it. He seemed to be awaiting my approval. Slowly, I took a deep breath and nodded. He pushed the button, and a deep gong echoed throughout the house. There was no turning back now.

After a few moments, a short and very thin girl wearing a servant's uniform pulled open the front door. Her dark hair was pinned up neatly, and she stood perfectly straight as her eyes appraised us.

"Good morning, Miss," Mr. Withermyer began. "Is the gentleman of the house at home?"

"No, I'm sorry, Mr. Lyons has gone out for the day, and I don't know when he'll be back," the girl answered.

"Is the lady of the house at home?" Mr. Withermyer questioned again.

The maid looked uncertain about how to reply. Finally, she answered, "Mrs. Lyons is here, but I haven't been made aware of any visitors today. You'll have to send word of your arrival and plan your visit another time. Good day." The maid began closing the door, and anxiety flooded my chest. We had come all this way.

"Please, ma'am, if we could only have a few minutes of her time. I have information about her missing son," I cried without thinking.

The servant paused, and a female voice inside the house suddenly spoke.

"Let them in."

Almost reluctantly, the servant swung the door fully open and stepped back to allow us entry. Cautiously, Mr. Withermyer and I stepped over the threshold. The entrance to the house was grand. A large chandelier hung in the center of the room, a dull gold with large crystals hanging from all sides. On the floor was a long oriental rung stretching down the vast hallway in front of us. On the walls were expensive paintings in large, gilded frames. Every inch of the room screamed out with lavish expense.

A woman emerged from the shadows in a fine blue gown with a high lace collar. The dress had to be made from valuable silk, and the sleeves and hem were adorned with white lace. She appeared to be in her late forties or early fifties. Her hazel eyes held sadness, and her auburn hair, so like Robert's, was streaked with gray.

"Did you say you had news about my son?" she asked, coming toward us. Her eyes focused on me.

"Yes, ma'am. I believe I might if your son's name was Robert," I replied.

Upon hearing the name, the woman looked as if she were going to faint. The servant rushed over and grabbed hold of the woman's arm to steady her. After a few moments, the woman became stable, and she turned to smile at the girl.

"I'm fine, Martha. Please prepare some tea for our guests and bring it into the sitting room," she instructed.

Martha looked like she'd rather not leave her mistress's side, but following orders, she disappeared down the hallway.

"Please follow me," Mrs. Lyons stated, leading us through an open doorway on the left.

We proceeded behind her into a bright and beautifully decorated sitting room. One wall was covered in floor-to-ceiling windows that let in the morning light. Baby blue draperies hung on both sides of the windows. Beautifully carved oak end tables stood on both sides of a settee that was upholstered with a light blue fabric. A long coffee table of the same wood and design was in front of the sofa, and on the other side were two large armchairs of the same color. A brass standing fan was currently blowing a light breeze throughout the room.

Mrs. Lyons indicated the settee and then sat in one of the armchairs. We took a seat, and Mr. Withermyer cleared his throat.

"My name is Phillip Withermyer, and this is my sister, Jane. She's employed as a maid, and I believe that's where she met your son."

"You know my boy, Robert?" Mrs. Lyons exclaimed, and I saw the unfortunate hope flare in her eyes. "Where is he? Why hasn't he come with you?"

"Mrs. Lyons," I began, unsure how to tell her. "I knew your son Robert very well. He and I worked together."

"My son works at a manor?" she replied, sounding slightly appalled. "Please tell him to come home. I've missed him greatly and never thought I would see him again."

"I know Robert wanted to find his home, and more than anything, he wanted to return here. Unfortunately, that isn't going to be possible because Robert passed away over a year ago," I said, tears springing to my eyes.

Mrs. Lyons raised her hand to her mouth. Her face glazed over, and tears glistened in her hazel eyes. I couldn't imagine what she must be feeling. She lost her son on a crowded street when he was only six. Hearing I had news of her son probably sparked some hope inside her, only to crush it so soon.

"I'm sorry to bring you this terrible news. I'm deeply saddened by his passing. Robert was very important to me," I said, wiping a tear from my cheek.

"I suspected he passed a long time ago. I never wanted to accept it, and I always hoped he would just show up on the doorstep. My husband always accuses me of being foolish, but how can a mother lose hope in her children?" Mrs. Lyons said, pulling a handkerchief out from the sleeve of her gown. She dabbed her eyes. "We searched for days and didn't find any trace of him. My husband and I had been visiting friends in a town several miles from here. We had taken Robert along because they had a son who was only a few years older. It was Robert's first vacation."

Mrs. Lyons was interrupted as Martha entered the sitting room with a tray. There was a large pitcher filled to the brim with amber liquid. Ice cubes floated on the top, and condensation ran down the sides. Martha placed a glass in front of each of us.

"I hope you like iced tea. I find it most refreshing on a hot day like this one," Mrs. Lyons said.

"Thank you very much," I replied to Martha as she poured me a glass.

"Yes, thank you. I do enjoy iced tea," Mr. Withermyer stated.

Martha finished pouring and then removed a small plate of tea sandwiches from the tray, placing it in the middle of the coffee table.

"Thank you, Martha. That will be all at the moment," Mrs. Lyons said politely.

Martha eyed us wearily while she backed out of the room. Mrs. Lyons turned her attention back to Mr. Withermyer and me.

"Miss Withermyer, is it? How did you come to know my son?"

"He came to work as a stable hand at my mistress's manor. We often worked together," I replied before sipping the iced tea.

"I thought you were a maid in the household?" Mrs. Lyons replied curiously.

"I am, ma'am, but my mistress assigns many jobs around the house. I'm very versatile in my list of tasks."

"How odd! I've never had any attendants of mine completing different chores. Each of my girls has a job all their own."

"My mistress has different views regarding the manor's chores," I replied as politely as possible.

"So, you worked beside my son and got to know him well?" Mrs. Lyons asked.

"Yes, ma'am, I did. Like I said, Robert was very special to me," I stated.

Understanding seemed to dawn in Mrs. Lyons' eyes, but before she could reply, a young girl burst into the sitting room.

The girl appeared to be about ten years old, with strawberry blonde hair and bright hazel eyes. Something about her reminded me of Robert, even though she didn't have the same hair or eye color. She came rushing up to Mrs. Lyons with a large smile on her face.

"Mama, mama, I can't wait to tell you…." She stopped short as her eyes landed on Mr. Withermyer and me.

"Ann dear, as you can see, I have company. So, I'm sure whatever you have to tell me can wait, can't it?" Mrs. Lyons said calmly.

"I'm sorry, mama," Ann said, looking down at the floor.

"Now run along and play for a little longer, and if you behave, I'll tell Martha to fetch you some ice cream," Mrs. Lyons responded sweetly.

Ann's eyes lit up with joy at the mention of ice cream, and she happily skipped from the room. Mrs. Lyons smiled as she watched Ann leave, then turned back to me.

"I was blessed with Ann four years after Robert's disappearance. She barely leaves my sight, and we hardly ever leave the grounds. Ever since I lost Robert, I've been so afraid of losing Ann."

I nodded in understanding as I sipped my iced tea again. Mrs. Lyons was silent for a moment, and then her hazel eyes slowly met mine. Tears glistened and threatened to fall as she took a deep breath.

"How did my Robert die?" she asked solemnly.

I could feel my own eyes welling up. We had come to the difficult part of the conversation, and I wasn't sure if I was ready to discuss Robert's death. I knew I couldn't tell the entire truth, but I wanted her to know her son had saved my life.

"My mistress's daughter was getting married, and Robert and I were instructed to serve the guests at the wedding. During the wedding reception, a fire broke out in the house. Robert was very brave. He saved my life and helped me to escape the fire, but he didn't manage to get out," I said as my voice cracked, and I began to cry. Mr. Withermyer offered me his handkerchief, and I dabbed at my eyes.

Mrs. Lyons's tears also began to fall, and she touched her cheeks with the cloth in her hand.

"Your son was the bravest person I've ever known, and I wouldn't have survived without him," I choked out as an image of Robert's smiling face flashed in my mind. The loss of him pierced my heart again, and I struggled to keep myself composed.

"It's obvious how much he meant to you," Mrs. Lyons said with a tearful breath. "Tell me more about my son."

I took several deep breaths and cleared my throat before I spoke again. "Robert was quiet at first, but the more time I spent with him, the more I got to know him. He was very polite and chivalrous, and he was always a gentleman. He was also very determined and hardworking. Robert always talked about his family, and he wanted to find you again. That was his main goal in life."

Mrs. Lyons nodded as she dabbed her eyes again. "I've always wanted him to come home. I never lost hope I would see him again. Do you think he was happy?" she asked, full of hope.

I didn't want to tell her about the abuse Robert had endured or how hard his life had been. Working at the manor had been hard as well, but I wanted to believe Robert had found a small shard of happiness with me as I had with him.

"Robert wanted nothing more than to return to you, but I know his life was greatly improved by coming to work for my mistress. I loved Robert, and I believe he loved me as well," I managed to get out before I began to cry again.

Mrs. Lyons and I both cried silently for a few minutes. Mr. Withermyer placed his hand on my back in comfort, and I found myself leaning slightly into his touch. I finally completed what Robert had asked of me in my nightmares.

When Mrs. Lyons finally composed herself, she spoke again. "I'm glad my son had someone who loved him." She reached out her hand across the coffee table, and I leaned forward to clasp it in mine. We sat for a moment, finding comfort in each other's touch, until suddenly, we heard a noise at the front door.

A man strolled into the sitting room and instantly gazed at

Mrs. Lyons's and my clasped hands. He looked so much like Robert that it took my breath away, but he had light blonde hair. Even though his brown eyes were the same shade as Robert's, they held none of the chocolate warmth. Mrs. Lyons dropped my hand and sat back in her armchair.

"Gabriel, you've arrived home early," Mrs. Lyons exclaimed as he walked toward her.

"Yes, I have a few hours to spare, so I thought I would enjoy lunch at home. I wasn't aware you had company," he replied.

"I wasn't expecting visitors, but allow me to introduce you to Mr. and Miss Withermyer," Mrs. Lyons began," Phillip and I rose to shake Mr. Lyons's hand. His eyes scrutinized us as his wife continued to explain. "Miss Withermyer was acquainted with our son, Robert."

Mr. Lyons froze, and then his focus settled fully on me. "You claim to have knowledge of my son?" he questioned with a confused look.

"Yes, sir. We both worked at a manor together," I replied.

"How can we believe what you're saying is the truth? My son disappeared when he was six years old. Though we have looked for him, we've never had anyone claiming to know him until today. How can my wife and I even trust you?" Mr. Lyons said harshly.

Mr. Lyons's accusations seemed to have struck a chord with Mrs. Lyons, who was now staring at me suspiciously.

"My wife and I are very wealthy people, so if you think you can come here and demand some kind of compensation for knowing the whereabouts of our son, then you're greatly mistaken. I highly doubt you even knew him," Mr. Lyons said defensively.

I was startled by Mr. Lyons's accusations and reaction. I remembered Robert's ring was tucked under my blouse, and I pulled on the chain to reveal the ring. I unclasped the necklace and held the band up to the light.

"You have to believe me because Robert gave me this," I said as the silver ring twirled on the chain in my hand.

Mr. Lyons quickly snatched the necklace from me and stared intently at the ring. "This is our family ring with our crest. How did you even get this?" Mr. Lyons asked, his eyes blazing. "In what form of mischief did this come into your hands?"

"Robert gave it to me. It was the only thing he had to remember his family by," I said, frustrated tears coming to my eyes. Mrs. Lyons had been so kind, but Mr. Lyons was defensive and making outrageous claims.

"My sister is not a thief if that's what you mean. She's telling the truth," Mr. Withermyer spoke up defensively.

Mr. Lyons glared at us, but suddenly, Mrs. Lyons spoke up. "Gabriel, Robert was wearing your ring when he went missing. He wanted to wear the family crest, so you allowed him to have it, but since his fingers were too small, you placed it on a chain for him. I remember now," she said in a small-sounding voice.

Mr. Lyons briefly looked at his wife, and when he turned back to us, some of the fire in his eyes had subsided. He clutched at the chain and slid the ring off, fitting it onto one of his fingers. It looked similar to the one he had on his middle finger. I gazed at Robert's ring with longing. It was the only thing I had left of my beloved. Mrs. Lyons must have noticed my expression.

"Gabriel," she said in the same soft tone. "give the girl the ring back."

"Why would I do that? This is my family ring, and it's made of solid silver. Why should a maid get to keep my family heirloom?" Mr. Lyons spat out as he angrily eyed his wife.

"Miss Withermyer told me she was in love with Robert, and he loved her too. I'm sure it was his reasoning for giving this young woman our family ring. Our son saved Miss Withermyer from a fire, but he perished inside," Mrs. Lyons replied.

"So, my boy is dead?" Mr. Lyons asked, covering the ring with his other hand.

Mrs. Lyons nodded tearfully, and she lifted her handkerchief. "Yes, I was just informed that he passed away over a year ago."

"I loved Robert and wanted to honor his memory by completing his goal to find his family. I came all this way to let you know what happened to him—not because I wanted anything in return, but because I really loved him," I said sadly.

Mr. Lyons made no move to take the ring off but instead stood there silently, taking in the information about his son. He ran a hand through his blonde hair and sighed deeply. Finally, he looked at Mrs. Lyons and spoke. "I always knew we would discover he was dead. Now, we've just confirmed what we always knew. Robert was gone the moment you didn't keep an eye on him."

Mrs. Lyons paled, and a feeling of embarrassment came over me. I looked down at my hands while Mr. Lyons continued speaking.

"I told you your hope was foolish. Our son is gone!"

Mr. Lyons began to pace. Martha walked into the room carrying a small tray. She paused, taking in the scene: her mistress pale as death and the gentleman of the house pacing in front of her. Mr. Lyons caught sight of her and turned to face her.

"Yes, Martha?" Mr. Lyons inquired.

"I'm sorry, sir. I don't mean to bother you, but I was given this letter. I was told it was urgent," Martha replied, holding out the tray toward Mr. Lyons.

Mr. Lyons lifted the letter from the tray and held it out to examine it. My eye caught the wax seal stamped on the back of the envelope, and suddenly, I couldn't breathe. Heat rose to my cheeks, and my hands began to shake. The wax seal was in the shape of a hexagon with a giant, stripped insect set in the middle. I had seen the seal several times, and each time had sent a shiver down my spine. Its appearance here could only mean one thing. Mr. Lyons was a member of the W.A.S.P.

5

AN ESCAPE

MR. WITHERMYER MUST'VE NOTICED the seal on the letter because he grasped my shaking hands and leaned toward me. His green eyes met mine, and his gaze implored me to act naturally. His presence and touch slightly calmed me, but fear had settled deep in my heart. The appearance of the letter and its evil wax seal had shaken me to my core.

Mr. Lyons ripped open the letter, and his eyes darted over the words. I tried to keep my face neutral. I couldn't appear alarmed or make it apparent I had recognized the seal. Mrs. Lyons's pale face studied her husband as he read the letter's contents. Mr. Lyons abruptly finished, folded the letter, and placed it in his jacket pocket.

"You'll have to excuse me, but I must be on my way. Unfortunately, my job has called me back on urgent business," Mr. Lyons stated with a scowl.

Slowly, Mr. Withermyer rose to his feet and tugged on his coat jacket. "We should be on our way as well. My sister and I do not want to overstay our welcome. Jane has completed her wish to inform you of your son. I am so sorry, but the news she bears is not what anyone had hoped. I'm sorry for your loss. Let us not encroach on your family's grief, and we'll be on our way."

Mr. Withermyer reached out his hand, and I grasped it as he pulled me to my feet. I felt a little unstable, so I placed my hand in the crook of his arm. My only thought was that we needed to get out of this house. Mrs. Lyons also rose to her feet, gazing at us from across the coffee table.

"Thank you for telling me about my son," she whispered, and Mr. Lyons shot a glare her way.

"I can show you out," Mr. Lyons stated, walking toward the front door.

I could feel myself beginning to sweat. I gripped Mr. Withermyer's arm, and we followed behind Mr. Lyons. My palms felt clammy, and my heart fluttered with anxiety. If Mr. Lyons was a member of the W.A.S.P., how many pixies had he tortured and killed? My stomach was sick, and I fought to focus on getting to the front door. How could my sweet and gentle Robert be related to these people?

Mr. Lyons flung the front door open and stepped to the side so we could pass by. His dark brown eyes looked us over, and a chill ran down my spine. He glared at me for a long moment, and I felt self-conscious under his harsh stare. He seemed to examine every detail of my face now that I was closer to him. I kept my eyes adverted and allowed Mr. Withermyer to pull me along.

We stepped onto the porch, and my eyes wandered to Mr. Lyon's hand, now baring Robert's ring. The ring was the last thing I saw before Mr. Lyons slammed the door. My heart felt like it was sawed in two. I wanted to crumble onto the porch in tears, but I couldn't do such a foolish thing. The other part of me wanted to run far away from the potential danger. Since I could do neither of those things, I walked as calmly as possible beside Mr. Withermyer.

Our carriage had been moved down the driveway, so we had to walk further to reach it. My anxiety was building with each step, and I kept glancing over my shoulder. I didn't know whether it was ghosts or a real-life threat, but I felt as if something was going to reach out and grab us at any moment. I found myself walking closer to Mr. Withermyer. What if the Lyons realized what we truly were and attacked us?

Mr. Withermyer sensed and understood my anxiety. He placed his hand lightly on top of mine. He gently squeezed my hand to reassure me we would escape this situation unharmed. Finally, we reached the carriage, and Mr. Withermyer helped me up. My legs shook as I pulled myself onto the seat. Mr. Withermyer quickly climbed up and flicked the reigns.

The garden didn't look so beautiful as we went down the drive. My nightmare plagued my thoughts, and I could visualize the dead flowers. The ghostly girl's warning echoed in my head. Now I knew she had been trying to tell me the Lyons family was connected with the W.A.S.P. I gazed behind me, expecting us to be followed, but the path was empty.

Mr. Withermyer was tense, and I knew he was just as worried as I was. Finally, we got to the end of the drive, and I was glad to see the large black gates were still open. We rode through them, and I wanted to feel relieved, but a nagging feeling in my stomach kept my senses alert. I wanted to get as far away from Peach Glen as possible.

We rode through the tiny town, and when we reached the wooded outskirts, Mr. Withermyer pulled the carriage off the road and stopped.

"Why are we stopping?" I asked as panic rose in my voice. "We need to get away from here. I don't have a good feeling about our parting with the Lyons family."

"My intuition is telling me the same, which is why we'll be faster if we leave the carriage behind," Mr. Withermyer replied, unhitching the horse. "We'll ride back to the hotel and collect our belongings. We should leave Gettysburg as well, just to be safe. Don't worry about another carriage. I'll figure something out, but for now, we must move quickly."

I didn't wait for Mr. Withermyer to help me, and I jumped down. He glanced around the deserted forest and quickly plucked a summoning charm from his pixie dust case. I watched as he conjured a saddle and horse blanket. Then, I helped him outfit the Clydesdale. The sheer size of the horse was intimidating, and Mr. Withermyer had to give me a leg up onto the saddle. My skirt rode up my legs, but I didn't care about propriety at the moment. Mr. Withermyer climbed up behind me, wrapping his arms around me so he could grip the reigns.

"Grab onto the saddle horn and hold on tightly," he instructed, his voice close to my ear.

As Mr. Withermyer steered the horse back onto the road, I held on for dear life. Within moments, the horse was moving at a gallop, and the woods were flying by. My heart thundered as fast as the horse's hooves on the road. Feeling slightly self-conscious, I leaned into Mr. Withermyer to have a more stable position in the saddle. The further we traveled down the street, the better I began to feel. I was grateful for Mr. Withermyer and knew he would protect me.

The wind tugged at my hair, and I could feel my braids loosening as the horse carried us toward our destination. Mr. Withermyer was an excellent rider, and he expertly steered the Clydesdale through every turn on the road. We rode for a while, Mr. Withermyer occasionally slowing to give the horse a break. It didn't seem to take as long as the morning trip. We arrived at an alarming speed. It wasn't long before we reached our hotel, and Mr. Withermyer pulled the horse to a stop.

Hurriedly, Mr. Withermyer dismounted and reached to help me down. My dismount wasn't as graceful, and I clumsily fell into Mr. Withermyer's arms. He caught me effortlessly and gently placed me on my feet.

"Run up to the room and gather our belongings," he said, pressing the key into my palm. "I'll try to find another carriage."

I nodded, closing my fingers around the key. While

Mr. Withermyer headed off down the street, I entered the hotel. Mrs. Hansen was behind the counter, and she greeted me. I uttered a nice reply before I raced up the stairs to the room. I couldn't explain the strange feeling I had; I only knew I would feel better when I distanced myself from this town.

Turning the key in the lock, I entered the room and went straight to my suitcase. For the most part, I had kept my things neatly packed, so I only had to toss my brush, hairpins, and clips into the suitcase. Mr. Withermyer's belongings were neatly stowed on his side of the room. I pulled his heavy bag toward the door and placed mine beside it.

My stomach rolled with anxiety, and I rushed into the bathroom. I retched for a moment over the sink. Finding out Robert's family was connected to the W.A.S.P., the anxiety, and the rapid horseback ride had made me ill. I rinsed out my mouth and glanced around the sink vanity. My eyes rose to the mirror, my flushed face and terrified eyes peering back at me. Then, I saw something over my shoulder that almost made me lose the contents of my stomach again.

Reflected in the mirror was the girl from my dreams. I stifled a scream as her dead eyes gazed at me. Her face was a pale gray, and her frizzy hair stuck out in all directions. Her mouth opened, and I distinctly heard her utter one word.

"Hurry!"

When I turned around, no one was standing behind me, and when I looked at the mirror again, the girl was no longer reflected in the glass. A panic rose in my chest. I rushed back to the room. A few moments after entering, a sharp pounding sounded on the door. Was Mr. Lyons coming after us? Had he sensed what we were? The apparition had told me to hurry. Was I too late? My heart pounded so hard I could hear its rhythm in both ears. Unsure of what to do, I stayed crouched on the floor next to the suitcases.

The pounding sounded again, and I heard a muffled voice through the door. "Jane, it's Phillip. Please open the door."

My anxiety slightly subsided as I lurched for the knob. Mr. Withermyer quickly strode into the room. "I've found another carriage, and we should be on our way. I'll grab the bags. If you could, please turn our key in at the front desk and act as naturally as possible. I have parked the carriage in the next alley, so meet me there right away," he said, grabbing the suitcases and heading back out the door.

My small bag was the only item left in the room. I grabbed the key, threw my bag over my shoulder, and hurried out. I tried to walk as calmly and naturally as possible, even though every cell in my body begged me to run. I managed to make it down the staircase, fixing a smile on my face as I approached the counter. Mrs. Hansen was still standing there.

"My brother and I would like to check out of the hotel," I said calmly, extending my hand holding the key.

"Your brother has paid until the end of the week," Mrs. Hansen exclaimed. "Why are you in such a rush to leave?"

"We have received urgent news that our mother is unwell, and we've been asked to return at once," I replied, thinking quickly as Mrs. Hansen reached for the key.

"All of the payments are nonrefundable," Mrs. Hansen insisted, hesitating to take the key from me.

"That's fine," I stated distractedly. I just wanted to leave the hotel and find Mr. Withermyer.

Mrs. Hansen took the key, and I mumbled my goodbyes as I walked toward the front door. I almost made it to the alley when I noticed a group of men on the opposite side of the street. Leading the group was Mr. Lyons. My breath caught in my throat, and I rapidly ducked into the shop next to me.

Why had Mr. Lyons followed us to Gettysburg? Had I been correct in assuming he sensed we were pixies, or had he just been suspicious enough to investigate? Maybe neither of these things applied, and his letter from the W.A.S.P. had brought him here. Either way, Mr. Withermyer and I had to escape. My intuition, along with the spirit girl, made my stomach clench. I watched through the shop's front window as Mr. Lyons and the two large gentlemen walked by. They hadn't seen me, and I sighed.

"Excuse me, can I help you?" a voice asked from behind me, and I almost jumped out of my skin.

I turned around to find a hunched-over elderly woman staring at me. I realized the shop was full of antique objects, and the woman thought I was a customer. I forced a smile and cleared my throat.

"I'm sorry. I was just looking around," I replied, pretending to look at the objects in front of the window.

"Let me know if you see anything you like," she said sweetly, and I expressed my thanks.

Once the woman had shuffled deeper into the store, I glanced out the window again. I could see Mr. Lyons had stopped outside the hotel where we'd been staying, and I watched his group slip inside. Now was my chance to move. Quickly, I dashed out the door and into the street. In a very unladylike fashion, I ran toward the alleyway, my footsteps sounding loud to my ears. I slowed as I reached the alley, and with a glance over my shoulder, I darted into the opening between the buildings.

My body collided with another, and we almost tumbled to the ground. I was relieved to see the dark hair and familiar green eyes. Mr. Withermyer caught me against his chest.

"Mr. Lyons is here! I just saw him go into the hotel!" I sobbed.

Mr. Withermyer held a finger to his lips and looked at me intently. He then took me by the hand and led me to the carriage he managed to acquire. He helped me board and gracefully climbed up beside me.

"I saw Mr. Lyons while I was waiting for you. We need to

get to someplace where we can teleport. There are too many eyes around here, and it isn't safe," Mr. Withermyer whispered, snapping the reigns.

The horse trotted down the alley, and we exited onto the next street over. Mr. Withermyer steered the animal onto another road, and we began heading toward the edge of town. He kept the horse at a trot since we would probably draw too much attention if he had brought the horse to a gallop. My entire body was a bundle of nerves, and with every moment, I expected to hear shouting behind us. I gripped Mr. Withermyer's hand, my anxiety threatening to eat me alive with each passing second.

Finally, we reached the tree line and headed into the woods. Mr. Withermyer coaxed the horse to a faster pace and asked me to help him look for a path off the main road. I scanned the trees as we flew past, and after a while, I spotted a trail that forked into a heavily wooded section of the forest. Mr. Withermyer steered the horse in that direction, and we slowed since the path wasn't as smooth as the main road. Once we were a decent way down the trail, Mr. Withermyer slowed the horse to a stop.

"This area seems secluded enough," he said, searching his pockets for his pixie dust case.

I took deep breaths, watching him pull the case from his jacket pocket. It took a moment for him to enlarge it before placing his pointer finger on the lock. Mr. Withermyer began sorting through the case in search of a teleportation charm vial. As he continued to look, I got a prickly feeling on the back of my neck. I scanned the forest for any signs of movement.

Suddenly, I heard the sound of hoofbeats in the distance. Then, I could distinctly make out the yelling of men. I wasn't sure if the voices belonged to Mr. Lyons or someone else, but I didn't want to stay to find out.

"Hurry, Phillip. I hear someone coming!" I cried out just as Mr. Withermyer wrapped his hand around a teleportation charm.

"Hold on tightly, Jane," he deplored, whipping the cap off the vial.

The voices and sounds were getting closer as I gripped the edge of the carriage. Sweat trickled down my brow. Any moment now, I expected Mr. Lyons to crash through the trees, followed by those two grisly-looking men. Mr. Withermyer tossed the charm into the air, and the pixie dust surrounded us. My world went black, and I squeezed my eyes shut.

6

THE BEACH HOUSE

A SHARP, SALTY BREEZE stung my nose, and I slowly opened my eyes. Mr. Withermyer and I were no longer in a forest. Instead, I beheld a stretch of beach with ocean waves rolling into the shore. I gasped at the picturesque landscape. Never before had I seen an ocean or a beach. The sight was absolutely breathtaking.

"This was the first place I could think of," Mr. Withermyer replied, rattling the reigns for the horse to move up a hill toward a cute little house on the ridge. "My family sometimes comes here on vacation, and as far as I know, the cottage is empty."

"It's beautiful here," I replied, continuing to look around me. The calming sounds of the waves hitting the shore, coupled with the ocean breeze, calmed my nerves. Our escape had rattled me, and this place was already helping calm my mind.

Mr. Withermyer stopped the horse outside the little cottage and then jumped down from the carriage. Once he helped me onto my shaky legs, he unloaded our suitcases. I stood staring out at the ocean, still in awe at the sight of it. Mr. Withermyer must've found the key to the place, and I heard him opening the front door. I sunk onto the sandy grass and tried to catch my breath.

We had been so close to being caught. I felt so overwhelmed, and tears sprang to my eyes as all the emotions of the day poured out of me. I had met Robert's family, relived his death as I told his mother, discovered his family was connected to the W.A.S.P., and had been overcome by anxiety as we escaped. Tears began flowing down my cheeks, and the sea breeze blew through my hair.

"I've placed your suitcase," Mr. Withermyer began, and then he must've spotted me sitting on the ground. I could hear him hurrying towards me, but I didn't turn my head to look at him. "Jane, are you okay?" he cried, crouching beside me and touching my shoulder.

I shook my head. "I feel so overwhelmed and shocked," I stated, my shoulders shaking with sobs.

Mr. Withermyer sat beside me and placed his arm around my shoulder. "You're okay. We're safe now. Nothing can harm you here," he said in a soothing voice.

I leaned into his shoulder and used my hand to wipe at my tears. "I hoped to find Robert's family, and I did, but discovering they're members of the W.A.S.P. is devastating. Robert was such a sweet person. How could he be related to people who are so evil?" I asked, shuddering with emotion.

"I don't know, Jane,' Mr. Withermyer said, gently rubbing my shoulder.

"If Robert had never been separated from his family, he would have grown up hating pixies. He would have hated me!" I sobbed.

Mr. Withermyer reached into his jacket pocket and produced a handkerchief. He handed it to me and continued to hold me as I cried. Finally, when my tears subsided a bit, Mr. Withermyer spoke again. "Jane, you know Robert loved you. Don't torture yourself with what-ifs. He was separated from his family, and he did fall in love with you. You can't think about what he might have become.

Sometimes, things in life happen for a reason. Most of the time, we never know what the reason is."

I nodded, staring out at the ocean. When I got my emotions under control, I spoke in a shaky voice. "You must think of me as weak and emotional." This was not the first time I had come undone in his presence.

"No, I could never think that of you. I can't imagine what you must be feeling. You've been so strong the entire day. You were able to tell Robert's mother he had passed, and you remained so calm when Mr. Lyons received that letter. I don't believe anyone could tell how anxious you were since you acted so naturally. I don't know how you managed to get through it. There were times when I thought we would be apprehended, but I told myself I had to get you to safety," Mr. Withermyer said, his green eyes looking to the waves on the sand.

"When I saw the W.A.S.P. insignia stamped onto that wax seal, I thought I was going to faint. I'm glad I wasn't alone," I replied, my cheeks going red as I dabbed at my eyes again.

I took a deep breath, and Mr. Withermyer dropped his hand from my shoulder. "Would you like to go inside and get off this hard ground?" he asked.

I nodded. Mr. Withermyer stood to his feet and dusted the dirt off his pants. He grasped my hand firmly and pulled me up. I followed him through the front door. The cottage was small, but it had a very homey feel. There was a small kitchen on the left and a tiny table in the middle with six chairs around it. The floor plan was open, so to the right was a living area with a few sofas and some chairs. A large bay window looked out to the ocean, a pictur-esque view. Three doors were across the room, and Mr. Withermyer walked over to the open one on the right.

"I've placed your suitcase in this room. It's the bigger of the two bedrooms and has an ocean view. There's another bedroom through the far-left door. The middle door is the bathroom," Mr. Withermyer explained.

"Thank you," I said, my eyes taking in the pretty blue comforter on what must be a king-sized bed. The furniture in the room looked like it had been aged by the sea, and even though it was worn, I thought it was lovely. "You said your family vacations here?" I asked.

"Yes, this cottage is owned by my family, and we sometimes come here. We used to vacation here often when I was a child. We came less and less as I got older and my mother passed away. This was my mother's special place, and my father can't bear to part with it, but he hardly comes here anymore," Mr. Withermyer said sadly. "I know it reminds him of her and how painful it is. Every summer, I stop here for a week or so to keep the place in order and repair anything that needs fixing."

"Well, I've only been here for a few minutes, and I love it. It's so relaxing, and I've never seen an ocean before," I replied, gazing out the bay window to the rolling waves.

Mr. Withermyer walked to the table and sat on one of the chairs. "I wanted to discuss our plans for the next week. You don't have to collect your school supplies right away. We can stay here, or I'll take you to the Jewel Caverns early, and you can stay there. I'll do whatever you would like," Mr. Withermyer said.

I contemplated the options he'd given me as I looked back toward the sparkling sea. Something about this place felt right, and I didn't want to leave it so soon. "If you don't mind, I would like to stay here," I replied.

Mr. Withermyer let out a breath and then smiled at me. He stood from the chair. "In that case, I'll have to get a few supplies for the week." He pulled out his pixie dust case and set it on the table. I recognized the summoning charm as he pulled out several vials and placed them on the table. He picked up one of the vials and sprinkled it over the kitchen table. Within moments, multiple cans of food and salted meats appeared. Then fresh fruits and vegetables materialized until the table was full. I stood back, opening my mouth in awe.

"I can't help being surprised by our magical abilities. The only time I get to use magic is at the Jelf Academy, and it's usually only for lessons," I said.

"Just wait until you enter the pixie world after school and can use your magic every day. You'll need help finding someplace to live and work in the pixie community," Mr. Withermyer said. I nodded, but I wasn't sure what my life would be like in the future. I didn't have money and nowhere to go but the manor.

With a smile, Mr. Withermyer reached for another summoning vial. "I almost forgot," he said, casting the charm. A few dark blue and white garments fell onto the table, and I looked at them with curiosity. One looked like a short-sleeved dress with white stripes around the waist and hem and tiny buttons down the front. I saw a matching set of pants that had to go with the dress because they were feminine and of the same pattern. The other outfit was for a man. The shirt was stripped and sleeveless, and the pants looked like they would come to a man's knees. Both sets of clothing were made out of light, airy material.

Mr. Withermyer handed me the feminine set. "These should fit you. We can't be at the beach for a week without you having a proper bathing suit," he said, studying my confused expression.

"Thank you. I've never owned a bathing suit. I learned to swim in a pond by the manor," I said, thinking about how I used my undergarment for bathing. I'd never owned a specific outfit for the leisurely activity of swimming.

"After we put the food away, we can change and head down to the water if you like," Mr. Withermyer suggested.

I nodded in agreement, placing the bathing suit to the side. I helped Mr. Withermyer take the food to the pantry, which was through a tiny door on the floor that opened to reveal an underground storage room. The room was colder than any pantry I'd ever been in, and the air was dry. Shelves lined all four walls. I handed Mr. Withermyer the canned goods, salted meats, and fresh produce, and he arranged everything on the shelves before climbing back up. Carefully, he closed up the pantry and picked up his bathing suit.

"We can head down to the water for a while, and we'll prepare dinner later," he suggested, heading for the smaller room.

Following his lead, I picked up the other bathing suit and entered the additional bedroom. Quickly, I changed into the navy suit. It fit perfectly, and I wondered if it was made from pixie material. When I gazed in the full-length mirror in the corner of the room, I saw that the bathing outfit was a bit more revealing than my regular clothes, but not as much as my undergarments. I felt self-conscious, and my hair was a mess. I took a moment to fix my hair, then returned to the main room.

Mr. Withermyer stood in the living room, waiting for me. Quickly, I cast my eyes to the floor. I had never seen him dressed in anything other than a suit, and it had been dark when he'd worn pajamas. His skin was slightly tanned, and the muscles in his arms were prominent. The pants of the swimsuit came down to the tops of his knees. He cleared his throat, and I looked up at his face.

"The bathing suit looks very nice on you."

"Thank you," I replied, shifting my weight, and the dress swayed back and forth. "Shall we head to the beach?"

Mr. Withermyer held the front door of the cottage open, and I walked outside. The sea breeze caressed my face, and I breathed in the scent of the ocean. We walked side by side down the gentle slope to where the sand met the path. Mr. Withermyer gave me a slight grin before he kicked off his loafers and ran across the sand toward the water. Laughter bubbled in my throat, and I kicked my little shoes off beside his.

The sand was surprisingly hot beneath my feet, and soon I

found myself running toward the water. I stopped when my feet hit the wet sand, and a wave encompassed my ankles. I couldn't stop myself from yelping about the coldness of the water, and I jumped out of the next incoming wave. Mr. Withermyer began to laugh.

"You didn't tell me how hot the sand was," I said, wiggling my toes between the wet sand.

"Why did you think I was running?" he replied with a laugh.

Mr. Withermyer began to walk into the waves slowly. He jumped each time the crest of the waves smacked into his legs. He had gone out to where the water reached his mid-thigh and then turned around to look at me.

"Are you coming?"

I took a few tentative steps toward him. "Yes. I'm getting used to the water," I replied.

"You should just jump right in," he cried, throwing himself back into the next wave. His dark head disappeared for a moment, and then he resurfaced, his hair dripping with water.

I chuckled and took another step. The sand shifted beneath my feet, and I couldn't help smiling. Standing in the ocean water made me feel better than I had in a while. Despite everything that happened, I was delighted Mr. Withermyer brought me here. The water splashed up on my legs with every step, and soon, I was submerged up to my waist. Mr. Withermyer was still a few feet away from me. The waves were up to his chest. He turned around to check on me.

"The trick is when each wave comes, jump, and you'll float over them without getting splashed in the face," he called back to me.

I followed his instructions and soon made it out to where he was standing. The water was up to my shoulders, and I continued jumping as each wave rolled in. The cool water felt good as the sun beat down on us.

"Thank you for bringing me here. This place is wonderful," I said, swimming out a little further.

"I'm glad you like it. This is one of my favorite places. I figured you deserved to be in a serene setting such as this one. You've been through challenging times, and I believe the ocean has healing properties," he responded.

I couldn't agree more as I tilted my head back and floated on top of the gentle waves. I tried to clear my head and not think about the W.A.S.P. or Robert's family. Mr. Withermyer and I stayed at the beach for the rest of the afternoon. After we swam for a while, we walked on the beach collecting seashells. When the sun began to set, we both agreed it was time to head back and start dinner.

We walked up the sand, which didn't feel as hot as before, and I picked up my shoes from where I'd left them. Mr. Withermyer's pockets were full of shells, and they rattled against his legs as he walked. He levitated his shoes into his hands, and we climbed the slope to the house.

"There is a facet on the left side of the house where we can wash the sand off," Mr. Withermyer explained, showing me where it was located.

We both washed the sand off our feet before entering the cottage. Mr. Withermyer dumped the shells onto the coffee table, and I headed to my room to change. I stripped out of my slightly damp bathing suit and found a simple cotton dress in my suitcase. I felt so refreshed from swimming and walking on the beach.

Mr. Withermyer was still in his room when I came out of the bedroom, so I opened the pantry door. I descended into the cool basement and scanned the shelves. On one shelf was a small chicken, and I grabbed it along with some potatoes and carrots. I levitated the vegetables from the pantry and carried the chicken up the stairs. Once the items were on the counter, I went back into the pantry to collect garlic, parsley, and lemons. After sorting the ingredients, I turned to ensure the pantry door was shut. Checking each drawer and cabinet in the kitchen, I searched for the utensils I needed to prepare dinner.

Mr. Withermyer came out of his bedroom and surveyed the kitchen. "What did you decide on?" he asked, walking toward me.

"Roasted garlic and lemon chicken with potatoes and carrots, if that's okay?" I replied. "I was just about to light the oven."

"Here, let me," Mr. Withermyer said, coming around the kitchen table. He found a fire charm, and the oven sparked to life instantly.

I began chopping the garlic and lemons and stuffing them inside the chicken.

"What do you need help with?" Mr. Withermyer asked.

"Nothing. I'm fine. I can prepare dinner," I replied.

"I can help you. You always have to do chores like this when you're at the manor. So the least I can do is help," he offered.

"You've done so much to help already. I can never repay you for your kindness, so please allow me to take care of our meals while we stay here," I insisted.

"Okay, but may I offer one small bit of advice? You can use your magic here," he said, demonstrating by levitating a knife and commanding it to chop one of the potatoes.

A smile spread across my face. "I've never used magic to cook," I replied.

"You have complete freedom here, Jane. You can do whatever you want," he said with a wink, retreating into the living room.

It took me a few minutes, but I mastered the ability to chop up the carrots and the potatoes simultaneously. I levitated the chicken into the pan and spread the potatoes and carrots around it just by thinking. Then, without my hands, I opened the oven door and slid the roasting pan inside. I laughed when I realized I had just prepared an entire meal without physically touching anything. I checked the little clock on the wall before I pranced into the living room.

"You're going to spoil me this week," I announced, sitting on one of the sofas.

Mr. Withermyer was hunched over the coffee table, sorting through the shells we had collected. "Good, you deserve it," he replied, his green eyes glancing up at me.

"What are you doing?" I asked, leaning forward to watch him.

"I'm trying to decide what to do with these shells. There are books on the shelf if you want something to amuse yourself with as we wait for dinner," he offered.

I rose from the sofa and walked over to the bookshelf. Scanning the bindings, I chose *Pride and Prejudice* and settled back onto the sofa. I got lost in the world of the Bennet family, and every so often, I would check on the roasting chicken. I couldn't remember a time I could sit and read for pleasure. I did have freedom at the Jelf Academy, but most of it was spent studying. I was amazed at how comfortable and at home I felt in the Withermyer's summer cottage.

When the chicken had finished cooking, I called Mr. Withermyer to the table. He insisted on carving, and I let him serve the food. He instructed me to sit at the head of the table and took the chair next to mine.

"Everything looks delicious, Jane," he exclaimed, cutting into his chicken.

"Thank you. I hope you enjoy it," I said, picking up my fork and knife.

"Having dinner at this table reminds me of when my family used to come here every summer," Mr. Withermyer commented as we ate. "My mother used to cook meals like this after we'd spent the day playing in the ocean. I don't think her chicken was ever this tasty, though." He smiled at me before placing another forkful into his mouth.

"You're just saying that."

"No, I'm not. I guess I can trust you with the meals for the rest of the week," he teased.

"I learned to cook at a very young age. One of my first jobs was helping Ellen, the cook. It's part of my daily routine."

"Your father must've been very successful to have maids and servants employed in the house. I was thinking of how impressive it was when I came to retrieve you."

"I believe the farm does well. My father always took good care of it. I have no idea how Marie runs it now. My father was never outrageously wealthy. The manor is nothing compared to what Mr. Doyle's mansion used to be," I replied.

"Mr. Doyle is the man your stepsister married, right?" Mr. Withermyer asked in between bites.

"Yes, and he's very wealthy. I'm sure it was why Emily married him, and it doesn't hurt that he's easy on the eyes. Emily is a very shallow person."

Mr. Withermyer chuckled. "She seemed disappointed when she found out I came to the house for you."

"Knowing Emily, she probably thought you were easy on the eyes, too," I said with a joking smile.

Mr. Withermyer's cheeks were red, but I couldn't tell if it was because we'd been outside for the afternoon. Finally, he spoke. "I should probably shave off this beard. People will think I let myself go this summer." He reached up to touch the stubble along his jawline.

I shook my head, stabbing another potato. "I think the facial hair is becoming on you. It looks rather nice," I said encouragingly. "I wouldn't say you let yourself go."

"Well, that's nice to hear. Maybe I won't get rid of it just yet."

We continued to eat, and after a while, our conversation turned to our private lessons.

"We can go over a few things while we're here. Since we just had a close encounter with the W.A.S.P., it's imperative we continue your training," Mr. Withermyer stated, sitting back in his chair, his plate empty.

"Yes, I would love to. Today was so unexpected, and I shudder to think what would've happened if Mr. Lyons had caught us."

"That's why I want you to be prepared. If something like this were to happen when you're on your own, I want to be sure I taught you as much as I could."

I nodded, and we both agreed for a few hours each day, we would have lessons. Mr. Withermyer promised we'd still have time to swim in the ocean. He insisted on helping clean up the dishes, and then we spent the rest of the evening with Mr. Withermyer teaching me how to play gin rummy, a card game. With each hand, I got better, and it wasn't long before I was winning.

It was later when we both agreed it was time for bed. Mr. Withermyer put the cards away and wished me a good night before disappearing into his room. I closed the door to mine, and without any lamps, I made it to the bed by the moonlight shining through the window. My body felt exhausted, and I quickly drifted off to sleep. It was the first time in a long while I didn't dream at all.

7

SELF-DEFENSE LESSON

"STRIKE WITH THE outer edge of your hand and aim for the side of my throat. Focus your magic the same way you levitate something. Imagine that power on your hand and land the blow on my neck," Mr. Withermyer instructed.

We had been practicing self-defense on the beach for most of the morning. Sweat dripped down my face as the harsh sun blazed and refused to disappear behind the clouds. We'd chosen the beach as our practice area, and Mr. Withermyer reviewed each self-defense strategy I had learned before. Then, we focused on adding my magic to the counterattacks, making them more powerful.

I focused my energy on my right hand and struck Mr. Withermyer's throat. He partially blocked my swing, but my magic took him off balance, and he stumbled to his right. I waited while he steadied himself.

"That was better, but I want you to put more energy behind it. Don't worry about hurting me. My shield charm should protect me from the severity of your attack," he said.

"I do worry about hurting you. I've done it before," I replied, recalling the lesson we had last year.

"I'm sure I can fix anything you do to me," he said with a slight smile. "I'm going to attack you randomly, and we'll see how you go about escaping."

Without allowing me time to think, he reached out and grabbed ahold of my wrist. He didn't hurt me, but his grip was firm. I remembered I needed to relax my wrist and have a stable stance. Then, I quickly rotated my wrist toward his thumb, and I could feel his grip loosening. Concentrating my magic on my arm, I rapidly retracted my hand, and it slipped from his grasp. He nodded but instantly advanced on me again. My instincts had me raising my hands until the heel of my right hand collided with his nose. I remembered at the last minute to put magic into the attack, and Mr. Withermyer flew backward onto the sand.

"I'm sorry," I said, rushing to his side, but Mr. Withermyer stuck out his leg, causing me to trip and lose my balance. I fell on top of him, and his body cushioned my impact. Gently, he rolled me over until he pinned me to the ground. A look of triumph came over his face.

Not wanting to lose, I quickly hooked my right leg around his left one. I shifted my body to get him off balance, then focused on sending magic to my hips. Before I gave him a chance to counter my movements, I thrust my hips and tossed him to the right. Slowly, I sat up, slightly out of breath from our small struggle. Sand clung to my sweaty body, and I tried brushing it off my fingertips. Mr. Withermyer lay sprawled on the sand, staring at the sky and breathing rapidly. Cautiously, I took a step toward him.

"You're not going to knock me down again, are you?' I asked.

He shook his head and raised his hand in mock surrender. I approached and stood over him, my shadow blocking the sun from his eyes. The sand was dusted through his dark hair. His skin glistened with sweat, and he looked tanned from being out in the sun for the past few days. After a few moments, he smiled at me and opened his brilliant green eyes.

"That was very good. You're getting better with the techniques and using your magic," he said with a groan as he sat up.

I extended my hand to help him to his feet. He grasped my hand, our sandy fingers causing friction on our skin. I pulled on his hand when suddenly, he tugged me down onto the sand.

"I thought we had a truce," I exclaimed, landing on the sand beside him.

He laughed as I pushed myself up into a seated position. "We did, but I couldn't resist seeing the look on your face."

I scowled at him and playfully punched him on his forearm. I still couldn't believe the change I'd seen in him over the past year. A few years ago, I wouldn't have thought Mr. Withermyer was capable of laughing. He used to hate me and treated me more harshly than any other student. Now we were sitting on a beach, enjoying ourselves while he made jokes and laughed. I never would've imagined that I could be so comfortable around him. Ever since I lost my temper during a lesson last December, Mr. Withermyer began to understand what I'd been through. He became kind to me and even shared his feelings about my mother. If it weren't for Dr. Tweedle insisting on my private lessons, I wouldn't have gotten to know the man Mr. Withermyer truly was.

We both agreed to end our lessons for the day and went for a swim to cool off and wash the sand from our bodies. I closed my eyes and drifted on the waves, relishing the feel of the water. We would be leaving for the Jewel Caverns tomorrow, and as much as I enjoyed the caverns, I couldn't help feeling sad about leaving this place. I never felt so rejuvenated, and I pushed all my troubled thoughts about Robert's family to the side of my mind. My dreams hadn't haunted me this week. The cottage had been magical for me, and I didn't want to leave.

Mr. Withermyer and I left the beach later because I wanted to spend as much time as possible in the water. I made a simple dinner we both enjoyed, and we spent the evening playing cards again. We played through a couple of games, but my mind wasn't entirely on the cards. Mr. Withermyer shuffled and dealt the next hand before pausing to look at me.

"Jane, what's wrong? You've been pensively staring out the window the entire time we've been playing."

I shook my head and looked down at the cards in my hand. I already had a run of three cards, which I plucked from my hand and laid on the coffee table. Mr. Withermyer smirked, drawing a card from the deck and contemplating his next move. When he looked up at me, his face had become serious again.

"You can tell me anything. I hope you know that by now," he stated softly, placing a card on the discard pile.

I sighed deeply and shifted slightly on the sofa. "This is going to sound ridiculous, but I'm afraid of leaving this place. I've been so relaxed here, and I've finally been able to sleep. My nightmares seemed to be kept at bay because of this place, and I'm so afraid that everything will come rushing back once I leave. I'm excited to return to the Jelf Academy and see my friends, but I know they'll ask questions about Robert's family. I'm not sure if I want to talk about their connection with the W.A.S.P. Josefina will worry, Taylor will be terrified, and I'm not sure what Miguel and Kairi will do. All I know is everyone will judge humans more harshly, and none of them will understand that not all humans are bad. Not all humans are members of the W.A.S.P.," I said breathlessly.

"I know that not all humans are members of the W.A.S.P. It's just hard for pixies to understand when most human interactions end in death for us," Mr. Withermyer replied softly.

"Doesn't anyone realize how much it hurts my heart when humans are judged so severely? Everyone always seems to forget human blood runs through my veins. No matter how talented I am at magic, I'll always be half of my father."

"I'm sorry, Jane. You know your friends love you for every-thing that you are. They accept you, and so do I. I'll admit I was a fool blinded by hatred; for that, I'm ashamed, but I believe I've come to know you after our time together. You're correct. Pixies shouldn't judge all humans because of the actions of the W.A.S.P.," Mr. Withermyer stated.

"They do accept me, and I'm fortunate for all of them," I said. However, since I was part human, it amazed me that someone at the Jelf Academy talked to me, let alone became my friend.

"Yes, and I'm sure they'd all listen if you explained your feelings. You have nothing to be afraid of. Maybe your nightmares have ceased because you've completed the task Robert wanted. I know how you feel about this cottage because I feel the same way. I never like leaving this place. Perhaps sometime in the future, I'll be able to bring you here again."

"I would like that very much," I replied, drawing another card from the deck.

"Please don't be sad on our last night here. When we escaped Gettysburg, I thought of this place because it makes me happy. I hoped it would have the same effect on you," he said, placing his cards on the table. "I have an idea. Let's take a final walk on the beach. I'm sure it will make you feel better."

"It's dark out," I said with a laugh. "How would we even see where we're going?"

Mr. Withermyer quickly summoned a goblin fire lantern, and I couldn't help smiling. He extended his arm to me, and I bounded off the sofa.

"Wait until you see the stars over the ocean, my lady," he said with a grin, escorting me to the door.

❦

The moon was a full orb in the sky, casting some light as we walked down the path toward the beach. The gentle sea breeze swirled through my hair, softly pulling the loose ends out of my braid. We reached where the sand met the gravel road, and Mr. Withermyer held the lantern aloft as he kicked off his shoes. I removed my shoes as well and plunged my toes into the sand. The sand felt nice and cool compared to the middle of the day. I moved my toes around, savoring the feeling of freedom. As the wind blew around my face, I reached up and released my hair from the constraints of the braid. On this final evening, I wanted to feel completely free and at ease.

Mr. Withermyer stared at my blonde hair, blowing wildly in the wind. I shook my head and began running down the sand. My skirt swirled around my ankles as I breathed deeply and kicked up the sand beneath my feet. I stopped before reaching the water and spun around, laughing to see Mr. Withermyer trailing after me with the lantern. While I waited for him, I looked back at the ocean and the night sky. The stars took my breath away, and I stood there in awe.

"It's beautiful, isn't it?" Mr. Withermyer asked. When I turned around, I discovered he had summoned a blanket that he was currently sitting on.

"Yes, it is," I replied, dropping onto the blanket beside him.

Mr. Withermyer turned a knob on the lantern, and the goblin fire dimmed. The stars looked so much brighter without the blazing flame. I gradually lowered my head onto the blanket, my hair creating a fan shape around my head. Mr. Withermyer followed my lead, and we both gazed at the stars, the waves crashing on the shore. Neither of us said anything for a while. The only noises were the sounds of our breathing and the rolling of the ocean. It was so peaceful I hated to break the silence.

"The stars are so much brighter here," I murmured, my voice only a whisper.

"There is Ursa Major and Ursa Minor," Mr. Withermyer said, pointing his hand to the sky.

I learned about a few of the constellations when I had Zodiac Signs, and I pointed out the summer triangle, Canis Major, Scorpio, and the position of Venus in the night sky. I traced each constellation in the air, and Mr. Withermyer nodded.

"It's good to see you're learning something in other classes besides mine," he said with a laugh.

"What is that supposed to mean? Are you trying to say your class is the only one worth learning or that I'm not smart enough to retain information from other classes?"

"What I'm saying is I think you're very intelligent and have the ability to be the top student in your class."

I could feel my cheeks getting hot and was grateful it was so dark. "Thank you, and thank you again for bringing me here."

"It was my pleasure. It's nice to see you smile every once in a while."

I smiled and then gasped when a shooting star streaked across the sky. Its bright white tail flashed in the midnight sky. Mr. Withermyer saw it, too, pointing to the vanishing end of it.

"Do you know what they say about shooting stars? You're supposed to make a wish," Mr. Withermyer said.

I tilted my head toward him. "What are you going to wish for?" I asked.

"If I told you, it wouldn't come true," he replied with a wink in my direction.

I stared into his bright green eyes and contemplated what I should wish for. There were so many things I hoped for, but I knew they would never come true. I'd seen many things happen because of magic, but I'd never seen anyone be brought back to life. Was the magic from wishing on a star so powerful that it could make anything happen? I closed my eyes and concentrated hard. If I was being honest with myself, all I really wanted was to feel as happy as I'd been this week.

8

SCHOOL SHOPPING WITH
MR. WITHERMYER

THE MORNING SUN broke through my window and roused me from my sleep. It was hard to believe how fast the night had gone. I arose from the bed and crossed the room to my suitcase. Sifting through my clothes, I chose a comfortable outfit and slowly opened the door to my bedroom. The cottage was quiet, and I silently slipped into the bathroom. The knobs on the shower creaked as I turned them to regulate the water temperature. Once I had the perfect blend, I hopped under the water and scrubbed my skin. The water did wonders at waking me up, and I rinsed the soap from my hair.

When I finished, I turned the squeaky knobs again and reached for a fluffy white towel. I patted my body dry and wrapped my hair in the towel. I chose a plain white blouse and a light blue skirt. I dressed and headed out of the bathroom. The strong smell of coffee beckoned from the kitchen where Mr. Withermyer was seated at the table, a cup in his hands.

"Good morning, Jane," he said, turning to face me,

"Hello, Phillip," I replied, strolling into the kitchen and pouring myself a cup. I acquired a taste for it this week when Mr. Withermyer explained that other ingredients could be added to make the drink more pleasant.

"Do you have your school list with you?" he asked, taking a sip of his coffee.

I blew on my mug and nodded. "Yes, I have the letter and the supply list in my small bag. I haven't even opened it yet."

Mr. Withermyer nodded, finishing the last of his coffee. "I'm going to get a shower, and as soon as you have everything packed, we can leave for the Jewel Caverns."

He quickly rinsed his mug in the sink before heading for the bathroom door. I placed my cup on the kitchen table to cool for a few moments and walked to my bedroom to take the towel off my head. I combed through my damp blonde hair and swirled it into a bun atop my head. Then, I pulled the loose stands and curled them around my face with my finger.

The coffee was the perfect temperature when I took a sip, and I stared out the bay window while I drank it. The sky was a beautiful shade of blue with hardly any clouds. The waves mildly rolled into the shore, the white foam slowly creeping up the sand. I sighed deeply, inhaling the coffee aroma as I lifted the cup for another sip.

I'd just finished my coffee and was cleaning the cup in the sink when Mr. Withermyer exited the bathroom. He wore a white button-up shirt, black pants, and a black tie. His dark hair was combed back, and I was happy to see he'd left the beard and the mustache alone. He strolled across the kitchen area and gave me a grim smile.

"Do you have everything ready?" he questioned.

"Yes, my bags are packed in the other room," I replied, placing the coffee mug back in the cupboard.

Mr. Withermyer disappeared into my bedroom and returned with my bags. He placed them near the front door and turned toward me. "I'll grab my bags and load everything in the carriage. Then, I'll come back inside."

I nodded and crossed the room to the bay window seat. I sat down to wait. I wanted to view the ocean for as long as possible. Two seagulls soared across the sky, and I watched as they dipped toward the water. They were both splashed by the salty spray and quickly returned to the sky. Both were free to go wherever they pleased. I inhaled deeply and tried not to feel sad. At least I wasn't returning to the manor just yet.

Mr. Withermyer reentered the cottage and stood by the door. "Are you ready, Jane?" he asked.

I turned toward him and smiled, rising from the window seat. "Yes, I guess it's time to return to the real world," I commented, crossing the room toward him.

He nodded as he held the door open for me, and I blinked in the bright sunlight. The brown Clydesdale waited patiently as Mr. Withermyer helped me into the carriage seat. The day felt warm, and I longed for the ocean, but the week was over. It was hard to believe we were running from Mr. Lyons and the W.A.S.P. only a week ago. Now, I needed to focus on my fourth year at the Jelf Academy.

As Mr. Withermyer climbed aboard, I reached behind me for my small bag. Unclasping the latch, I found my letter. I replaced the bag as Mr. Withermyer pulled out the teleportation charm. I inclined my head in his direction as he uncorked the vial. Clutching the letter and the side of the carriage, I took one last look at the magnificent ocean before the black dust encircled me and obscured my view.

⋙

The mountains encasing the Jewel Caverns differed drastically from the ocean we had just left. It was strange not hearing the roar of the waves after having listened to that sound for a week. The mountain forest seemed so quiet. Mr. Withermyer steered the horse up the path until we stopped before the familiar rock face. It was a bit bizarre since I wasn't with Dr. Tweedle. Mr. Withermyer swiftly found the rocky lever and pulled it to open the cavern.

The rocks made a grinding noise as they lowered into the earth. Once all movement had ceased, Mr. Withermyer flicked the reins, and we moved inside. It took my eyes a moment to adjust to the darkness as the wall rose back into place behind us. Blues, greens, yellows, and reds from the sprites danced before my eyes as they illuminated the path. Finally, a larger light glowed at the end of the tunnel.

It wasn't long before we burst into the open cavern full of shops and houses. I smiled at the pixies walking along the spiraled street.

"Dr. Tweedle told me I could get your school money from the bank. Let me see your school list so we can decide where to go first," Mr. Withermyer suggested.

I pried open the wax seal and pulled out two pieces of paper, spreading the pages out on my lap.

Dear Jane Fitzgerald,

I am eager to welcome you back to the Jelf Academy of Magic for your fourth year. Enclosed is the list of books and items you will need for your classes. Classes begin the last week of August. As headmaster of the Jelf Academy of Magic, I wish you a wonderful fourth year and anticipate your return.

Sincerely,

Dr. Oliver Tweedle

Headmaster of the Jelf Academy of Magic

SCHOOL SUPPLIES:

- *Restock the 12 Astrological Gemstones*
- *Restock all the ingredients in pixie dust case as needed.*
- *Additional materials (notebooks, pencils, etc.)*

BOOKS:

- *Mixing Stone Powders Volume IV-* Randolf Talc
- *Magical Creatures of the World Volume III-* Natalie Tame
- *Pixies of the American and French Revolutions-* Alyson Bashita
- *Connecting with the Spirit Realm and Similar Divinations-* Joan Clearfield
- *Transfiguration and You: Changing Appearance at Will-* Stephan Meta
- *Introduction to Teleportation: How Not to Leave the Important Bits Behind-* Dr. Oliver Tweedle

OPTIONAL:

- *A small pet to keep in your dormitory.*

I blinked and reread the book list. Had Dr. Tweedle really written one of the textbooks? I asked Mr. Withermyer as much.

"Yes, Dr. Tweedle is quite an expert at teleportation. He's written a few textbooks on the subject. He insists on teaching that class even though he is the headmaster. You can't expect to learn teleportation from anyone better than the master of the subject," Mr. Withermyer explained.

"I had no idea Dr. Tweedle taught classes," I replied, my eyes scanning down to the bottom of the page.

We reached the bottom of the cavern, and Mr. Withermyer disappeared into the bank. I looked over my school list again while I waited. Suddenly, I heard a familiar fake laugh and looked up to see Betty Ann Barber coming out of the bank. She was accompanied by a man with salt and pepper hair, who I knew was her father. I had seen them in the Jewel Caverns before. There was also a woman with them. She had the same hair color as Betty Ann, except it was cut in a short bob. I assumed she was Betty Ann's mother.

Betty Ann spotted me sitting in the carriage and scowled in my direction. Her father also noticed, and the three of them walked in my direction. I hadn't forgotten Betty Ann's threats at the end of last year. I arranged my expression to look indifferent as the family drew parallel with the carriage.

"Good morning, Jane. Mother, this is one of my classmates," Betty Ann said in a sickeningly sweet voice, confirming my suspicions.

I extended my hand to shake her mother's, even though I'd rather not, but I wouldn't be openly rude. Her mother's face looked pinched, and her eyes seemed to narrow. She scrutinized everything about me, and I wondered if she knew I was half-human.

"Mom, this is Jane Fitzgerald," Betty Ann said with a fake smile.

"I'm Kelly Ann Barber, and this is my husband, Arnold," Betty Ann's mother said with an air of superiority.

"Yes, we've met," I replied, releasing my hand from her grip.

"Jane is Rachel McCalski's daughter," Betty Ann added, and I could've sworn I watched Mrs. Barber wipe her hand off on her dress. A tight smile crossed her face. I subtly dragged my hand along the carriage while looking down at them. I wanted all three of them to go away. I wondered how to make that happen without being blunt or impolite. What was taking Mr. Withermyer so long?

"Picking up your school supplies?" Mr. Barber asked gruffly.

"Yes, I am," I replied, trying not to fidget on the seat. I didn't want to show any discomfort. I also wanted my responses to be short in hopes they would get the message that I had no desire to talk to any of them.

"We just came from the bank, and I didn't see Dr. Tweedle. Your family is human, so they couldn't bring you to the Jewel Caverns," Betty Ann said, emphasizing the word human. "Doesn't he normally bring his favorite student to get her school supplies?"

I decided not to reply because I saw Mr. Withermyer crossing the street toward me. His eyes shifted back and forth, taking in the Barbers with a look of confusion. Mr. Barber must've noticed my gaze because he turned to see what had caught my attention.

"Ah, Mr. Withermyer, fancy seeing you here," Mr. Barber said, reaching out to shake Mr. Withermyer's hand.

"We've just come from the bank and didn't see you inside. We must've just missed you," Mrs. Barber said snootily.

"Yes, I suppose so," Mr. Withermyer answered politely.

"How're things going at the Jelf Academy? Are you ready for the upcoming year?" Mr. Barber asked.

"As ready as I can be. I haven't stayed at the school this summer. I've been consumed with running errands for Dr. Tweedle," Mr. Withermyer replied, taking another step toward the carriage.

Mr. Barber's eyes widened in understanding, stepping to the side to let Mr. Withermyer pass. "Guess one of those errands was to oversee Miss Fitzgerald's school shopping," he chuckled as if Mr. Withermyer assisting me was a joke.

"Have you talked to Blair? Is she enjoying the Jelf Academy?" Mrs. Barber asked.

"I haven't seen her since the spring," Mr. Withermyer said. "She seems to be settling in. I'm sorry to cut our conversation short, but I really must be on my way."

"Oh well, it was nice seeing you. Tell Blair I said hello," Mrs. Barber answered, the three of them stepping away from the carriage. Betty Ann squinted her eyes at me while Mr. Withermyer climbed up beside me.

Mr. Withermyer shook the reins, and the Clydesdale turned and headed up the road. I waited until we were out of earshot before I turned to Mr. Withermyer.

"Who is Blair?" I asked.

"Blair is Ms. Pregmon," he answered.

I blinked in surprise. "How do the Barbers know Ms. Pregmon?" I asked.

"Kelly Ann Barber's older sister married Lawrence Pregmon, and they had Blair," Mr. Withermyer explained.

It took me a moment to process the information. "Do you mean to tell me that Blair, I mean Ms. Pregmon, is Betty Ann's cousin?" I practically yelped.

"Yes," Mr. Withermyer said again.

"So that's why Ms. Pregmon favors Betty Ann in class! It's because they're related!" I exclaimed.

"Well, she's not supposed to let her personal emotions get involved with teaching," Mr. Withermyer said, and I looked at him quizzically.

"This, coming from the man who carried a torch of hatred for me?" I stated.

"Jane, how many times must I apologize?" Mr. Withermyer asked, looking stricken.

I laughed and swayed into him. "I'm sorry, I can't point out the irony?" I asked, and Mr. Withermyer shook his head. "The Barbers acted like you are well acquainted with Ms. Pregmon." I had never seen them exchange words.

"I'm not very close with Blair. We just went to school together," he answered.

"Wait, did she know my mother?" I inquired.

"She started the Jelf Academy when Rachel was in her fourth year and I was in my third. She knew of your mother, of course, but

Blair wasn't our friend. Besides, Rachel was so busy with her internship and her complicated classes that I don't even know if they ever spoke," he commented, steering the horse to the side of the road.

"How do you know the Barbers, then? From their interaction, I assumed they knew you on a personal level."

"Everyone knows the Barbers. Since Mr. Barber works for the Pixie government, he sometimes takes interns from the school. So that is how we're acquainted. Also, some of the Academy staff help with government projects during the summer months. I can't say I'm the biggest fan of the family, but Mr. Barber is influential since he donates money to the school," Mr. Withermyer sighed. Then he gestured to a building where he stopped the carriage. "How about we stop at *Paper and Ink* first?"

I nodded, looking up at the bookstore carved into the cavern wall. When I stepped inside, I breathed deeply, loving the smell of freshly printed books. Then, taking out my list, I began searching for the books I needed.

Mr. Withermyer picked up a basket and followed me around the store, letting the basket levitate behind us. It was easy to find *Mixing Stone Powders Volume IV* and *Magical Creatures of the World Volume III*. I plucked them from the shelves where they sat with the previous volumes.

Dr. Tweedle's face smiled at me from the back cover of the Teleportation book. He had never mentioned writing a textbook or teaching Teleportation. I placed his book in the basket along with the rest. I only needed to find one more book on my list.

Finding the Predicting the Future textbook was more complicated than the others. Mr. Withermyer helped me look through all the shelves in the reference section. When we didn't find it after a while, I finally asked someone who worked in the store. They pointed me toward the back to what they called the occult section. All the bindings in this section looked eerie, and I quickly searched through the titles. Finally, I found *Connecting with the Spirit Realm and Similar Divinations*. A chill coursed through me as I took in the front cover. There was a ghostly-looking girl shrouded in mist, and something about it reminded me of the dream I had about the Lyons' estate. With a shiver, I purchased my textbooks and hurriedly left the store.

Our next stop was *Jewels and Powders*. Mr. Withermyer helped me refill my astrological gemstones. He insisted on getting extra ingredients because we would use them in my private lessons. Once the basket was full to bursting, we paid and returned to the carriage. Mr. Withermyer pointed the carriage toward the *Leaf and Lily Inn*.

I was excited to see Irene again and almost leapt from the carriage when we stopped in front of the cozy inn. Goblin fire candles glowed softly in all the windows, and the partial glass door was etched with the inn's name and two lilies on each side of the text. Mr. Withermyer came around and helped me down. Then he retrieved my bags.

"It's been a long time since I've seen Irene," he commented, carrying my bags to the door.

"She'll be happy to see you," I said, holding the door for him.

The inn always felt cozy, and I couldn't help smiling. Irene stood behind the counter, and when she saw us come in, she let out a yelp of excitement.

"Phillip, is that really you?" she asked, coming around the counter. Mr. Withermyer placed my luggage on the floor before she flung her arms around him. They hugged for a few moments before Irene stepped back to look at him. "I haven't seen you since you were thirteen or fourteen. How have you been? What have you been up to?" she asked him.

"I've been well. After the Jelf Academy, I continued my education so I could teach students at a school like the Jelf Academy. When I finished my training, Dr. Tweedle immediately contacted me and offered me a position. I've been teaching there ever since."

"That's wonderful! I'm so glad to hear it. Jane mentioned you were teaching at the Jelf Academy. You look so grown up, and you're still so handsome," Irene commented, and Mr. Withermyer blushed a little. "What brings you to the *Leaf and Lily*? You've never stopped in before."

"Other matters detained Dr. Tweedle, so I've brought Jane," he replied as Irene's eyes found mine.

"Hello, Jane, dear. Forgive me; I didn't see you standing there," she said, coming over to hug me. I stepped into her warm embrace, and I could've sworn she smelled like freshly baked cookies. "It's so nice to see you! Are you both going to have dinner?"

"Yes, I suppose so. If you give me the number to Jane's room, I can run the bags up and be right back," Mr. Withermyer replied.

Irene went back behind the counter and handed Mr. Withermyer a key. "I think Rachel would be so happy to see her school friends reunited and in the company of her daughter," Irene sighed before Mr. Withermyer headed up the granite steps to the second floor.v

Once Mr. Withermyer returned, Irene seated us in her small restaurant. After handing us the menus, she promised she would stop over in a while. I smiled as she went to check on her other guests.

"It's so strange seeing Irene again after all these years," Mr. Withermyer stated, his eyes scanning the menu.

"Weren't you friends with her? Why haven't you come by?" I asked. I didn't mean to pry; if he didn't want to answer, I wouldn't push the question.

Mr. Withermyer shrugged and cleared his throat. "We were friends in school, but Irene was older than your mother and much older than me. It was Rachel who held our friendship together. Irene and I lost touch after the Jelf Academy. She got married, and I focused on becoming a teacher. As the years went by, it became harder to make an appearance. I knew she would talk about Rachel, and I didn't think my heart could handle it."

His facial expression looked pained, and I touched his hand over the table. "I'm sorry. I wasn't aware of how hard it was for you."

"No, I'm fine. Talking about Rachel with you has eased the pain. I should've stopped in to see Irene before today," he replied.

One of Irene's waitresses took our order and brought two glasses of water. The cold drink felt like heaven to my parched throat, and I drained half the glass. As I put the glass back down, Irene came to the table and sat beside me.

"Did you get all your materials?" she asked me. "Time moves so quickly. It seems like yesterday you were getting ready to begin your first year."

"Yes. I collected everything Dr. Tweedle had on my list," I replied.

"You get to start Teleportation this year. That class is exciting. Hopefully, you won't make the same mistakes I did. I was in the hospital wing a few times for botched teleportation," Irene said with a chuckle.

I was glad I stopped drinking my water because I would have choked on it. "What do you mean by botched teleportation?" I asked cautiously.

"If you don't make the charm and use it correctly, you can leave parts of yourself behind," Mr. Withermyer explained. I was sure my face had gone pale. "Don't worry, Jane. I'm sure when you practice, nothing terrible will happen. You've done well with every charm you've created. I'm sure teleportation won't be any different."

"There is a first time for everything," I gulped. "With my luck, it would be the first charm I didn't master."

"It doesn't hurt that much when it happens, and a botched teleportation can almost always be fixed. You'll feel a numbness and some tingling in the body parts that were left behind," Irene said, patting me on the back.

"Yes, it definitely sounds pleasant," I sighed sarcastically.

"Don't be uneasy. Phillip is correct. You are your mother's daughter. You'll be mastering teleportation in no time," Irene said, rubbing my arm affectionately.

Our food arrived, and we began eating. Irene stayed at the table a while longer until she was called away to the front desk. Mr. Withermyer and I talked about tomorrow and hypothesized about the school year. I wondered about classes and how my friends spent their summer vacations. When we finished, Irene returned to the table and declared the meal was on her.

"No, let me pay for the dinner. You have a business to run, and you can't make any money if you're giving food away," Mr. Withermyer objected, pulling out his wallet.

Irene waved her hand in a dismissing motion. "It's the least I can do for an old friend," she replied sternly.

"Please allow me to pay. I haven't been a supportive friend over the years, and I'm very sorry I haven't visited sooner. I'm a coward. I couldn't bear to talk about Rachel's death, and I was sure you would want to. You knew how important she was to me, and it was too hard to face the memories I knew would resurface if I came to visit. I'm sorry if my absence has offended or hurt you. I didn't stay away because of you," Mr. Withermyer explained.

"Phillip, I'm not hurt or offended. I understand that life has a way of separating people. You were busy with your life, and I was busy with mine. Neither of us had any intention of hurting the other. I'll accept your apology, although it was not needed. However, I will not accept your money. I'm just glad we got to see each other again, and maybe you won't be such a stranger in the future," Irene said as they hugged each other again.

"Well, Jane, I must be on my way," Mr. Withermyer said, pausing by the front door.

"You're not going to spend the night here?" I asked.

"No, I must be on my way to prepare for tomorrow," he replied.

"Oh," I said, slightly disappointed. I'd spent so much time with him over the past two weeks. I just assumed he would be staying.

"Get a good night's rest, and I'll see you at the academy tomorrow," Mr. Withermyer said, touching my shoulder.

Without thinking, my arms encircled his middle. "Thank you so much for the last two weeks. I appreciate everything you've done for me and what you continue to do with my private lessons," I mumbled into his chest. He smelled like sandalwood and the crisp scent of ocean breezes. His arms came around me momentarily, and then we released each other. He handed me the keys to my room, his fingertips grazing my palm.

"Good night. I'll see you tomorrow," he said with a smile, placing his hand on the doorknob.

"Good night," I echoed, watching him leave the *Leaf and Lily Inn*.

After a few moments of staring out the door, I took a deep breath and headed up the granite stairs to the second floor. The goblin fire sconces on the wall lit up the hallway and illuminated the room numbers on each door. I easily found the room corresponding with the key in my hand and turned the key, pushing the door open. The room felt so dead, so empty. Typically, I loved everything about the *Leaf and Lily Inn*, but I felt so alone for some reason. I changed into my pajamas and crossed the room to where Mr. Withermyer had placed my suitcase. I lifted the bag onto the bed and popped the latch open. On top of my clothes was a bulging envelope that hadn't been there this morning when I had packed. Curious, I picked up the envelope and tore it open. A bracelet made out of shells fell into my palm, along with a letter.

Dearest Jane,

I made this bracelet out of the seashells we collected on the beach. You'll always carry a piece of the ocean when you wear it.

Love,

Phillip Withermyer

I smiled and clasped the bracelet onto my wrist. Mr. Withermyer had only been gone for a few moments, but I was surprised by how much I had missed him already.

9

My Fourth Year Begins

THE WIND BLEW through my hair as I looked out the carriage window. The ground below looked so small as the winged horses gained altitude. Their white feathered wings shimmered in the morning sun as they flew up, up, up into the clouds. As the horses continued along the familiar route to the meadow, I settled into my seat.

It would be wonderful to see my friends, and my heart skipped a beat when I thought of my dragon, Thistle. She had stayed at the academy the summer before, so I hoped she'd still be there when I returned. I worried she would take off into the sky and disappear one day. No one had ever kept a dragon, so even Mrs. Rowley wasn't sure what Thistle would do. My dragon was the only one who had ever stayed. All the others had taken to the sky when they had reached a certain age. I held on to the fear that Thistle would be gone someday.

The winged horses swooped through the sky, and my stomach dropped from the shaking carriage. Looking out the window, I could tell the horses were starting to descend. Other carriages filled the sky around me, aiming for the meadow beneath. It wasn't long before my carriage landed with a slight bump, and I bounced up off my seat. The horses slowed to a stop, and I waited another minute before I stood up to open the door.

There was a flurry of activity around me as the other carriages landed and students emerged. I levitated my luggage and checked to ensure my seashell bracelet was still on my wrist. I smiled and lightly touched the shells before scanning the field of arriving students. Since I didn't see any of my friends, I floated my bags behind me as I went in search of them.

So many new faces passed by. Several of them looked so nervous that it was easy to see this was their first time arriving at the meadow. I smiled at those anxious faces, picking my way through the crowd, on the hunt for anyone familiar. The warm sun shone on my back, and if it weren't for the cooling breeze blowing across the meadow, I would be sweating. I shielded my eyes and spun around, looking in all directions. Finally, a musical laugh caught my attention. I turned toward the sound, and my eyes landed on Kairi.

"Jane," Kairi's melodic voice called out when she saw me. "It's so good to see you."

Kairi's reddish-brown hair shone in the sun. Her brother, Zachary, stood to her left, and Taylor to her right. I discovered that Kairi was half-pixie and half-mermaid last year. She needed the wheelchair because of her tail, which she kept hidden beneath long skirts and the blankets across her lap. No one besides a few teachers and I knew Kairi's secret. I'd accidentally discovered it and had promised to keep it to myself. Due to her pixie blood, Kairi could be on land in her mermaid form. Only one week, during a full moon, Kairi's tail transformed into legs.

Zachary smiled at me when I approached, his teeth gleaming white in the sunlight. He was really Kairi's half-brother; his mother had been a pixie. Zachary was very grateful I kept his sister's secret. He's very protective of Kairi, especially since she'd been treated poorly at their previous school, the Capra Academy of Magic.

Zachary had been expelled for defending his sister. Many pixies frowned upon anyone who was a half-blood, which was why Kairi wanted to keep her heritage unknown.

As I stood before them, I realized both Zachary and Kairi had eyes that were different shades of the ocean. Zachary's were an aqua blue, while Kairi's were a fitting shade of sea green. Their skin looked tan, and I was sure they had been near the ocean this summer. Their father was in the cruise ship business, and he was an excellent sailor.

I placed my suitcases on the ground nearby and then looked at Taylor. I was surprised to see her usually pale skin was slightly red, as if she had also spent the summer in the sun.

"Hello, everyone," I said, hugging Taylor first before embracing Kairi. Zachary encircled his arms around me next, which surprised me because he'd been slightly standoffish last year. I couldn't blame him. They had been new students, and he was unsure if he could trust anyone after what happened at the Capra Academy.

"We've missed you, Jane," Taylor said.

"You all look well. Have you three been enjoying the outdoors this summer," I asked.

"Taylor's family allowed her to accompany us on our father's ship this summer. She was only going to spend a few weeks with us, but we were having so much fun we begged for the entire summer," Kairi exclaimed.

I was glad to hear Taylor was able to have some fun. Her past wasn't happy, and she'd been so withdrawn when she first arrived at the Jelf Academy. After Robert's death, Taylor had confided in me about the W.A.S.P.'s execution of her twin sister, Tammy. Twins have an exceptional bond in the pixie world, and Taylor felt all of her sister's pain through the bond. I didn't think anyone else in our group of friends knew about Taylor's sister. It seemed I was the keeper of secrets.

"We wished that you would have been able to join us as well,"

Zachary added, a blush coloring his cheeks as he nudged his sister's arm.

"Yes, of course, Jane. I'm sorry. It was very insensitive of me to talk about our vacation while you were trapped in that manor," Kairi apologized.

"No, you have nothing to be sorry about. On the contrary, I'm glad to hear about your summer," I replied, and Kairi's eyes strayed to my bracelet.

"Wow, your bracelet is beautiful!" Kairi commented, reaching out and grabbing my wrist. She touched the shells and closed her eyes as if listening for something. "These shells are from the eastern coast, maybe North or South Carolina. Either you managed a visit, or you have a secret admirer sending you gifts from that area," Kairi said with a wink.

I felt my cheeks going red, but I didn't want her to think it was because of her latter guess. "I've had a fascinating couple of weeks, but I'll tell you all about it when we find Miguel and Josefina," I said.

Kairi looked slightly disappointed that she had to wait, but Taylor smiled and began talking about where they had cruised and what they'd done. I listened with interest as they laughed and explained their trip. Taylor's light blue eyes seemed to sparkle more than I'd ever seen, and I also noticed how they kept sliding over to Zachary. A slight grin touched the corners of my mouth, and I couldn't help but wonder if Taylor had begun to fancy him.

The meadow filled with students, but there was still no sign of Miguel and Josefina. Though I continued my light-hearted conversation, I was beginning to worry. The twins had never been late before. Usually, the Martinez family were the first friendly faces I found.

Suddenly, the magical cloud began to descend. Everyone in the meadow began forming a line.

"Does anyone see Josefina and Miguel?" I asked, panicked as the crowd jostled to form a line.

Taylor, Kairi, and Zachary also began looking, their eyes filled with concern. With the W.A.S.P., no one was safe, and nothing was certain. My heart began to pound with dread. I feared I would lose my mind if something happened to my two dearest friends.

The students around us began moving toward the cloud, but I stayed rooted to the spot, gripping my luggage and scanning the faces that passed.

Suddenly, Zachary let out a shout. "There they are. Here they come now!" he exclaimed, raising his arm in the air and waving it.

Relief came crashing down upon me, causing a rush to my head. I swayed to the side, feeling slightly dizzy. Taylor grasped my hand, and I was grateful for her steadying presence. I still couldn't see them, but Zachary was taller than me. Finally, after a few minutes, Josefina and Miguel broke through the crowd. Josefina had a large smile as she embraced me. Her dark hair was curled in ringlets down her back, and a matching red ribbon adorned her hair. She released me from our embrace, her dark brown eyes meeting my violet ones.

"Jane, what's wrong? You look so pale," Josefina questioned.

"You and Miguel weren't here. I was so worried," I said as Miguel greeted me.

"We are fine. Only running a little late," Josefina said, rubbing my arm.

"Without Juan pushing Josefina along, she wasn't ready on time," Miguel said with a smirk.

I remembered their older brother, Juan, and friend, Lena, had graduated from the Jelf Academy last year. It was strange to see the twins without their brother accompanying them. Juan had been like a paternal figure in our group, and I would miss him and Lena. I wondered what they were doing now.

Josefina and Miguel greeted the rest of our friends, and we got in line. Since we were looking for the twins, we were now toward the end of the line. Slowly, we inched along with the crowd.

Josefina and Miguel began discussing their summer as we waited for the line to move.

"I attended the summer History classes Mr. Collyworth offered to students who want to pursue a career in History," Miguel said. "The classes were only in July, but the lessons were so stimulating I wouldn't have minded if they lasted all of August too. My father wasn't happy about sending me, but my mother convinced him. He finally relented and let me attend. I know he wants me to be a part of the family business, but he already has Juan for that."

"So, Juan is working with your father in the gem mine?" I asked.

"Yes, they both leave the house early, which was why Juan wasn't around this morning to make sure Josefina was on time," Miguel teased his sister.

Josefina shot him an evil glare as the line moved forward again. "I don't need Juan to be on time. We didn't miss passage on the cloud," she huffed.

"Did many students take the summer history class?" Taylor wondered.

"No, there were only ten from our year and a small handful from the year above us. I was glad Andrew took the class, too, because at least one of my friends was there," Miguel answered, squinting in the sun. "Has anyone seen Andrew?"

"Yes, I did," Taylor commented. "A younger cousin of his is beginning their first year. Andrew wanted to make sure he got onto the cloud. I spoke with them earlier."

"That's good," Miguel answered, looking relieved. "Andrew is close to all his cousins since he is an only child."

We all grew quiet, remembering one of Andrew's cousins and an aunt and uncle had been murdered by the W.A.S.P. It happened in our second year when the W.A.S.P. discovered several pixie families. It had been the largest number of pixie murders in several years.

Kairi's lilting voice filled the air. "What did you learn for a whole month?"

Miguel smiled down at her before he continued speaking again. "We looked at artifacts from different periods and had to date them. It was fascinating."

"Yes, and if a month of examining artifacts wasn't enough, we visited Uncle Fernando and Aunt Teresa for two weeks," Josefina added.

Miguel chuckled as his sister rolled her eyes. I knew the time spent with her aunt and uncle consisted of Miguel discussing history.

"You act like you didn't have a wonderful time," Miguel scoffed.

"I did. I'm only saying you spent the summer consumed with the past instead of the present," Josefina commented.

"Which is wonderful since it's Miguel's favorite subject," Kairi chimed in, coming to Miguel's defense. "Anyway, Jane told us she had a few interesting weeks this summer but refused to say any more until you two arrived."

"Did you manage to do it? Did you find Robert's family?" Josefina asked, her eyes going huge.

The whole group turned to stare at me.

"How did you manage to leave the manor?" Taylor asked in a soft voice as everyone looked dumbfounded.

I smiled slightly and looked at each of their faces. Mr. Withermyer's help had been a secret. Only Josefina knew of the role Mr. Withermyer played in helping me. I swallowed the lump in my throat and took a deep breath.

"If I tell you, you can't tell anyone. I wouldn't want to get the other person involved in trouble," I said. We had almost reached the cloud. Every one of my friends vigorously nodded, and I began. "I received a clue on the whereabouts of Robert's family at the end of the last school year. Lena recognized the crest on the Lyons family ring." I reached up to where the chain usually hung beneath my blouse, then realized I no longer had the ring.

"Wait. How did Lena recognize the crest? She doesn't remember anything about the past," Zachary questioned.

"She must have finally recalled something because I was able to find Robert's family," I said.

"How? Did he help you?" Josefina gasped.

"Who?" Kairi inquired.

"Will you just let Jane tell the story?" Taylor said gently.

Everyone quieted down and turned to me with impatient stares. "To answer Josefina's question, Mr. Withermyer helped me find them."

I waited for another interruption, but they all remained silent. After a moment, I continued. "Dr. Tweedle didn't want me to search for Robert's family. He said it was too dangerous. In a way, he was right, but I'll get to that in a moment. Through our private lessons, Mr. Withermyer understood how important it was to me, so he offered to help. When I received the lead from Lena, I told Mr. Withermyer, and he promised to follow up on it.

"Two weeks ago, Mr. Withermyer came to the manor. He convinced Marie that I needed to attend a social lesson. She allowed me to leave. We teleported to Gettysburg because Lena told us she'd seen the crest in Peach Glen, a smaller town nearby," I said.

"Peach Glen is where Lena's family used to live," Josefina whispered.

"Yes, and that was where we found Robert's family. I met Robert's mother, his younger sister, and his father. I was able to tell them about his death, but I didn't mention Mr. Wicker. Thankfully, I told them he died in a fire," I sighed.

"Well, of course, you weren't going to tell them he was murdered while defending you from a member of the W.A.S.P.," Miguel stated.

"Correct, plus the story was very complicated. It was also good that I didn't because Mr. Lyons received a letter while we were there. Before he opened it, I spied the wax seal on the envelope. The stamp in the wax was an insect surrounded by a hexagonal shape, which can only mean one thing. Mr. Lyons is involved with the W.A.S.P."

10

CLASSES OLD AND NEW

THEY ALL STARED at me with open mouths while the cloud descended and stopped a few feet ahead of us. Mentally, I lifted my luggage and boarded my friends, scrambling after me to do the same. I knew my friends would want me to continue the conversation, so I moved further away from the other students since I knew my friends would like me to continue. I started to resume my story when Taylor interrupted me.

"How did you escape?" she asked. Her tan face had gone pale and frightened. I knew this story would upset her the most.

"Mr. Withermyer noticed the seal, too, and made an excuse as to why we had to leave. We quickly rode back to Gettysburg, but I could sense something was wrong," I explained as the cloud lifted us into the sky.

For a moment, we focused on retaining our balance. Then, once I had centered myself, I took a deep breath and continued speaking.

"Mr. Withermyer had the same feelings of dread, and we agreed to leave Gettysburg as soon as possible. However, shortly after returning to the hotel, I noticed Mr. Lyons coming down the street.

I wasn't sure if Mr. Lyons realized what we were, but it was apparent he had followed us to Gettysburg.

"Mr. Withermyer managed to get us out just in time," I finished, explaining our escape through the woods.

The castle rose before me, and it wasn't until this moment that I realized what a relief it was to see it again. During my week at the beach, I almost forgot the fear I felt in Gettysburg, but talking about it now brought it to the forefront of my mind.

"If Mr. Lyons was a member of the W.A.S.P, they probably know who you are by now. They'll be looking for Jane Fitzgerald everywhere. It will only be a matter of time before they find you," Josefina said, fear rising in her voice. "Dr. Tweedle will be furious if he finds out after all the hard work he's done to protect you."

"Are you going to tell him?" I asked her. It was Josefina's fault that Dr. Tweedle discovered I had been in love with a human.

Josefina shook her head, and I could tell she could sense where my train of thought had headed. "No, Jane. I would never! It's just that…."

"I think my sister is trying to say if the W.A.S.P. are looking for a Fitzgerald, then wouldn't it be best if Dr. Tweedle was aware? Maybe he wouldn't send you back to the manor for your safety," Miguel offered.

"I didn't introduce myself to the Lyons family as Jane Fitzgerald. I told them I was Miss Withermyer. We posed as brother and sister. Besides, Mr. Lyons might not have realized we were pixies. He accused me of wanting money in exchange for information about his son. Perhaps there was another reason he came after us. Also, the manor was my father's home, and I would have nowhere else to go. I wouldn't want to be a burden," I said.

Josefina still looked slightly uneasy, but Kairi said, "We're glad you made it away safely. Did anything else happen?"

"Mr. Withermyer teleported us away just in time to his family's summer cottage on the beach. It was the first safe place he could think of," I said, dropping my voice to a whisper as we got closer to the school.

"Oh, so that's where you got the shells," Kairi commented, gesturing to my wrist.

I nodded as we reached the steps. Zachary wheeled Kairi toward the ramp while we walked up the stairs. The front doors magically swung open for us, and we stepped into the main entrance. Our bags followed behind us. Dr. Tweedle stood just outside the entrance to the dining hall.

"First-time students, please enter the dining hall for orientation. All others, please proceed to the fourth floor to get your schedules and dormitory assignments," Dr. Tweedle instructed.

Josefina, Miguel, Taylor, and I climbed the stairs while Zachary and Kairi went to the unique dumbwaiter system, which she used to navigate the multiple stories. We climbed up the stairs because the line for the dormitory assignments was so long.

"So, you at least got to go to the beach?" Josefina asked, and I shook my head, looking around.

"Let's not discuss it here. I'll tell you all about my week at the beach later," I replied.

"Oh, you were there for a week?" she exclaimed, and I glared at her as Miguel laughed softly.

"You should know by now how impatient Josefina is when it comes to gossiping about something," Miguel said.

"It is not gossip! I'm just curious about my friend's summer," Josefina insisted as the line moved forward again.

We finally made it to the top of the stairs. Mr. Withermyer was seated at a table with a long list of student names and a stack of envelopes containing class schedules. He assigned each student to a dormitory and paired them with a classmate.

Josefina and I approached the table, and Mr. Withermyer looked up. "Good morning, Miss Martinez and Miss Fitzgerald," he said.

I blinked at the formality. He hadn't called me Miss Fitzgerald for the last two weeks, which sounded strange now. I should've realized that our informal banter would have to end with our return to the Jelf Academy. It wasn't acceptable anymore.

"Good morning, Mr. Withermyer," I replied, and if he felt the same way as I did, he didn't show it. "Josefina and I would like to share a room again."

He nodded as if he expected as much and found our names on his roster. "This year, you'll be in room 444 on floor number seven," Mr. Withermyer said, marking our room number on his papers. Then he sorted through the remaining stack of envelopes to the ones addressed to us. "Here are your schedules. I'll see you both in Charms class," he said as he looked up at me.

Josefina and I thanked him as we moved to the side to allow Taylor and Miguel access to the table. Taylor shared a room with Kairi, and Miguel requested to be with Andrew again. Then, the four of us took the stairs to the seventh floor.

Josefina and I looked for our room, and we didn't have far to search because it was at the beginning of the first hallway closest to the stairs. I placed my hand on the pad next to the door and waited for the uncomfortable pinch. Then the door rattled off my information, followed by Josefina's. When the door was finished recognizing her handprint, it slid open to allow us access to the room.

"You were saying you got to spend a week on the beach," she said, slyly raising one of her eyebrows.

"Yes, it was the first time I've seen the ocean," I replied, pulling out my other supplies for classes.

"What was it like being with Mr. Withermyer alone all that time?" she asked, rifling through her suitcase.

"It was surprisingly normal. While we were in Gettysburg, he made sure I was protected. We didn't run into trouble besides meeting Robert's family," I explained.

"Did you meet his family? Is he married?" Josefina asked.

"No, it was only us. I don't believe he's married, but he did tell me about his father and two younger sisters. His mother passed away when he was young," I said.

"He probably isn't married. I've never noticed a wedding band. I'll have to look when we have Charms today," Josefina said with a laugh. "What did you do for the second week on the beach?"

"I got to swim in the ocean, and Phillip and I practiced some self-defense for my private lessons," I replied. Josefina's smile broadened.

"I guess you and Mr. Withermyer are on a first-name basis now?"

My cheeks felt hot, and I gave Josefina a stare. "We both agreed to call each other by our first names since we pretended to be brother and sister. However, now that we are back here, the informalities will have to end. It's not like he called me Jane when he greeted me today, but I believe we've become friends over the last few weeks. He's a changed man," I said, grabbing the envelope containing my schedule. "We should open our schedules before we're late," I added before she could tease me any further.

I ripped open the envelope and spread the schedule out on my desk.

Charms- *8:00 a.m.-8:55 a.m.*

Transfiguration- *9:00 a.m.-9:55 a.m.*

Teleportation- *10:00 a.m.-10:55 a.m.*

Lunch- *11:00 a.m.-12:30 p.m.*

History- *12:35 p.m.-1:30 p.m.*

Magical Creatures- *1:35 p.m.-2:30 p.m.*

Predicting the Future- *2:35 p.m.-3:30 p.m.*

"I have Charms first," Josefina said. "I guess I don't have to wait too long to see if Mr. Withermyer, or should I say, Phillip, is wearing a wedding ring."

"Can you stop it?" I asked, even though I found myself smiling. I packed up my Charms, Transfiguration, and Teleportation books for the first half of my day and then slung my bag over my shoulder.

"You spent two weeks with the youngest and most handsome teacher at this school, and you expect me not to tease you?" Josefina chuckled as we exited our room.

"Well, I have Charms first, too, and I would appreciate it if you acted like you didn't know we spent time together," I replied, walking down the stairs to the second floor.

We entered the room, choosing a seat at one of the long tables toward the front. Miguel, Andrew, Kairi, and Taylor were also in this class, and of course, Betty Ann, to my displeasure. She came slinking into the room right before the bell sounded and sat behind me.

"Good morning. I'm sure you're all glad to be back at the Jelf Academy. For your fourth year, we will discuss and prepare charms that deal with your senses. Some examples would be the *super sight charm* and the *heightened hearing charm*. We'll also learn the *invisibility charm*, which will be harder than anything you've ever made before, but don't be discouraged. We will also be learning a few fun charms like the *color-changing charm* and the *lucky charm*," Mr. Withermyer said, turning to the chalkboard. The words *heightened hearing charm* appeared on the board along with the page number in our books.

"Since classes are short, I would like everyone to turn to page fifteen and begin reading about the heightened hearing charm," he instructed.

Everyone reached for their book. I spent the remainder of the class reading about the history and theories behind the charm. Ancient pixies discovered the charm which helped them hunt for food. Depending on the strength of the charm, a pixie could hear sounds from miles away. The charm was also used for spying, and it was an advantage in some pixie and human wars. I was halfway through the chapter when the bell sounded.

"I have Transfiguration next," I mumbled to Josefina.

"I do, too," she answered, and we began heading for the door, but Mr. Withermyer stopped me.

"Miss Fitzgerald, could I see you for a moment?"

Josefina raised her eyebrows. "Yes, Mr. Withermyer?" I replied, stopping in front of the desk.

"When do you wish to continue our private lessons? Last year, we met on Mondays, Wednesdays, and Thursdays. Do you want to keep meeting on those days? If so, do you want to have a lesson this evening? We can wait until Wednesday if you'd like since it's your first day back," he said.

"Those days are fine for lessons, and we can meet tonight if you want to. I'm sure I won't have too many assignments," I replied.

"Okay, I'll see you in my office around eight o'clock then?"

"I'll see you then," I replied with a smile as I hurriedly left the room. Ms. Pregmon's class was next, and I knew she wouldn't be happy if I were late.

Rapidly, I raced down the hall. I entered the room just as the bell rang. Ms. Pregmon glared at me, her hateful brown eyes shooting daggers.

"Late on the first day, Miss Fitzgerald," she tsked.

"I don't believe I was late, ma'am. I arrived just as the bell rang," I said sweetly. Now that I knew she was a cousin of Betty Ann's, I could see some similarities.

"You're not in your seat and ready to begin; hence you are late. If you would prefer to argue with me, you can spend your first day in Dr. Tweedle's office. I suggest you find your seat. They are in alphabetical order by last name," Ms. Pregmon sneered.

Sure enough, the only remaining seat was next to Betty Ann. Ms. Pregmon's eyes continued to glare in my direction, and I straightened my spine, defiantly staring back.

"Now that you've all arrived, we can begin. From this moment on, I will not accept tardiness. Once the bell rings, the door to this classroom will close," Ms. Pregmon said, raising a hand toward the door. It swung shut, and I heard the lock click into place. "The door will be locked, and you will not be able to gain entry. Don't even think about banging on the door. I will not let you in; all you'll be doing is disrupting the others who were decent enough to arrive on time. If you're late, your class points for the day will be docked, and any assignments due will receive a zero. Do all of you understand?"

The class murmured in affirmation, and Ms. Pregmon paced the front of the room.

"Good. Last year, most of you learned how to transform objects. We'll review that charm for the next week before we get into the new material. This year will be more complex. Instead of transforming objects, some charms consist of changing your clothes or physical appearance. You'll need to study and pay close attention since these charms are complicated. Only a few of you may prove to be gifted with this type of magic. Not only do the charms have to be prepared properly, but they also require a strong use of the mind. This evening, I want you to review the transfiguration of objects charm and read the first chapter in *Transfiguration and You*," Ms. Pregmon continued, holding up the textbook for this year.

The bell sounded, and Ms. Pregmon looked annoyed. "Everyone, stay seated for one more moment," she snapped. "Be prepared to create a *transfiguring objects charm* tomorrow. We will start with that first and then discuss the first chapter of your textbook. You are now dismissed." She waved her hand toward the door, causing the latch to unlock and the door to fly open.

"Does anyone know where the Teleportation classroom is located?" I asked.

"It's on this floor and in this wing at the end of the main hallway," Taylor said softly.

Miguel led the way.

"Why did Mr. Withermyer want to speak with you after Charms class?" Josefina whispered, walking closer to me.

"We're going to resume our private lessons this evening," I responded as we approached the end of the hallway.

The last room on the left was the Predicting the Future classroom, so the one on the right had to be Teleportation. When we entered, it was strange to see Dr. Tweedle standing before the blackboard. A smile came over his face when he saw me, and his blue eyes crinkled at the corners. It was also peculiar that this was my first time in his presence since last spring.

"Good morning, Dr. Tweedle," I said, walking by him and choosing a desk in the front.

"Hello, Jane. I'm sorry I couldn't retrieve you from the manor. Unfortunately, some pressing business had me detained. However, I see Mr. Withermyer managed to get you away successfully. Perhaps he was better suited at charming your stepmother than I," Dr. Tweedle replied, winking while the rest of the class settled into their seats.

Dr. Tweedle paused briefly, pushed his glasses up the bridge of his nose, and then turned to face the class. The words Teleportation appeared on the board behind him.

"Good morning, everyone, and welcome to your first class on Teleportation. I know you all know me as the headmaster and have never seen me in a classroom environment. Most of you don't know that I've been teaching Teleportation for a little over forty years, and even though I acquired the headmaster job about ten to fifteen years ago, I didn't want to give up teaching. Since I'm considered a master of Teleportation, I decided to maintain both positions so my students could benefit from my knowledge of the subject. As you might have realized, when shopping for your school supplies, I have written the textbook we'll use this year. Chapter One discusses the history of the *teleportation charm*. Please review the chapter this evening, though don't worry about reading every page. I want you to have an idea about what we'll be discussing tomorrow.

"Teleportation is the most complex form of magic, and it requires a lot of practice. It's essentially taking every particle of your body and moving them all to a different area in a matter of moments. This type of magic takes great mental ability and a lot of focus. Therefore, it should always be taken seriously. Teleportation can be dangerous, so we'll learn it one step at a time," Dr. Tweedle said, his blue eyes glancing at each face in the room.

I remembered what Irene had said about leaving parts of yourself behind, and I could feel a lump rising in my throat. What if that happened, and I couldn't be fixed? I shuddered at the idea of missing body parts. Dr. Tweedle mentioned particular pages we should focus on when the bell sounded. My knees felt shaky as I stood to collect my books. I was sure Dr. Tweedle would be an excellent teacher, but there was no doubt that Teleportation would be the most challenging class I'd ever had.

11

MENTAL STAMINA

THE REST OF the day went by in a blur. I enjoyed lunch in the dining hall with my friends, and it was strange that Juan and Lena weren't seated at our table. During lunch, we discussed our schedules. I discovered we had the same classes together. History was after lunch, and Mr. Collyworth was next, and he droned on about discussing the American and French Revolutions this year. Miguel seemed excited as always, but I didn't feel as enthusiastic.

Next, we had Magical Creatures, which was more exciting. Mrs. Rowley informed me that Thistle had remained at the school. Therefore, I could visit her when classes were over. Mrs. Rowley reviewed a few things we would discuss this year and assigned a few readings. Not long after she gave us the assignment, the bell rang. Before leaving the outdoor classroom, I told Mrs. Rowley I would be at the barn to check on Thistle before dinner.

My final class was Predicting the Future. Ms. Crescent emerged from her office, her arms covered in bangle bracelets. She jingled as she paced around the bottom of the amphitheater-like room. In her wispy mythical voice, she explained that this year's focus would be receiving visions from the spirit realm. A shiver coursed through me as I listened to her talk about the different ways we would attempt to contact ghostly apparitions. Once the students were feeling thoroughly spooked, the bell rang, ending our last period. Everyone in the class jumped in their seats at the sound, and a few people let out nervous laughter when they realized it was only the bell.

"I'm going down to the barn to see Thistle before dinner. Do you want to come?" I asked Josefina.

She nodded, pushing her books aside. "What time do you have lessons with Mr. Withermyer?" she asked.

"I'm supposed to meet him in his office at eight o'clock. We'll have an hour or so after dinner before I have to meet him. We can go to the library to review Transfiguration," I suggested.

Josefina nodded in agreement. "Ms. Pregmon is going to make things difficult," she whispered, walking closer to me as we descended the stairs.

"I have to tell you what I learned about her," I whispered. "when we get out to the barn."

The barn loomed in the distance, and we followed the path past the Magical Creatures classroom. I could feel a flutter of excitement in my chest. I hadn't seen Thistle for three months. Last year, on my birthday, I received a saddle and had been training her to carry me on her back. We had yet to take to the skies, but I hoped it would happen one day.

We entered the barn, and it took a moment for my eyes to adjust to the dim light. Mrs. Rowley kept the magical creatures we studied in class here. As we walked by one of the stalls, I saw a parander lift its head. Its eyes grew larger, and it instantly transformed into a tree. Paranders had the ability to transform into trees or rocks as a type of camouflage.

Thistle's stall was the largest one at the end of the building. Thistle's purple head poked out as we drew closer, sensing that I was here. I couldn't stop the huge smile from spreading over my face. Thistle had grown slightly over the summer but was still larger than the biggest horse I'd ever seen. Her scales were an array of purple, and she had an elegant row of spikes from her head down to her neck like a horse's mane. I reached up and patted her nose. Then, I unlatched the stall door.

Thistle jumped around in excitement, circling me. Josefina and I laughed while she attempted to lick my face. I raised my hands to shield myself from her tongue. When she calmed down, I ran my hands down her neck, and she let out a happy growl.

"I've missed you," I murmured, leaning into her leg and scratching her neck.

Josefina stepped forward and allowed Thistle to smell her outstretched hand. Her tongue darted out to lick Josefina's hand. Josefina giggled, running her hand down the other side of Thistle's neck. Then, after a few moments, Josefina spoke.

"What did you want to tell me about Ms. Pregmon?"

"When Mr. Withermyer and I were in Jewel Caverns, we ran into Betty Ann and her parents. Her mother asked after someone named Blair was and if she was adjusting to the Jelf Academy. Later, when I asked who Blair was, he explained that she was Ms. Pregmon. The Barbers know Ms. Pregmon because she's their niece and Betty Ann's cousin."

Josefina's mouth gapped open. "No wonder Ms. Pregmon's always so nice to Betty Ann. That's unfair. I wonder if Dr. Tweedle knows."

"I'm sure he does. He probably hired Ms. Pregmon because everyone is familiar with the Barber family. Also, since Mr. Barber is involved in the government, he helps students get internships," I replied.

"Guess we won't be receiving any internships if Betty Ann's father has a say in it," Josefina joked.

"Maybe not, but Dr. Tweedle probably has a say too. I'm going to grab Thistle some dinner, so I'll be right back," I said, heading out to the ice chest. I selected a frozen cow leg and levitated it out.

Thistle's eyes lit up when she saw her dinner, and she leapt around the stall while I laid the huge hunk of meat in the center.

"Stand back," I warned Josefina as Thistle approached.

A flame burst from her mouth and engulfed the leg. We stepped back from the fire, the heat washing over our bodies. Beads of sweat broke out on my forehead, and I waved my hand in front of my face. Thistle's flame evaporated, and she sniffed at the meat. She must have deemed it cooked because she dug into it, ripping off a chunk.

Josefina told me more about her summer, and even though not much happened during mine, I talked about Marie, Emily, Preston, and Mr. Doyle. After a while, we realized it was almost dinner time and decided to head back to the castle. Thistle was still gnawing on the bones when I rubbed the top of her head.

"I'll be back tomorrow," I told her, and her big violet eyes looked into mine as if she understood. "We need to get back to training with the saddle soon," I said, grabbing the stall door. I could have sworn Thistle nodded as I slid the door closed.

The dining hall doors were open, and other students filed in. Josefina and I joined the throng and got in line for the buffet. I could smell the roasted turkey and gravy, my stomach rumbling.

It wasn't long before our friends arrived. I told them about visiting Thistle, and Josefina whispered what I discovered concerning Ms. Pregmon. We made sure to keep our voices low as other students walked by.

"Well, I wouldn't be a positive person if I had Betty Ann as a family member," Kairi whispered, and we all laughed.

"I have some time before I have to meet Mr. Withermyer. Does everyone want to go to the library and focus on Transfiguration?" I asked.

"Yes. That's an excellent idea. I could use some help reviewing transfiguring objects," Taylor said.

"I can help with that," Zachary insisted, and I caught Taylor's smile, but his aqua eyes were on me.

Though Zachary was a year ahead of us, he typically joined us for study sessions in the library. He usually sat at the next table over to keep an eye on his sister. Zachary never offered to help with studying before, and I was glad for his help since he had the class last year.

Josefina and I quickly climbed the stairs to our room. When we reached the top of the seventh floor, I paused to catch my breath before placing my hand on the panel outside our room. The door slid open, and I gathered the books spread across my bed. I put the ones I didn't need on the shelf and took my Transfiguration book and the materials for Mr. Withermyer's lesson.

"Already studying on the first day of school?" Miss Pierce said as we walked past the main desk of the library. We nodded and held up our textbooks. "Just remember to keep your voices down," Miss Pierce reminded before returning to the book on her desk.

Kairi and Zachary were already seated at a table toward the back. Taylor had gone to retrieve their books. We waited for everyone to arrive. Since I felt comfortable with the *transfiguring objects charm*, Zachary and I walked the others through the steps. I explained how to picture the object transforming and keeping the vision in your mind before casting the charm. Zachary nodded in approval of my explanation. He helped organize the ingredients before each pairing up to create the charm. We practiced for an hour before I had to be on my way.

Mr. Withermyer's office was the second door on the left in the west wing, and I raised my hand to knock. The heavy oak door opened inward, and Mr. Withermyer stood in the doorway, his broad shoulders filling the space.

"Come in," he said, stepping back into the room.

I entered his neat office. The desk was clear of papers, and the bookshelves behind the desk were organized. I sat in front of his desk and placed my bag beside my legs.

"How was your first day back at the Jelf Academy?" he asked, his richly toned voice filling the room.

"Overall, it was exceptional. My classes are more complicated this year, especially Transfiguration and Teleportation," I replied.

"If you ever need assistance with any classes, I'd be happy to help. As you would expect, your fourth and fifth years will be the most difficult at the Jelf Academy. Transfiguration and Teleportation's foundation are Charms, so if there is anything I can do, just let me know."

"Thank you, Mr. Withermyer. You've helped me so much already, but I might have to take you up on that offer," I replied.

"During our private lessons, you can call me Phillip," he said gently. "These lessons are informal, so you can address me by my first name, Jane. I see you found the bracelet I made," he said with a slight smile.

My hand automatically went to the shells on my wrist. "Yes, thank you. It's beautiful. I wanted to tell you earlier," I said, swirling the bracelet around my wrist.

"I'm glad you like it. I know how much you enjoyed staying at the beach, so I wanted to give you something to remind you of it. I thought it was a good use for the shells we collected. Now you can have the ocean with you," he said, looking down at his desk.

"This bracelet was so thoughtful, and I'll cherish it forever," I replied, lowering my arm to my lap. "The week we spent at the beach was one of the best in my life. I've never been so relaxed."

"Then I promise one day you'll get to be there again. It was nice to see you happy," he replied.

I could feel myself blushing. "What did you have in mind for our lesson?" I asked.

"Our lesson…," he repeated. "I thought we could go up to the exercise room and continue what we practiced at the beach. I've debated introducing you to another charm, but let's start with a familiar lesson since it's only the first day."

"Okay," I replied, rising to my feet and picking up my bag.

We climbed to the uppermost floor of the Jelf Academy. My legs ached, and I let out a sigh as Mr. Withermyer pushed open the door leading to the swimming pool.

"Are you out of breath already?" he asked. "We're going to have to get you into better shape if you're ever confronted with the W.A.S.P. again."

"I just feel like I've been up and down stairs all day," I answered, following him across the pool room to the exercise room.

We entered the ample space, and I placed my bag along the wall. Quickly, I secured my hair with the clip Mr. Withermyer had given me while keeping him in my sight. While we were at the beach, he would spring an attack when I wasn't ready to see how I would react. I watched while he used a shield charm on himself. Then, he advanced toward me. I backed away, and he quickly rushed forward, grabbing my arms. I kicked out with my legs, aiming for his knees and remembering to put magic behind the attack. My foot connected, and Mr. Withermyer flew back, landing several feet away.

"Very good," he praised, getting back to his feet.

He didn't give me much time to think as he sprinted toward me again. He grabbed my wrist this time, and I managed to shake him off before I sent my right hand flying up into his nose. He stumbled back a few steps but quickly grabbed ahold of me again. In a flash, he spun me around so my back was to him. His arms held me tightly. I jumped up and threw my weight down onto his arms. I could feel his grip on me loosening. As I continued to toss my body, I felt his pushing against mine. I reached out with my mind and levitated him over my head on my next thrust down. Mr. Withermyer slammed onto the floor in front of me. He stared up, looking stunned.

"Are you okay?" I asked in alarm.

"Yes," he groaned. "I'm just a little surprised. The shield took the brunt of the impact, but I never thought you'd do that." Slowly, he sat up, moaning with each movement.

"I'm sorry. I just wondered what would happen if I levitated you," I stammered.

"Well, it's very effective," he said as I pulled him to his feet. "Let's run through it again."

We spent the next few hours practicing with levitation until we were both tired. Breathlessly, we leaned against the wall, and Mr. Withermyer summoned two glasses of water.

"You have powerful mental ability. Your ability to levitate with your mind is amazing!" Mr. Withermyer exclaimed between exhausted pants. Sweat was running down his face, and he took a long gulp of water.

"I thought all pixies had the ability to move things with their minds," I replied.

"They do, but the mind is also a muscle in that sense. You have to work on strengthening it. Usually, an untrained pixie isn't able to move larger objects for long periods. How much you are able to lift or move depends on the strength of your mind. Just like any other muscle in the body, the mind can become tired," Mr. Withermyer explained. "Spending several hours tossing a full-grown man around should be exhausting. I'm not sure I know many pixies who would have the strength and stamina you do for someone your age."

"I had no idea there was a limit to what my mind could lift," I said. "I've always managed to levitate anything I've needed to."

"No, not everyone has the ability that you do, Jane," he assured me.

I leaned my head back against the wall and thought about all the times I used magic to levitate things or make them easier to carry. I had done it so many times that it was second nature. It was the only magic I could subtly do at the manor house.

"On the day my father passed away, I was so overcome by grief

I made every door in the manor slam shut," I said before taking another gulp of water.

I could feel Mr. Withermyer's eyes on me, and I turned to look at him. "You moved every door in that house simultaneously?" he asked in awe, and I nodded. "I wouldn't understand the magnitude of that statement if I hadn't just been to the manor. That house has more than just a few doors," he exclaimed.

His green eyes appraised my face, and I felt self-conscious under the intensity of his stare. "Yes, and I remember how loud the sound was, too."

"When that happened, did your stepmother know you had done it?" he asked with concern.

"Yes, I think a part of her sensed it. In the moments after, Marie grabbed me by the arm and dragged me from my father's bedside. I claimed I didn't know why she was so upset, but I knew what I had done. It was then Marie confessed she had noticed toys moving without being touched. She kept dragging me down the hall, her grip like a vice on my arm. Again, I used magic to heat my skin to escape her. Marie did drop my arm but managed to grab my hair. She hauled me to the attic by my hair and tossed me onto the floor. From that day forward, the attic became my bedroom, and I became her slave," I said. I'd never told another person about the events that occurred on the day of my father's passing, not even Josefina.

Mr. Withermyer brushed his hand against mine. "I'm so sorry, Jane. That's horrible," he said. We sat in silence for a moment before Mr. Withermyer spoke again. "So, your stepmother knows what you are? She knows you're a pixie?" he asked.

"She doesn't know the term, pixie, but yes, she believes me to be a freak," I replied.

"Is Dr. Tweedle aware your stepmother knows what you can do? I don't think it's safe to return to the manor. What if she tells someone and the W.A.S.P. finds out?"

"Marie's embarrassed about what a freak like me could do to her reputation. So, she always threatens me to keep my abilities a secret. If she were ever to see or sense an ounce of magic, she would throw me out of the house. Trust me, Marie would never tell anyone. She'd be too ashamed of what people would think of her," I said.

"What about Marie's children?" Mr. Withermyer questioned.

"Emily feels the same way as her mother. I'm a blight to their family; she often pretends I'm not even there during public gatherings. Preston was only two when my father passed, so I doubt he even remembers anything from that day," I said.

"And the staff?"

"I don't remember seeing many people around the manor then. Marie hired new people once my father passed away, and I'm sure some of them didn't even realize my father owned the house. Only a few staff members, like Ellen, the cook, remain from when my father ran the place. I don't think the new staff knows I'm Marie's stepdaughter. Besides, don't you think the W.A.S.P. would have come for me by now?"

"I suppose you have a point," Mr. Withermyer sighed. "I'm just concerned about how vulnerable you are in that manor, surrounded by humans."

"Well, that's what these lessons are for, so you have nothing to worry about," I said, playfully nudging him with my arm.

"Indeed," he murmured, but his uneasy expression didn't fade.

12

MR. O'DOHERTY

I
T WAS STILL unbearably hot for the middle of September. I pushed the piece of clothing up and down the washboard into the soapy water of the tub. My hair clung to the back of my neck, and I rubbed my arm across my forehead in an attempt to keep the sweat from rolling into my eyes. The heat radiated over my skin, and the only relief was when I dipped the laundry into the water to rinse out the suds. Slowly, I rose to my feet and hung the material on the clothesline. My back ached from being bent over the washtub. I stretched for a moment before returning to the task.

The number of clothes seemed endless this morning, but I only had a few more articles to clean. I took a deep breath and plowed forward, feeling motivated that the end of the task was near. I stared at the manor and could have sworn I saw Marie gazing down at me from the sitting room window. Keeping the grimace off my face, I plunged the clothing along the washboard, each time imagining that it was Marie's head I was thrusting into the filthy water instead. I knew I shouldn't have such horrible thoughts, but sometimes I couldn't help it.

I finished the last bit of laundry and hung it on the clothesline.

Then, I carried the heavy washtub and dumped the dirty water toward the woods. When the tub was empty, I lugged it back up the hill towards the kitchen door. Ellen was mumbling something under her breath when I entered. She was making tea and hustling to get everything together on a tray.

"Are you finished with the laundry?" she snapped when she saw me.

"Yes, I was just returning the washtub to the storage closet," I replied.

"Good. When you're finished putting that away, run this tea tray to the sitting room," Ellen demanded, putting tea sandwiches on a plate.

I rapidly carried the tub to the storage closet and returned for the tray. Marie and Emily were both sitting on the sofa. I went around it and placed the tray on the coffee table before them. Emily scrunched up her face as she looked up at me.

"What is that awful smell? I feel as if I'm going to vomit," she said, aghast.

"You certainly are a mess, Jane. You think you would take some pride in yourself and clean up before coming in here," Marie said snidely.

"I'm sorry, ma'am, but I've just finished with the laundry. Unfortunately, Ellen didn't give me any time to be presentable," I replied.

"Since you insist on being so filthy, here's what I want you to do next. We need to prepare the fireplaces for the winter season, and since our chimney sweep isn't coming today, you can do it. The equipment is located in the staff quarters. I expect every fireplace in this house to be thoroughly cleaned by dinner time," Marie ordered.

I didn't say a word before walking out of the sitting room. A young man usually came to the house to clean the chimneys. Marie might have asked me to clean around the fireplace, but never up the chimney before. I went to the storage room and poked around for the chimney sweep brush. It wasn't hard to find. The wire bristles stuck out in a circle and were attached to a series of long poles that folded in on themselves. I lifted it onto my shoulder and found it slightly heavier than expected. Using levitation so the brush was propped against my shoulder, I balanced it in my arms before heading to the sitting room.

Marie and Emily gave me an evil glare when I came in, but other than that, they ignored me. I dropped the chimney brush on the floor by the fireplace and knelt next to it. Emily and Marie continued their conversation while I grabbed the first handle and inserted it into the fireplace.

"I've just been feeling sick lately," Emily was saying. "Sometimes certain smells make me want to gag."

I looked over my shoulder to see her eyes on me. I ignored her and continued pushing the brush upward, the metal wires scrapping along the sides. Soot trickled down onto my hands, and I coughed slightly.

"Do you have other symptoms? Is your throat sore, or are you achy? Do you feel like you have a fever? Maybe you just have a stomach bug," Marie suggested, sipping her tea.

I moved the brush up further and snapped the next rod into place. Black soot rained down on me as I moved the brush up and down.

"No, I don't have a fever, but sometimes nausea just comes over me. Maybe there's something wrong with the food," Emily sniffed.

"Your brother and husband don't seem ill, and I haven't noticed anything of the sort," Marie commented.

"Do you think someone is poisoning me?" Emily asked, and I was glad to be facing the fireplace so she couldn't see me roll my eyes.

"I'll have a talk with Ellen," Marie replied.

"I've just felt so out of sorts lately. My clothing also feels constricting," Emily complained.

I kept shoving the chimney brush upward as I listened to the long list of ailments Emily thought was wrong with her. The soot continued to rain down in a thick coating, and I turned my head away from the fireplace. Finally, I felt the brush reach the top and slowly began pulling it back down. I would have to get a broom and a dustpan to sweep up the ash and debris that had fallen into the fireplace.

Carefully, I folded each rod as I pulled the chimney sweep down. My hands had turned black, and I tried not to touch anything besides the rod. Mindful of the dirt, I slowly rose to my feet and went to get the broom and dustpan. When I returned to the sitting room, Marie and Emily were hunched closer together on the sofa.

"What about your monthly courses?" I caught Marie whispering, and I paused in the doorway.

"Nothing happened last month, but I didn't think anything of it. I've never had the most regular courses," Emily answered.

"Now that you're married, you need to pay attention to those kinds of things," Marie hissed. "Does Drake come to your room regularly?"

"Mother! I refuse to discuss that with you. If you're wondering about that possibility, yes, it's possible."

"You need to pay attention. When is your next monthly supposed to happen?" Marie asked.

"Sometime next week," Emily replied.

"We won't know for sure until then. Come see me right away if you begin to bleed. Once it's several days past expected, you need to tell me," Marie demanded.

They both settled back onto the settee and stopped whispering. I waited another second before breezing into the room, brandishing the brush and dustpan. I didn't want them to realize I'd overheard their conversation. Quickly, I began sweeping up the soot. Then, I collected my equipment and moved on to the fireplace in the ballroom.

As I monotonously cleaned each fireplace in the house, my mind kept straying back to their conversation. If Emily really was experiencing nausea and if she had missed her monthly courses, could that mean she was pregnant? It really wouldn't be so hard to believe. She'd been married to Mr. Doyle for over a year. If Emily was indeed pregnant, what would that mean for me and my list of duties?

I was completely covered in filth by the time I finished with all of the fireplaces. My arms ached from pushing the wire brush up all the chimneys. My hands were black and caked with soot. The dirt had traveled up both arms to my elbows, and I couldn't even imagine what my face looked like. Sweat trickled down my face as I walked back downstairs, lugging the cleaning equipment in my hands. I was leery of each step, not wanting to touch anything with my hands or the wire brush. I had already cleaned so much today that I didn't need to accidentally get ash or dirt on anything.

I replaced the wire brush in the staff supply closet and walked into the kitchen. Ellen took one look at me and narrowed her eyes.

"Get out of here! You're filthy! I will not have you in my kitchen looking like that. I won't need you for another hour. Get cleaned up," she yelled, shooing me out the back door.

Once outside, I looked at my blackened hands. It would probably take multiple buckets of water in my little washtub to get all the grime off my skin. I wasn't sure how many times I would need to empty and refill it. The air was still hot and humid outside, so I decided the lake was the best option.

I headed in the direction of the woods and found the familiar path between the trees. I hadn't been out to the lake last summer because of the amount of work Marie had assigned me. Also, the lake reminded me of Robert. It wasn't long before I reached the glittering clear water. The lake wasn't gigantic and was secluded by the tall trees surrounding it. I walked over to the flat rock near the water and sat down to unlace my boots. I placed the boots to the side and unbuttoned my blouse.

I removed my filthy blouse and skirt, then leaned off the rock to submerge them in the water. I scrubbed them with my hands to remove most of the dirt before laying them on the rock to dry. Slowly, I waded into the lake, the water feeling slightly cold against my skin. I took a deep breath and dove beneath the cool blue surface. I opened my eyes and propelled myself toward the center. It felt good to swim, to feel free for a little while.

Coming up for air, I swirled in the water and ran my hands along my arms to scrub off the filth. The dirt came away, and I saw my clean, pinkish skin. I reached up and tugged at my hair to remove it from its braid. My blonde tresses tumbled into the lake, and I submerged myself again. My hair swayed back and forth around my shoulders, and I ran my hands through it. I could understand how Kairi felt so free moving through water.

I resurfaced again and floated on my back. Staring up at the blue sky, I watched puffy white clouds roll overhead. Waving my arms like wings, I propelled myself in a circle. Breathing deeply, I filled my lungs with air to keep buoyant in the water. My body floated, and I allowed myself to relax. All the while, I kept an eye on the sun's position so I wouldn't stay out too late.

When goosebumps began to break out on my arms, I paddled back to the rock and rose from the water. Making sure not to get water on my drying clothes, I sat on the other side of the boulder. I wrung out my underclothes the best I could while wearing them and coiled my hair to the left side of my body to squeeze the water from it. Slowly, I stretched out on the rock to dry off a bit before getting dressed again. The sun broke through the trees and warmed my skin. I let my eyes flutter closed and allowed my shoulders to loosen.

It only seemed like a few moments had gone by when I heard the sound of hoofbeats moving through the forest. I leapt from the rock and scrambled to grab my clothes. The horses sounded like they were getting closer. I managed to pull on my skirt and begin buttoning up my blouse before I heard a man's voice.

"What do we have here?" the stranger asked, and I looked up to see two men on horseback. The strange man led his horse into the clearing, and Drake Doyle followed him. Mr. Doyle's dark eyes scanned my body, and I wrapped my arms around my chest.

The stranger's expression wasn't any more chivalrous. He had large hazel eyes and dirty blonde hair. He was a broad man, and his presence was intimidating. There was a scar on his left cheek and a handlebar mustache above his upper lip. I supposed most women would consider him roguishly handsome, but there was a sinister look in his eyes.

"Drake, you didn't tell me anything about exquisite young maidens that rise from the lake shore like Aphrodite," the man barked, his eyes also traveling over me.

"This is Jane, a maid in my mother-in-law's household," Mr. Doyle responded.

"None of the maids in my household look like this: such strange violet eyes and such an innocent expression. How do I find help like this?" the man chuckled.

"Seth, I have a hard time believing you can't find beautiful housekeepers," Drake said. Then, his eyes focused on me again. "What are you doing here all alone?" he questioned.

"I was taking a walk," I replied. I tried to look confident. Marie never said I couldn't go into the woods, so I wasn't breaking any rules. I kept my hands crossed over my chest. My wet hair was the only indication I hadn't just been out for a walk, but I couldn't bring myself to say that I'd been swimming.

The man called Seth leered at me. "We must've just missed the part where you fell into the lake," he said sarcastically. "If only we'd arrived a few minutes earlier." He winked one of his hazel eyes at me, causing me to shudder.

"Come on, O'Doherty. Stop teasing my wife's maid," Mr. Doyle said seriously, but I could tell he was enjoying my discomfort. His mouth turned up in a mischievous manner.

I shifted my weight and rolled my shoulders back to appear taller. I dropped my arms into a more relaxed stance and tried to summon the confidence I did not feel. "If you two gentlemen would excuse me, I must be on my way back to the house. I'll need to begin dinner preparations," I said, trying to put authority in my voice.

Seth O'Doherty and Drake Doyle shifted on their horses, but neither moved out of my path. They both looked at each other, and I could feel panic rising in my chest. I didn't want to be in the woods anymore. All I wanted to do was run back to the house, but I felt trapped. I tried to keep my feelings from showing on my face. It wouldn't help to let them know I was scared. If they attacked me, would I be able to use self-defense to escape? Mr. Withermyer hadn't trained me for the possibility of more than one opponent. A sickness settled into my stomach.

Suddenly, Mr. Doyle let out a loud laugh, and within seconds, Seth O'Doherty began laughing too. They shifted their horses off to each side of the path. Slowly, I walked between them, my senses on edge, waiting for the attack. Every inch of my body willed me to run, but I fought the impulse.

"Be careful on your way back up to the house, Jane. You never know what is lurking in these woods," Mr. Doyle warned with a smile.

I didn't say anything as I followed the path out of the woods. The sound of hoofbeats moved off into the distance and didn't come after me, but I remained on edge. I didn't understand their motives. Had they intended to harm me, or was it a game to intimidate me? I kept my ears alert to hear if they would turn the horses around, planning to hunt me for sport. I allowed myself to shudder in repulsion when the manor house finally came into view. One thing was obvious. I knew I had left the woods today because they had let me.

13

FIRST FLIGHT

The sun began to set earlier each day as summer faded into autumn. I headed down to the barn at the Jelf Academy. I wanted to get a lesson in with Thistle before it became too dark. Since it was a Tuesday, I didn't have a private session with Mr. Withermyer, and I didn't have many assignments to complete for my classes. Josefina decided to come along, and she walked beside me on the path. She was the only person I told about Drake's strange behavior a few weeks ago.

Josefina listened to my story, and for once, she didn't interrupt. I didn't really want to share my experience with everyone. I could predict their reactions, and I wasn't sure if I could stand to see the alarm on everyone's faces. The incident had been terrifying, and seeing the horror in their expressions would make it even more real. However, I needed to tell someone, so I turned to Josefina. She warned me to be careful and advised me to avoid the woods and Mr. Doyle if I could.

Every lesson with Mr. Withermyer seemed even more critical. I focused most of my energy on perfecting what he was teaching me. I wanted to become more confident when protecting myself, and I didn't want fear to cloud my abilities. If Mr. Withermyer had sensed my determination, he didn't say anything about it.

Josefina and I reached Thistle's stall, and I opened the latch. Like always, my dragon was excited to see me. I rubbed her nose to calm her down, and Josefina stepped up to pet her. While Josefina stroked her hand down Thistle's nose, I walked over to the riding equipment. I grabbed the riding blanket first, and gently, I tossed the blanket over Thistle's back. She stood very still as I straightened the covering.

"Did you see the advertisements for the Harvest Festival?" Josefina said, stepping away from Thistle.

"Yes, I can't believe it will be the middle of October soon. It seems as if we've only just started back at the academy," I replied, retrieving Thistle's special saddle.

"Do you think you'll be able to go this year?" Josefina asked.

"Probably not. Unless Dr. Tweedle is somehow able to convince Marie, since Mr. Withermyer took me away for two weeks, I couldn't see her agreeing to my absence," I said sadly.

"I wish you'd be able to attend. Do you think Dr. Tweedle could at least try? Unfortunately, you've only been able to come to one dance with me, and everyone else misses you too," Josefina said, referring to our group of friends.

"I suppose I could ask him, but I can't make any promises. Marie's been on edge lately. I've told you that Emily might be pregnant, and Marie watches her like a hawk."

"What do you suppose will happen if Emily is pregnant?" Josefina asked.

"I'll probably be even more under Emily's thumb," I said, securing the saddle on Thistle.

Before coming to the barn, I had changed into the riding outfit I'd received for my birthday last year. The pants were much more comfortable than a skirt. I reached up, gripped the saddle horn, and placed my left foot in the stirrup. Swinging my right leg over, I managed to pull myself up. Since I didn't have a bridal for Thistle, I'd been training her to follow my leg nudges and voice commands. Once I strapped myself into the saddle, I commanded Thistle to move forward.

Slowly, Thistle obeyed. Josefina walked beside us to the fenced-in area Mrs. Rowley used for Magical Creatures class. Josefina opened the gate for me, and I rode Thistle inside the fence. Josefina climbed atop the highest rail and took a seat to watch our lesson.

I eased Thistle into a trot and circled the fence a few times. Then, Josefina summoned obstacles for Thistle to jump over. Once we were comfortable with the lower jumps, Josefina increased the height. I praised Thistle for every obstruction she leapt over, and she grunted at my approval as if she understood every word I was saying. Soon, we were galloping, and Thistle was vaulting every hurdle Josefina put in front of us. I was so pleased that my dragon was obeying my commands.

After several quick laps, Thistle was breathing heavily, and I slowed her down for a break. When she came to a stop, I summoned a tub of water for her to drink. Thistle's pink tongue enthusiastically lapped up the water. Then, I stood by the fence with Josefina while Thistle rested for a moment.

"She's so beautiful," Josefina sighed, gazing at my dragon. "I wish my dragon would've decided to stay," she said sadly.

"I wish it would've happened, too," I said. "Then we could have ridden together."

"Thistle is so special, and you are too. That's probably the reason she stayed," Josefina said.

"You're important too. I don't know why Thistle stayed behind," I replied.

Thistle trotted over to me and rubbed her head against my arm, almost knocking me over with her enthusiasm. I steadied myself before reaching up to get back in the saddle.

"I wonder why she hasn't flown yet," Josefina commented, looking up at me.

"Mrs. Rowley told me she checked Thistle's wings, and nothing appears wrong with them. Maybe she's scared, or she just isn't ready yet," I replied, patting the side of Thistle's neck.

Using my knees, I gently turned her around, and we began trotting around the fence again. I leaned low in the saddle, continuing to rub the scales of her neck.

"Hey, Thistle," I whispered while crouched in the saddle. "Are you scared to fly? Is that why you haven't done it yet? I'm scared, too, but I'm right here with you. We can do this together. I know you'll be able to do it," I continued to whisper in her ear.

Thistle began to gallop, slightly flapping her wings as she leapt over the first jump. I encouraged her as I clung to the saddle. We rounded the opposite end of the pen, and I urged Thistle onward, racing toward one of the higher jumps. Thistle's beautiful wings moved as she ran, and she leapt to clear the jump. She soared over the obstacle, continuing to flap her wings. It took me a moment to realize she wasn't landing. A cry of excitement escaped my lips, and I clutched the saddle tighter. Butterflies exploded in my stomach, and I checked that the straps were secure. Thistle gained altitude, and the ground became smaller.

"You're flying!" I exclaimed, patting the side of Thistle's neck.

Thistle shook her head as if understanding as she flexed her wings again. We glided among the clouds. I realized with excitement and a slight fear of how high we were in the sky. If the Jelf Academy sat on clouds above the earth, Thistle and I were thousands of feet in the air. However, I tried not to think about it as the Jelf Academy disappeared in the clouds.

Thistle continued onward, and the wind whipped my hair. The loose strands fluttered around my face, but the majority of it was secured in my braid and my hair clip. As Thistle flew, I became more confident in the saddle, loosening my grip. I could feel elation bursting through my chest, and my body couldn't contain my emotions. Boldly, I stretched out my arms, and the air blew through my fingers and across my hands. Thistle's wings stretched out on both sides, too, as we glided forward.

A whoop escaped my lips, and I flapped my arms, enjoying the feeling of freedom. I couldn't even wrap my mind around the fact that I was flying. I pinched my left forearm to make sure I wasn't dreaming. I could never have imagined my life would bring me to this moment. I was a pixie currently riding a dragon through the skies.

We continued for a few moments, but Thistle suddenly banked to the right. I grasped the saddle horn and was relieved that the straps had kept me securely in place. Thistle began descending lower, and I soon saw the Jelf Academy in the distance. I patted her side, shouting my praise as we approached the school. As we swooped closer, I could make out the Magical Creatures' enclosure and Josefina, who only looked like a speck from this high up. Thistle circled the school grounds, continuing to descend. My heart raced as she neared the fenced-in area. Her front legs slammed into the ground, and I was jostled by the impact. Once again, the saddle straps kept me upright, but the landing still jarred me.

It took Thistle a moment to stop, and when she did, we had reached the end of the fence where Josefina stood, looking amazed. Slowly, I unbuckled the straps, my hands shaking. Josefina opened the padlock and ran toward me.

"Jane, are you all right? I didn't expect that to happen! Are you okay?" Josefina exclaimed, rushing to my side.

"Yes, I'm fine," I replied, taking another moment in the saddle. My mind was still reeling from the flight, and my body was still shaken from the landing. Slowly, I swung my right leg over and lowered myself to the ground. My knees felt wobbly, and I kept a hand on Thistle's side.

"That was amazing!" I sighed, rubbing Thistle's neck. She

nuzzled her snout into my shoulder. "We have to do that again sometime, but the landing needs a little work."

I chuckled as Josefina put her hand on my shoulder. "I didn't know what to do when Thistle took off. I wasn't sure if you would be safe or if I should get Mrs. Rowley," Josefina gasped.

"I was perfectly safe. The saddle straps were very effective and kept me secure for the entire ride. I wasn't afraid and knew Thistle wouldn't allow any harm to come to me," I said, leading Thistle through the open gate and toward the barn.

Josefina fell into step beside me. "What was it like?" she anxiously asked as I opened Thistle's stall door and ushered her inside.

"It was like being in the carriages pulled by the winged horses but a thousand times better. I felt so free, and the wind blew through my hair. Everything looked so small from the sky. I can't really explain it. You'll have to try it sometime," I replied, working on removing Thistle's saddle and riding blanket.

Josefina looked nervous, but she chuckled. "I'll have to ask for a riding outfit like yours for Christmas. Somehow, I don't think taking to the skies in a skirt would be appropriate," she said with a laugh.

I filled Thistle's water trough and then rubbed her scales with a towel to remove the sweat where her saddle had been. I still needed to get her something for dinner, so I headed to the icebox.

"Are you going to be down here for a while, or will you head back to the school soon?" Josefina asked as I levitated a large hunk of meat into Thistle's stall.

"I'm going to let Thistle eat, and then I have to muck out her stall. You can head back up to the school if you don't want to wait," I said.

"Are you sure? I'm feeling a little exhausted, and my heart hasn't stopped racing since Thistle took off with you on her back. Also, it's getting late," Josefina said.

"You don't have to wait for me. Go back to our room. I just want to spend a few more moments out here," I replied.

Josefina said goodbye and left the barn. I watched Thistle as she attacked her dinner, and then I began cleaning out her stall. This type of work was familiar, and my muscles settled into the routine. By the time I had finished, Thistle had consumed her dinner, and she followed me around as I scattered fresh hay for her. I couldn't help laughing as she gently nudged the sides of my neck with her nose.

"You did a great job today," I told her, scratching around her ears. She leaned into my touch, and I felt so happy to have her in my life. Training her was always an incredible experience. I kissed the bridge of her nose as she leaned her head toward my shoulder. Then, after several more scratches and pats, I stepped away from my dragon. Her purple eyes glanced at me in understanding. "It's getting late, and I have to head back," I said out loud.

Thistle dropped into the fresh hay, and I gave her one last touch before exiting the stall. I hated leaving her, but I needed to return to the castle. I knew students really weren't supposed to wander around after dark unless given permission by a teacher. I left the barn and walked up the path to the academy. The moon was out, but it was only a crescent, and I was glad the way was lit by lanterns.

My heart still thrummed with excitement. I felt energized and wondered if Mr. Withermyer was still in his office. Somehow, I found my feet headed in that direction. I was sure he would want to hear about my experience, and I hoped it wasn't too late. Softly, I knocked on his office door.

In moments, the door slowly creaked open. Mr. Withermyer's green eyes gazed out at me. His dark brows knitted in confusion. "Jane, what are you doing here? Is everything okay?" he whispered with concern.

"Yes. Something amazing happened to me tonight, and I just wanted to share it with you," I whispered back.

"I was just on my way to my staff quarters," Mr. Withermyer began, and I cut him off.

"Oh, I'm sorry. I didn't mean to bother you. I'll just tell you tomorrow during our lessons. Please forgive me for calling on you so late," I replied, turning to go.

Quickly but gently, his hand shot out and landed on my arm. "No, it's okay. Come on in," he replied, opening the door wider and ushering me inside.

The office was primarily dark, with only one goblin fire candle burning on the desk. Mr. Withermyer's desk was cleared off, and it was apparent that he was just finishing up for the night.

"I'm sorry for the lack of lighting. As I was saying, I was just about to retire to my staff quarters. I would offer you something to drink, but I have nothing in this office. My personal quarters are only down the hall if you would like a cup of coffee or tea," he offered.

"That would be lovely, as long as you have decaffeinated coffee. I'm so invigorated already; I probably won't be able to sleep if I have caffeine," I replied.

Mr. Withermyer opened the office door again and pressed his finger to his lips. "Students don't typically enter the staff quarters," he whispered. "Follow me and be as quiet as possible."

I followed Mr. Withermyer further into the west wing. Some staff rooms were off the main hallway, down a short hall to the right, and Mr. Withermyer stopped at the first door on the left. Similar to the student rooms, there wasn't a doorknob. Mr. Withermyer placed his hand on the panel next to the door. The door slid open, and I quickly ducked inside.

Mr. Withermyer's personal quarters were brightly lit, and I looked around. There was a small living space with a couch and a few chairs. To the left, against the wall, was a large bookshelf, and on the right was a small kitchen area. Two open doors were at the back of the room: one revealing a bathroom and the other a bedroom. Mr. Withermyer walked into the small kitchen and began brewing coffee. I took a seat on the sofa while I waited.

"This seems like a very nice living space," I commented.

"Thank you. Being employed at the Jelf Academy of Magic does have its benefits. The staff quarters are spacious," Mr. Withermyer replied, pouring the freshly brewed coffee into two cups. I watched as he added a lot of milk and sugar to my cup before crossing the room to hand it to me.

I thanked him as he sat in one of the chairs across from me. He took a long sip of coffee while his eyes glanced up at me over the rim of the cup.

"What couldn't you wait to tell me?' he asked, wrapping both hands around the mug.

"Tonight, I went to the Magical Creatures barn to train with Thistle. I was riding her around the padlock, training her to leap over a series of jumps, when the most wonderful thing happened!" I said with excitement. "Thistle finally flew!"

Mr. Withermyer leaned forward in his seat. "Were you in the saddle when she took flight?" he asked, astonished.

"Yes, and it was amazing! When we leapt over an obstacle, Thistle was flapping her wings. It took me a moment to realize she hadn't touched back down. It was the most incredible feeling," I exclaimed. I lifted my cup to my lips and blew on the scalding liquid.

"How high did she fly? How far did you go?" he asked, continuing to lean forward in his chair.

I blew on my coffee again before I answered. "The school looked small when we soared up through the clouds," I replied before taking a sip of my coffee. The liquid warmed a path down my throat, and I shifted into a more comfortable position on the couch. "I don't think we were in the air for too long."

A smile crept over Mr. Withermyer's face, and he settled back into his chair. "So, the saddle was safe? You were strapped in, correct?"

"Yes, I always strap myself in. I felt perfectly safe. I do trust

Thistle, and I don't believe she would do anything to harm me," I replied, taking a deeper sip from my cup.

"I'm glad Thistle finally flew. Just be careful when riding her. I wouldn't want you to get hurt," he said with concern.

"I'll be careful, but I've never felt so free before. I would never have imagined something like this could happen to me. My experiences at the Jelf Academy have exceeded my wildest dreams. Only four years ago, I thought I was the only person who could do magic. I would never have believed dragons existed or that I would be riding one," I proclaimed.

"Yes, I can imagine your point of view. Everything must seem so enchanting to you. Sometimes, it would be nice to see the pixie world through your eyes," Mr. Withermyer said with a slight grin.

"Sometimes I feel as if this part of my life is a dream, and one day I'll wake up, and the Jelf Academy won't exist. Marie will be banging on the attic door, and I'll jolt awake, realizing I imagined all this. Is that crazy?" I asked while he stared at me intently.

Mr. Withermyer shook his head, leaning forward to place his empty coffee cup on the table. "No, it's not crazy to believe your happiest moments are dreams, but I can assure you all this is real. This school and your magic won't disappear. Your life here exists, as does everyone who cares about you."

I smiled back at him. "I know that, but sometimes, on days like today, it just seems surreal. Soaring into the sky with Thistle was incredible. It was better than a carriage pulled by the winged horses! The wind was in my hair, and as I told Josefina, I wouldn't be able to describe the feeling properly. You'll have to try it!" I exclaimed.

"I would be honored. I cannot say I've ever ridden a dragon before."

"I think you're going to like it!" I replied with a laugh, finishing my cup of coffee.

Mr. Withermyer rose from his chair and took my empty mug. "Would you like another cup?" he offered.

"No, thank you. I guess I'll be on my way. I've probably already taken up too much of your evening. I don't want to overstay my welcome and be a bother. Thank you for the coffee," I stated, rising from the couch.

"You are never a bother, Jane," he replied, placing both cups in his tiny sink. "I really appreciate that you told me about Thistle. We'll have to pick a date for me to experience flying." Mr. Withermyer walked me over to the door.

"Thank you again for listening," I said.

"Anytime. Just remember to be quiet on your way upstairs. It's later than I realized. Good night, Jane," he whispered as the door slid open.

"Good night, Phillip," I murmured, stepping out into the hallway.

14

WHAT EMILY'S EXPECTING

"THERE IS GOING to be an important dinner tonight," Ellen sighed as I came down to the kitchen after ensuring the household had been served breakfast. "I was told the other Mrs. Doyle is coming this evening."

I paused on my way to the closet with the cleaning supplies. If what Ellen claimed was true, then Drake's mother would be arriving. There was always tension when Catherine Doyle paid a visit because Marie and Emily highly disliked her. I didn't mind because their focus wasn't on me, and their hatred was centered on someone else. Mrs. Doyle always pointed out Marie's mistakes when it came to running a household, and I would be lying if I said I didn't enjoy Marie's discomfort.

I collected the mop and broom and proceeded to go about my regular weekend chores. Of course, if Mrs. Doyle was coming for dinner, Marie would expect the house to look perfect. "Is she just coming for a friendly visit to see her son?" I asked Ellen.

Ellen let out a chuckle. "I don't know if I would call her visits friendly. Mr. Doyle was the one who invited her, of course. From what I could gather, he has some kind of announcement planned," Ellen said with a shrug.

I was going to reply when suddenly Marie burst into the kitchen. Ellen rapidly closed her mouth and intently returned to her task. Marie's cold eyes landed on me. "Jane, what are you doing standing about? I'm sure you've heard about our special dinner guest. Get to work immediately!" she snapped at me before she turned to Ellen. "Please tell me you're planning something astonishing for dinner this evening!"

Quickly, I carried the mop, broom, and bucket out of the kitchen and into the foyer. I began sweeping the floor and, afterward, grabbed the mop. I pondered what Ellen had meant about an announcement as I drew the mop back and forth across the floor.

I continued my cleaning routine, and thankfully, Marie left me alone for most of the morning. I managed to tidy up the downstairs rooms without anyone interfering, and I was glad Preston didn't ruin any of my efforts. After cleaning the floors, I made sure all the furniture was appropriately dusted and all the light fixtures were spotless. I didn't see Marie again until late afternoon when she inspected my hard work.

"I guess what you've completed will have to do. Come with me upstairs," Marie demanded, storming up the main staircase.

Obediently, I followed Marie to her room. She sat down at her vanity and looked at me through the mirror.

"Jane, go into my closet and retrieve my dark green dress with the white lace around the collar," she barked. Her gray eyes looked like cold, hard stone.

I hurriedly entered her closet and began searching through her many dresses. When I found the one she requested, I pulled it from the hanger and gently held it up and away from myself so I wouldn't wrinkle it. When I returned to the bedroom, Marie let her hair down from its severe bun, brushing it with an ivory comb. I laid the dress across her bed. She thrust the brush into my hands when I walked over to her. I managed to grasp it, then resumed brushing where she had left off.

"As you know, that awful woman is coming to dine here this evening. So, everything needs to go perfectly tonight. I don't need that witch harassing me under my own roof," Marie sneered.

I couldn't help thinking that with Marie's wiry black hair streaked through with gray, she was the one who looked the part of a witch. I kept my face neutral while running the brush through her hair. Marie sat as still as a statue.

"How would you like to wear your hair this evening, ma'am?" I asked, scooping her hair into my hand.

"Part it in the middle, and then poof it on both sides. Then, roll it up and pin it at the base of my neck," Marie snapped.

Her steely eyes scrutinized my every move. I carefully pinned her hair so she wouldn't have anything to complain about and ensured I didn't push the pins too deep into her scalp.

"I wonder what our wonderful guest will lament over this evening," Marie said sarcastically. "I swear she does it just to irritate me. Make sure she has nothing horrible to say, do you understand? Greet her at the door, take her coat, and do whatever you must. I'll blame you if she makes one negative comment about the state of this house," Marie stated.

"Yes, ma'am. I understand," I replied. I wondered what punishment I'd receive since I had no control over Mrs. Doyle's comments.

"Good. Now, help me get into my dress. After, you are to head over to Emily's room right away," Marie said, leaning toward the mirror and gently patting her hair.

I picked Marie's dress up and unbuttoned the back. Gracefully, she stepped in, and I pulled it up, holding it out in the front so she could slip her arms into the sleeves. I gingerly buttoned each button, ensuring I didn't pinch her skin. Once Marie was finished, I darted down the hall to Emily's room.

On the second knock, Emily demanded I enter the room. I

found her deep in her closet in only her undergarments, furiously searching through her dresses. I was glad she wasn't tossing the clothes onto the floor this time.

"I am here to help, ma'am," I stated, entering the closet.

"Excellent," Emily barked, tossing a pale blue dress toward me. "Help me into this! This evening is crucial," Emily huffed as she stood ramrod straight.

I managed to get two of the buttons closed, but the third one wouldn't come together. I tugged on the fabric but couldn't get the button through the hole.

"What are you doing back there?" Emily screeched.

"I can't get the buttons together," I replied, grasping the fabric again.

"What do you mean?" Emily snarled, spinning around to face me.

"What I'm saying, ma'am, is that the dress appears too tight. Therefore, I cannot fasten the buttons up the back," I stated matter-of-factly.

"Try again," Emily demanded.

"Ma'am, I don't think…," I began, but Emily glared at me, and I reached for the buttons.

I pulled on the fabric, afraid it would rip, but to no avail. Finally, Emily gave up and took off the dress. She tossed it at me and demanded I bring her the pale pink dress. I brought the pink dress from the closet and helped her step in. I began clasping the buttons but encountered the same problem after the first few. Emily obviously gained weight, and I couldn't get the buttons to close. I cleared my throat and took a deep breath, preparing for the worst.

"Ma'am, this dress needs to be let out as well. Do you have any dresses that were loose on you before?" I asked slowly.

Emily spun around so quickly that I couldn't even react in time. She shoved me so hard that I fell into the dresser. The edge of the furniture dug into my right side, and I crumpled to the floor. I let out a gasp as pain sliced through my body. Emily leered at me as she stepped out of the pale pink dress.

"Get up off the floor and fetch my orange dress. Stop being so dramatic; I barely touched you," she said with a laugh.

I placed my left hand on my side and rocked back and forth momentarily, trying to block out the pain. My ribs and hip flared in agony as I gripped the dresser with my right hand and pulled myself to my feet. I gritted my teeth, hobbling into the closet, hoping none of my ribs were broken. I found the third dress Emily requested and prayed to the gods that this dress would fit.

I was grateful when the gods answered my prayers, and I was able to button the dress up. Then, I steeled myself to fix her hair. I felt like a horse had kicked me, and I struggled to breathe through the pain. Emily demanded I braid her hair on both sides of her head and twirl the braids into two buns. I worked as quickly as possible, finishing just as the front doorbell echoed through the house.

Before she could object, I excused myself from Emily's room and raced to the front door. My body ached in agony, but I ground my teeth against the throbbing in my side. I took a second to compose myself before I reached for the front door. Then, with a deep breath, I pulled it open.

Mrs. Doyle stood on the stoop in a wide-brimmed hat and a handsome tweed coat over her elegant dark blue dress. Her gray hair was neatly styled, and she stared at me with large, dark eyes.

"Good evening, Mrs. Doyle, and welcome. Would you like me to take your hat and your coat?" I asked, bowing to her. I managed not to cry out at the pain in my side.

"Yes, very well," she replied as I helped her out of the coat. "It's good to see that someone around here has been trained in manners," she huffed under her breath.

"Greetings, Mother." Drake's voice boomed as he briskly came down the stairs. "I see you're being well taken care of." His eyes, just as dark as his mother's, looked me over and then winked. My cheeks began to heat as I turned from him to hang his mother's coat in the front entryway closet.

"Yes, it appears your wife's family does have some good help around here," she answered.

"Now, Mother, please behave," Drake chuckled as Mrs. Doyle handed me her hat.

I placed the hat on the shelf above the clothing rack. As I closed the closet door, I saw Marie, Emily, and Preston descending the stairs. Marie tilted her face toward the ceiling as she descended the stairs. Emily looked annoyed, and Preston flashed his regular mischievous smile.

"Good evening, Mrs. Doyle. How wonderful for you to join us for dinner," Marie said in a fake voice.

Emily sighed deeply at her mother for addressing the old Mrs. Doyle with her new moniker. Mrs. Doyle gazed up at the descending family and then glanced at her son.

"What a pleasure to be invited," she replied in an equally forced voice, and I breathed a sigh of relief, even though it caused my ribs to ache.

The family walked toward the dining room, and I followed behind them. I was glad Ellen had already set the table, and Mr. Doyle pulled out a chair for his mother. Emily waited expectantly, and he pulled out a chair for her once his mother was seated. I rushed into the kitchen to get a water pitcher and began pouring out the glasses.

"So, my son, you invited me here for this special dinner. I'm dying to know the reason," Mrs. Doyle said.

"You have a knack for getting right to the point, don't you, Mother?" Drake said with a slightly nervous laugh. "We haven't even been served our drinks, let alone our dinner."

Mrs. Doyle looked down her nose at her son. "You should know by now that I don't like beating around the bush. So why make me wait until the end of the dinner service? If you have some good news, let me hear it," she demanded.

Drake grabbed Emily's hand and cleared his throat. "Mother, Emily, and I have some very exciting news. We'll be expecting our first child sometime at the end of April or the beginning of May," he said with a smile.

I struggled to keep the water pitcher straight as I hovered over Preston's glass. So, Marie's suspicions were correct. Emily was pregnant. Mrs. Doyle looked so shocked it was probably a blessing she wasn't in the middle of eating, or she actually might have choked. It took her a moment to compose her features before she commented on their announcement.

"Congratulations," Mrs. Doyle finally said. She paused for a second before continuing to speak. "You must be in your ninth or tenth week then."

"Yes. It's the end of my tenth week," Emily replied.

"Have you seen a physician yet?" Mrs. Doyle questioned.

"No, Mother. We wanted to be certain," Drake replied.

"I'll have my daughter see someone soon," Marie chimed in.

"I have just the doctor in mind," Mrs. Doyle said, holding her hands up to silence everyone.

"Oh, really?" Marie sighed and rolled her eyes.

"Yes, I'll make an appointment for you to see him," Mrs. Doyle proclaimed. "I don't want some stranger taking care of my grandchild."

"You act as if I'm incapable of finding my daughter the proper doctor," Marie spat out.

"I want my grandchild to have the best possible care! Dr. Bradley is the best money can buy, and I don't want to risk my first grandchild coming into this world. Hopefully, it will be a strong boy to carry on the Doyle name."

"Mother, Dr. Bradley's office is several days away," Drake said.

"Yes, which is why we should leave this Friday. I'll make all the arrangements," Mrs. Doyle insisted.

"How can we be sure Dr. Bradley will be a good enough doctor for Emily?" Marie asked haughtily.

"Dr. Bradley delivered my Drake into the world, and I wouldn't trust anyone else with this matter. He's one of the best doctors!" Mrs. Doyle said, her face the color of a ripe tomato.

Marie was about to retort when Emily cleared her throat. "If Drake believes Dr. Bradley is the best option for our baby, then I will see him."

Drake looked over at Emily and smiled. "If my mother believes him to be the best, then I'm sure he is. So, there is no need to worry about a thing. My mother and I will make all the arrangements. We'll leave on Friday morning, and you should be able to see the doctor by Monday or Tuesday."

"Make sure the details include Preston and me," Marie spoke up. "I believe Emily's family would be a great comfort to her on this trip."

Mrs. Doyle didn't look too pleased by this statement, but before she could say anything, Drake spoke again. "Then it's all settled. We shall all leave Friday morning."

Slowly, I slipped into the kitchen to bring out the dinner. I couldn't help smiling through the pain in my ribs. With the recent turn of events, it seemed that I could attend the Harvest Festival after all.

15

SWORDS AND SOARING

MY RIGHT SIDE was still sore as I headed to Mr. Withermyer's office for our Monday lesson. I didn't think any bones had been broken, but a sizeable blackish-blue bruise ran under my breast all the way down to my hip. I hadn't told anyone that Emily had harmed me, and I tried not to wince or show any signs of pain.

I told my friends I would be able to attend the Harvest Festival, and Josefina was elated. Dr. Tweedle promised to take me to the Jewel Caverns on Friday after classes so I could find a dress. Perhaps with Emily having a baby, my life wouldn't be so bad if she had to make weekend trips with the entire family to visit a doctor. I was thrilled that I would be able to attend another dance. I did have an excellent time at the last one.

A part of me felt guilty about attending. I still missed Robert and felt like everything about him was slipping away. His father had taken the ring from me, and when I thought about Robert, I couldn't remember the sound of his laugh or the glint in his eyes. My nightmares didn't plague me like they used to, and sometimes, I feared I would forget Robert's face.

I knocked on Mr. Withermyer's door, and he immediately answered as if he'd been waiting just on the other side of the door.

"Good evening, Miss Fitzgerald," he said, gazing down at each end of the hallway. "We can go up to the ninth floor."

I nodded, stepping back from the door to allow him to exit the office. We climbed to the ninth floor. I waited patiently while I watched Mr. Withermyer pull out his pixie dust case, and I wondered what we'd be going over today. I wasn't sure if I could handle physical self-defense at the moment.

"Today, I'll summon practice weapons, and we'll begin reviewing some defenses with those. You seemed to have excelled at the other techniques and have been adding magic to those tactics. I think it would be good for you to learn to defend yourself with a sword or something like it," Mr. Withermyer explained, summoning two wooden swords. "We can use these to practice and begin training. I'll summon metal swords once you've mastered the techniques."

He handed me one of the wooden swords, and my side throbbed slightly as I reached for it. The wooden weapon felt heavy in my hand, and I winced as I held it up. Mr. Withermyer faced me and held his sword aloft.

"The first thing we're going to work on is a stance," Mr. Withermyer explained, holding the sword upright so it was perpendicular to the ground. He also positioned his left foot slightly ahead of his right foot.

I mirrored his position, wincing as I lifted the sword. Mr. Withermyer circled me, examining my stance. He made a few slight adjustments to my shoulders before he nodded his head.

"Good. You should obtain this stance when you are about to fight with a weapon like this. You have the sword in the ready position, allowing you to maneuver in any direction. Positioning your feet this way will help you maintain balance. Now that you're in this position, you can try a basic attack like a lunge," Mr. Withermyer explained, positioning himself in my line of view.

"A lunge is very simple; all you have to do is bring your right foot forward and thrust the sword with your right hand. You'll want to do this quickly while keeping your left foot grounded. Give it a try."

He demonstrated, then stepped to the side to observe. I lunged forward, and my right side twinged with pain. I hissed as the sword flew from my hand, and I clutched my ribs.

"Jane, what's wrong?" Mr. Withermyer asked, coming to my side.

"It's nothing," I replied, taking a deep breath.

I started forward to retrieve the sword.

Mr. Withermyer laid his hand on my shoulder, stopping me. His green eyes searched mine. "They've hurt you again, haven't they?" he asked gruffly. I began shaking my head when Mr. Withermyer spoke again. "You don't have to be ashamed. You can tell me."

I took another breath and looked up at him. "It's just a bruise. I'm sure it will heal soon," I replied.

"Have a seat against the wall," Mr. Withermyer said, gently taking my left arm and guiding me to the side of the room.

Slowly, I lowered myself and rearranged my skirt. Mr. Withermyer sat beside me and began digging through his pixie dust case. He summoned a glass of water and poured white pixie dust into it. He swirled the charm around and then handed it to me.

"Drink this. It's a pain-relieving charm with healing properties," Mr. Withermyer said.

I stared at the murky water for a moment and then raised the glass to my lips. The water tasted bitter, and I quickly gulped it down. I stuck out my tongue as I handed the glass back to Mr. Withermyer, and he added more water so I could get the taste out of my mouth.

"I know the charm isn't pleasant, but it will help to get rid of the pain, and it will also help heal the bruising. Where does it hurt?"

"The pain goes from here to there along my right side," I said, indicating my ribs and hip.

"What happened?" he asked softly, pulling two more charm vials from his case.

"Emily pushed me, and I fell into a dresser," I said with a sigh, glancing away from him.

I did feel ashamed of what my stepsister had done to me. I wished I could've retaliated, but Marie would've done something worse. Who knew what physical punishment she would have imposed on me? Then, she probably would have expelled me from the house.

Mr. Withermyer lightly touched my chin and tilted my face in his direction. "You have nothing to be ashamed of, especially in front of me. I understand why you felt you could do nothing. You've already told me of the threats your stepmother has made," he said softly.

"I don't have anywhere else to go. I have no other family, and I won't become a burden to anyone. Even though my stepfamily is awful to me, the manor is still my home. All my memories of my father are there. I have no money to my name, and I'm too proud to accept charity," I replied.

Mr. Withermyer held up the two charm vials he had taken from his pixie dust case. They appeared to contain the pain-relieving charm he just gave me. "I understand how you feel. Your mother was the same way. I don't mean to insult you, but I want you to have these charms. Take them for the pain," he replied.

"Phillip, I can't take your charms…." I began, but he cut me off.

"Jane, stop being ridiculous." He pressed the two vials into my palm and curled my fingers around them. "This isn't charity. Eventually, I'll teach you how to create this charm, and then you can pay me back," he said with a smile.

"Thank you. I promise to pay you back. You do too much already. I don't need to take your charms, too," I said.

"Don't worry. I'm sure you'll make good on your promise," Mr. Withermyer said with a chuckle and a shake of his head. "We won't continue this lesson until you're fully healed."

"Are you canceling my lessons for the week?" I asked, worry creeping into my voice.

"Only if you would like me to. We could take a break from the physical lessons, and I could show you how to make other advanced charms," Mr. Withermyer offered.

"A break from the physical lessons sounds fine, but please continue to teach me. There is so much I need to learn in case the W.A.S.P. finds me," I answered.

"Alright, we'll begin on one of the charms on Wednesday. As for today, I think we should do something fun. How about changing into your riding uniform and meeting me at the Magical Creatures barn? Didn't you tell me last week that Thistle flew with you on her back?" Mr. Withermyer asked with a smile as he made the water glass disappear.

Mr. Withermyer rose to his feet and extended his hand to me. I placed my hand in his, and he helped me to my feet. "I can meet you in ten minutes," I replied as we exited the exercise room.

I hurried to my room. The bedroom was empty, and I was sure Josefina had gone to the library to study. I crossed the room to my closet and pulled out my riding uniform. When I lifted off my blouse, I glanced at the bruise for a moment in the full-length mirror. My skin was still discolored, but some of my pain was receding. I was thankful for the pain-relieving charm, but I needed to learn how to create one so I could pay Mr. Withermyer back. I fastened my boots before turning toward the mirror again.

Quickly, I secured my hair before leaving the room. I was excited Mr. Withermyer had suggested this outing. It would be nice to take to the skies again. I tried not to run down the multiple staircases to the massive front doors.

Mr. Withermyer was waiting outside the barn doors. He held

the door for me when we entered, and I hurried toward Thistle's stall. Her purple head peeked out over the door. When she saw me, she puffed smoke rings and tossed her head. I giggled as I threw open the stall door and threw my arms around her neck. I heard Mr. Withermyer laughing behind me.

"She seems happy to see you," he commented while I walked toward the riding equipment.

"Yes. Thistle always acts like this when I come to see her," I replied, tossing the saddle blanket over her back. She quieted down when she realized I was getting ready for riding. "I love spending time with her."

Mr. Withermyer grabbed the saddle off the wall. He lifted it onto her back and helped fasten it in place. When Thistle was outfitted, I led her from the stall. Every once in a while, he reached out to pat Thistle's neck, and she blew contented smoke rings every time. We walked beside her into the fenced-in area, and Mr. Withermyer closed the gate behind us. Thistle stood perfectly still while she waited for my instructions.

"You can ride her if you'd like," I said to Mr. Withermyer as he came up beside me.

Slowly, he approached Thistle and held out his hand. Thistle's nose skimmed over his palm before she nuzzled him with her nose. Mr. Withermyer murmured gentle words as he slowly swung himself into the saddle. Thistle didn't object and stood very still while Mr. Withermyer situated himself. I stepped forward to praise her, but suddenly, Mr. Withermyer leaned toward me and extended his hand.

"What are you doing?" I asked hesitantly.

"I have no idea what I'm doing. I've never ridden a dragon before. Come with me," he said with a grin.

A laugh escaped my lips, and I shook my head. "Riding Thistle is like riding a horse. There isn't much difference except she has wings and might take flight," I replied.

Mr. Withermyer defiantly kept his hand extended and stared

at me intently. "Oh, come on!" he said again, wiggling his fingers. "Thistle doesn't have a bridal, and I don't know what commands you've taught her. There's enough room on this saddle, and the straps will be able to secure both of us. It would be safer if you just joined me," he stated.

I let out a soft sigh and approached his outstretched hand. Tentatively, I placed my fingers in his palm and then put my left leg in the saddle's stirrup. I gripped Mr. Withermyer's hand to steady myself as I swung my right leg over. Finally, I settled onto the saddle in front of Mr. Withermyer. He reached around and handed me the straps after securing them around his legs. Mr. Withermyer kept his hands loosely at his sides, and I could tell he was leaning back to maintain a polite distance.

Once we were situated, I used my knees to coax Thistle into a trot. We did a few turns about the fenced-in field before I leaned forward slightly and persuaded her into a gallop. Her membranous wings began flapping, and I knew it was only a matter of time before she would lift off the ground. Mr. Withermyer's intake of breath alerted me to the fact that we were no longer on the field. I laughed as his hands gripped my shoulders while he tried to gain his balance. Before raising my arms, I checked that the saddle straps held us in place.

Thistle rose into the sky, into the shadows of the approaching dusk. Clouds whipped by as Thistle soared around the Jelf Academy, and then she ascended higher. Butterflies raged in my stomach at the sensation, and I let out an excited cry to extract some of my emotions.

"This is incredible!" Mr. Withermyer breathed, and his warm breath tickled my earlobe. "I can see why you were so energetic the other night. I've never experienced anything like this."

I smiled, turning my head slightly. I could barely see him over my left shoulder, but I could tell he was grinning from ear to ear. I leaned my left knee somewhat into Thistle's side, and my dragon banked left, causing Mr. Withermyer to cry out in alarm as he gripped the tops of my shoulders again. I laughed, leaning into the turn, my hair whipping around my face. Mr. Withermyer chuckled when he realized we weren't in any danger.

"Could you let me know if you're going to do that again?" he exclaimed, shifting slightly in the saddle.

Thistle blew smoke rings as if Mr. Withermyer's reaction had amused her. I patted the side of her neck, and she continued to flap her wings. "Did you hear that, girl? We must behave," I scolded gently as she extended her wings into a smooth glide.

My heart raced as Thistle glided back toward the Jelf Academy. The sun was very low on the horizon, and the sky was alit with a beautiful array of colors. I had never seen a sunset from this position, and I sighed deeply.

"It's beautiful, isn't it?" I asked, stretching out my arm to indicate the sky in front of us.

"Yes, it is," Mr. Withermyer responded, leaning over my right shoulder to better view the sky.

"Doesn't it feel so free up here?" I asked. "I feel like all my worries are below me, and if I could just keep flying, I could escape all my troubles. At least Thistle allows me to escape for a while, and everything seems so small. I can feel completely free for a moment." I sighed deeply again, taking in the bright pinpricks of the first few stars becoming visible in the sky.

We continued toward the setting sun in silence as the night grew darker and the bright colors faded to blue and purple hues. Finally, as Thistle began her descent back to the field, Mr. Withermyer cleared his throat, breaking the silence.

"Jane, one day you will be free from your stepfamily, and I'll do anything I can for you to find a way to accomplish this. Eventually, you won't have to be chained to them, and you won't have to suffer from their abuse. You'll be able to escape without becoming a burden to anyone, and I'll try to figure out a way for you to do it. I promise."

16

THE HARVEST FESTIVAL

FRIDAY NIGHT ARRIVED quickly, and I waited for Dr. Tweedle in the front entrance hall. Josefina offered to come with me even though she had already chosen a dress for the Harvest Festival. I was grateful she was accompanying me because I valued her opinion. We sat at the bottom of the staircase, discussing what colors would look good on me. Suddenly, our discussion was interrupted by the clearing of a throat.

"Good evening, Miss Fitzgerald and Miss Martinez. I don't mean to intrude on your conversation. Dr. Tweedle sent me to find you. Unfortunately, he has been called away by pressing business, and he won't be able to take you to the Jewel Caverns," Mr. Withermyer began.

What would I do now? I supposed I could wear the same one I wore to the Valentine's Day dance last year. I hung my head and glanced at the floor, feeling disappointed.

"That's why he sent me in his place. I'll be the one to take you if that's okay. Are you ladies ready to go?" he asked with a smile.

I glanced at him and then at Josefina, trying not to look hopeful. "Are you sure it is not a bother?"

"Not at all. I didn't have plans, so I don't mind in the least," Mr. Withermyer replied, coming down the remaining steps.

We crossed the hall to the front doors, and Mr. Withermyer held one open.

"Dr. Tweedle seems to be very preoccupied lately. It seems unusual since he has always been available in previous years," I commented.

"He's become more involved with some aspects of government this year," Mr. Withermyer responded as we walked toward the cloud.

"Does it have anything to do with the W.A.S.P.?" I inquired.

Mr. Withermyer glanced over at me before he replied. "Yes. Some of the issues he has been assisting with deal with the problem of the W.A.S.P."

Josefina and I shot worried looks at each other. "Has there been any recent W.A.S.P. activity?" Josefina asked with an anxious tone in her voice.

"There have been some disappearances far from here, but pixie officials haven't been able to determine if it was because of the W.A.S.P. The missing pixies could just be on a long holiday or some other matter without cause for concern," Mr. Withermyer explained.

The cloud descended into the meadow where a carriage awaited us. Mr. Withermyer helped us board, and we held on as he cast a teleportation charm. The night sky was bright with stars when we appeared outside the caverns. It didn't take long for us to travel to Mr. Murray's store, and Mr. Withermyer parked the carriage.

Josefina smiled as we walked into the shop. Mr. Murray greeted us warmly and showed us the racks with all the evening dresses.

"I'll just be seated on the bench over there," Mr. Withermyer said, pointing to the bench he was referring to. "I'll be right here if you need anything."

Josefina began helping me browse through dresses, and it wasn't long before she was holding onto several. She chased me into a dressing room and began lining up dresses for me to try. I began trying what Josefina had picked, starting with an emerald A-line with a V-neck collar. It was pretty, but I didn't feel it was the right dress for me.

The next several minutes were consumed with trying dress after dress. Even though they all fit perfectly, I wasn't crazy about any of them. I finally grabbed the wine-colored dress I had picked out. It was an off-the-shoulder ballgown with swirling lace across the chest and on the short sleeves. The bottom of the gown had many layers, making the dress full. I slipped it over my head and slid my arms through the sleeves. Then I straightened out the skirt. Slowly, I stepped out of the dressing room.

Josefina's face lit up, and she applauded. "You look wonderful, Jane!"

I swished the skirt in front of the full-length mirror and bit my lip. "What do you really think about this one?"

"I think it's perfect! The color of the dress says autumn! Men are going to fall over themselves to get dances with you!"

"I don't know about that," I laughed, staring at my reflection.

"I can prove it to you! Mr. Withermyer is a man," Josefina exclaimed as if she had just realized it. "Let's ask his opinion!"

"Josefina, no," I cried, but she had already darted away.

I could feel my face becoming increasingly hot, and I was sure it was almost the same color as the dress. It wasn't long before Josefina came back around the corner with Mr. Withermyer in tow.

"Tell Jane what she looks like in this dress," Josefina exclaimed, stepping to the side.

Mr. Withermyer glanced up at me, and he paused. His green eyes met mine before they traveled down the length of the dress. Then, quickly, he closed his mouth since he had been gaping at me. It took another minute before he began speaking.

"Miss Fitzgerald, you look absolutely stunning," he finally managed to say.

"Thank you," I murmured, keeping my eyes on the floor.

"I told you the dress was perfect! Mr. Withermyer was almost speechless," Josefina commented, and I looked up just in time to see Mr. Withermyer's red face disappear around the corner.

"Okay, I suppose this is the dress," I said, quickly stepping back into the dressing room.

I purchased the wine-colored dress, and Mr. Withermyer transported us back to the Jelf Academy. We didn't speak much on the way back to the school, but Mr. Withermyer did offer to carry my garment bag for me. Then, he followed Josefina and me to our room before handing me the dress and wishing us a good evening. I thanked him again for escorting us, and Mr. Withermyer said he would see us at the dance.

"Can I expect you'll take a dance on my card?" I asked with a smile.

Mr. Withermyer nodded and smiled in return. "Of course, Miss Fitzgerald. I promise to seek you and Miss Martinez out. Good night, ladies," he replied again before backing down the hallway.

Josefina noticed my smile as the door slid closed, and I ignored her as I hung the garment bag in my closet. She was still smirking when I turned around, her big brown eyes aglow.

"What are you grinning like a Cheshire cat for?" I demanded, sitting on my bed.

"Oh, nothing. Mr. Withermyer thought your dress was stunning."

"Well, you did ask the man his opinion. Will you stop looking like that? Mr. Withermyer is a dear friend of mine, so quit being silly. At least I'll have one guaranteed dance on my card tomorrow," I replied, grabbing my nightclothes and heading off to the bathroom, Josefina's giggles following in my wake.

The next evening arrived in the blink of an eye. Josefina and I helped each other get ready for the Harvest Festival. I ran the brush through Josefina's long, dark hair and began pinning it.

"I'm hoping my dance card will be full for the entire evening," Josefina sighed, gazing at me through the mirror.

I chuckled, securing a loose curl at the nape of her neck. "Won't you be tired if every dance is promised?"

"I've had such an amazing night's sleep I feel as if I could dance all night," she commented while I finished up with her hair.

Josefina leaned forward on the vanity chair to get closer to the mirror so she could put on makeup. I watched as she outlined her dark eyes and added a bit of rouge to her cheeks before picking up dark red lipstick and outlining her lips. When finished, she rose from the vanity chair and turned to me.

"It's your turn," Josefina said, indicating the vanity chair.

I took a seat, and Josefina began working on my hair. First, she curled and pinned it into a low bun. Then she picked up a wine-colored ribbon. Josefina took a few moments to create a pretty bow before pinning the ribbon into my hair. When she was finished, she took a step back to admire her work.

"You look lovely, Jane. I believe my ribbon matches your dress perfectly. First, let me apply your makeup, and then we can put on our dresses."

Josefina picked up her powders and accessories and began on my face. I followed her instructions when she told me to close my eyes and pout my lips. Josefina lightly brushed rouge over my cheeks, and when she was finished, she instructed me to look in the mirror. Slowly, I turned to glance at myself.

My face looked flawless, and the makeup on my eyes made them look brighter. My cheeks were a delicate shade of pink, and Josefina had selected a mauve color for my lips. Like the dance I attended last year, I felt gorgeous. I softly touched my pinned curls and stood up from the vanity chair.

"Thank you so much. I feel so pretty," I said, smiling at Josefina.

"You are always pretty, Jane," she said with a grin as she went to her closet to pull out her dress.

Josefina's dress was a pumpkin orange empire style with a light tan ribbon around the waist. The dress had a Queen Ann neckline, and the sleeves were made from orange lace, the same color as the dress. Josefina's dress looked like it belonged at the autumn dance. I retrieved my dress from my closet and laid it on my bed while I helped Josefina into hers. My heart began beating faster as Josefina helped me with my dress. Once we were both fully dressed, we stood side by side before the full-length mirror.

"You look so beautiful," I exclaimed, patting Josefina's hand.

"Thank you. We're going to have such a wonderful night," Josefina replied, taking a deep breath. Her eyes trailed over to the pixie clock on the nightstand. "Are you ready to go down?"

I nodded, and we headed to the door. There weren't many students in the hallway as Josefina and I headed for the staircase. Slowly, we glided down the stairs, and I was careful not to step on the hem of my gown. When we reached the second floor, we could hear the clamor of the party beginning downstairs. With an excited breath, we rounded the top of the balustrade leading down to the first floor.

The railings of the stairs were twined with garlands of fall leaves in reds, oranges, and yellows. The leaves shimmered in the light as if sprinkled with glitter. On every third step down was a lantern containing a flickering candle of goblin fire. On both sides at the bottom of the stairs were several artfully stacked haybales decorated with an array of pumpkins. Scattered around the haybales were more fall leaves. Some students were milling around the front entrance hall, talking excitedly, and I could hear music beginning in the dining hall.

Josefina and I descended the stairs. Similar to other dances I attended at the Jelf Academy, all the tables were pushed from the middle of the floor, leaving room for dancing. Each table was covered with orange tablecloths and sheer gold overlays. The long tables had leaf-shaped runners, while the round tables had golden cloth circles in the centers. Each round table had a lantern or a carved pumpkin with a candle inside as the centerpiece. The long tables had golden candle holders, each with goblin fire candles. Scattered around the centerpieces were leaves, acorns, berries, and sunflowers. Cornstalks, haybales, and giant pumpkins stood in the room's corners.

Josefina and I picked up new dance cards and sat at one of the round tables.

"I just let Miguel know where to find us. Andrew and Miguel should be here soon," Josefina said, watching the students' arrival through the dining hall doors.

It wasn't long before Zachary and Kairi arrived. Kairi was in a black velvet A-line dress with an illusion neckline. The sleeves were a little past her elbows, but they were made of sheer fabric, just like her neckline. I knew there wasn't a full moon this week, so Kairi couldn't dance. Even if there had been, the dance was not a masquerade ball, so she couldn't conceal her identity. Kairi spotted Josefina and me, and she let her brother know. Zachary began guiding her wheelchair in our direction.

Zachary's aqua eyes trailed down my body, and he grinned. "Jane, you look dazzling," he remarked when he arrived at our table.

I could feel my cheeks growing red at his praise. "Thank you. You look dashing as well," I responded, looking up at him from under my eyelashes.

"Just ask her to dance already," Kairi burst out, causing Josefina and me to laugh. Zachary shot his sister a scowl as he tugged on his suit jacket.

"Jane, may I have the honor of the first dance?" he asked, his serious aqua eyes back on me.

"Yes, of course," I replied, passing him my dance card.

"Are you going to ask Josefina too?" Kairi inquired. "It would be rude not to."

Zachary gave her another aggravated look. "Dear sister, I was going to ask Josefina. Unfortunately, I can only ask one person at a time," Zachary replied, handing me my card and reaching for Josefina's. I looked down and was surprised to see he had requested three of my dances.

I had little time to ponder on it when Miguel and Andrew arrived at our table. They greeted everyone and then began asking for dance cards. Miguel's eyes flitted to Kairi as he wrote his name on Josefina's and my dance cards. When he finished, he took a seat beside Kairi.

"Would anyone like something to drink? I was going to go to the buffet tables," I inquired.

"Jane, have a seat! Miguel, Andrew, and I will retrieve refreshments for everyone," Zachary offered, jumping to his feet. Miguel reluctantly rose from his chair.

"Thank you, gentlemen," Josefina exclaimed as the three of them headed toward the refreshment table.

While we waited for the drinks, Taylor arrived. She was wearing a moss-green empire gown with an asymmetric neckline. There was gold beading along the waistline of the dress, which sparkled when she moved. Her wavy hair was pinned up in a side bun, and some curly waves of her blonde hair fell flatteringly around her face. She gently pushed her square glasses up the bridge of her nose.

"Good evening, everyone," Taylor's soft voice sounded. "Where are our gentlemen friends?" Her blue eyes searched the crowded room.

"They went to get drinks for the table," Josefina replied. "They should be back soon."

Suddenly, I felt a tap on my shoulder. I smiled as I turned, expecting to find Mr. Withermyer or Dr. Tweedle asking for a dance on my card. Instead, my eyes landed on Jonathan Hillman.

His black hair looked like it hadn't been combed in days and stuck out at odd angles. He smiled a very toothy smile at me.

"Good evening, Jane. You're looking so lovely this evening," he lisped.

"Hello, Jonathan. It's nice to see you," I replied automatically, not wanting to be rude. "Thank you for the compliment."

I caught Josefina's smirk, and her eyes rolled to the ceiling.

"I was wondering if I could have the pleasure of seeing your dance card," Jonathan asked as spittle flew from his mouth.

I swallowed the lump in my throat, slowly handing him my dance card. Even though I didn't want to dance with him, I couldn't bring myself to be disrespectful. I knew my card was nowhere near full, and it would be impolite to refuse. I prayed he would only take one dance. His hand curled around my card.

"Thank you for accepting, Jane. I'm sure you remember my excellent dancing at the Valentine's Day dance last year. I await our first dance with delight," Jonathan said, placing his hand over his heart before bowing to me. He put my dance card back on the table before he walked away.

"Did he say first dance? How many did he take?" Kairi asked, leaning to see my card. "It was bad-mannered not to offer anyone a dance."

"Consider yourself lucky," I said, glancing at my card. "He took three dances," I stuttered.

"Three dances!" Josefina blurted out. "That's so many! If he asked for more than that, it would seem improper. Does he have intentions to propose next?"

"So, the future Mrs. Hillman, what do you have to say about that?" Kairi chuckled.

"Please do not call me that," I replied, not wanting to tell Kairi her brother had also taken three dances.

"See, that's what you get for being so nice all the time," Josefina chided. "If you were a little rude, you wouldn't be in this situation."

"What situation?" Miguel asked, returning to the table with Zachary and Andrew. Zachary had remembered to get a drink for Taylor, too. He asked for her dance card after handing her a glass of cider. Taylor blushed prettily as she gave him her card.

"Jonathan Hillman has taken a lot of space on Jane's dance card. He marked himself down for three dances," Josefina responded to her brother.

I couldn't help but notice the scowl on Zachary's face while Miguel laughed. I wondered why he appeared upset by the number of dances Jonathan had requested. I pretended not to notice as I sipped my cider. The musicians announced the first dance, and Zachary rose to his feet, extending his hand to me. I allowed him to lead me onto the dance floor, and the first waltz began.

Zachary was a decent dancer. It was easy to follow his lead, and soon, we had settled into a comfortable rhythm.

"You do look lovely tonight," Zachary commented as he spun me around.

"Thank you," I replied, knowing a blush was rising to my cheeks.

"I want to thank you again for keeping my sister's secret. It means a lot to me that you would help protect her. I've discovered the pixie world can be cruel to people like my sister," he whispered, leaning closer.

"I would never do anything to hurt Kairi. I know what it's like to be shunned in the pixie world. Kairi has become one of my most special friends, and I would protect her secret with my life," I responded.

Zachary beamed as we swirled around the dance floor. "I'm glad to hear that. I know my sister feels the same way about you," Zachary said as the dance ended.

What are your feelings about me, Zachary? I thought as he led me off the dance floor.

17

BELLE OF THE BALL

Miguel took my hand and led me back onto the floor after I had taken a quick sip from my glass.

"You seem to be in high demand this evening," he teased, and I gave him a slight punch on his arm before the dance began.

"I wish my card would've been full before Jonathan Hillman asked me to dance. Then I could've politely refused him," I sighed as we danced.

"Now that I know, I'll have to take more dances on your card, so Jonathan won't be able to have any," Miguel said with a laugh.

"Oh, Miguel, what would people think then?" I quipped. "More dances on my card will have people wondering what your intentions are."

"Let them wonder. I don't give a damn. You're one of my best friends, and they can think all they like if it saves you from dancing with Mr. Hillman. All that matters is that you'll know my true intentions," Miguel said.

"I might not be able to attend another dance. I've only been able to come to this one because Marie and her family are away," I replied.

"Then what are you worried about? Your final dance with Jonathan tonight could be your last one," Miguel responded with an impish grin. "Why didn't you say that before I promised to fill up your card at the next dance?"

I had to suppress the urge to punch him again. As we continued around the floor, I noticed that Miguel's eyes would shift to our table occasionally. When I followed his gaze, I saw Kairi seated alone. Everyone else was on the dance floor. She smiled as she watched the dancers, but I felt a pain in my heart that she couldn't join us.

"I wish I could ask Kairi to dance," Miguel said, voicing my unspoken wish.

I nodded. "I hate to see her sitting alone."

"Kairi is such a special person, and I want her to have a nice time. I wish there was something I could do," Miguel sighed.

The dance ended, and we walked back to the table. Miguel sat beside Kairi, and they began discussing different dance types. I excused myself and walked over to the hors d'oeuvres table. I started helping myself to a few things when, abruptly, Mr. Withermyer was at my side.

"Good evening, Miss Fitzgerald," he said with a slight wink as he placed a tiny sandwich onto his plate. "I've been looking for you so I can request the dance I promised you, but you were occupied each time I wanted to approach."

"Yes, it seems so," I replied with a sigh.

"Is there still room on your card?" Mr. Withermyer inquired, and I handed it to him.

Mr. Withermyer glanced down with a bemused grin. "It appears that you are much sought after for dances, especially from Mr. Hillman and Mr. Walsh. Unfortunately, there aren't too many dances left to choose from. I suppose I found you at the right time, or I wouldn't have been able to keep my promise."

"I was not aware my dance card would be so coveted," I replied, blushing again.

Mr. Withermyer wrote on my card before handing it back. I looked to see what dance he'd taken and was surprised to discover he had requested two. My eyes went to his in bewilderment, and he laughed at my expression. He leaned in closer before he began whispering.

"I can't let my favorite student have empty spaces on her dance card. Shh, don't tell anyone I said that." His green eyes winked again before he moved off toward the beverages.

What is in the water tonight? I wondered as I walked back to my friends. Taylor, Kairi, and Josefina were chuckling over something Andrew said when I placed my plate on the table. I sat in the empty seat and had just enough time to eat a tiny sandwich before Jonathan came to collect me. I tried not to cringe as I took his extended arm, and he led me away from the table.

"How are you doing this evening?" Jonathan asked, and I fought the urge to lean away from him.

"I'm well, thank you. How are you?" I replied politely as the song began.

"Better now that I'm dancing with the most beautiful girl in the room," Jonathan lisped, and spittle flew toward me.

Jonathan dragged me around the dance floor. He was moving so quickly that I had to run to keep up with him. We almost bumped into other couples twice, and I gave them embarrassed, apologetic looks. I tried to pull on his hand to slow him down, but he was surprisingly strong despite his appearance.

"Jonathan," I gasped. "Don't you think we ought to slow down a bit?"

"No love, we have to keep up with the tempo of the music."

Jonathan spun me around so fast that I began to feel dizzy. The room swirled, and my stomach felt sick. It was a relief when the song finally ended, and I could catch my breath. My head felt woozy, and I wanted to get something to drink. When I reached the edge of the dance floor, I briefly closed my eyes in hopes that the room would stop spinning.

When I opened my eyes, Jonathan was still holding my arm. I tried to shake him off gently, but he grasped my hand and lifted it to his lips. He placed a sloppy kiss on the back of my hand and smiled at me.

"I will await our next dance with pleasure," he announced before walking off.

My stomach felt even worse after his gesture. I hurried to my table to grab a napkin and wipe off the back of my hand. Whatever affections Jonathan felt, I certainly didn't return them. I dreaded the next dance with him, but I knew I needed to be honest. Maybe he would stop what he thought were romantic gestures if I told him I had no interest. I settled down in my seat and reached for my cider.

"Jane, are you okay?" Taylor asked as she returned to the table with Kairi. "You look awfully pale."

I nodded, taking another sip of my drink. "I'm fine. Just a bit flustered, that's all. I've just had my first dance with Jonathan Hillman."

"What happened? You're as white as a sheet," Kairi stated.

"Unfortunately, he's a horrible dancer. He spun me so quickly, and now I feel dizzy. That's probably the reason I look so pale. When I asked him to slow down, he insisted we had to keep up with the music, but I knew we were moving too fast for the song. Also, it is becoming obvious that Jonathan has some sort of affection for me," I said.

"Well, that was obvious when he requested three dances," Kairi responded with a little laugh, but then she looked at my face. "Was he inappropriate with you?"

"Not entirely. Despite the horrible dancing, he hasn't done anything other than kiss my hand," I replied.

"Don't let him ruin your evening. I know you have two more dances with him, but just get through those and then ignore him. Look forward to your other dances," Taylor said as Josefina, Miguel, and Zachary returned to the table.

"Jane, it's time for our second dance," Zachary said, extending his arm.

I gradually rose to my feet and grasped his hand. Zachary smiled down at me as we walked away from the table. I smiled back and decided to take Taylor's advice.

"Jane, are you feeling alright? You look troubled," Zachary asked.

"I'm all right. I just needed to catch my breath after my last dance," I explained, looking up at him.

Zachary held me in a ballroom hold, and when the foxtrot began, he effortlessly led me in the dance.

"You dance very well," I complimented.

"Thank you. I'm glad you think so," Zachary replied.

"Honestly, any dancing would be better than my last partner's," I giggled.

Zachary's aqua eyes lit up as he laughed, though his laugh was not quite as musical as his sister's. "Who was this awful dance partner?" he asked.

"Jonathan Hillman," I whispered.

"Gods and this is the fella who requested three dances?" Zachary exclaimed, not missing a step.

"Yes, how will I ever survive?" I joked as Zachary led me into a promenade step and then an underarm turn.

"You seem like the type who can survive anything. I'm sure a few more dances with Jonathan Hillman aren't going to kill you."

"It just might," I said with a laugh.

"Where did you learn to dance so well?" Zachary asked.

"Actually, I learned from watching my stepsister and her party guests. Then, I would pretend to dance with someone alone in my attic bedroom. I'm sure that I am not that good of a dancer.

I've only been to a few dances like this with an actual partner," I responded with a slight blush. I had never admitted to my childish make-believe of dancing in the attic. No one had ever asked me before.

"You're very graceful and have a great sense of rhythm. Your pretending has paid off," Zachary said with a deep chuckle. "You've spoken too highly of me about my dancing. It wasn't a particular interest of mine at the Capra Academy of Magic."

"Did the Capra Academy host dances?" I asked curiously.

"Yes, they had several during the year, but I had no desire to attend any," Zachary said, lifting his arm so I could turn beneath it.

"So, what were you interested in then?" I asked, coming back around from the turn.

"Sailing and being near the ocean. The ocean was closer to the Capra Academy than here, but I still couldn't accompany my father on his ships. I can't wait until my education is finished so I can be on board the deck of a ship again," Zachary said.

"I've only seen an ocean for the first time this year, and it was lovely. I've never been on board a ship before," I replied.

"You'll love it!" Zachary exclaimed enthusiastically. "Maybe you could join my family sometime like Taylor did last summer."

"I can't make any promises. My stepmother usually doesn't allow me to go anywhere, but it would be wonderful to experience sailing on a ship," I answered as the dance ended.

Zachary beamed, placing my hand in the crook of his arm. "Anything can be possible," he added as we walked off the dance floor.

I smiled, but my attention was pulled away by the figure we were walking toward. Mr. Withermyer stood at the edge of where the tables met the dance floor. I knew he was waiting for me since he was my partner for the next dance. I watched as he reached up to straighten his tie, his eyes never leaving my face. When we drew nearer, Mr. Withermyer stepped into our path.

"Good evening, Mr. Walsh. By my calculations, it's time for the fifth dance of the evening, and Miss Fitzgerald is to be my partner. May I?" he asked smoothly, extending his arm.

Zachary paused only a moment. "Of course," he replied, handing me off to Mr. Withermyer. "Thank you for the captivating dance, Jane."

I nodded to Zachary as he walked to our table, and Mr. Withermyer placed my hand on his arm. We walked to the middle of the dance floor and waited for the music to begin. According to my card, the fifth dance was supposed to be a tango. Mr. Withermyer grasped my left hand with his right one and then placed his land on my back for a ballroom hold. I gently rested my right hand on his left arm. He held my body tightly but not too close.

When the music began, Mr. Withermyer started with the basic steps. He moved gracefully, and his hold on my body allowed me to know exactly what he would do before executing the move. I danced with trust and confidence as we went down the dance floor, and he turned me so effortlessly when we reached the end of the dance floor. Mr. Withermyer danced with an intensity I had not observed in my other partners. He guided me into more complicated steps, and I executed each one perfectly. From my perspective, the dance seemed so precise, and I wondered if that was how the people watching us perceived it.

Mr. Withermyer turned me into a promenade to get around other dancers on the floor, and then he smoothly settled back into the basic tango step. His cheek was only inches from mine as he led me into several spins. I followed as if I was reading his mind. The dance ended, and he dipped me backward for a moment. I was breathless when we walked off the dance floor.

"Are you feeling well?" Mr. Withermyer asked, leaning toward me.

"Yes. You were amazing. Where did you learn to dance like that?" I exclaimed as I gasped for air.

Mr. Withermyer chuckled as he led me to the beverage table. I waited for him to pour me a glass of cider and gratefully accepted it.

"Honestly, the reason I learned to dance at all was due to your mother. Rachel and Irene were always dragging me to these school dances, so it was your mother who taught me all the steps. As you know, I also have two sisters who used me to practice and learn for their school dances," Mr. Withermyer explained.

"I've never danced like that before," I said after taking a sip of cider.

"I would never have been able to tell. You danced beautifully," Mr. Withermyer replied.

I blushed. "It was only because you were such a great partner. My mother must've been a wonderful dancer if what you say is true, and she really did teach you."

"She was. She danced like an angel," he replied.

"I wish I could've seen her dance," I smiled wistfully. "Every day, I wish I could have known her."

"Yes, I understand how badly young women need their mothers. Unfortunately, my sisters didn't have a motherly figure to turn to," Mr. Withermyer said sadly.

"I believe everyone needs their mothers in some way or another, no matter what age they are. Some people are just more fortunate and are allowed a longer time to cherish them," I replied, placing a comforting hand on Mr. Withermyer's left forearm.

Mr. Withermyer nodded. "Has anyone ever told you how incredibly intelligent you are?" he asked.

I sighed and then shook my head. "You know, I have heard that a time or two, but I'm not sure that's...."

I was interrupted by a rapping on my shoulder. Slowly, I turned to see Jonathan Hillman standing there.

"Jane, it's time for our next dance," he exclaimed with a large, toothy grin.

"Oh, I suppose it is. Pardon me, Mr. Withermyer. Thank you

again for the dance," I said with a bob of my head as Jonathan dragged me onto the floor.

We stopped along the outer edge of the dance floor, and Jonathan pulled me tightly to him. His body was too close to mine, and I tried to step backward. The song began, and we started to dance the foxtrot. Jonathan took such large steps that he would tread on my feet every so often. I couldn't move out of the way because he held me so tightly. I cried out when he stepped on my toes for the fourth time.

"You keep stepping on my feet," I said.

"I'm sorry, but I'm just following the flow of the dance. You have to move backward while I'm moving forward. That's how the steps are in the foxtrot," Jonathan said condescendingly as if it were my fault and my feet were in his way.

I glanced up at him with an annoyed expression. He didn't seem to notice, and I didn't say anything else. This dance was almost over, and I had one more to endure with him. It was amazing how drastic the difference was between my last dance and this one. While Mr. Withermyer had been graceful and elegant, Jonathan was clumsy and awkward.

When the dance ended, I was eager to get away, but Jonathan tugged on my elbow. "Jane, could I have a word with you in the hallway?" he asked.

I couldn't imagine what he wanted to say, but I nodded. It was apparent that he was enamored with me, and I needed to explain that I didn't share his feelings. Perhaps if I was honest, he would stop being so forward and pursue someone else.

Jonathan didn't let go of my arm as he led me out into the hallway. There were only a few other students outside the dining hall. Jonathan didn't stop until we reached a quiet corner. Finally, he let go of my arm and turned to face me. His face was dimly lit by the soft glow of the goblin fire candles in the entrance hall.

He took a deep breath, and when he released the air through his mouth, spittle accompanied it.

"Jane, first let me say how beautiful you are. I've never seen someone with such exquisite violet-colored eyes," Jonathan said, touching my left hand.

"Thank you, Jonathan. I really appreciate the compliment, but..." I began though Jonathan started speaking over me.

"I love you, Jane," he blurted.

"What?" I responded in confusion. I had expected him to tell me he fancied me and maybe wanted to court me, but... love?

"Yes, I love you. You're so beautiful and special. Plus, you're one of the best pixies in our class," Jonathan sighed, gripping my hand.

"But you hardly know me. How can you possibly love me?" I stammered. I was feeling very uncomfortable. Jonathan paused for a moment before he edged closer.

"What isn't there to love about you?"

"Jonathan, we never really talk in classes. You really don't know anything about me, nor have you ever attempted to get to know me in the past three years. So, I wouldn't say that constitutes falling in love with someone," I replied, leaning back to get away from him, but my back touched the wall behind me.

"I know we haven't talked much, but I know I love you. You're so smart and talented. I knew from the moment I laid eyes on you that I had to make you mine," Jonathan said.

"I don't think you should classify your feelings as love. It's more of an infatuation. I don't mean to hurt your feelings, but I can't say I feel the same, and I will never be yours," I faltered.

"Don't say that. I'm sure you could come to love me, too," Jonathan insisted.

"I'm sorry, Jonathan, but I am not sure I can develop those feelings for you," I said softly.

"I'll just have to convince you," Jonathan said, and before I realized what he intended, he gripped my shoulders, pushed me into the wall, and smashed his lips into mine.

I couldn't breathe as Jonathan's mouth pushed down on my lips. He held me against the wall, and I struggled to move. Panic set in when I felt his tongue pressing against the seam of my mouth, and I fought to keep my lips closed. My training with Mr. Withermyer sprung to the forefront of my mind, and using all my strength combined with magic, I pushed Jonathan away. Jonathan flew across the front entrance hall and landed several feet away with a loud crack.

His glasses were slightly askew, and he rolled around in pain while clutching his elbow. I wiped the back of my hand across my mouth, disgusted by what had just occurred. I resisted the urge to spit as a chill ran through my body. Jonathan groaned, continuing to cradle his arm. A few students who had been in the entryway looked at me in surprise. Then, suddenly, Josefina came rushing into the room, followed by Mr. Withermyer.

"Jane, are you okay?" Josefina exclaimed, taking in the scene. Jonathan was lying on the ground a few feet away from me.

I nodded slowly, but my hands were shaking, and I felt like I was going to cry.

Mr. Withermyer approached me and gently touched my arm. "What happened?"

Jonathan groaned again. "She threw me across the floor. That is what happened! I was only being nice to her!" he cried out.

"Tell Mr. Withermyer what really happened!" Josefina yelled. "I saw it with my own eyes! You were taking advantage of Jane!"

Josefina wrapped her arms around me. Mr. Withermyer glared at Jonathan while he struggled to his feet.

"It was only a little kiss. I wasn't taking advantage of anything, and besides, I was only doing what Jane wanted," Jonathan said.

"It was most certainly not what I wanted," I replied hotly.

"Now, don't be such a tease, Jane. We both know what was going on here," Jonathan snarled.

"That is enough, Mr. Hillman!" Mr. Withermyer roared. "Do not talk to Miss Fitzgerald in such a way. You are dismissed from the Harvest Festival. See yourself up to your room or the hospital wing if that is what you require. You can count on detention with me starting Monday right after classes. There is no need for further discussion."

Jonathan scowled as he slinked up the stairs. I breathed out a sigh of relief as Josefina began talking.

"I saw him pull you out of the dining hall, so I waited a moment before I followed. When I came into the entrance hall, I saw he had you cornered against the wall. I didn't know what else to do, so I ran to find Mr. Withermyer," Josefina explained.

"Thank you, Josefina," I said as I patted her arm. "That was not at all how I expected that conversation to go. Thank you, Mr. Withermyer, for coming to my rescue."

"I didn't do anything, Miss Fitzgerald. It would seem you're quite capable of taking care of yourself," Mr. Withermyer replied.

I found myself beginning to smile. "We both know it is no credit of mine."

"Let's return to the dining hall. I'm sure we could all use something to drink, and there is plenty of dancing left to do. Don't let Mr. Hillman's actions ruin the evening," Mr. Withermyer said, gesturing toward the dining hall.

Josefina threaded her arm through mine, and we returned to the dining hall. Mr. Withermyer retrieved two glasses of cider for us, and I began to feel better once I'd consumed the liquid. When we returned to the table, Josefina and I explained what had happened and why Jonathan Hillman was no longer at the dance. My friends were disappointed to hear how forward he had been with me but were glad he'd been removed from the dance. With Jonathan gone, I could finally relax.

I finished my cider and then glanced at my dance card. My next dance was with Miguel, and I was relieved to be dancing with a trusted friend. I placed my empty glass on the table and reached for Miguel's arm. Just as he was about to lead me onto the dance floor, Dr. Tweedle came rushing into the room. I hadn't even noticed that he hadn't been present. He walked quickly toward the podium and raised his hand to silence the band from playing the next song.

The room fell into an eerie silence as Dr. Tweedle cleared his throat. "Attention, students! I'm sorry to disrupt your evening of festivities, but I just received word of a W.A.S.P. attack in the pixie town of Celestial Heights. Our officials are searching the town at this very moment, but the outcome doesn't look promising. I'm sorry to report that there might be no survivors."

18

A W.A.S.P. ATTACK

EVERYONE IN THE dining hall stared in shock. Dr. Tweedle continued speaking. "I believe the pixie government is declaring a 'code yellow' or medium threat warning, but I'm unsure about the closing of the school. Everyone should retire to their rooms. I'm sorry this evening has to come to a close in this manner. When I receive more news, I'll inform everyone," Dr. Tweedle said sadly as he stepped down from the podium.

Dr. Tweedle made eye contact with me, and I dropped Miguel's arm. I murmured a few words to my friends and slowly followed Dr. Tweedle out of the dining hall. He paused in the entrance hall and turned to face me.

"Jane, as you already suspect, you should come with me."

I could feel a lump building in my throat, and I struggled to swallow. There must've been another letter. I dreaded what the message would be. Carefully, I lifted the hem of my gown as I followed Dr. Tweedle up the stairs. My body was shaking with each step up to the second floor.

Dr. Tweedle opened his office door and allowed me to enter. With my heart pounding, I walked toward the blue settee and lowered myself onto it. I rearranged my skirts as Dr. Tweedle came behind his desk.

"What has the W.A.S.P. threatened now?" I asked, spying the letter with the red wax seal shaped like a honeycomb. My voice trembled slightly as I studied the horrible impression of a wasp inside the hexagonal shape.

Dr. Tweedle picked up the letter with a sigh. "The W.A.S.P. still demands we hand over Rachel McCalski's daughter."

"Have they discovered who I am or where I live?" I asked with distress.

"No. Thankfully, they have not, but their movements are becoming more drastic. Celestial Heights was a town entirely inhabited by pixies. No humans resided there, and they had no way of accessing the area. "Dr. Tweedle said with a shake of his head.

"What do you mean when you say that humans don't have access to the area?" I asked.

"Celestial Heights is similar to the Jelf Academy in that it can only be accessed by cloud," Dr. Tweedle said solemnly.

My heart raced as my mind processed the information. How was it even possible? Places like the Jelf Academy and the Jewel Caverns were protected with pixie magic and hidden from the human world. How could a human gain access?

As Dr. Tweedle and I pondered these recent events, a knock sounded on the office door. Dr. Tweedle glanced toward the door; his blue eyes looked tired behind his round glasses.

"You may enter, Phillip," Dr. Tweedle called, and Mr. Withermyer strode into the room with a look of panic.

"Has there been another letter?" he asked, glancing at Dr. Tweedle, then me.

Dr. Tweedle held up the thick parchment.

"Have they discovered anything new about Jane?" Mr. Withermyer asked.

"No," Dr. Tweedle said, opening the letter. "It states that if we do not hand over the daughter of Rachel McCalski, more destruction will follow."

"They've threatened this before," Mr. Withermyer exclaimed.

"Yes, and even though the other letter came months ago, it looks as if they've finally followed through on the threat," Dr. Tweedle sighed.

Suddenly, another knock banged on the office door. I jumped at the noise, my heart racing with anxiety.

"Come in, Mr. Barber. I've been expecting you," Dr. Tweedle announced. The door flew open, and Betty Ann's father entered the room. His salt-and-pepper hair was slicked back, and he was wearing another of his expensive suits.

"Good evening, Oliver, Phillip," Mr. Barber said, his eyes passing over me.

"What was discovered about the tragedy at Celestial Heights?" Dr. Tweedle asked.

"We scouted the entire area, and it was as we suspected. There are no survivors," Mr. Barber announced sadly.

Dr. Tweedle gripped the edge of his desk to steady himself.

"How did this happen?" Mr. Withermyer asked with a gasp and a shake of his head.

Mr. Barber ran his thumb and forefinger over his mustache before he answered. "From the evidence recovered at the scene, it appears the W.A.S.P. utilized a pixie to gain entrance to Celestial Heights. Mr. Baker was discovered on the outskirts of the town. From what we can surmise, Mr. Baker was tortured into revealing the town's location. Once he provided the W.A.S.P. entrance, they disposed of him."

I shuttered at the recounted information. An entire town of pixies had been wiped out because the W.A.S.P. was searching for me. I could feel myself becoming lightheaded. Mr. Withermyer came behind the couch and placed a steadying hand on my shoulder.

"Perhaps we should excuse Miss Fitzgerald. She's looking pale," Mr. Withermyer said.

Mr. Barber turned and finally looked at me. His eyes narrowed, and his mouth shaped itself into a scowl.

"Ah, Miss Fitzgerald. You seem to be the common denominator of our current problems. Perhaps we should put an end to this meaningless slaughter and finally give the W.A.S.P. what they're asking for," Mr. Barber said snidely.

"Arnold, how can you suggest such a thing?" Dr. Tweedle demanded just as Mr. Withermyer shouted the word no.

"The W.A.S.P. wants the heir of Rachel McCalski. Miss Fitzgerald is that heir. The W.A.S.P. will continue to end pixie lives in their search for this one girl. Do you deem this girl's life more important than all pixie lives? Especially when this heir is half-human?" Mr. Barber spat out.

"How dare you," Mr. Withermyer cried, moving from behind the sofa to stand in front of me. "Handing an innocent woman over to our greatest enemies wouldn't do any good. Apologize immediately for your degrading comments about Miss Fitzgerald's heritage!"

"Phillip is correct. We do not tolerate discrimination at the Jelf Academy. Miss Fitzgerald's parentage shouldn't signify anything, nor should it be discussed. The W.A.S.P. has been attacking and hunting pixies for centuries. Handing Miss Fitzgerald over to them isn't going to prevent anything," Dr. Tweedle said sharply, his face colored with anger.

"My apologies, Miss Fitzgerald," Mr. Barber murmured, glancing around Mr. Withermyer at me. His apology didn't seem sincere, and I narrowed my eyes at him. "Something must be done about these increasing W.A.S.P. attacks, though," Mr. Barber continued.

Mr. Withermyer still glowered at Mr. Barber, but he sat beside me on the sofa.

"I agree something must be done, but not something that will sacrifice lives. If only we could find a way to penetrate the W.A.S.P.'s network. Then we could discover how they're acquiring information and their future plans."

"I will discuss ideas with other members of my department. If you can come up with any solutions to this problem, feel free to contact me," Mr. Barber stated.

"What about the Jelf Academy? I'm unsure whether to close the academy until this threat passes. The last I heard, the government was on a yellow alert," Dr. Tweedle said.

Mr. Barber shook his head. "Keep the school open. The W.A.S.P. attacks have been distant. There is no need to deprive our children of their education. Another attack might not happen in the near future. I'll keep you updated if the status changes."

"Thank you, Arnold," Dr. Tweedle replied solemnly.

Mr. Barber nodded and then left Dr. Tweedle's office. Mr. Withermyer glared at his back as he disappeared out the door. Once the office door clicked shut, Mr. Withermyer turned to Dr. Tweedle.

"The nerve of that man! Suggesting we give Jane over to the W.A.S.P. How dare he suggest such a thing and then comment on Jane's parentage," Mr. Withermyer raged.

"Yes, what he said was certainly uncalled for. I dare say the Barber family is known for being uncouth. I apologize for his words, Jane," Dr. Tweedle said, looking at me. "I don't know why Mr. Barber would even consider it. As I said earlier, the W.A.S.P. has always hunted pixies. Handing you over to them isn't going to accomplish anything."

"So, Mr. Barber believes the W.A.S.P. tortured a pixie to gain access to Celestial Heights?" I asked, my voice sounding very small.

"It seems so. I know what you're thinking, and it's not your fault. Whether the W.A.S.P. was looking for you or not, they would still do despicable things to pixies. So don't you dare blame your-self!" Dr. Tweedle said.

"I can't help but blame myself. The W.A.S.P. is looking for me and torturing others in the process," I said.

"Yes, and that's exactly why I don't think you should return to your stepfamily. You're unsafe, surrounded by humans, and so far from anyone who could help you," Dr. Tweedle began.

"I can't just leave the manor. I have nowhere else to go and refuse to accept anyone's charity, even yours. You've already done so much for me, Dr. Tweedle, and I'm already in your debt. Please don't injure my pride any further," I said, rising from the loveseat.

Mr. Withermyer let out a soft chuckle as he leaned on the arm of the couch. "Does she remind you of anyone, Oliver?"

"You said yourself that the W.A.S.P. hasn't gained new information about my identity. I haven't had a threat from the W.A.S.P. since Mr. Wicker," I said.

Dr. Tweedle took a deep breath before he finally replied. "Okay, Miss Fitzgerald." His blue eyes stared at me over the top of his glasses. "I will continue to return you to your family home, but if the W.A.S.P. gains any more information or other attacks happen, promise me you will agree to stay here indefinitely."

I paused before I answered. It would be nice to escape Maire and her family, but I couldn't become a burden to Dr. Tweedle. I had no money and no way to earn any. I couldn't properly pay for my room and board. It would be deplorable if I mooched off Dr. Tweedle's generosity.

Also, I couldn't fathom leaving my father's property. If you didn't count the Jelf Academy, I had never lived elsewhere. Even though my life at the manor was terrible, I was afraid to leave it. If I no longer stayed there, would I forget my father? Would my childhood memories fade away?

"If I'm put in immediate danger because of the W.A.S.P., I will agree to accept your offer on one condition. You must allow me to pay my way with something," I said determinedly.

"Jane, don't be ridiculous," Dr. Tweedle began, but he stopped talking when I started to shake my head.

"You'll have to allow me to clean or do some tasks, or else I won't be able to stay here if it comes down to our conditions."

Dr. Tweedle looked at the ground, and then he nodded. "Okay, we'll negotiate how you'll earn your stay when the time comes. So, we are in agreement that if any danger arises, you will forgo your human home and live in the pixie world where you truly belong."

I bobbed my head affirmatively. Then, I reached out my right hand towards Dr. Tweedle. Understanding my intentions, he raised his hand to meet mine. He gripped my hand tightly, looking into my eyes, and we shook in agreement.

19

MORNING SICKNESS

THE ATTIC WAS chilly, and I pulled my shawl around me as I rose from the bed. November had arrived with a frosty gust, eliminating all the leaves on the trees. I dressed quickly into one of my long-sleeved serving gowns and tried to ignore the bitter cold and my stiff hands. I stuffed my hands into my dress pockets and headed down the staircase to begin my day.

The last few weeks at the manor had been brutal. Emily awoke with morning sickness almost every day, and more often than not, she never made it to her bathroom in time. I constantly cleaned up vomit and scrubbed the stains from clothing, sheets, and rugs. A minor odor would upset her stomach, and she would run from the room, retching. The bouts of sickness did nothing to improve her mood, of course. She was like a ticking time bomb, and I never knew what would set her off next.

It didn't help that Mrs. Doyle visited more often now that Drake and Emily had announced the baby. She constantly referred to the pregnancy and suggested what Emily should do. Mrs. Doyle tried to dictate what Emily should eat, how much exercise she should get, and how often they would visit the doctor. Emily accepted some of Mrs. Doyle's suggestions, which made Marie furious. Since the announcement of Emily's baby, the house had been full of tension.

I steeled myself for the day as I entered the kitchen. Ellen was working on the breakfast preparations. Since Mrs. Doyle demanded a strict diet for Emily, Ellen had to prepare something special for her. The green herbal tonic for morning sickness was already on the tray. The bacon and eggs were for the other family members, and Ellen poured hot oatmeal into a bowl for Emily. Once everything was ready, I grabbed the tray and made my rounds.

I left Emily's room as the last one in my cleaning routine, in case I had a huge mess to clean up, and quickly distributed the meals to everyone else. When I arrived at Emily's room, I closed my eyes and prayed it wouldn't be awful. I clutched at the tray and knocked on the door. I heard muffled moaning from within, so I gradually pushed the door open.

"Mrs. Doyle, I have brought your breakfast," I called, placing the tray in the sitting area. I could tell the bed was empty, and the moaning was coming from the bathroom.

I tapped on the bathroom door before opening it. Emily was on her knees near the toilet. She had almost made it this time, but there was a trail of sickness leading up to her. Her black hair hung in lanky strands around her face, and her cheeks were bright pink. Her gray eyes narrowed when she saw me.

"What are you looking at?" she snapped. "Get over here and hold back my hair."

"Come on. Let's get you cleaned up," I said, crossing the room.

I helped Emily to her feet and then removed her dirty night-gown. I began filling a bath with warm water as Emily shivered on the bathroom tile. She looked weak and pathetic, and I handed her a towel to wrap around her naked body while she waited for the bathtub to fill. Next, I gathered a few rags from the closet and mopped up Emily's sickness. A few times, I thought I would be sick myself, but I managed to thoroughly clean up the floor.

When the tub was full, I assisted Emily as she stepped into the water. She latched onto my arm so she could keep her balance. Her nails dug into my arm as she lowered herself into the water. When she released me, I could see tiny crescent moon shapes on my skin. Emily leaned her head back and rested it on the edge of the tub. She let out a sigh and then turned to look at me.

"Wash my hair, Jane," she demanded.

I went around the tub and reached for the soap. I lathered my hands and began massaging Emily's scalp. I mixed the soap with her long tresses, then piled her hair atop her head to spread the soap throughout. Emily closed her eyes as I poured water over her head.

"Everything hurts all the time, and I feel so ill," Emily mumbled as I washed the soap from her hair. "I'm so tired."

"Perhaps you would like to lie down after your bath," I suggested. If Emily stayed in her room, she wouldn't be around to interfere with my daily chores.

"As much as I want to, I can't. Mrs. Doyle insists on exercise, and she'll be disappointed if I appear to have gained a pound," Emily sighed.

"Surely she'll understand the baby is growing," I allowed myself to say.

"Mrs. Catherine Doyle brags about how she didn't start showing with Drake until her fifth or sixth month. She expects me to do the same. Indulgences are not good for the baby. Plus, it won't do for Drake to constantly order new gowns for me. I don't know why I'm telling you any of this. It's not like you understand any of it anyway," Emily said, slowly leaning forward so I could reach her back.

I gently ran the washcloth over her skin and left her to soak while I ran the dirty laundry downstairs. Once I placed it in the bin to be washed, I headed back toward the stairs. Marie was on her way down and paused when she saw me.

"I'm finished with my breakfast dishes, and I'm sure Preston and Drake are as well. What is taking you so long?" Marie snapped.

"Emily was ill again this morning, ma'am," I stated. "I was aiding with her bath."

"Make sure Emily eats something. I swear the diet that old hag has her on is making her sick. Speaking of Drake's mother, she'll be arriving this afternoon for tea. I want everything dusted, cleaned, and organized before her arrival at one o'clock. Drake and Preston are out hunting today and won't return until evening. I don't want any complaints from that evil woman, so you better get to work," Marie insisted.

"Yes, ma'am," I said, keeping my head down. I returned to Emily's room and helped her out of the bathtub. It took her a few moments to get her legs over the rim of the tub, and she gripped my arm again.

As she toweled herself dry, I went into her closet and picked out several lovely dresses for her to wear to tea. When she came out of the bathroom, her eyes scanned my selections.

"Why have you pulled these out? One of my casual gowns will suffice," Emily snapped.

"I thought you'd want to look nice for tea with the older Mrs. Doyle," I said quietly.

"She's coming here today?" Emily shrieked.

"Yes, ma'am. Your mother has just informed me," I replied.

Emily began pacing the room. "I can't believe she's coming today. I thought her visit was scheduled for tomorrow. Hurry and dress me in the dark blue gown," she cried, pointing to the dresses.

I rapidly grabbed the dress and held it open for her. She kept a scowl on her face the entire time I did up the dress and worked on her hair. I was glad she didn't lash out at me, and I managed to make Emily presentable while she sat in solemn silence. When I was finished, I left Emily to pick at her oatmeal while I collected the breakfast trays from the other bedrooms. Quickly, I rushed the dirty dishes down to the kitchen and washed them. After everything was put away, I braced myself and returned to Emily's room.

Emily had barely eaten her breakfast, and she thrust the tray at me as soon as I entered.

"Get this disgusting sludge away from me, or I swear I'll be sick again," Emily snipped, walking by me and out her bedroom door.

"Of course, ma'am," I responded.

I waited until she had gone down all the stairs before I followed her. If she truly was going to be sick, I didn't need to clean it up on top of all the preparation I had to do before Mrs. Doyle arrived. I disposed of Emily's leftover breakfast and then cleaned the remaining dishes. As I finished in the kitchen, I made a mental checklist of everything I needed to accomplish.

✧

By the time one o'clock arrived, I was exhausted. I came down the main staircase and was on the way to the kitchen to start the tea when a knock sounded at the front door. I rapidly straightened my skirt and grabbed the door handle. I pulled the door open to reveal Drake's mother, as expected. A fur coat clung to her tiny frame, and she clutched a small handbag. A velvet hat covered her gray curls. Her dark eyes glanced at me as she stepped through the door.

"Oh, good. It's you. The only one with any manners around here," Mrs. Doyle said, shrugging off her coat. "Take this and hang it in the closet."

I took her coat, which was actually quite heavy, and hung it up in the front entrance closet. While I did so, she carefully removed her hat and handed it to me.

"Allow me to show you into the sitting room," I said once her belongings were neatly stowed in the closet.

Mrs. Doyle followed me as I led the way into the sitting room.

Just as I suspected, Marie and Emily were already waiting. Emily sat on the sofa, and Marie was in one of the straight-backed chairs. Mrs. Doyle claimed the other straight-backed chair closer to the fireplace. After they had greeted each other, Marie turned to me.

"Go fetch us the tea and sandwiches, Jane," she demanded.

"Yes, ma'am," I said before dipping into a curtsy.

When I entered the kitchen, I was relieved Ellen had already put the teapot on the burner. She was just finishing the tea sandwiches and stacked them neatly on a silver tray. I reached into the cupboard and pulled down three teacups and saucers decorated with tiny roses. I added those to the tray along with the sugar, milk, and lemon wedges. Then, I retrieved three teaspoons while I waited for the tea to whistle.

I didn't have long to wait for the pot to reach boiling, and I placed the kettle alongside everything else I had prepared. Then, using magic, I balanced the tray and carried it out to the sitting room. The three ladies looked at me expectantly as I placed the tea tray on the coffee table.

"Mrs. Doyle," I began, addressing Drake's mother. "How do you take your tea?"

"Two lumps of sugar and just a dollop of milk," Mrs. Doyle responded.

I poured out her tea and prepared it as she requested. I handed her the cup and then went about preparing Marie and Emily's tea. Once everyone received their cups, I went around with the tray of sandwiches so each of the ladies could take one. Then, I took up my usual place in the corner if they needed anything.

The ladies spoke about the weather and current events until the topic of conversation finally turned to Emily's pregnancy. Mrs. Doyle inquired about the next doctor's appointment and Emily's exercise routine.

"You must remain active for the baby's sake. Some exercise to keep the excess fat off never hurt anyone. You'll want to maintain your figure. As I've told you before, no one could tell I was pregnant until my sixth month. Drake was such an easy baby. How are your bouts of sickness?" Mrs. Doyle inquired.

"It comes and goes, but I believe Emily has been feeling much better, right?" Marie snapped.

"Yes, I've been better," Emily said, taking a large breath.

"That's good. I assume it's because you're eating the food I have instructed. I'm glad you're listening to my suggestions. I want my grandson to be a healthy boy," Mrs. Doyle chirped.

"Why are you so certain Emily will have a boy? She could easily be carrying a girl," Marie said haughtily.

"Call it a woman's intuition. Not all women have it, obviously, but I can feel it in my bones that Emily is carrying a Drake junior," Mrs. Doyle insisted.

"Speaking of names, my mother and I did prepare a list to share with you," Emily said.

"Yes. Jane, run along and fetch the list of names. The paper is in my office. It should be right on top of the desk," Marie commented with a wave of her hand, shooing me.

I left the sitting room and crossed the entrance hall. My father's office was down the corridor. I would never consider the room as Marie's. I walked down the dimly lit hallway and went to the first door on the left. Thankfully, the curtains had been drawn open, and light spilled into the room and across the desk.

With hurried steps, I crossed the room to my father's large oak desk. Papers were strewn all over the top, but luckily, as Marie had claimed, there was a parchment right on top with a list of boy and girl names. I carefully plucked the paper up and turned to go when the stack of mail beneath the list caught my eye.

A letter addressed to Mr. Drake Doyle was on top of the pile. The design of the envelope and the handwriting of the address caught my attention. Both seemed familiar, and I was certain I had seen them before. Slowly, I took another step back toward the desk. My heart was pounding, and I knew Marie was expecting me, but my hand reached out to clasp the unopened envelope. My pulse sounded in my ears at the feel of the familiar thickness of the envelope, and I reluctantly flipped it over.

My eyes took in what I had already expected. Splashed in bright red was the wax seal. Embossed in the wax was a hexagon with an ugly insect in the middle. I fought to swallow the lump that had risen in my throat. Finding a letter like this at the manor could only mean one thing. Drake Doyle was a member of the W.A.S.P.

20

GLAMOUROUS TRANSFIGURATION

THE SICK REALIZATION of what I discovered about Drake Doyle still revolved in my head on Monday morning. I still couldn't comprehend that I was living under the same roof as a member of the W.A.S.P. I felt sick, but I was confident that Drake had no clue who or what I truly was. If he knew that I was a pixie, let alone the one his organization was searching for, he probably would've murdered me or turned me over by now. I felt safe at the moment, but I had to be really careful.

Dr. Tweedle had been serious about my staying at the manor after the last W.A.S.P. attack. If he were to discover whom I was living with, he would never let me return to my father's home. Perhaps it wouldn't be so bad to never see Marie, Emily, Preston, or Drake again, but I would feel ashamed to become a burden to whoever would take me in, especially in the summer months. These facts plagued my mind and made it hard to concentrate.

Mr. Withermyer knew I was distracted during Charms, my first lesson of the day. He didn't say anything, but I noticed his worried expression. When the bell sounded at the end of class, he kept trying to catch my eye, but I ignored him and quickly shuffled out of the room with Josefina. We hurried down the hall to Transfiguration, but I knew Mr. Withermyer would question me during our private lessons this evening. I wasn't sure what to tell him, and I sighed as I entered Ms. Pregmon's classroom.

Ms. Pregmon was seated at her desk, glaring at us. We took our seats, mine at the front of the room and Josefina's toward the middle. I pulled out my materials for the class and waited for Ms. Pregmon to begin. Betty Ann Barber sauntered into the room, and I hoped Ms. Pregmon wouldn't make us work in groups today. Since I was seated next to Betty Ann, she was forced to be my partner for assignments.

When the bell rang, Ms. Pregmon rose to her feet and paced the front of the room. "Good morning. Today, we will create a type of transfiguration charm called the *color-changing charm*. We will test our efforts by changing the color of our hair. This is not a specific charm just for hair; it can be used to change the color of anything. Talented pixies can use this charm to change eye and hair color simultaneously, but I'm only asking for one today. Please note this charm can only change colors. It cannot change features. You must mix a *color-changing charm* with a *transfiguration charm* to completely change your appearance. Don't worry; we will get to that later in the year if you all prove to have the abilities to accomplish it," Ms. Pregmon said with a smirk.

She turned to face the chalkboard, and the ingredients magically appeared in writing. There were four components, so I knew the charm was going to be complex. I flipped through my textbook to the correct page and glanced over the long list of steps while Ms. Pregmon continued talking.

"The effects of the charm last as long as the pixie can concentrate. Most pixies can hold a glamor for five to eight hours. Ten to twelve hours isn't unheard of, but any longer than that is extremely rare. Usually, a pixie will just recast the charm if they want to maintain it. This is also common when you mix the color changing with the transfiguration charm. Today, you won't be graded on how long you can hold the glamor. I just need to see the color change so you can receive credit. You may begin."

I started by collecting the ingredients and then measured them. I needed four cups of fluorite, one cup of amber, a half cup of limonite, and a fourth cup of orpiment. I crushed all the ingredients to fine dust and slowly began reading the next set of instructions. I had to measure so much of each component and add them together at a specific time. I was so paranoid I would miss a step or mix the wrong things that I read each step three times before completing it.

Ms. Pregmon was harsh when grading students, and she never gave me perfect marks, even when my charms were completed correctly. I wanted to excel so I could receive some credit. For some reason, Ms. Pregmon always found excuses to give me a lower score than other students. Since I discovered that Betty Ann was Ms. Pregmon's cousin, I noticed that Betty Ann received higher scores on her assignments than she probably deserved.

Every so often, I kept an eye on the clock to ensure I didn't run out of time. About halfway through the class period, Ms. Pregmon began handing out hand-held mirrors. I took that as a sign that she wanted us to finish the charm soon. I read the third line from the bottom and mixed two cups of fluorite with the mixture of amber and orpiment. I concentrated very hard on the charm's last two steps, making sure I was adding the ingredients at the correct time.

When the *color-changing charm* was completed, I bottled it and began putting my mixing bowls away. I was among the first to finish the charm, and Ms. Pregmon approached my desk with the little smirk she always wore.

"Well, Miss Fitzgerald, you were the first to complete this complicated *color-changing charm*. Perhaps you can go first with casting it. I want you to change your blonde hair to black," Ms. Pregmon requested with a chuckle.

Slowly, I shook out some of the pixie dust into my palm. Then, I picked up the mirror and gazed at my reflection. Before casting the *color-changing charm*, I focused on what Ms. Pregmon asked me to do. With a tiny sigh, I tossed the dust over myself and imagined what I would look like with black hair. Holding that image in my mind, I gazed into the mirror. At first, I didn't notice any difference, but gradually, my hair began to change. It started at the roots and grew darker and darker until the color cascaded down the entire length of each strand. Soon, my hair was as black as Emily's. The dark hair made my face look paler, and my violet eyes looked bigger. I stared in disbelief at my transformation.

Other students began to gasp as they took in my now-dark hair. Ms. Pregmon glared at me with an open mouth for a moment. I continued to concentrate on my new glamor and could understand what Ms. Pregmon meant about holding onto it. I knew if I stopped thinking about the change in a part of my brain, my hair would revert to blonde. However, I was sure if I practiced, I'd be able to hold a glamor for a while, and it would become second nature.

"Very well, Miss Fitzgerald. I suppose you'll receive full credit for today's assignment." Ms. Pregmon said begrudgingly.

Ms. Pregmon looked so disappointed about giving me full credit that I almost wanted to laugh. She couldn't come up with a reason to take points off. When the bell rang to end Transfiguration, I couldn't help feeling like I had won a small victory.

I managed to hold onto my glamour until classes were over for the day, a total of six hours. I had wanted to see how long I could go before I felt the illusion slipping away. Over dinner, my friends praised me for conquering the *color-changing charm* and silencing Ms. Pregmon.

"I'm glad you were able to maintain it for so long," Kairi exclaimed. "You should've seen her face during lunch when you still had dark hair."

Other students had been successful during the class period, but it seemed I'd been the only one to keep the charm for hours.

"In our next lesson, she'll probably find a way to deduct points. As satisfying as it was, I'm sure Ms. Pregmon will find a way to punish me for upstaging her expectations," I replied.

"She's delighted when students don't accomplish the assignments she gives out," Taylor said quietly as she cut another piece of turkey.

"Ms. Pregmon is always on a power trip. Every day, she wants to prove she's smarter than the students," Josefina sighed in annoyance.

"She should be smarter than the students," Miguel added. "She's a teacher, after all, but I agree. It's almost like she lords it over us."

"I've never had a problem with her, though I agree that she seems overconfident at times," Zachary said.

"Of course, she isn't nasty with you!" his sister commented. "I've noticed that she talks down to girls more often. It's almost as if she sees females as a threat. Since you're a boy and a handsome one, Zachary, Ms. Pregmon isn't going to be unpleasant with you."

"Kairi does have a point. Ms. Pregmon will be snippy with Josefina and won't react the same with my work," Miguel noted.

"There's only one female who receives her praises. As we all know, Betty Ann is her cousin," I stated before finishing the rest of my mashed potatoes.

"It isn't fair that Ms. Pregmon is teaching her family member. She's biased," Josefina said with aggravation.

"Nothing will be done about it. I'm sure Dr. Tweedle knew who Ms. Pregmon was related to when he hired her," Miguel said solemnly.

"All we can do is work hard and complete the transfiguration charms correctly," I said.

After dinner, my friends went to the library to work on transfiguration. I climbed the stairs to the second floor to meet Mr. Withermyer in his office. We were working on advanced charms, and I wasn't sure if we'd use the exercise room today.

"Come in, Miss Fitzgerald," Mr. Withermyer called after I had knocked on the door.

I entered the office and took a seat across from him. Mr. Withermyer put aside the papers he'd been grading and looked up at me.

"I'm glad to see your natural hair color has returned. I'll admit I wasn't fond of your black hair," Mr. Withermyer said with a chuckle.

"I can't say I was either, but I was making a point," I replied, shifting on the seat.

Mr. Withermyer laughed a little louder. "What point were you making?"

I could feel myself blushing, and my lips curved into a slight smile. I had never discussed one teacher with another.

"Perhaps I shouldn't say," I replied, looking down at my hands.

"Jane, you can tell me anything, but I think I already know what you mean. From the comments I've overheard, Blair Pregmon isn't the easiest of teachers," Mr. Withermyer responded.

I allowed myself to grin. "Yes, I suppose that's the truth. She doesn't believe students can complete anything correctly, so I kept up the *color-changing charm* as long as possible."

"How long were you able to maintain it?" he asked.

"For about six hours," I replied.

"That's marvelous, Jane! Usually, the first time a pixie attempts to change their appearance, they can only maintain the glamour for an hour or two."

"Ms. Pregmon didn't tell us that. Instead, she claimed most pixies could maintain the charm for five to eight hours," I said.

"Yes, that's true for pixies who have practiced transfiguration multiple times," Mr. Withermyer replied.

"No wonder why we always feel like failures. Ms. Pregmon purposely doesn't tell us the right information about charms, so we feel inadequate when we don't live up to her expectations," I sighed.

"Jane, from what I've seen, you always appear to surpass everyone's expectations," Mr. Withermyer said.

I knew I was blushing again. I examined my fingernails before looking up at Mr. Withermyer again. "I'm not that special," I answered with a shrug.

"You're a very experienced pixie, and that's something to be proud of," Mr. Withermyer stated. "Which is why I didn't understand why you seemed so distant in Charms this morning."

My eyes slowly slid to his, and I swallowed. My success in Ms. Pregmon's class allowed me to forget what had been bothering me. I didn't even know what to say.

"It was nothing. I was just tired," I finally responded.

Mr. Withermyer squinted his green eyes at me. "Jane, I've been in your company long enough to know when you're tired and when you're distressed. I don't believe you were tired this morning," he said pointedly.

"Phillip, I don't want to talk about it. I already know what your reaction will be," I said.

"Have you done something wrong?" he asked, concerned.

"No, I haven't done anything," I sighed.

"You were obviously upset about something. Whatever it is, I would like to help fix it."

"There's nothing you can fix," I said.

Mr. Withermyer sighed profoundly and rested his chin on his hands. "I understand you don't want to discuss whatever is going on. I was only asking because I'm worried."

Slowly, he leaned across his desk and grabbed his copy of the volume four charms book. I breathed deeply, but my anxiety had returned. Drake was a member of the W.A.S.P., and I hadn't told anyone. What if something were to happen to me? No one in the pixie world would know what had befallen me if I was discovered. Maybe telling Mr. Withermyer would help ease some of my anxiety.

"If I tell you," I began with a deep sigh. "Will you promise not to fly off the handle?"

Mr. Withermyer put the book down and stared at me. "Well, that depends. I don't know what you're going to tell me. I don't know if I'll be able to keep that promise."

"If you cannot remain calm, then I don't know if I can tell you," I said.

"Jane, it must be awful for you to be acting like this," he replied.

"It is awful, but I want your word that you'll keep composed when I tell you. If you can't, I fear I will break down," I said quietly.

Mr. Withermyer hesitated before he finally nodded. "I promise to do my best."

Tentatively, I looked into his eyes and took a deep breath before I spoke. "Emily's husband, Drake Doyle, is a member of the W.A.S.P."

It was as if time stood still for a moment. I could see the fear in Mr. Withermyer's eyes, and he opened his mouth to speak but quickly closed it. He closed his eyes and put his pointer fingers to his temples. It took him a long time before he finally responded.

"How do you know this?" Mr. Withermyer asked with a cough.

"I found a letter addressed to him with the W.A.S.P. insignia embossed on the wax seal," I replied.

"Do you know for certain?" he asked.

"The letter was addressed to him. It was the same scenario as Robert's father receiving a letter," I said.

Mr. Withermyer nodded gravely. "Was this the first time you discovered a letter from the W.A.S.P. at the manor?"

"Yes, but I normally don't go through the papers in the office. It's possible that Drake has been a member of the W.A.S.P. the entire time I've known him," I replied. "Mr. Wicker, the man who attacked me, was invited to his wedding after all."

"Were you able to read the contents of the letter?"

"No, the wax seal was unbroken. He hadn't read it yet, and I was too terrified to try," I confessed.

"Do you suspect Mr. Doyle knows who you are or suspects you're a pixie?" Mr. Withermyer asked.

"No, I don't believe so. If he knew, he would've harmed me already. I have always been cautious at the manor. After the attack from Mr. Wicker, I have been cautious."

Mr. Withermyer leaned back in his chair and pondered for a moment. I had no idea what he was thinking or what he was going to say next. I was sure he was worried, and I didn't know what he would do now that I had told him. After a few long moments, he finally stood from his desk and stared at me.

"This is an alarming but interesting turn of events. I believe we need to see Dr. Tweedle."

21

A New Proposition

"No, Phillip, please don't tell Dr. Tweedle. It will shame me if I'm taken from the manor and become someone's burden. He made it very clear after the attack on Celestial Heights," I begged. "This is why I didn't want to tell you."

"Jane, calm down. Don't get worked up. I understand you don't want to be a burden, and I might have an idea that could help your situation," Mr. Withermyer said, coming around his desk.

"What do you mean?" I asked.

Mr. Withermyer crouched in front of my chair and held my gaze. "Do you remember when Mr. Barber visited Dr. Tweedle after the attack on Celestial Heights? They discussed what they could do to discover information about the W.A.S.P. The W.A.S.P. has grown stronger over the past decades, and our government is nervous. They're gaining more information about pixies, and their tactics for destroying us have been more effective. If there was a way to discover how they're doing it, we would be able to save pixie lives. With you living in secret among the humans, especially a member of the W.A.S.P., you could be our answer, Jane."

"How could I be useful?" I questioned.

"You would have access to letters between members. You could spy on Mr. Doyle and gain as much information as possible about their organization. This could help our government know where the W.A.S.P. plan to strike next and how much they truly know about pixies."

"So, you're saying I could spy on Emily's husband and report on his plans and who the other members of the W.A.S.P. are?" I asked.

"Exactly! Consider how many pixies' lives we could save if we discover the W.A.S.P.'s plans," Mr. Withermyer said.

"Do you really think I could do this?" I stuttered.

Mr. Withermyer gave me a serious look. "Jane, what I'm proposing is dangerous, and I understand your hesitations, but I believe that you have the talent, the skills, and the matter of circumstance to gain the advantage we've been looking for. I would continue to work with you during our lessons and ensure you would be prepared if anything were to happen," Mr. Withermyer insisted.

I stared off into space, pondering what Mr. Withermyer was proposing. Perhaps discovering that Drake was a member could work to our advantage. If I was able to read Drake's correspondence, I could notify the Pixie government in enough time to stop future attacks. The pixies could finally be one step ahead of the W.A.S.P.

"I believe in you, Jane, and I know you would be able to be our spy," Mr. Withermyer said, breaking through my thoughts.

I cleared my throat and glanced back into Mr. Withermyer's eyes. "Okay," I said slowly. "I could try, but something tells me Dr. Tweedle isn't going to agree with this."

"Well, you'll have to help me to convince him," Mr. Withermyer said with a wink as he took my hand and pulled me up from the chair.

✍

"No, no, absolutely not!" Dr. Tweedle hollered a few minutes later when we had gone to his office and explained our proposal. "You are not putting one of my students in danger, especially Jane, who is already being hunted by those damn people!"

I'd never seen Dr. Tweedle so angry before. He paced in front of his desk, his face bright red, and his hands clenched into fists. The desk began to shake, and the papers fluttered like a breeze blew them. While at the Jelf Academy, I'd never seen a teacher's emotions show so much that their magic unleashed and affected the objects around them.

"Dr. Tweedle," I began softly. "This could be a good opportunity for me to discover the W.A.S.P.'s plans. I could save pixies."

"It is too dangerous! My answer is no! I will not allow it!" Dr. Tweedle huffed.

"Oliver, if you would just listen," Mr. Withermyer stated, but Dr. Tweedle turned on him.

"You're supposed to teach the girl how to defend herself if the W.A.S.P. comes looking for her. You are not supposed to be filling her head with silly ideas and throwing her into a W.A.S.P. nest, for the gods' sake!"

"Mr. Withermyer is not throwing me into a W.A.S.P. nest," I proclaimed.

"No, apparently, you already live in one. That ends today! You agreed that you would leave the manor if anything else happened with the W.A.S.P. Living with one of them definitely constitutes a good enough reason," Dr. Tweedle raged.

"Dr. Tweedle, please. If I could spy on Mr. Doyle, I could report on their agenda. What happened in Celestial Heights doesn't need to happen again. You and Mr. Barber were hoping for a way to infiltrate the W.A.S.P., and I could be that answer," I said.

"Jane, you're far too young, and it's far too dangerous! What don't you understand about the word no?" Dr. Tweedle spat out. His face was so red that I was afraid he was going to combust.

"I am not a child anymore! I've almost reached my twentieth birthday. Didn't my mother work for Waldrick the Great, protecting pixies when she was my age?" I stated. "How am I any different?"

Dr. Tweedle stared at me with his mouth agape. "That's beside the point!" Dr. Tweedle said after a moment. "Yes, your mother worked for Waldrick, and it was dangerous. I'm just trying to protect you. I don't want the same thing that happened to your mother to happen to you!"

"Oliver, if I didn't think Jane was qualified or had enough experience, I wouldn't have suggested this to her. I've been working with Jane for a year, and I'm well aware of her strengths and weaknesses. I do believe she's capable. Jane is brilliant, and she has excelled in everything I've taught her so far. She's great at thinking on her feet, which is a good attribute for what I'm suggesting. I believe you should summon Mr. Barber here and get his opinion. I'm sure he would agree and award Jane with an internship. She could make money by spying on the W.A.S.P. If she ever needed to leave the manor, she'd at least have some money. Then she wouldn't feel so much like a burden," Mr. Withermyer stated.

My ears perked up at his words. He hadn't told me I could be paid to spy on Mr. Doyle. If I could be paid, as Mr. Withermyer stated, I wouldn't feel so inadequate. I looked to Dr. Tweedle, awaiting his answer.

"I know an internship would be a wonderful opportunity for Jane, but I'm still not sure it's the right situation…." Dr. Tweedle stated, but Mr. Withermyer held up his hand.

"It pains me, Oliver, that you no longer trust my opinion. I care about Jane just as much as you do, and I would never put her in any situation I didn't think she was prepared for. This Mr. Doyle obviously has no idea Jane is a pixie or Rachel McCalski's daughter. She's been living under his nose for quite some time, and it would be a shame if we ignored this opportunity. The gods have handed us an ideal opportunity, and we'd be foolish not to take it. Please have as much faith in Jane as I do," Mr. Withermyer responded.

Dr. Tweedle sighed deeply and stared at Mr. Withermyer. He had gone from looking incredibly angry to extremely tired, and he circled the desk, throwing himself down heavily on his chair.

"Jane, do you believe you could do what Mr. Withermyer suggests?" he asked, looking defeated.

"Yes, sir," I said more confidently than I felt. "Every weekend, I clean the manor and have access to every room. So, I don't think it would be difficult to snoop through some mail or listen in to Mr. Doyle's conversations."

"You do realize the risk you would be putting yourself in?" Dr. Tweedle asked, removing his glasses and rubbing his eyes.

"Yes, sir, but technically, I have already lived in danger unknowingly. Mr. Doyle has lived at the manor for over a year. At least now, I won't be blindsided."

Dr. Tweedle leaned forward and grabbed a blank piece of paper from a stack on his desk. He jotted down a note and proceeded to fold the paper into the shape of a bird. When finished, he rifled through his pixie dust case and pulled out a charm vial. The paper bird disappeared as soon as he tossed the pixie dust over it.

"Have a seat, Phillip…, Jane. I'm sure we'll be waiting for a few minutes," Dr. Tweedle sighed.

Mr. Withermyer and I sank down onto the blue sofa. I wasn't sure to whom Dr. Tweedle had sent the message, but I assumed we were awaiting a response. Dr. Tweedle looked exhausted, and I never fully noticed how old he was until this moment. I hadn't meant to upset him, but if I could help the pixie world, I had to try. I glanced over at Mr. Withermyer, and he gave me a reassuring smile.

After a few moments, there was a sudden knock at Dr. Tweedle's office door.

"Come in," Dr. Tweedle called out, and the door creaked open.

Mr. Barber strode into the room wearing a top hat and an overcoat. He reached up to remove the top hat as he came to stand before Dr. Tweedle's desk.

"You summoned me here with an idea of how we can penetrate the W.A.S.P.'s network. What is it that you propose?" Mr. Barber asked.

"It has just come to my attention that Miss Fitzgerald might have a way to gain information about the W.A.S.P. I'm not sure if you're aware, but on the weekends, Miss Fitzgerald lives in the company of humans. She has just discovered her stepsister is married to a member of the W.A.S.P. Against my better judgment, Miss Fitzgerald believes she can gather important information that could save pixies from future W.A.S.P. attacks," Dr. Tweedle explained.

Mr. Barber turned from Dr. Tweedle to look at me. "What makes you so sure you'll be able to accomplish this?" he demanded.

I rose from the sofa and glared at him. "I discovered a letter with the W.A.S.P. seal at the manor. Now that I know my stepsister's husband is a member of the W.A.S.P., I could uncover the contents of other letters. In addition, I have access to every room of the house, so I could look through Mr. Doyle's other belongings. Then, I could report my findings," I responded.

Mr. Barber looked at me, and then he started to chuckle. "Do you honestly expect me to trust someone as old as my daughter with a task of this nature?"

I crossed my arms over my chest. "I'm the best hope you have of receiving any information about the W.A.S.P. In my situation, no one will suspect me. My stepsister's husband doesn't have a clue that I'm a pixie. It would be easy to gain access to any correspondence. You wanted a way to penetrate the W.A.S.P. organization, and I might be your only way," I replied.

Mr. Barber stared at me, curling his lip up in a menacing way. "How can I be sure that you'll be helping the pixie world? You are half-human, after all," Mr. Barber said snidely.

As soon as the words left Mr. Barber's mouth, Mr. Withermyer was out of his seat. His fist collided with Mr. Barber's face, sending Mr. Barber spiraling backward. Before Mr. Withermyer could land another blow, Dr. Tweedle rose from his seat and used his magic to separate the two men.

"That is enough!" Dr. Tweedle shouted.

He must've kept a firm barrier around each man because Mr. Withermyer was struggling to move. Mr. Withermyer's green eyes blazed wildly as he glared at Mr. Barber. Mr. Barber's nose leaked blood onto his graying mustache, and he wiped it with his hand.

"I will not tolerate insults or physical violence in my office or my academy," Dr. Tweedle continued. "Miss Fitzgerald would never ally herself with the W.A.S.P., Arnold. Your insinuations are insane. The W.A.S.P. has murdered people Jane loves. Any information she procured would be to help the pixie world."

"Then, if Miss Fitzgerald can manage to spy on the W.A.S.P., the job is hers. It does seem fitting that she contributes since the W.A.S.P. are slaughtering our kind in an attempt to find her," Mr. Barber spat.

Dr. Tweedle glanced at Mr. Withermyer, who was still struggling against the force holding him back. Then, he took a deep breath before speaking. "If you agree that Jane shall spy and gather information on the W.A.S.P., then an internship with the Department of Defense should be awarded along with a salary. Jane will be putting herself in great danger. She should be compensated for her efforts."

Mr. Barber pouted at the request, but then he nodded. "I will mail you a copy of the job description, and we can agree on a sum."

"Very well, Mr. Barber. I expect to reach an understanding by the end of the week. Again, thank you for your time, and I certainly hope Miss Fitzgerald will be an asset to our cause," Dr. Tweedle replied.

Mr. Barber placed his top hat on his head and made his way to the door. Dr. Tweedle must've removed the magic holding him in place. Once he left the office, Dr. Tweedle also released Mr. Withermyer.

"Your behavior was a disgrace, Phillip. What Mr. Barber said was insulting, but attacking the man was no way to behave. I hope this was all worth it, putting Jane in danger."

"I believe it was," I said, speaking up to defend Phillip as he had defended me. "By doing this job, I'll be able to support myself, and the information I collect could save our lives. Mr. Withermyer's idea is brilliant. They'll never suspect what I'll be up to."

"Your judgement about this matter better be flawless, Phillip, or I fear this decision is something we might both come to regret," Dr. Tweedle said with a worried expression.

I hoped Phillip was right to have such faith in me.

22

APPREHENSIVE ESPIONAGE

Y HEART POUNDED as I entered my father's office. The red curtains were pulled tight, and the room was dimly lit by the brass sconces on the wall. I crept toward the large oak desk, focusing on the stack of papers directly in the center. When the mail arrived today, I wondered if there had been any letters for Drake, and now was the perfect opportunity to investigate. The family had just retired to their rooms for the evening, and Marie had given me a long list of chores.

I came around the desk and began shuffling through the stack of papers. On top of the pile were some accounts Marie had of the manor's expenses and revenues. I barely glanced at them, placing them to the side and continuing to look for envelopes or letters. My hands shook slightly, so I took a deep breath and held it until my lungs felt like they would burst. Slowly, I let the air out between my lips in a quiet sigh. I had to calm down and focus on what I was looking for.

I searched through the stack without any luck. There hadn't been one letter among what I'd searched through. However, I was certain the mail had been delivered today. Slowly, I opened the top compartment of the desk. It made a slight creaking noise, causing my pulse to jump. I paused to listen for any sounds from upstairs in case the family heard the noise. I stood frozen for several moments, my heart thundering, but I didn't hear anything. I breathed again as I began searching through the top compartment.

There wasn't anything of interest in the drawer. Mostly, there were pens, ink bottles, sealing wax, and wax seal stamps, one of which had the W.A.S.P. emblem embossed on the bottom. Carefully, I closed the drawer so it wouldn't make another loud noise and opened the next drawer. This drawer was larger and filled with file folders. Each section was marked with a year, and from my first glance at the documents, they appeared to be more accounts of the manor. It would be interesting to see what Marie was doing with my father's money, but not tonight. The drawer slid closed easily, and I reached down toward the next one.

I pulled on the drawer handle, but it wouldn't budge. Bending down, I examined the drawer and discovered a keyhole. Feeling frustrated, I dug into the pocket of my dress for my pixie dust case. I knew it was dangerous to use a charm, but I had to access whatever was locked in the drawer.

I enlarged my case and began searching for an unlocking charm. The room was dark, so I had to hold up each vial to read the label. Finally, I found the *unlocking charm*. I sprinkled a pinch of the dust onto my palm and blew it into the tiny keyhole. With satisfaction, I heard the lock click and tested the drawer to see if it would open. As soon as my pixie dust case was hidden in my pocket, I turned my attention back to the unlocked drawer.

The house was silent around me, but I waited for another few breaths before crouching back down to the drawer's level. The drawer slid open smoothly without a sound, and I peered at the documents inside. Heavy parchment caught my eye, and I reached down to pull out the first of many pages. My heart sped up again when I recognized the W.A.S.P. insignia at the bottom of the page.

The letter was addressed to Mr. Doyle, dated June two years ago. I positioned the paper toward the light and paused to read the print.

Dear Mr. Doyle,

On behalf of the World Association for the Slaying of Pixies, I am conveying our deepest condolences on the loss of our fellow member, Mr. Alastor Wicker. It brings us great sadness to hear about the passing of one of our Majors. It must have been disheartening to have him pass away on what was supposed to be such a happy day, your wedding day. We are also sorry to hear about the loss of your family home. The fire must have been devastating. Please know the W.A.S.P. stands beside you in your time of crisis.

In lieu of Mr. Wicker's passing, we are currently in need of a new Major for the Northeast American region. Since your father is no longer with us, you are the perfect candidate for the position. It is with our hope that you will accept. You are a very bright and promising young man, and we are sure that with your dedication, you could rise to the rank of colonel or even general of the Northeast American region. We await your prompt reply.

Sincerely,

Dorrin Getla

Secretary of the World Association for the Slaying of Pixies.

I swallowed the lump in my throat as I moved on to the next piece of parchment. The next letter was a congratulatory note for accepting the position of Major. I took note of the wording, recalling that the first letter had mentioned a Secretary, a General, a Colonel, and a Major. I wondered how the W.A.S.P. was structured and how many regions they had. I was curious if these letters would be able to give me any insight or if they only mentioned the Northeast American region.

I paused to listen for any noises, and when I didn't hear anything, I continued paging through the letters. They were in order by date. I knew I didn't have time to read every letter, so I quickly pulled out the last one. It was dated a few days ago, so I assumed it had arrived today or yesterday.

Dear Major Drake Doyle,

My unit and I are continuing to follow up on the new lead you have provided pertaining to another secret pixie location. Unfortunately, our progress is not going as expected. However, we will continue to track down certain individuals who can lead us to another pixie community, especially if we are "charming" enough. I will update you again on our progress at our next monthly meeting on Wednesday, November 30.

Sincerely,

Captain Seth O'Doherty

I stared at the letter for a few moments, trying to absorb the vital information. The name Seth O'Doherty sounded so familiar to me. I knew I had heard it before. After several seconds, a face surfaced in my memories. Drake had been horseback riding with a large blonde man, and I was sure he had called him Seth. I read over the most recent letter again. Mr. O'Doherty had mentioned a monthly meeting and a potential lead to another pixie town. I wondered where the meeting was being held.

As I leaned down to replace the letter, footsteps sounded in the corridor. I almost passed out from fear. I'd been so consumed that I hadn't heard the footsteps descending the stairs. I had just enough time to close the drawer and pull a dust rag from the pocket of my dress when the doorknob to the office jiggled. The door glided open, and standing in the doorway was none other than Drake Doyle.

"Oh," he exclaimed. "I had no idea anyone was in here."

"I'm sorry, sir, I was just doing a bit of late-night cleaning," I replied, running the rag over the exposed surface.

My heart was pounding so hard I could swear he could hear it. I swallowed and tried to look as if I hadn't been up to anything.

"If you excuse me, sir, I'll be out of your way," I said, keeping my eyes down.

"There is no need for you to leave. I'm sure this room needs to be dusted like any other. Don't leave on my account," Drake said smoothly, coming around me to stand behind the desk. His shoulder brushed mine, and I knew he had done it on purpose. There was plenty of space to move around me.

"No, sir. I wouldn't want to bother…." I began when he gave me a stern look.

"You can start with this desk," he said, gesturing grandly as he took a seat in the chair.

The blood pounded in my veins, and I longed to run from the room, but I had no choice. Trying to remain as calm as possible, I ran the rag along the desk as Drake watched me. I tried not to look at him, even though I could feel his eyes on me. Carefully, I lifted all the papers off the desk and dusted the surface beneath.

"You've worked here for a long time, haven't you?" Drake asked, breaking the silence.

"Yes, sir," I replied, replacing the papers.

"Do you know anything about the family who owned the manor previously?" he questioned.

I could feel sweat breaking out all over my body.

"No, sir. I was too young," I responded.

He hadn't asked about my father by name; for all I knew, he could've been asking about the family who owned the land before my father.

"I was just curious as to how Marie acquired this manor. You don't need to look so scared, Jane. That's your name, isn't it?"

"Yes, sir," I answered, dusting one of the bookcases.

"People believe Jane is a plain name, but you are anything but," Drake commented.

My cheeks felt hot, and I ignored the urge to look at him. Instead, I picked up my pace, hoping he would allow me to leave the room once I had dusted all the surfaces. My heart pounded loudly when I heard the chair scrape across the floor. I quickly looked up to see Drake coming toward me. He stopped in front of me, using his pointer finger to lift my chin and force my eyes to meet his almost black ones.

"You have such soft features, a tiny nose, full lips, and such stunning eyes," he said, a sly grin spreading across his mouth. I tried not to shudder. Even though only one finger was beneath my chin, I found it difficult to turn my head. Drake rose above me like a feral animal, and I feared what he would do.

"Thank you, sir, but I feel it would be impolite to accept such compliments from you, as your pregnant wife is only just upstairs," I replied softly.

Drake barked out a harsh laugh. "A man of my station should be allowed to compliment the beauty of any woman he pleases, even if he is married. I'm only sharing my opinion on your gorgeous face. It's not as if I'm doing anything indecent," he purred.

However, the fact that he had me cornered alone in a room seemed indecent to me.

I took a step backward and managed to gracefully maneuver away from him. I forced a laugh and a smile as if we were only playing a harmless game. "Oh, Mr. Doyle, you jest," I replied.

"No, I would never. Not when you are one of the most beautiful women I have ever seen," he replied.

I glanced at the ground, pretending to look shy but pleased by his compliments. I had to play this situation out in the right way.

"Marie must've kept you hidden," he mused.

"No, sir," I said, forcing another laugh. "I'm only a mere servant. I'm no match for any man of high standing."

"Perhaps not for marriage, but certainly for fun," Drake whispered, edging closer. He reached out, grabbing a loose strand of my hair and twirling it between his fingers.

My stomach churned at his touch and what he was implying. I wanted to back away, but I also didn't want to make him angry. I kept my eyes on the ground as I answered. "Whatever do you mean?"

Drake laughed softly as he released my hair. "Oh, so innocent," he murmured, stepping back. "Perhaps I will explain my meaning another time. I wouldn't want to contaminate your purity so soon. I've always found that everything of value is worth the wait."

He stalked behind the desk and sat down again. I watched as he pulled a small key from the chest pocket of his dark blue vest. Then he bent down toward the drawer I'd been in earlier.

I pretended to continue my work, even though I kept an eye on him. As he turned the key in the lock, a puzzled expression flashed across his face. I knew I'd left the drawer unlocked, and I was sure he hadn't heard the lock click open. I held my breath as Drake pulled on the drawer, and it slid out. I prayed that I had replaced the letters exactly as I'd found them.

"I thought I locked this," he whispered to himself while bending over the drawer. He shook his head, pulling out a few letters from the back. My heart pounded even harder, if that was even possible. After a few moments, I realized nothing appeared to be amiss because Drake didn't look surprised. I let out a slow breath, running the rag over the other bookshelf.

Just as I calmed myself down a bit, Drake cleared his throat.

"Jane," he began.

Slowly, I turned to face him. My stomach filled with dread.

"Yes, sir," I said hesitantly.

"I've changed my mind. You may leave now. I'm finding your presence too distracting, and I have business to attend to."

Though I knew the business was W.A.S.P. related, I didn't need to be told twice. Quickly, I bowed and hurriedly left the office. I shuddered once I was down the hall now that I was free of Drake's eyes. Adrenaline coursed through my body at the thought of Drake's actions, and what I had, most likely, just narrowly avoided.

23
DISGUISES AND DISCOVERY

M R. BARBER PACED IN front of Dr. Tweedle's desk while I sat on the plush blue sofa with Phillip. Dr. Tweedle had requested Mr. Barber's presence so I could relay what I had discovered from Mr. Doyle's letters.

"So, you found some sort of W.A.S.P. hierarchy?" Mr. Barber stated.

"Yes, sir. From the letters, I've discovered that Mr. Doyle's title is Major. He received a letter two years ago from someone called Mr. Getla confirming his position. Mr. Getla had the title of Secretary," I explained.

"We don't know how high up in the chain of command a Major is, though, do we?" Mr. Barber asked.

"No, I have yet to discover the specifics, but a Mr. O'Doherty was writing to Mr. Doyle as if he was a subordinate. I believe he had the title of Captain," I said.

"You believe?" Mr. Barber said snidely.

"I'm certain Mr. O'Doherty had the title of Captain," I responded.

"Well, what of their future plans?" Mr. Barber exclaimed.

"I haven't discovered any letters with a location. I know the W.A.S.P. is planning something. They have a monthly meeting on November thirtieth."

"Where is the location of this meeting?" Mr. Barber asked.

"The letter didn't say, sir," I replied.

Mr. Barber threw his hands in the air. "So, we don't know the location of the W.A.S.P. meeting or any of the W.A.S.P.'s plans! What do we actually know?" Mr. Barber sighed angrily.

"Arnold, calm down. This is Miss Fitzgerald's first report. You can't expect her to discover everything we need in one try. She's putting herself in danger to gather what she can," Dr. Tweedle stated, slowly blinking his eyes. He looked drained.

"There are more letters in Mr. Doyle's drawer. I just didn't have time to read them all. Perhaps I'll get another chance, and they'll provide more information," I said.

"Good. If you could find out more about the meeting next week, that would be grand," Mr. Barber said in a demeaning tone.

"Jane is doing her best," Phillip muttered, and Dr. Tweedle shot him a stern look.

"I'll transfer Miss Fitzgerald's weekly wages into the account you set up for her, Oliver. If there's nothing left to discuss, I'll be on my way," Mr. Barber said, placing his top hat on his head. "You know how to get in touch with me if you discover anything else."

Mr. Barber straightened his coat as he came around the sofa and headed toward the door.

"Good evening, Arnold," Dr. Tweedle called as Mr. Barber opened the door.

"Goodbye," Mr. Barber responded, leaving the office.

Dr. Tweedle waited a few moments before speaking. "Are you sure you can handle this, Jane?"

"Yes, of course," I responded, trying not to think about Drake's actions.

"If this ever becomes too much for you, you won't have to

do it anymore. I'm sure Mr. Barber could find someone else," Dr. Tweedle said reassuringly.

"I'll be fine. I'm in the best possible position to gain information. I'm being extremely careful. I understand the dangers, which is why Mr. Withermyer and I should get to our lessons," I said, slowly standing.

"Yes, Miss Fitzgerald is correct. We should be off to her lesson," Phillip added, standing as well.

Dr. Tweedle nodded. "Yes, you should get on with it, I suppose. Excellent work this week, Jane, although I can't say I'm not worried about this."

"Thank you, Dr. Tweedle, for your concern. I do appreciate how much you care about me," I said.

"Yes, and that's why you need to be extra careful," Dr. Tweedle said.

⁂

Phillip and I left Dr. Tweedle's office and climbed to the ninth floor. We entered the exercise room, and Phillip immediately summoned the dummy I used to practice. I instantly slammed my palm into the figure's nose and followed it with a few kicks. It felt good to hit something since I was frustrated with Mr. Barber.

"That man infuriates me," I cried, slamming my fist into the dummy's face again.

"I assume you're referring to Arnold Barber," Mr. Withermyer said with a slight chuckle.

"Yes, he doubts everything I say and then demands the impossible. If only I could do something to get him to close his mouth," I snarled.

"You're doing your best and gaining information that could help us in the future," Phillip replied.

"Yes, but it doesn't seem good enough," I sighed. "If only I could discover the location of the W.A.S.P. meeting."

Phillip didn't say anything for a while, causing me to stop. I looked over at him, and he appeared deep in thought.

"What are you thinking about?" I asked.

"From what you've gathered so far, we know Mr. Doyle has been involved in the W.A.S.P. for a long time. You said one letter mentioned his father," Phillip mused.

"Yes, and?" I prodded.

"Well, you've found evidence that he was promoted when his house burnt down. So, he must've attended these monthly meetings the entire time he's been living with you. Can you remember when Mr. Doyle would leave the house?" Phillip asked.

I closed my eyes and tried to remember. There had been so much going on in my life when Mr. Doyle had moved into the manor. Marie had been complaining about his absences, and Emily insisted he had meetings and work to attend to.

"The meetings must happen in the evenings because I can recall times when Mr. Doyle didn't have dinner with the family. He would leave the manor beforehand," I replied.

A smile crept across Phillip's face, and I stared at him in confusion.

"If Mr. Doyle leaves the manor to go to the W.A.S.P. meetings, then it might be possible to follow him. We could discover the location of the meetings and even find out what's being discussed at them," Phillip said enthusiastically.

"How do we accomplish that?" I asked. "The meeting takes place on a Wednesday. So, I would be here."

"After the final class on Wednesday, we could leave the academy, and I could teleport us to the manor. As long as we don't arrive too late, perhaps we could follow Mr. Doyle to the meeting," Phillip suggested.

"Do you really think that would work?" I asked, my voice rising with hope.

"Yes, and if we can accomplish that, maybe we could gain access to the information being discussed," Phillip replied.

"There's one problem with that," I said. "Mr. Doyle knows what I look like. I can't very well show up at a W.A.S.P. meeting without him wondering why I'm there." I punched at the dummy in frustration.

Phillip started to laugh at me. "Jane, we're pixies. Have you forgotten we have magic? We would just need a *transfiguration charm* to change our appearances."

"Ms. Pregmon hasn't taught a *transfiguration charm* that can change a person's appearance. So, I don't know how to do it," I said.

"You don't think I could teach you?" Phillip asked. "What are these lessons for if not to teach you advanced charms?"

I blushed. "I wasn't implying that you couldn't teach me. Do you think I could master the *transfiguration charm* by then?" I asked.

"Of course! You'll probably pick it up during our first lesson. We can actually begin now. We don't have a lot of time until the thirtieth."

"If we attempt this, it's going to be dangerous. I don't think Dr. Tweedle will approve. He already disapproves of my spying at the manor," I said.

"That's why we won't let him know until we've already gone," Phillip said with a wink. "Get out your pixie dust case, and let's begin."

⚬

The *transfiguration charm* to change appearance was difficult to create and even harder to maintain, but I learned it just in time. On November thirtieth, my stomach was a ball of nerves by the time the last bell rang. I already informed my friends that I wouldn't be joining them for dinner.

Phillip answered the door on my first knock and practically pulled me inside.

"Are you ready?" he asked anxiously.

"Yes," I answered with a deep breath.

Phillip nodded and then peered out into the hallway.

"Okay, the hallways are clear. If we run into anyone, we'll just say we're going to the Magical Creatures barn to take care of your dragon," he whispered.

I followed Phillip down the hall. The hallways were practically empty because most students returned to their rooms between the last bell and dinner time. We made it across the lawn without being stopped, and I breathed easier when we boarded the cloud. I caught Phillip glancing at me out of the corner of my eye.

"You look nervous, Jane. Are you sure you want to do this?"

"Yes," I said with a reassuring smile. "I just thought Dr. Tweedle was going to catch us."

Phillip smiled back. "Okay, I just assumed you were having second thoughts. Don't worry, Jane. I'll keep you safe," Phillip said as the cloud landed in the meadow.

Before Phillip teleported us to the road outside the manor, we needed to get into our disguises. During my lessons, we had agreed to disguise ourselves as a middle-aged couple named Francis and Jenny Smith. I had practiced my transfiguration many times and hoped to perfect it today.

Phillip insisted I cast my charm first, and I pulled the vial of pixie dust from my pocket. I closed my eyes so I could concentrate. I tossed the pixie dust over myself when I gained the focus I needed. Slowly, I felt my features transform. My nose grew longer, and my cheeks became fuller. My body felt heavier, and when I looked down at my hands, they were wrinkled.

"Good job, Jane," Phillip said, handing me a small hand-held mirror so I could examine my transformation. I took the mirror and gazed into the reflective surface. My violet eyes were now blue, and my blonde hair was a light gray. I was happy to see that the image in the mirror was how I had imagined.

Phillip's transformation was almost instantaneous. His dark hair became a dark gray, and his green eyes changed to a very light shade of blue. Wrinkles formed around his eyes, and a long gray beard grew in place of his short, dark one. It was bizarre to gaze at a stranger's face, but know it was Phillip underneath the glamor.

"I'm going to have to get used to this," I said, and Phillip chuckled before reaching for the reins.

"Well, Mrs. Jenny Smith, are you ready to go?" he asked.

"Yes, Mr. Francis Smith," I answered, grabbing the side of the carriage.

"Just remember to keep a part of your mind focused on your glamour at all times. Hold on now," Phillip said, casting his *teleportation charm* into the air.

When the dust cleared and the darkness turned to light, I saw the woods, not very far away from the road that went by the manor's property. Phillip glanced over at me; seeing his smile on a stranger's mouth was so odd. The horses slowly pulled the carriage out of the underbrush and onto the road. When we got close enough to see the manor's driveway, Phillip directed the horses to the side of the road, pulling them to a stop.

"Now we wait," he announced, leaning back in the seat.

I shifted in an attempt to become more comfortable. "What time is it?" I asked.

Phillip glanced down at his pocket watch. "It is a quarter after four."

"Hopefully, we didn't arrive too late," I said, continuing to stare at the entrance to the manor's drive.

Phillip and I sat silently for a few moments before he spoke again.

"Are you cold? I can get a blanket for you."

My body involuntarily shivered at his mention of the cold,

and I nodded. Phillip disappeared around the back of the carriage to discreetly summon a blanket. In a few moments, he returned carrying a large quilt, which he draped over both our legs. Phillip edged a little closer to me, and I could feel the warmth radiating from his body. We continued to sit and wait, our eyes never leaving the entrance to the driveway.

Time seemed to drag by as we huddled in the carriage. Dusk started to fall, and the woods grew dark. I pulled the blanket tighter to ward off the cold. I was beginning to feel tired, and I could feel my head starting to bob. Maybe we had arrived too late, and Drake had already left the manor.

I was about to tell Phillip we should give up when he stirred beside me. I shook myself to attention and followed his gaze. A light was coming down the manor's driveway, and an automobile came down to the end of the drive, turning onto the road. I almost leapt out of my seat with excitement.

"That's Mr. Doyle's automobile!" I told Phillip. "Follow him."

Phillip flicked the reins. We followed behind at a slight distance, keeping him in our sight. I held my breath as we traveled along every curve and bend in the road. There was a moment when I thought we would lose him, but we crested the hill and could see him again. We followed the automobile all the way to a small town. More carriages and automobiles were on the road, so it was harder to keep up, but we managed to see where he had parked his vehicle.

We quickly pulled the carriage over and watched as Drake walked down the street, entering a tavern. Phillip leapt from our carriage and hitched the horses to a post. He helped me down, and we rushed toward where Drake had disappeared. My heart was pounding wildly as Phillip opened the door for me, and I entered the tavern.

The tavern was dimly lit, but I saw a bar to the left. The room wasn't large, but it was long, and tables crowded the space. The place didn't seem very busy, and my eyes scanned the room, looking for Drake Doyle. Finally, my eyes landed on the back of his dark head. He was leaning over the bar, conversing with the person behind it. I strained my ears to hear what they were saying.

"Let me show you to the back room," the bartender said before escorting him toward the back of the tavern.

Slowly, I followed a slight distance behind, watching them as they walked through a small doorway to a room in the back. Through the doorway, I could see other men gathered at a long table, one of them being Mr. Seth O'Doherty. They all greeted Drake enthusiastically, and I quickly sat at the closest empty table. Phillip joined me in the other vacant seat, his back to the room where the W.A.S.P. were meeting. Unfortunately, with the angle of the table, I could only see into a small corner of the room. I tried to listen, but hearing some of the conversations was hard. I was just about to whisper to Phillip when the bartender approached our table.

"Good evening, and welcome to the *Dew Drop Inn*. I haven't seen you in these parts before."

"My wife and I are only passing through," Phillip replied.

"Are you looking for lodging and a hot meal?" the bartender asked.

Phillip shook his head. "No, we've made other arrangements and are just looking for something to eat."

"I'll send a waitress over with menus," the bartender said before stalking off.

It wasn't long before a young brunette woman approached our table. We ordered a few sodas, and the waitress left us to peruse the menu. I glanced over Phillip's shoulder, trying to see what was happening in the back room.

"I can't hear what they're talking about," I whispered to Phillip.

Slowly, he reached into his pocket and pulled out two charm

vials. He slipped one across the table to me. I quickly hid it in my clenched fist.

"Put that in your drink," he muttered.

I uncorked the vial and upended it into my soda. Then, I followed Phillip's lead, taking a long drink. Suddenly, the room became deafening. I could hear what people were conversing about from across the room. My eyes grew wide in understanding.

"It's a *heightened hearing charm*," he said, and even though he was whispering, it sounded like he was talking loudly in my ear. "Just focus on a direction, and the sounds will become clearer."

I focused on the back room, and suddenly, I could hear the men. Drake's voice rang out above all the others, and the room quieted.

"Gentlemen, settle down. I believe Captain O'Doherty might have some news to share."

"Thank you, Major Doyle," Seth O'Doherty began. "I've just discovered a new and important location for us to infiltrate."

"How did you come across this information?" someone asked.

Seth let out a low chuckle. "I caught one of those disgusting pixie animals. It didn't take long for her to start talking. I can be very persuasive."

The rest of the men began laughing. "What did you do with her? The usual?" a man asked.

"Of course. It's amazing how much they look like us. Once I had weakened her magic, she was begging for mercy. By the time I was done with her, she was willing to tell me anything."

My stomach felt sick as the W.A.S.P. members broke out in laughter again. When the waitress returned to take our orders, I wasn't hungry anymore, but I just ordered a salad so she would go away.

"So, Captain, what did you learn from this pixie barbarian?" Drake asked, steering the conversation back to the information.

"She told me about an all-pixie town called Coillewood.

It's located somewhere in the forest east of here," Seth O'Doherty bragged.

Phillip's eyes widened, and he tapped my arm to get my attention. "Coillewood is an all-pixie town," he mouthed to me.

"Supposedly, the town is invisible, but just like those other hovels, there is a special way to gain access. With this place, there is a tree that will reveal the town," I heard Seth continue.

"Have you disposed of the pixie filth yet, or will we be using her to find this tree?" one of the men asked.

"She's still my captive, and since she has already given me the location, I'm sure I can persuade her to point out the tree and show us what we have to do," Seth said confidently.

"Excellent work, Captain O'Doherty," Drake said, slowly applauding. "Do you have any suggestions on when we should attack?"

"Just give me a few more days to convince my captive. Only a few units will be needed to finish the job. Coillewood doesn't seem to be a large town, and this will be such a surprise. It should go as easily as the last few."

"Are you sure you don't need a few more men?" Drake asked.

"No, I think my units should be more than enough, with your permission, of course," Seth replied.

There was a pause before Drake spoke again. "If you believe you can get the job done with your units, then permission is granted."

"Thank you, Major Doyle. You can count on my men. We'll attack in three days."

24

THE W.A.S.P.'S PLANS

THE CHEERING FROM the men could be heard even without a heightened hearing charm. A few of the other patrons in the tavern looked toward the back room. Finally, the waitress approached our table with our dinner.

"Those gentlemen are always excited about something. They rent out our back room at least once a month. I've always wondered what they are so enthusiastic about," she commented, placing the food in front of us.

Murder, I thought as a slight chill passed through my body. Phillip thanked her, and she moved off to another table. I picked up my fork and hovered over the salad. The W.A.S.P. members had quieted down, and Drake was calling for everyone's attention again.

"With that part of our agenda settled, let's move on," Drake demanded. "Can anyone make me a delighted man and tell me they have information on the McCalski heir?"

My fork almost flew out of my hand, and I gasped in alarm. Phillip reached across the table and touched my hand, but my mind was on the W.A.S.P. They were about to discuss the information they had about me. I could feel my pulse beginning to pound in my head.

Mumbled voices converged from the other room. It seemed like no one was willing to speak up at first. Finally, someone cleared their throat.

"We have not been successful in gaining more information about the girl. Every one of those savages we captured doesn't know anything about the name McCalski. If they do, they're talking about the woman we already disposed of," the man practically stuttered.

"We haven't gained anything new since we discovered the heir was a girl," Drake fumed.

"I know, Major, and we are doing our best. Those younger pixies gave us what we already know. Perhaps the girl we're looking for is around their age," the stuttering man replied.

"Perhaps…. Do we know any information on who might have fathered this McCalski heir?" Drake asked.

My heartbeat picked up as I waited for the response. "No. Every pixie we've tortured claims that Rachel McCalski disappeared without a trace over twenty years ago."

"This heir has to be somewhere," Drake thundered.

"We will keep looking, Major. As I said, we're doing our best to find her," the man simpered.

"I know these unnatural beings have magic, but I don't think they have the ability to spawn a child out of thin air. There has to be a father out there somewhere. The damn girl probably has her father's name, and that's why the name McCalski isn't eliciting any response. Keep looking, and we'll discuss this again later," Drake demanded. "I want that girl found."

Heat coursed through my body as my heart rate sped even faster. I felt lightheaded, and my vision began to grow cloudy. The man demanding my capture and possible death lived under the same roof as me. I felt extremely sick.

"Jenny, Jenny," I heard, but it sounded far away. A hand gripped my arm and squeezed. "Jane," Phillip hissed, finally calling my real name instead. I glanced up at him. He was quickly rising from the table. "We need to leave now," he said in a sharp whisper.

"No, I'm okay now," I replied, but Phillip pointed to my loose strands of hair. The gray was quickly transforming to blonde. Hearing the W.A.S.P. plan my capture must've caused my mind to lose focus. My *transfiguration charm* was beginning to fade quickly.

Phillip tossed a handful of bills onto the table, and I ducked my head down, pulling my coat around me. I rose from the table and hurried to the door. I could feel the charm fade as my nose shrank to its original size and shape. I heard Phillip following me, saying something about his wife being ill, before he dashed out behind me. I ran down the street and managed to climb onto the carriage just as the charm completely dissolved.

"That was close," Phillip sighed, leaning against the carriage. His breath was coming in short gasps. "I thought you were going to transform in front of everyone. Thank the gods, it was dark in that place."

"I'm so sorry. I didn't even realize I was losing it," I said, putting my head in my hands.

Phillip hopped up beside me and placed his arm around my shoulder. "Don't be upset. It's okay. I believe we got you out of there fast enough. No one followed us, so I assume no one saw a thing," he said in a soothing voice.

"There were so many W.A.S.P. members in the other room. If one of them had noticed, a mistake like that could have gotten us killed," I cried.

Phillip picked up the reins and coaxed the horses into motion. "Jane, we're fine. Like I told you earlier, I wouldn't let anything happen to you. You did well tonight, and we gained some important information."

I shuddered, recalling what the W. A. S. P. had discussed. In three days, they had plans to attack a town called Coillewood. "We have to stop them," I said. "That awful Mr. O'Doherty has some poor girl captive, and only the gods know what he's done to her. We have to send someone to save her and the rest of the pixies in that town."

"As soon as we return to the Jelf Academy, we'll have Dr. Tweedle summon Mr. Barber. I'm sure his department will take care of this. Unfortunately, we don't have much time to stop them," Phillip said, steering the horses on a trail that headed into the woods.

Once deep enough, Phillip steered the horses off the trail and into the underbrush. He allowed his glamour to disappear, and it was nice to see his familiar green eyes. He pulled his pixie dust case from his pocket and searched for a *teleportation charm*. I gripped the side of the carriage and waited for the darkness to settle over me.

It wasn't long before we were riding the cloud up to the Jelf Academy. My heart had finally slowed, but I wondered what Dr. Tweedle's reaction would be. The hallways were mostly empty, and no one looked our way as we climbed to the second floor. Outside Dr. Tweedle's office, I took a deep breath while Phillip knocked on the door.

When we heard Dr. Tweedle's voice calling us to enter, Phillip allowed me to enter the office first. He followed, closing the door softly behind him.

"Ah, Phillip and Jane. What do I owe this pleasure?" he asked with a slight smile. His blue eyes scanned us from head to toe.

"We discovered some information regarding the W.A.S.P., and we think it would be best if you summoned Arnold Barber here," Phillip said.

"Information about the W.A.S.P.? How did you two manage that?" he asked, pushing his glasses up the bridge of his nose.

Phillip took a deep breath and glanced at me. "Well, sir, Miss Fitzgerald and I discovered the location of the W.A.S.P. meeting," Phillip began.

Dr. Tweedle gave us a dumbfounded stare before suddenly rising from his seat. "Don't tell me you were foolish enough to attend," his voice roared through the room.

"Please don't be upset," I begged. "We took all the necessary precautions. We went in disguise."

"Have you lost your mind, Miss Fitzgerald? You are only a student who hasn't completed all of your training! Do you wish yourself dead? Do you want to end up like your mother?" Dr. Tweedle thundered.

I could feel tears forming in my eyes, spilling over onto my cheeks. I'd never seen Dr. Tweedle so angry before. His face was bright red, and sweat glistened across his forehead. I felt terrible to have upset him. I hated to see him so angry, especially because he had taken care of me for the last four years.

"Don't yell at Miss Fitzgerald. It wasn't her idea. It was mine," Phillip said, taking another step closer to the desk.

Dr. Tweedle's blazing eyes burned into Phillip. "I should fire you right now for endangering a student's life!" Dr. Tweedle spat.

"No, please! This isn't Mr. Withermyer's fault. He was only helping me. I wanted to discover the location of the W.A.S.P. meeting. I hadn't discovered anything of use in the letters, so I wanted to discover some beneficial information, and it's a good thing I did. The W.A.S.P. are planning to attack another pixie town. Coillewood will be attacked in three days!"

Dr. Tweedle's face dropped, and he took a deep breath. "Is this true?"

"Yes, sir, we both heard clearly," Phillip said. "Coillewood is the next location."

Dr. Tweedle took a seat. He quickly scrawled a note and cast a charm over it, making it vanish.

"Mr. Barber will be here momentarily. You might as well have a seat," Dr. Tweedle said, gesturing to the sofa. He looked defeated and overwhelmed.

It wasn't long before a familiar knock sounded on the office door, and Mr. Barber strode in wearing his usual black top hat.

"I received your message, Oliver. What is so urgent? I'm a very busy man. My department has been trying to track down information about the W.A.S.P. meeting that is supposed to occur today," Mr. Barber barked.

"I believe Miss Fitzgerald and Mr. Withermyer can help you in that respect," Dr. Tweedle replied.

"Whatever do you mean?" Mr. Barber asked, turning to glare at us.

"We discovered the location of the meeting and were able to spy on the topics being discussed," I stated.

"Really?" Mr. Barber asked skeptically.

"Yes, what Miss Fitzgerald says is true. We followed Mr. Doyle, and while in disguise, we were able to listen in on their conversation," Phillip spoke up.

"I supposed you discovered something of interest for Dr. Tweedle to summon me here," Mr. Barber said.

It made me mad that he still seemed so skeptical, as if what Phillip and I had to share would be worthless. I wasn't a child who didn't have a clue. I was risking my life to save other pixies from danger.

"The W.A.S.P. are planning to attack Coillewood in three days," I said.

Mr. Barber looked startled for a moment, but then he shrugged. "Coillewood is an all-pixie town hidden in a very deep forest. It's invisible and can only be accessed by a magical tree. Therefore, only a pixie would be able to use it."

"Captain O'Doherty has captured a pixie who will lead him right to it. He knew the name of the town and how to access it. He told the other members about the tree, and he has been torturing a pixie to gain this information," I cried.

"The W.A.S.P. has gained access to pixie locations before,"

Dr. Tweedle commented. "Celestial Heights could only be entered by pixies, and the W.A.S.P. managed to infiltrate it. They are getting bolder, Arnold. I wouldn't put anything past them.

Mr. Barber paced the room with a hand on his chin. "In three days, you say?"

"Yes, sir. Captain O'Doherty and Major Doyle agreed on three days. Major Doyle seems to be in charge. He was the one to dictate the meeting, and he gave Captain O'Doherty permission to attack," I replied.

"My department will have to act quickly, then. We'll do our best to evacuate Coillewood and set up an ambush," Mr. Barber said. "Good work on relaying this information."

"Captain O'Doherty is supposed to have the captive pixie with him. Will you be able to rescue her? I'm sure she has suffered greatly," I said.

"We will try to keep every pixie safe, but I cannot make any promises. If this intel proves to be true, I'll add a bonus to your account, and you'll be required to attend as many of these W.A.S.P. meetings as possible. You seemed to have proven yourself, so you are officially our spy, Miss Fitzgerald. Hopefully, you are prepared for all that entails."

I nodded, but I couldn't help but notice the distressed look on Dr. Tweedle's face.

25

COILLEWOOD

I HAD NEVER BEEN more nervous about returning to the manor than I was the following weekend. The attack would take place while I was there, and I wasn't sure if I should expect anything to happen. Would Drake be joining Seth O'Doherty? Would the attack be prevented, or would the W.A.S.P. claim more innocent lives?

I tried to hide my anxiety while I cooked and cleaned for the family. All day Saturday, I wanted to leap out of my skin. My eyes kept wandering to the door for the arrival of news. Instead, the day went by without Drake leaving the house. This did nothing to relieve my unease. Either he was not participating, or I had heard wrong about the date. I hoped my information was correct and Mr. Barber's department would be able to stop them.

Night fell at the manor without a word. I helped Ellen set the table and prepare food for dinner. Marie, Emily, Preston, and Drake gathered around the table as I poured the water. Emily's face had a little more color, but she still looked ill. Evidence of her pregnancy was becoming more apparent since she was almost twenty weeks along now.

I rushed back to the kitchen to bring out the first course. Ellen had made vichyssoise a few days ago and deemed it ready to serve. I carried the chilled bowls and placed them in the middle of the plates. Preston grabbed his spoon and began slurping noisily. Marie gave him a look before turning her attention to Drake.

"Have all the plans been finalized for next week?" she asked him.

"Yes, my cousin has agreed to host us for several months," Drake responded.

"So that means we are leaving next week?" Emily asked excitedly.

"Yes, dear. We will take the train down to Savannah, Georgia, where my cousin Douglass will meet us and take us to his estate," Drake replied.

"Trains again," Emily sighed. "Well, at least we'll get away from the freezing weather here. The baby and I can't take it any longer."

"Do you realize this is the first year I won't be hosting my annual Christmas party? I'm disappointed, but the warmer weather will be better for my grandchild," Marie stated.

I paused in the doorway, unsure if I had heard correctly. Was it possible they wouldn't be here for Christmas?

"Are there any crocodiles in Savannah? I want to hunt one for my collection," I heard Preston mutter through a mouthful of soup.

When I entered the kitchen, Ellen was putting the salmon filets on a platter.

"Did you know that the family is leaving next week?" I whispered.

"Yes, Princess Emily has been complaining about the cold, so Mr. Doyle has planned a winter holiday for the whole family. They're not expected to be back until the beginning of March. Emily claims that this winter weather is not good for her pregnancy," Ellen replied, thrusting the salmon platter into my hands.

I returned to the dining room with the tray and placed it in the middle of the table. Drake and Preston were discussing what they could hunt while in Georgia, and I cringed because I knew about his other hunting habits. Emily had barely touched her vichyssoise and made a face at the salmon. I went around the table collecting the soup bowls, but Marie spoke when I went to pick up Emily's.

"You didn't eat any of your vichyssoise soup," Marie barked.

Emily looked over at her and shrugged. "I'm not in the mood for it," she sighed.

"You need to eat! All you do is pick at your food. You're starving my grandchild when you don't eat," Marie snipped.

"Maybe my baby doesn't like this food, Mother," Emily spat.

"There is nothing wrong with this food," Marie snapped, spearing a salmon filet and putting it on her plate.

"Well, I don't want salmon today," Emily sniffed, pushing the plate away from her.

"What do you want, dearest," Drake asked, but his voice sounded tight.

"Umm…" Emily hummed, putting her right hand on her chin. Several minutes passed before she finally answered. "I would like eggs benedict."

Drake pointed at me and motioned for me to approach the table. I stood beside his chair, but I didn't come too close. He turned toward me with a skeevy smile.

"Jane, go into the kitchen and tell the chef to whip up some eggs benedict for my wife," he said.

I nodded, heading for the kitchen door.

"What?" Ellen snapped when she saw me.

"Emily has decided that she doesn't want to eat salmon. Instead, she would like eggs benedict."

Ellen rolled her eyes and went to the pantry. "When will these children realize that this kitchen is not a restaurant? I plan the meals for the week with Marie. If they'd prefer to eat something specific, perhaps they should discuss that with their mother!" Ellen huffed.

She hurried to prepare Emily's request while I grabbed the water pitcher.

"I assume Emily's dinner will be on its way out soon," Marie snapped as soon as she saw me.

"Yes, ma'am, of course," I replied, walking around the table and refilling the water.

Drake's eyes followed me the entire way, and every time I caught his dark stare, I wanted to shudder. Darting back into the kitchen to check on Emily's meal was a relief. Ellen was still mumbling under her breath as she plated the eggs benedict. With a deep breath, I carried the dish back out into the dining room. Marie glanced over the plate as I set it down before Emily. She must have found it satisfying because she didn't make any comments.

I sighed with relief as I retreated to a corner of the room. Dinner progressed without further incident, and besides discussing the upcoming trip, the family hardly talked. After dinner, everyone's plate was mostly cleared, but Emily's still had half her dinner. Again, I sighed as I brought the dishes into the kitchen and washed them.

As I worked, I wondered if Ellen wouldn't mind if I didn't return to the manor while the family was away. She had allowed it last year, but I wasn't sure if she would allow it again. I also considered what would happen with the W.A.S.P. meetings if Drake was gone for three months. Would the meetings be cancelled? I doubted the W.A.S.P. would stop hunting pixies just because he was taking a vacation.

I had just replaced all the cleaning supplies and turned off the lights in the front entryway when a loud banging sounded at the front door. I paused in alarm. If it hadn't been so loud, I would have thought I had imagined it. My heart thundered in my chest, and I wasn't sure what to do.

Before I could make a decision, the loud pounding sounded again, causing me to jump. I inched toward the door, hoping I'd be able to catch a glimpse of whomever it was through the tiny glass window. I was almost to the door when a loud voice boomed behind me.

"Who is at the door at this god-forsaken hour? Jane, are you going to answer it or not?" Marie burst out, and I turned to see her standing at the top of the stairs.

I broadened my steps to the door and reached for the handle. My breath caught in my throat when I beheld Seth O'Doherty on the front porch. His face was dirty, but somehow, the scar on his cheek stood out more. His dark blonde hair was a mess, and his clothes were torn. He was holding his right arm, which appeared covered in blood.

"I need to see Mr. Doyle right away," he hollered, shouldering past me and into the house.

"What is the meaning of this?" Marie began, but Drake Doyle soon joined her at the top of the stairs.

"I'm sorry for the late hour, but this must be a matter of urgency if Mr. O'Doherty came by. Return to bed, mother-in-law. I do apologize for the commotion. I will take care of this," Drake told Marie as he descended the stairs. "Jane, fetch some clean wet towels, a bowl of warm water, and gauze. We'll be in the office," he barked as he went by me.

I turned around and headed to the supply cupboard while Drake helped Mr. O'Doherty to the office. Why had Seth O'Doherty shown up in the middle of the night looking bloody and bruised? Had the attack on Coillewood occurred? I couldn't be sure, but Seth O'Doherty did not look like he had been victorious.

I collected the supplies and made my way to my father's office. Pausing outside the door, I leaned in to listen.

"We were surrounded," Seth groaned. "It was an ambush. It was like those bastards knew we were coming."

"What happened?" Drake demanded as Seth groaned again.

"The woods went black. They must've used a spell or whatever it is they do. We couldn't see anything. We fired our guns into the darkness but only managed to subdue a few," Seth said. "Where is that maid of yours?"

I waited for a few breaths before I entered. Seth was sitting in one of the armchairs with his right arm propped up. A long gash ran down his arm from his elbow to his wrist. Now that he was in the light, his face looked bruised, and he had a series of cuts all along his body.

"What happened next?" Drake asked, taking the bowl from my hands. Seth eyed me warily, and Drake sighed. "She's only a maid, and she doesn't have a clue what you're talking about. If she's a wise maid, she won't repeat anything you say," he said threateningly. "Jane, get over here and help me clean Mr. O'Doherty's wounds."

The thought of doing anything to help Seth made me ill, but I needed to know what had happened. I steeled myself and approached the chair as Seth began talking again.

"They were attacking us in the darkness, with you know," Seth said with another glance at me as I began wiping blood off his arm.

"Magic," Drake said snidely, and he cast a look at me as if daring me to call him crazy. Instead, I kept my head down and continued working.

"Yes, magic," Seth finally said. "It must've been some kind of explosive because I could feel myself being cut everywhere. I threw up my right arm to protect my face and neck. It was a good thing I did. I was thrown backward and must've landed thirty feet away. It knocked the breath right out of me, and I'll admit I laid there stunned for a few moments," he said with a groan and a hiss. "When I finally came to, the darkness was starting to lift, and the sight I beheld wasn't pretty."

I dipped the bloody towel into the warm water as Drake held Seth's arm down. He hissed again while I continued to clean the wound.

"How many?" Drake sighed, the question escaping his clenched teeth.

"More than half of my units have perished, and the other half ranges from slightly injured to severely wounded," he said, sounding defeated. Though I kept my eyes down, I noticed that Drake's eyes were blazing.

"How did this happen? You swore this would be an easy conquest," Drake seethed.

"It was supposed to be. My prisoner showed me the exact location. It was supposed to be an in-and-out mission, just like the last one. I don't know how they were prepared. It was almost like they had known," Seth said.

"Your prisoner, where is she? Are you sure she wasn't the one to warn them?"

Seth shook his head. "She perished in the onslaught of the attack, but there is no way she would've been the one to warn them. I kept her powers drained. I made sure she received her treatments and that she was weak. There was no possible way for her to get word to anyone."

"These people are sneaky. You have to keep a constant eye on them. We know more about them than ever before, but we don't want to start underestimating them. Hopefully, you remember that next time you keep a hostage. This couldn't have happened at the worst time," Drake spat. "You know I'm going away next week. I'll be gone for a few months!"

"I'm sorry, Major. This turn of events was most unexpected. I promise to get to the bottom of this. I'll discover how they knew. I promise that our next venture will be successful," Seth pleaded, and it almost looked as if Drake was about to hit him.

"You better," Drake muttered, turning away for a moment. "While I'm away, you better work harder than ever to find another location. Also, I want you to work double time searching for the McCalski heir. You need to start recruiting to make up for the men you lost. You'll be representing me at the next meeting on December twenty-first. I hope you have a good explanation for what went wrong today."

I began wrapping up Seth's arm.

"Yes, sir, you can count on me. I won't disappoint you again."

"I picked you to be my Captain for a reason. Your ruthlessness allows you to get the job done, which I admire, but I don't want to see another mistake like this. Our friendship will only get you so far. I expect to see results; believe me, you can expect my correspondence while I'm away," Drake said while I gathered the blood-soaked towels and red-stained water.

Drake strode toward the office door and held it open for me. As I walked out into the hall, he reached out and grabbed my arm, turning my body so I would face him.

"Thank you for your help tonight, Jane. Can I trust that the things you heard tonight will go no further than this room?" he questioned.

"Yes, of course, sir," I struggled to say without stuttering.

"That's a good girl," Drake murmured, stroking his fingers down my face and cupping my chin. It took everything in me not to shudder at his touch. "It's getting late, and you should run along to bed. Sweet dreams," he added before finally releasing my face.

I stepped away from him as he softly chuckled before returning to the office. My body was shaking so badly that it took all my focus not to spill the water bowl.

26

THE MARTINEZ FAMILY

MR. BARBER WAS SLIGHTLY more cordial with me the next time I saw him, but he wasn't any less moody. The information I managed to overhear had saved Coillewood from an attack, and Mr. Barber's department had gotten the upper hand on the W.A.S.P. I had been generously compensated for having the correct intel, but Mr. Barber expected me to continue delivering information. Though Coillewood had been saved, I wasn't happy to hear Mr. Barber's department attacked without trying to rescue Mr. O'Doherty's prisoner.

The Christmas season was quickly approaching, and with it, the midterm exams. My group of friends and I studied for weeks in the library, hoping to pass. Somehow, I managed to squeeze in classwork, studying, and my extra lessons with Phillip. Leading up to the midterms, we cut our lessons back to two times a week. In addition, I needed to be prepared for the next W.A.S.P. meeting scheduled for December 21st. Though Drake would not be in attendance, I was still expected to spy. Phillip had me practice my transfiguration charm again so I could hold the glamour longer.

Once Marie and her family left on their trip, I stayed at the Jelf

Academy again. As soon as Josefina learned Marie would be away for the Christmas holiday, she insisted I come to her family's house. I protested because I didn't want to inconvenience her family, but Josefina assured me it wouldn't be an issue since Kairi and Zachary were already coming. Their father was away on one of his ships and wouldn't be home for Christmas.

Josefina sent her mother a letter immediately, and her mother quickly responded that it would be wonderful if I joined the family for the Christmas holiday. I was happy the Martinezes invited me, but at the same time, I was nervous because I'd never met Josefina and Miguel's parents. I really hoped they would like me.

December passed quickly, and the midterm exams were soon completed. Josefina and I were giddily packing our suitcases.

"I'm so excited you're coming home with me for Christmas!" Josefina exclaimed, folding her dresses, skirts, and blouses.

"I can't wait to meet your parents and see Juan and Lena again," I replied.

"They can't wait to meet you. I talk about you all the time, and they know what a special friend you are to me. You're going to love my mom. She's the most caring person, and she will want to feed you the entire time. Don't be surprised if you gain a few pounds over the next few weeks," Josefina laughed.

"What about your dad?" I asked, collecting my pixie dust case.

"He can be quiet at times, but he's hilarious. He really is only serious regarding his business," Josefina replied.

"I could use some good food and some laughter," I said with a smile.

"This is going to be the best holiday ever. We're going to have so much fun spending every day together," Josefina exclaimed.

"Other than Wednesday, December twenty-first," I reminded her. "Mr. Withermyer is coming to get me so I can do my job for Mr. Barber." Even though the meeting for the W.A.S.P. wasn't until the evening, Phillip had agreed to pick me up around eleven o'clock in the morning so we could go to the Jewel Caverns. This was the first year I had money of my own, and I wanted to get my friends Christmas presents.

Josefina frowned slightly, clasping her suitcase closed. "I don't know if I like that you're spying for Mr. Barber. It's risky, Jane."

"I know, but I discovered where a few W.A.S.P. members have their monthly meetings. I learned their next plan of attack, and the entire town of Coillewood was protected," I said.

"I know, but something bad could happen to you. What you did helped save a lot of pixies, but do you really need to put yourself in danger again?" Josefina asked.

"The W.A.S.P. isn't going to stop attacking pixies because they were defeated outside Coillewood. They probably plan on doing much worse now that their efforts have been thwarted. I need to spy on the next meeting," I replied.

"The W.A.S.P. is hunting you, though. Can't Mr. Barber find someone else to do the job?"

"No, I need to be the one. I feel responsible for the attacks since the W.A.S.P. is looking for me, and besides, for the first time in my life, I'm finally making my own money. I've been practicing my *transfiguration charm*. The W.A.S.P. won't know who I really am," I answered.

"I'm glad Mr. Withermyer has been accompanying you. I just want you to be careful, Jane," Josefina said.

"I understand that you're worried. It will be okay. The last time we disguised ourselves, I wasn't actually in the same room with the W.A.S.P. I expect we'll do the same thing on Wednesday," I responded, lifting my suitcase from the bed.

Again, I promised to be careful, and we exited our bedroom and went down to the entrance hall. Most of the other students had left already, and the hall was quiet. Miguel, Kairi, and Zachary were already waiting, and Miguel glanced up as we descended the stairs.

"How many things did you have to pack? It seems like I'm always waiting on you," Miguel teased his sister.

"There are certain things that a woman needs to have with her, Miguel. We aren't like you men who can just throw on anything and head out the door," Josefina replied, approaching them.

"I believe the carriage is waiting for us in the meadow," Miguel responded, holding the front door open.

Zachary pushed Kairi out the door first, and the rest of us followed. The cold wind whipped around our faces, causing strands of my hair to flutter in the breeze.

"I wish Taylor was joining us too," Kairi said.

"I did invite her to stay with us, but she told me she had to be home for Christmas. Apparently, the holidays aren't a good time for Taylor to be away from her family," Josefina said.

I kept my eyes on the ground because I knew why. Taylor's twin sister was murdered by the W.A.S.P. Now, she was her parents' only child, and I was sure they wanted to keep her close.

"I'm going to miss her," Kairi said, and we agreed.

The ride down to the meadow was smooth, and a large carriage pulled by four winged horses was waiting for us. Zachary insisted that he would help his sister into the carriage by himself. Miguel tried to protest, saying he would be happy to help, but Zachary brushed him off. While Zachary helped Kairi, Josefina, Miguel, and I went around to the back of the carriage, where there was a compartment for storing luggage. Miguel began loading the suitcases, and Josefina and I helped by levitating each one up to him. By the time all the bags were packed, Zachary came around with Kairi's wheelchair.

Josefina and I boarded the carriage. I sat across from Kairi, and Josefina sat beside me. Miguel climbed in next, and instead of sitting next to his sister, he took the seat next to Kairi. Zachary climbed in last, and I caught the slight scowl on his face as he took the seat next to Josefina. As soon as Zachary closed the carriage door, we could feel the winged horses beginning to move. It wasn't long before we were soaring through the clouds.

On the way to the Martinez family home, we talked about our exams. Zachary was more talkative than usual. Occasionally, my eyes would catch his aqua-blue ones, and he would smile.

The carriage ride wasn't too long. We traveled for about an hour before the horses began to lose altitude. From what I could tell, we were in a mountainous area dense with forests. Finally, the foliage opened up, and a street with huge houses appeared. The horses swooped toward the street and landed on the cobblestones. They trotted down the road and turned up one of the wide driveways that led to a magnificent house.

The gate surrounding the property magically opened, and the horses pranced through it. The house seemed slightly larger than the manor. The driveway led up to the front and wrapped around a large garden. The garden was snow-covered, and the only things jutting out of the snow were two statues: one of a man and the other a woman. The flowers were probably lovely in the spring.

The house itself was a red brick colonial with many blue shuttered windows and a large front door also painted blue. Two pristine white pillars on both sides of the door supported a small balcony on one of the upper floors. The carriage pulled to a halt, and Miguel shifted in his seat.

"Welcome to our home," Miguel announced.

Zachary climbed out after Miguel, and he helped Josefina and me. His hand grasped mine firmly as he smiled at me warmly until both my feet were securely on the ground. Just as we were about to begin unloading our luggage, we heard a commotion coming from the front door.

"My two youngest are finally home!" a female voice exclaimed, causing Miguel and Josefina to rush around the side of the carriage.

Slowly, I came around to see the twins embracing a woman slightly shorter than Josefina. When their hug broke apart, I could see she had dark brown hair cut to her shoulders and light brown eyes. She had a sweet, round face with features that made it obvious that she was the twin's mother. Her eyes lit up when she saw me, and I gradually walked toward the family.

"Hello, you must be Miss Jane Fitzgerald," Mrs. Martinez said enthusiastically, warmly shaking my hand. "My children have told me so much about you. I'm so pleased to finally meet you."

"Thank you so much for inviting me to your home, Mrs. Martinez. I really appreciate being able to celebrate with Josefina, Miguel, and the rest of your family," I replied.

"Please call me Ana Luisa. Mrs. Martinez is so old-fashioned," she insisted as Zachary and Kairi approached.

"Mom, I would also like you to meet Kairi and Zachary Walsh," Miguel said, and Ana Luisa turned to shake their hands. She didn't seem at all phased that Kairi was in a wheelchair.

"It's so nice to meet the two of you. It's a pleasure to have you throughout the holiday season," Ana Luisa said.

"Thank you for having us, ma'am," Zachary replied.

"Yes, we are so grateful. With our father away, we would've spent the holiday alone," Kairi added.

"Miguel and Josefina's friends are always welcome here. Let me help you with the bags so we can get inside out of this cold weather," Ana Luisa said, coming around the back of the carriage.

Mrs. Martinez helped levitate the luggage and led us to the front door. As we approached, the door automatically swung inward, and we followed Mrs. Martinez into the house.

The front entrance had a marble-tiled floor stretching down the hallway beyond. The walls were tall with mahogany paneling. The top half of the walls were painted white, and large paintings of what I could only assume were family members decorated the space. A curved staircase was located toward the back of the hall, and each step was made from marble. The room was illuminated by a brass chandelier hanging in the center and from the two large windows above the front door.

As we crowded into the foyer, a tall man walked down the hallway. He had salt-and-pepper hair and very kind brown eyes. His skin was tan, and he had a beard and mustache the same color as his hair.

"Welcome to our home," he said in a booming voice, lifting his arms wide. "My name is Carlos Martinez."

The twins' father crossed the room and embraced his children. Then he shook everyone's hand as introductions were made.

"Miguel, why don't you show Zachary to the guest bedroom down the hall from Juan's room," Ana Luisa suggested. "Jane, you'll be staying in the room next to Josefina's, and we've made up a room on the first for Kairi."

Zachary looked hesitant to leave his sister, but Ana Luisa smiled reassuringly. "Go with Miguel. I'll make sure your sister gets settled in."

"Thank you," Zachary said politely. Even though he followed Miguel upstairs, I knew he hated to leave Kairi.

Ana Luisa gently pushed Kairi down the hallway, and Josefina motioned to me. "Jane, you can follow me. I'll show you to the guest room you'll be staying in."

I levitated my luggage, following Josefina to the second floor. We passed a door on the left, which Josefina informed me was hers, and we stopped at the next door. Josefina opened up the door, allowing me to enter the room.

The guest bedroom was spacious, with a large, comfortable four-poster bed in the middle. It was decorated in elegant light blue. I placed my suitcase by the bed and turned to Josefina.

"This room is lovely," I said.

"My mother loves having a full house around the holidays. My aunt Teresa and my Uncle Fernando are expected to arrive sometime this week," Josefina said as I opened my suitcase, placing some of my dresses in the closet.

Josefina helped me unpack, and then we went to her room. Josefina's room was decorated in light pink, and the furniture looked feminine. Her bed had a canopy above it, and sheet fabric hung down, enclosing the bed. She levitated her suitcase onto the cedar chest, and I helped her unpack her things. Once we were finished, we hurried downstairs to see if Kairi needed help.

Kairi's room was similar to mine but decorated in yellow. Ana Luisa had just finished helping Kairi unpack her suitcase when we entered the room.

"Thank you so much, Mrs. Martinez," Kairi said in her musical voice.

"Dinner should be ready soon. I'll let you settle in, and then I'll see you all in the dining room in about fifteen minutes," Ana Luisa said before she left the room.

"Your mother is so kind," Kairi commented, coming around the bed.

Josefina smiled. "I don't know about you two, but the journey has made me hungry. I can show you the house on our way toward the dining room."

Kairi and I agreed, and I pushed Kairi out of the room as we followed Josefina down the hall. She showed us the sitting room, a small library, the ballroom, and the restroom before finally reaching the dining room. Wonderful smells wafted into the room from the direction of the kitchen, and my stomach rumbled.

The dining room wasn't empty when we entered. Mr. Martinez, Miguel, Zachary, and Juan were already seated. They stood up when they saw us enter, and we greeted Juan. Though it had only been six months since I'd seen him, Juan looked older. He had started growing a short beard. Once the greetings had ended, we each took a seat. It wasn't long before Mrs. Martinez entered the room, levitating a few dinner plates, followed by Lena.

Lena looked radiant. Like Juan, she seemed older, but she looked so healthy and happy. She gazed adoringly at Juan as she helped Ana Luisa place the dishes on the table. When I realized there wasn't a housemaid to assist them, I stood up and insisted on helping.

Ana Luisa kindly shook her head. "Please sit back down. Lena and I have everything handled. You are our guest, Jane," she said sweetly.

Slowly, I sank back into my seat, though it felt strange not to help. Once all the food was on the table, Ana Luisa, and Carlos thanked the gods before we began eating. The meal was delicious, and the food was flavored with spices I'd never had before. Juan told us about his job in the gem mine, and you could tell how proud Carlos was that his son was learning the family business. It felt cozy and loving at the Martinez table, and I instantly felt at home. The family laughed and talked as I imagined a close family would. Though Kairi, Zachary, and I were guests, the Martinezes made us feel like we were part of the family.

Sitting on my right, Lena looked more relaxed than the last time I'd seen her.

"How are you feeling?" I whispered while the men debated which magical creatures they thought were most dangerous.

"I'm doing well," Lena replied with a smile. "Ana Luisa has been wonderful in allowing me to live here. She's become like a mother to me. Some memories have started to resurface since I've been here."

"That's great to hear," I replied.

"Yes, I'm starting to remember a few things about growing up. By living here, my mind is finally recalling some things I'd forgotten," Lena replied.

"Do you remember anything from the time you went missing?" I asked hesitantly, holding my breath. I didn't mean to pry, but Lena was the only person I knew who had managed to escape the

W.A.S.P. If she could remember anything about her imprisonment, it might help prevent future attacks.

Lena paused and shook her head. "No, that part of my memory has been blocked from me. I'm sorry, but I don't remember what happened or what they did to me," Lena said, her face clouding.

"I'm sorry to ask about your terrifying experience. I was only wondering because of the work I'm currently doing for Mr. Barber," I said.

"Just please be careful, Jane. The W.A.S.P. are dangerous, and even though I can't remember what happened to me, I know it was awful. I couldn't stand it if you were captured by them."

"I'm aware of the dangers, but I want to stay one step ahead of them. The job I'm doing for Mr. Barber has already prevented an attack. I feel responsible for the increased pixie attacks since the W.A.S.P. are searching for me," I answered.

"Jane, you shouldn't feel responsible. The W.A.S.P. has always hunted pixies. I just want you to be careful. Especially if you are working for Arnold Barber. I wouldn't trust that man. Promise me you won't drop your guard when working with him."

27

An Unexpected Meeting

THE NEXT FEW days were enjoyable. Miguel and Josefina's aunt and uncle had arrived, so the house was a flurry of activity. Uncle Fernando was Carlos's younger brother, and they looked very much alike, except Uncle Fernand's hair was darker. Aunt Teresa was a tall, thin woman with light brown hair and greenish-hazel eyes. They were both very kind and had brought a carriage full of Christmas presents. They didn't have any children of their own, so they spoiled their niece and their nephews.

Uncle Fernando had been living in Egypt for several years while working on an archeological dig, but now he was planning a new project. He wanted to find the lost city of Atlantis, and Miguel was in his glory talking about it. Carlos didn't seem pleased about his brother's plans and was even less so about the fact that his son wanted to join the expedition.

"Fernando, we both know the city of Atlantis is a myth and even if it existed, it was destroyed by magic thousands of years ago," Carlos scoffed. "Stop filling my son's head with nonsense."

Fernando just laughed and continued to discuss archeology with Miguel. Though Carlos disagreed with his brother's career choice, they got along fairly well. Every day at the house was full of laughter.

Despite all the fun activities, I still made time to practice my *transfiguration charm* so I'd be ready for Wednesday. What Lena told me made me slightly nervous, but I wasn't spying on the W.A.S.P. with Mr. Barber. Though I was doing the work for him, he wouldn't be joining me. I was confident Phillip would keep me safe, and I was lucky for his presence when I went to the *Dew Drop Inn*.

At eleven o'clock on Wednesday morning, Phillip arrived at the Martinez house to pick me up. I didn't realize how excited I was to see him until he walked through the door.

"Good morning, Miss Fitzgerald," he stated as I descended the marble staircase. "Are you ready to head out for the day?"

"Yes. Let me just grab my coat from the closet," I replied, walking over to the coat closet.

When I pulled my coat from the hanger, Phillip took it off me, holding it open so I could put my arms through. His fingertips lightly grazed the back of my neck when he pulled the coat onto my shoulders. I thanked him for his help and ducked into the sitting room to tell the Martinez family I was leaving. They all wore worried expressions and wished me luck.

Phillip held the front door open, then escorted me to his waiting carriage.

"How is your stay with the Martinez family?" Phillip asked, climbing up beside me.

"It's wonderful. They make me feel like I belong in their family," I replied.

Phillip shrugged his shoulders, snapping the reins. "You never know. It could be a possibility."

"What do you mean?" I asked.

"You spend a lot of time with Josefina and Miguel," Phillip began, and I suddenly knew what he was getting at. I started to laugh.

"You mean Miguel and me?" I said between chuckles. "No. As much as Josefina would love me to be her sister-in-law, Miguel and I are just friends."

"Sometimes friends can become the best matches," Phillip joked, steering the horses onto the road.

"Well, not for Miguel and me. We don't think of each other in that way. Josefina tried placing a *love charm* on us in our second year. We were both furious at her," I said.

Phillip chuckled, pulling his pixie dust case from his pocket. He pulled the horses to a secluded area and extracted a *teleportation charm*.

"Are you ready to go to Jewel Caverns?" he asked.

"Yes. Thank you again for picking me up early so we could travel there. This is the first year I have spent the holidays with my friends. Now that I've made some money, I would like to do something nice for all of them. So, I really appreciate you escorting me there."

"You're welcome, Jane. It's my pleasure," Phillip said, casting the charm, and the world darkened.

Jewel Caverns was lively because of the holiday season, and the streets were crowded. Phillip and I went into the different shops as I hunted for the perfect gifts. I found a lovely earring and necklace set for Josefina. The stones were a beautiful shade of red, her favorite color, and I also bought her a soft fur muff, which was charmed so the wear's hands would never get cold.

In the same shop, I found jewelry made from seashells, which I purchased for Kairi since I knew how much she missed the sea. I also found an aqua-green shawl that felt softer than silk between my fingers. It reminded me of the ocean, and the color was a mixture of both Kairi's and Zachary's eye colors. For Zachary, I purchased a navy-blue ascot cap with a matching scarf, and for Miguel's present, I was delighted to find a magnified glass set charmed to magnify even the smallest objects. I also found a few books I knew Miguel would love.

Though Taylor was not joining us for the holidays, I still searched for a present for her. I found a few books at *Paper and Ink* that I thought she would be interested in, and I also purchased a necklace with blue stones that matched Taylor's eyes. The necklace was simple, but it looked like something Taylor would wear.

Since the Martinez family had been so kind to host me over the Christmas holiday, I picked up a few things for Carlos and Ana Luisa, Fernando and Teresa, and Juan and Lena. Phillip patiently escorted me to each store and waited while I shopped for everyone on my list. When I was almost finished, Phillip told me he would find a place to have a late lunch/early dinner before the W.A.S.P. meeting. I agreed to meet him outside *Mr. Murray's* in ten minutes, and I smiled because his absence would allow me just enough time to find a Christmas present for him.

After much debating, I purchased a silver watch for Phillip. I'd never seen him wearing one and only remembered him having a small pocket watch, not a wristwatch. The watch was a smaller version of a pixie clock, able to display the date. I was surprised to discover that you could set the time of upcoming appointments, and the watch would remind you of your schedule. I hoped Phillip would like it. I wanted to get him something nice for everything he had done for me and continued to do.

I finished in the store and walked out onto the main road. I headed in the direction of *Mr. Murray's Clothing Store*. I knew I would be a few minutes early, but I'd rather be early than late. I rounded a corner, following the road. The sidewalks were not as crowded here, and I noticed Phillip was already waiting for me. He was slightly turned away, so he hadn't seen me.

I was just about to cross the street and alert Phillip to my presence when a young woman came running toward him, throwing her arms around him. I paused, startled by the display of affection this stranger was showing. He seemed startled at first, but then he recognized the dark-haired beauty. She pulled away from him and clutched his hands as she spoke animatedly. I was unsure of what to do. I stood on the opposite side of the street, frozen. My heart felt like it was beating in my throat, and for some strange reason, my neck and cheeks felt hot. Phillip had never mentioned a woman in his life. However, despite how close we had grown, I supposed it probably wouldn't have been appropriate for him to discuss his personal matters.

I wasn't sure why I felt sick all of a sudden. I took a deep breath and tried to talk myself into crossing the street, but my feet stayed immobile. My body had a strange desire to flee, but before I could analyze my peculiar feelings, I heard my name being called.

My head snapped up, and my eyes made contact with Phillip's. He had finally noticed me. He called my name again and beckoned me to cross the street. Thankfully, my legs snapped into action, and I quickly crossed the cobblestone road. I hoped he had only called me twice. I didn't want to feel even more mortified than I already did. It wasn't long before I stood before Phillip and his female companion.

The young woman had silky dark brown hair, stunning green eyes, and a small, perfectly shaped nose. Her waist was thin, and she was four or five inches taller than me. She was even more beautiful on this side of the street, and again, my heart lurched in my chest. I forced what I thought was a convincing smile and mentally reprimanded myself for feeling the way I did.

"Jane, you're right on time. I want to introduce you to someone very important to me," Phillip began as I stared between him and the woman.

My neck felt coated in sweat. After her show of affection in such a public setting, I should have already assumed this woman was important to him. Was she someone he had been courting or even a fiancé, perhaps?

"Jane Fitzgerald, allow me to introduce you to Charlette Withermyer, my sister," Phillip stated enthusiastically.

His sister? My mind took a moment to catch up, but thankfully, my hand extended toward Miss Withermyer.

"It's so nice to meet you, Miss Withermyer," I replied, my heart beginning to slow.

"Please call me Lettie. Everyone does," the young woman said sweetly.

Now that I knew they were related, I could see the similarities. They had the same green eyes, and she was as stunningly beautiful as he was handsome. This time, when I smiled at her, it was genuine.

"Lettie was telling me that she just finished her Christmas shopping," Phillip said.

"Yes, and I was so surprised to run into my brother! You never fully explained what you were doing here," Lettie said, giving Phillip a hard stare.

I was about to answer when Phillip cleared his throat. "I've had a few last-minute things to pick up myself, and Miss Fitzgerald needed transportation to the Jewel Caverns."

"Since when did you become so thoughtful, Phillip?" Lettie teased.

Phillip just shook his head. "Well, it was nice running into you, sis, but we should be on our way."

Lettie's hand darted out incredibly quickly and grabbed his arm. "Do you have somewhere pressing to be? We would love to have you join us for lunch. Dad would be so happy to see you, and Bridgette promised to stop over today," Lettie pleaded.

"Jane and I have an obligation," Phillip began, but Lettie was already turning toward me.

"Please come by for lunch! Everyone has to eat, so why not come over? Plus, I would love to get to know Miss Fitzgerald and hear how my brother has become such a gentleman all of a sudden," she replied excitedly. I couldn't help but smile. "I can tell you want to come!" Lettie added, smiling back at me.

"Now, Charlette, Jane, and I do have somewhere to be," Phillip began, and Lettie's mouth turned down into a pout.

"Not until this evening, though," I found myself saying, and Phillip turned to stare at me. Lettie's eyes brightened again. She had looked so hopeful, and something about her had tugged at my soul. I didn't want to disappoint her.

"I was trying to save you from the insufferable charms of my sister, Miss Fitzgerald, but it appears I've been overruled. Very well, we accept your invitation," Phillip sighed as his sister beamed with joy.

Charlette quickly looped her arm through mine and began leading me down the street to where Phillip had parked our carriage.

"I'm so glad that you agreed to come for lunch. I hardly ever see Phillip when he's working at the Jelf Academy. He's been so busy lately. You'd think he would have more time around the holidays," Lettie commented, prancing along by my side.

When we reached the carriage, Phillip placed my bag in the storage compartment before helping Lettie and me on board. I couldn't believe the slight turn of events and the fact I was seated across from Phillip's youngest sister. My heart hammered slightly at the thought of meeting Phillip's father and his other sister. I was completely out of sorts today, and I didn't understand why. Before I could analyze my thoughts, I was told to hold on as Lettie cast a *teleportation charm* over the carriage.

❧

"Father and Bridgette will be so pleased to see you," Lettie gushed as the carriage passed a snow-covered forest. "Like I told Jane, we hardly ever see you anymore."

"Dr. Tweedle has been keeping me busy, and other assignments have needed my attention," Phillip replied.

"Jane, as I'm sure you already know, my brother is a genius whose life has been wrapped up in his profession since he started the Jelf Academy. Dr. Tweedle can't have you working on too much. It is the Christmas holiday," Lettie said with a sigh while the carriage made its way up a short driveway.

We steadily approached a pleasant-looking house with a decent-sized porch attached to the front. The house wasn't enormous, but it looked homey and comfortable. I sensed Phillip watching my face as I stared out the window. This must've been the home he'd grown up in. As I returned his gaze, I could sense how important it was to him. When the horses slowed to a stop, Phillip leapt from the carriage.

"Welcome to my childhood home, Miss Fitzgerald," he murmured as I stepped onto the hard-packed snow.

Lettie bounded up the front steps and flung the front door open. "Father, you'll never suspect whom I ran into at the Jewel Caverns!" I heard her cry.

Phillip held my arm so I wouldn't slip on the front steps, and we crossed the porch. I stepped into the foyer, Phillip right behind me. The entrance hall was narrow because a set of stairs was on the left side. The parlor was on the right, and the entrance hallway led back to a kitchen. Phillip had only just closed the front door when a man approached. He had gray hair and hazel eyes. I knew he had to be Phillip's father because they had very similar features. He had a strong, confident gait; his mouth was only slightly curved, and I couldn't tell if it was a grimace or a smile.

"Good afternoon, Phillip. What do we owe this pleasure?" he asked, allowing his lips to form into a small smile.

"Lettie bumped into me at the Jewel Caverns, and she invited us to come by for lunch," Phillip responded.

"Are you going to introduce me to this delightful young lady, or are you just going to stand in my foyer all day?" the man demanded, faking a stern voice.

"Dad, this is Miss Jane Fitzgerald. Jane, this is my father, Brennon Withermyer," Phillip said as I extended my hand.

"It's a pleasure to meet you, sir," I replied, shaking the elder Mr. Withermyer's hand.

"The pleasure is mine if you can take credit for persuading my son to come to visit his family," Brennon Withermyer stated.

I could feel myself blushing slightly as I responded. "I'm afraid I can't take the credit for that. Lettie is the one who's responsible."

The elder, Mr. Withermyer, looked doubtful. "Yes, my youngest can be very influential when she really wants something. Miss Fitzgerald, allow me to take your coat, and you can head back to the kitchen. Bridgette is already here and is putting out lunch. Please make yourself at home."

Phillip helped me remove my coat and handed it to his father. Then, after he shed his ulster, he led me toward the kitchen. The narrow hallway opened to a bright kitchen with a large bay window facing the back of the house. Beneath the window was a cozy breakfast nook. Lettie was already seated at the table along with another gentleman.

The man had short, dirty blonde hair, trimmed sideburns, and a dark golden handlebar mustache. His blue eyes crinkled as he chuckled at something Lettie said. The man appeared to be in his early thirties, and I wondered how he was connected to the family. My eyes were pulled away from the table at the sound of an infant. A tall woman with black hair and hazel green eyes crossed the kitchen with a little dark-haired boy in her arms. Her eyes landed on Phillip, and she stopped short.

"Finally found some time to visit your family?" the woman said snidely.

"Bridgette, don't be so mean," Lettie chided, rising from her chair and taking the baby from her sister's arms.

Bridgette crossed her arms and glared at Phillip. "He's always too busy for us, so I'm wondering why today is different."

"Now, Bridgette dear, please don't start," the blonde man said. "It seems we also have a guest." The man rose from his seat, his blue eyes on me.

Phillip stepped to the side, allowing me to fully enter the room. "This is Miss Jane Fitzgerald. Jane, I would like you to meet my brother-in-law, Mr. Sawyer Lunsford, my nephew, Weston, and my other sister, Mrs. Bridgette Lunsford."

"It's a pleasure to meet you," Mr. Lunsford replied, crossing the room to shake my hand. His hand felt firm, warm, and friendly.

Bridgette still glared at Phillip as she stepped forward to shake my hand. Lettie bounced baby Weston on her hip and resumed her seat at the table.

"What is everyone standing around for?" Phillip's father asked, walking by us and into the kitchen. "Please have a seat, Miss Fitzgerald," he said, pulling out a chair for me.

I gratefully sat down. "Thank you. Please call me Jane," I insisted.

Phillip took the chair beside me, and Mr. Lunsford resumed his seat. Phillip's father helped Bridgette bring the rest of the food to the table. Then he sat down at the head of the table, leaving the chair between Lettie and Sawyer Lunsford open for Bridgette.

"I don't recall hearing the name Fitzgerald within the pixie community," Mr. Lunsford said curiously.

"Yes, you wouldn't have heard that last name," I replied. I paused for a moment, unsure of how Phillip's family would receive my heritage. Being a half-human was part of me, and I didn't think I should be ashamed, no matter what others thought. "My father was a human, and my mother was a pixie. Her last name was McCalski."

The sound of utensils hitting the floor had me gazing across the kitchen at Bridgette. She had a shocked expression as she stared at Phillip and me. "Did I hear you correctly? Your mother was Rachel McCalski?"

28

UNSIMILAR SISTERS

B RIDGETTE'S STARE WAS piercing as she waited for my
response.

"Yes," I said slowly. "My mother was Rachel McCalski."

"Oh, Phillip, wasn't Rachel that old school friend of yours,"
Lettie commented, oblivious to Bridgette's cold stare.

Phillip met his elder sister's eye and subtly shook his head
before he redirected his gaze toward his youngest sister. "Yes, she
was a friend of mine, Lettie," he replied softly.

Bridgette maintained her cold demeanor as she bent down to
retrieve the fallen silverware. She tossed them into the sink and
opened a drawer to collect clean utensils. Her mouth was a hard
line as she stalked toward the table. "You must be fairly young if
your mother was Rachel McCalski," she said.

I could feel color coming to my cheeks, and I wasn't sure why.
"I will turn twenty in two months," I replied. I couldn't understand why Bridgette seemed so hostile or why my age seemed like
a shameful thing.

"We were so sorry to hear about your mother's disappearance
and then her passing," Phillip's father said. His eyes were kind.

"Your mother was a dear friend of Phillip's, and he took the loss very hard."

I wondered if Phillip's father knew the extent of Phillip's feelings for my mother. However, from Bridgette's attitude, I was sure she knew. I tore my eyes away from Bridgette and looked toward Brennon Withermyer.

"Thank you for your kind words, Mr. Withermyer. I don't remember my mother. She passed away when I was only a year old. It's nice to be acquainted with people who knew her. I love hearing stories about her. Through others, I'm able to become close to her," I replied.

Lettie looked at me with understanding in her eyes, and I gave her a slight smile.

"My wife passed away twenty-five years ago. Phillip was ten, Bridgette was four, and Lettie was a newborn. You never get over a loss like that," Brennon Withermyer said with a shake of his head. "I've told my children stories about their mother, especially my girls since they were so young at the time. I'm sure your father has done the same for you."

I could see Phillip tense in the chair beside me, but I wasn't offended by his father's words. The Withermyers would have no way of knowing.

"Unfortunately, my father passed when I was five years old, so we didn't have much time together for him to tell me many stories," I replied.

The Withermyers all became somber. Lettie leaned across the table and touched my hand. "Jane, I'm so sorry," she said.

"Thank you. I'm sorry you've also lost a parent. I'm sure your mother was a wonderful woman," I said.

"As I'm sure the same could be said about your parents," Lettie said with a soft smile.

Bridgette took a seat and motioned for Lettie to hand her the baby. From her expression, I assumed she disagreed. She didn't glance at me but instead began bouncing the baby in her lap.

"So, Phillip, what brought you and Miss Fitzgerald to the Jewel Caverns?" Brennon Withermyer asked.

"Apparently, Miss Fitzgerald is turning your son into a gentleman. He supposedly offered to escort Jane while she finished her Christmas shopping," Lettie responded before Phillip could reply.

Brennon Withermyer chuckled deeply, pouring himself another cup of coffee. "I'm liking Miss Jane Fitzgerald even more by the second," he said, adding cream and a little sugar to his cup.

I thought I saw Bridgette rolling her eyes at her father's outburst, but it happened so quickly I couldn't be sure. When I glanced at her again, her focus was solely on the infant in her lap.

"Why do you all believe that Phillip isn't a gentleman?" I asked with a laugh.

Bridgette's eyes darted to mine, and I realized I had referred to Phillip by his first name. I could tell she was calculating how we could be on such familiar terms. I could feel my cheeks coloring slightly, but none of the other family members seemed to notice.

"My brother is moody and likes to be left alone," Lettie said in a teasing voice. "He is not one for social graces, which is why I was so surprised to see him at the Jewel Caverns, especially accompanied by someone else."

"Being too busy to venture out does not make me a cad, Lettie," Phillip responded. "Nor does being alone."

"I've never seen you volunteer to escort the fairer sex out shopping before," Lettie pressed.

"My Christmas shopping isn't the only reason I was being accompanied today," I said in Phillip's defense before I speared a piece of fruit on my plate.

"Oh, that's right! You did mention an obligation," Lettie said excitedly.

"It's just something Dr. Tweedle assigned," Phillip quickly answered. "Nothing to be overly concerned or excited about."

I glanced briefly at Phillip and continued eating the turkey sandwich. I wasn't sure why Phillip would lie to his family about what we'd be doing tonight. Dr. Tweedle certainly didn't approve of me working for Mr. Barber. Perhaps he didn't want to worry them.

"So secretive," Lettie tsked, but she didn't press for more information.

For the remainder of lunch, the family discussed their plans for Christmas. Phillip commented on how big Weston was getting, and Lettie gossiped about neighbors and distant family members. For the most part, the Withermyers were very warm and welcoming. Bridgette was the only one who didn't say very much. When lunch was over, Bridgette headed upstairs to put Weston down for a nap, and I offered to help Lettie clean up the dishes. The men excused themselves to the sitting room.

Lettie's personality was so infectious it was easy for me to like her instantly. She loved to talk, and as we cleaned, she told me about her family while also asking questions about me. I was amazed at how easy it was to open up to her, and our conversation flowed so easily. She seemed to be the complete opposite of her sister. I was glad we had run into her at the Jewel Caverns and that she invited us to lunch.

When we finished the dishes, Lettie and I sat back down at the kitchen table.

"Thank you for your help," Lettie said.

"You're welcome. I should be the one thanking you for inviting us. It was delicious," I responded.

"It's so nice to see Phillip. We really do wish he would visit more often. I understand he's busy at the Jelf Academy, and finding the time is hard. Though our father would never say it, I know he's proud of Phillip. Our mother's death was difficult for everyone, and I know it strained their relationship," Lettie said with a slight shake of her head.

"I'm sorry to hear that," I replied. "I'm glad I met you today. Family is so important, and I'm pleased that we convinced Phillip to come for lunch."

Lettie smiled widely, causing her dimples to show. "I was so surprised to see Phillip. Like I said earlier, he likes to keep to himself. I've never seen him look so happy in public," Lettie commented. "Honestly, he hasn't seemed happy in a long time."

"When we first met, he wasn't pleasant," I said with a grin.

"I can imagine," she laughed. "Have you known him long?"

"I've only been acquainted with him for three and a half years, and for most of that time, he wasn't very personable. However, I've noticed a big change in him recently," I commented.

We both sat in contemplative silence for a few moments.

"You're very pretty," Lettie said out of the blue, startling me.

"Thank you," I stammered, feeling myself redden.

"Your eyes are such a nice shade of violet. I think I've only seen that eye color one other time," Lettie mused.

"You've met someone with violet eyes like mine?" I asked.

"Yes, I was very young at the time, maybe four years old at the most, and it was around the holidays. I could be wrong since it was such a long time ago, but I think some friends of Phillip's stopped by to wish him a Merry Christmas." Lettie shook her head, her eyes lost in memory.

"Do you remember anything else about them?" I asked.

Lettie shook her head. "All I remember is that one of the girls had eyes just like yours."

"It was most likely my mother. I've never heard of anyone else having eyes like mine," I replied.

"I'm sorry I can't remember much," Lettie said.

"That's okay. It was a long time ago," I replied.

"Since Phillip started at the Jelf Academy at such a young age, I don't know much about his life or friends. He's also ten years my senior, so even if he had attended school at the proper time, I still probably wouldn't know," Lettie said with a shrug.

Just as I was about to inquire about Phillip's life after the academy, Phillip walked back into the kitchen.

"You ladies aren't gossiping about me, are you?" he asked, his green eyes glinting knowingly as if he'd caught us doing something horrible.

"So, what if we are?" Lettie said defiantly. "Are you worried about Miss Fitzgerald finding out something embarrassing?"

"I'm sure you've managed to cover all that in your first few minutes alone with Jane, dear sister," Phillip responded.

Lettie laughed. "I'm sure I could think of a few more things to tell her."

Phillip shook his head, and his green eyes found mine. "I hate to interrupt whatever information my devious little sister is divulging, but we should really be on our way."

Lettie frowned as I rose from my seat. "So soon, Phillip?" she grumbled. "I was rather enjoying Jane's company."

"Unfortunately, we must be on our way. Lunch was wonderful, and I appreciated the invite," Phillip replied.

"This is still your home, Phillip. You're welcome at any time, even more so if you bring Jane along," Lettie said, and I could feel myself blushing.

"It was very nice meeting you. Thank you for having me," I said, turning toward Lettie.

"It was my pleasure. Don't be a stranger, Jane. I'm so glad to have met you. Let me know if you ever need anything," Lettie said with a smile. "Let me give you this address. Perhaps we can finish our conversation in writing or with a *calling charm*." She glanced at Phillip with a wicked expression before she darted off to get paper.

"Maybe coming here was a mistake. I forgot how bad an influence my sister can be," Phillip said, shaking his head but smiling.

I followed him down the hallway toward the front door, and Phillip retrieved my coat from the closet. Mr. Withermyer and Mr. Lunsford stood in the front entryway, and Bridgette and the baby were behind them in the sitting room. Apparently, Weston had refused to lie down for his nap.

"It was our pleasure to meet you, Miss Fitzgerald," Mr. Withermyer stated, grasping my hand. Mr. Lunsford nodded in agreement, but Bridgette stayed in the sitting room with the baby.

"Thank you for lunch. It was delicious, and it was positively delightful to make your acquaintance," I replied.

Phillip reached for the front door as Lettie came bounding back down the hall. She thrust a folded paper into my hands and threw her arms around me. I returned the hug, and after a moment, Lettie stepped back with a smile.

"Goodbye, Phillip, we love you," Lettie called as Phillip held the door open for me.

"I love you too. Goodbye," Phillip replied before closing the door behind him.

We walked to the edge of the porch, and Phillip extended his arm to me. I rested my hand in the crook of his elbow, and we descended to the waiting carriage. I glanced back at the Withermyer house and felt sad we had to leave. For the most part, Phillip's family had been so welcoming, and I'd enjoyed talking with Lettie. I wondered why Phillip didn't visit as often.

Once Phillip had flicked the reins to get the horses moving, I turned to look at him. "Your family seemed lovely," I said.

His eyes flicked to mine while he steered the carriage down the driveway. "They have their moments," he replied with a shrug.

"Well, I had a wonderful time, and I'm glad you agreed to go. Your sister, Lettie, is so delightful."

Phillip chuckled, adjusting his grip on the reins. "I don't know if you should be that generous."

"Why do you say such things? Lettie was so welcoming and sweet," I replied.

"My family is overwhelming sometimes. Lettie can be outrageous, and Bridgette can be aloof. My father was in a decent enough mood today, but we don't get on very well most days. He criticizes my career choice, and it always seems like he's expecting more from me. He doesn't act like that toward my sisters. Everything they do is always perfect. Then they wonder why I don't come home very often."

"Lettie told me your father was proud of you. You have a very successful career at the Jelf Academy. Why would your father be upset about that?" I asked.

"My father has never told me he was proud of me. Since I attended the academy at a young age, my father anticipated something great. He wanted me to get a job in the government or work as a healer, anything he thought was important. When I told him I wanted to become a teacher, he wasn't happy," Phillip said. His eyes held a faraway look. He seemed disheartened to be talking about his father's opinions.

"Well, if it's any consolation, I think you're a great instructor," I said, lifting my hand to his arm.

"I don't think you always had that opinion of me," Phillip said.

I hesitated a moment before I spoke again. "No, I didn't, but you've changed. I wouldn't be able to do some of those advanced charms without your tutelage. Besides, your self-defense lessons could save my life one day."

"Let's pray to the gods that you'll never need them and that my charm lessons will be enough," Phillip said, pulling the carriage into the woods. "We should begin preparing for tonight's meeting and have faith that nothing goes wrong."

29

A Nest of Information

THE *Dew Drop Inn* appeared darker inside than the first time Phillip and I had been there. We were disguised as a younger couple this time and picked a table toward the back, as near to the back room as we could manage. My blonde hair was now a dark shade of brown, and my violet eyes were a light hazel. Phillip had transformed into a thinner man with long reddish-brown hair that he tied away from his face. His eyes looked small and droopy and were a light shade of blue.

My eyes darted to the back room. From my vantage point, it looked empty. Phillip and I had arrived early this time in hopes of noting how many men would attend and what they looked like. I wondered what tonight's discussion would be about and if the W.A.S.P. had selected another location. In a month, had Seth O'Doherty found another pixie captive?

The same waitress from the first time came over to take our order. We ordered something to drink, and she hurried to collect our beverages. It wasn't long before she returned, both of us choosing something light to eat. I wasn't terribly hungry after my big lunch with the Withermyers. As soon as the waitress left, I pulled a *heightened hearing charm* out of my coat pocket and subtly tipped it into my drink before handing the remaining charm to Phillip. It didn't take long for the charm to take effect. The *Dew Drop Inn* became increasingly loud, and I practiced focusing on different areas of the room while we waited for the W.A.S.P. to arrive.

My attention was pulled to the door a few minutes later when a group of men entered. They were all wearing ulster coats in varying shades of gray, brown, and blue. Most of the men wore bowler hats, which some removed upon entering the tavern. The bartender appeared to recognize the group, and I heard him greet them warmly.

"Welcome! Here for another monthly meeting?" he asked pleasantly.

One of the men nodded in agreement. "Yes, I assume Mr. Doyle told you of our arrival and booked the private room in the back."

"Yes, he did. Mary will show you back," the bartender answered as the waitress appeared at his side.

Mary collected a handful of menus and led the group toward the back. I noticed a lot of the men were younger, probably ranging from twenties to mid-thirties. Only a few seemed to be in their forties and fifties. I tried not to blatantly study them as they walked by. However, I noticed on the lapel of each man's coat was a tiny pin in a honeycomb shape with an insect pictured in the center: the symbol of the W.A.S.P.

My eyes scanned the group, counting about ten to twelve of them. I didn't get a good look at each man since they were in such a large group, but I did notice that Seth was not among them. My ears perked up, trying to decipher the many conversations going on at once, but I didn't catch anything about pixies or magic. I was sure they wouldn't discuss those topics where human ears could overhear.

I heard the scrapping of chairs as each man took a seat at the table, and then I heard Mary's voice as she began passing out menus and taking drink orders. I caught Phillip's eyes across the table. I could tell he was concentrating, too. Even though Phillip was wearing a stranger's face, he somehow managed to produce a familiar expression as he reached for his glass.

"You have the blankest stare. Try to act naturally," Phillip whispered, his voice obviously sounding louder.

"I'm sorry," I replied with a smile. "It's so easy to get lost in thought."

"I know, but we don't need to draw attention to ourselves," Phillip whispered back, and I nodded.

I was trying to think of a topic of conversation so it would look like we were discussing something when the door to the tavern opened. Seth O'Doherty strode in with a confident air. A bowler hat covered his blonde hair, and he wore a gray coat similar to the other men. Even in the dimly lit room, the scar on his left cheek was visible. He reached up, removing his hat and running his hand through his slicked-back hair.

"Mr. O'Doherty, good to see you again," the bartender called out.

Seth nodded and said hello as Mary emerged from the back room. I noted how Seth's eyes flicked to the waitress as she approached with a smile.

"Mr. O'Doherty, your party is already situated in the back room. What can I get you to drink?" she asked.

"Scotch, and you know just how I like it, darling," Seth responded with a wink.

Mary moved behind the bar, and Seth continued toward the back room. I tried not to look at him as he came closer. His gait had a swagger, and I wondered if it was part of his personality or if he had new information. Then, at the last second, my eyes betrayed me and floated upward toward his face. They met his evil hazel ones, and he gave me a slight smirk before disappearing into the back room. My body involuntarily shuttered.

"Captain O'Doherty, you've finally arrived," one of the men said.

"Yes, and it seems like this meeting can begin since everyone else appears to be here. As you all know, during Major Doyle's absence, he has named me the overseer of these meetings until his return. Our first order of business is new recruits. Has anyone been successful?"

"A few boys have come of age recently in my hometown. I've been trying to convince them to join our cause," someone said.

"So, you haven't convinced them?" Seth replied condescendingly.

"No, Captain. It's been hard procuring enough evidence to win them over."

"That is not acceptable, Lieutenant Davis. If you were better a pixie hunter, you would have enough proof to convince anyone that pixies exist and must be exterminated. Major Doyle won't be impressed with your efforts. Has anyone else been successful?" Seth spat out.

Even though I wasn't sure which man was Lieutenant Davis, I filed away that name in my brain.

"I have a few men who have pledged themselves to my units," a gruff voice said.

"How many are a few, Captain Johnson?" Seth demanded.

"Ten," Johnson replied stiffly.

"Ten is better than Lieutenant Davis's 'potentials,' but ten is still not a large number. Has no one managed more than ten new recruits?"

The room fell silent. After a few moments, someone coughed, but no one else admitted to obtaining more than ten new members.

"This is very disappointing, gentlemen. Major Doyle will be most annoyed to hear of this when I send him this meeting's minutes," Seth said after a long sigh.

"We require new members because of the last disaster. If I recall, wasn't that attack planned around intel that you received from a filthy captive of yours?" one of the men said.

"The folly of Coillewood was not something we have on the agenda for tonight," Seth spat.

"However, that disaster is why we lost so many men. You were the one leading the attack. Tell me, Captain O'Doherty, how many men you have found for replacements? It's your fault that we need them," the same man answered.

"I'll have you know, Lieutenant Marchberg, I have a gala planned to recruit over one hundred new men to the cause. I've been working my ass off to replenish our lost resources. I've already discussed Coillewood with Major Doyle, and it is not on our agenda. Don't forget that I outrank you, Marchberg. Until you produce suitable results concerning anything in this association, you don't have the authority to question me!"

The room fell silent, and I wondered if it was because of Seth's outburst or because Mary had returned with a large tray of drinks.

"Here, gentlemen, don't mind me," the waitress said sweetly.

I heard the clink of glasses, but none of the men continued speaking.

Finally, after a few moments, Mary spoke. "I'll be back in a few moments if anyone would like to order something to eat. Let me know if you need anything else."

I watched Mary emerge, and she stopped at our table to refill our drinks. Phillip and I exchanged a few words so it would look like we had been in the middle of discussing something. By the time Mary left our table, the men in the back room had resumed the conversation.

"Has anyone gained information on a new location?" Seth questioned.

"I've been tracking a family that I'm pretty sure are pixies. I haven't mounted an attack yet. Once I know for certain, I plan to capture them for questioning," the man I was sure was Lieutenant Davis said eagerly.

"Hopefully, this venture is more fruitful than your plans for recruitment," Seth sneered. "When you are certain of these people, please let me know. I would be happy to assist in their capture and questioning."

"Of course, Captain O'Doherty. You will be the first to know. I have much to learn from your methods of questioning."

"How are you investigating this family?" Seth questioned. "We wouldn't want them to suspect anything before you're ready to strike."

"The daughter is very comely for a potentially vile creature, so I've visited under the guise of trying to court her," the man answered.

"Very well, Lieutenant Davis. That's not a bad way to gain access to the family's home. It's amazing how some of these beasts seem so pleasing to the eye. I often wonder if it's simply a spell they have us under to lull us into a false sense of security," Seth mused.

"I know they look human, but I don't find the women attractive at all," a man who sounded like Lieutenant Marchberg said snidely.

"You've never seen the ones I've captured then," Seth boasted.

The room fell silent, and I noticed Mary enter with another tray full of drinks and appetizers. I heard the sound of glasses and dishes being placed down and the rustle of her skirt as she made her way around the table. Some men murmured thank you.

"The appetizers are complimentary. I can't have my most loyal customers going hungry in the middle of their monthly meetings. Do you need anything else at the moment?" Mary asked.

"No, that will be all for now," Seth replied, and a few seconds later, Mary exited the room.

There was a pregnant pause as the men listened to Mary's footfalls fade away, and Seth cleared his throat.

"Please tell me there is progress on discovering the McCalski heir."

The room held its silence, and I could hear pacing footsteps.

"Major Doyle was most adamant. He wants this job to be our primary focus."

"How can we even begin to look if we have no information to go on?" Marchberg asked stiffly.

"The McCalski heir has to be somewhere in this general area. The mother was captured in the northeast region," Seth said.

"That doesn't mean anything. It's been years since the General exterminated the woman. The child could be anywhere by now."

I could feel a cold sweat breaking out all over my body. Hearing them discuss my mother so callously made me ill. If the general in this region murdered my mother, did that mean Mr. Wicker had been the general? Before his demise, Mr. Wicker admitted he had not worked alone. Did he give the orders, or had he taken them from someone else?

"No, I'm very certain we're closing in. The girl has to be nearby. My last few captives swore we were close," Seth insisted.

"Maybe the pixies you interrogated were lying. They could've told you anything in an attempt to protect the girl," Lieutenant Marchberg debated.

"Not with how I question my captives," Seth replied with an evil laugh. "Perhaps you should join me next time. I'm currently working on a more powerful device," Seth boasted.

"A more powerful device than the one we already use?" Lieutenant Davis asked in awe.

"Yes. I'm working on something with a more powerful pulse. When I'm finished, we should be able to block pixie magic for a longer period of time, inflict the most pain, and maybe even siphon their powers for our own personal use," Seth said.

"Impossible!" Marchberg cried out. "We've been trying to steal their magic for years, and nothing has ever worked! All we've managed to do is subdue their powers and weaken them long enough for questioning. Each one always succumbs in the end. What makes you think we can suck the magic out and use it for ourselves?"

"Technology is always progressing, Lieutenant Marchberg. If it hadn't been for the discovery of electricity, we would've never been able to subdue these monsters, and it definitely made disposing of them so much easier. You've been questioning me the entire evening, and it's starting to grate on my nerves," Seth seethed.

"I'm only playing the Devil's advocate," Marchberg said nonchalantly.

"I think you've been trying to undermine my authority this entire time! Major Doyle put me in charge and made me his first captain for a reason. He's heard of my plans, and I've informed him of my ideas for a more devastating device. His opinion is the only one you should be worried about, and he's already approved of my suggestions," Seth ranted.

I could tell the rest of the room had fallen silent, and I held my breath, listening for what Seth would say next.

"My apologies, Captain O'Doherty. It was not my intention to undercut your authority," Marchberg replied, but he didn't sound particularly sorry.

"You'll do well not to question me again; otherwise, I'll mention it to Major Doyle. When my new weapon is finalized, I will happily have you along for the first test. By then, Lieutenant Davis should have made some progress with the potential pixie family, and I would love nothing more than to be able to test it on them. So, no one has any leads on the McCalski heir?"

The room was silent for a moment, and Lieutenant Davis spoke. "What age do you believe the heir would be?"

"The mother was exterminated almost twenty years ago. So the girl has to be in her early twenties, if not older," Seth responded.

"The girl I have my eye on is in that age range. Perhaps she'll have information that will prove useful," Davis said enthusiastically.

"Good. Put all your focus into finding out if the girl is a pixie. Perhaps if she's the same age as McCalski's heir, we'll be able to use her. Once you're sure the girl is indeed a pixie, notify me immediately. As I stated earlier, I don't want anything to go wrong with this assignment, especially if you think it could lead us to the heir. I hope for your sake that something comes out of this. Major Doyle will be very pleased if we can make some progress while he is away. If I were you and botched this, I wouldn't consider coming to the next meeting."

30

CHRISTMAS SURPRISES

PHILLIP AND I were quiet as we rode away from the *Dew Drop Inn*. The W.A.S.P. meeting hadn't lasted much longer. The W.A.S.P. didn't seem any closer to discovering my identity or learning of another all-pixie location. As the members cleared out of the backroom, Phillip and I tried to note their appearances without being too obvious. However, the men were silent, and it was hard to determine who was who. Even though we hadn't learned of plans for future attacks, the evening wasn't entirely fruitless.

I shuddered and wasn't entirely sure if it was from the information we had gathered or the cold night. I hoped the poor girl Lieutenant Davis was "courting" was not a pixie. Chances were slim that she actually was since pixies tended to limit their contact with humans. However, there was still a possibility. I wondered what sort of device the W.A.S.P. already used on pixies. Lieutenant Marchberg mentioned that it subdued our powers, and the pixies they used it on perished. What could this weapon do, and how did the W.A.S.P. use it? Unfortunately, I could think of one person who would probably know.

Phillip must've noticed my shiver because he straightened the carriage blanket and reached over to touch my hand.

"They haven't discovered anything new about you. You're still safe, Jane. I promise to do anything that keeps you that way," Phillip insisted, squeezing my hand.

"I know, but it's just so awful. How can they callously kill pixies when we are so similar? Just to hear them talk about their plans and devices makes me sick," I spat out.

"They refer to our kind as beasts. To them, it's as if they're hunting an animal for sport. You don't have to do this anymore if this is too disturbing. We don't need to spy for Mr. Barber. I'll tell him it's too dangerous," Phillip said softly, his thumb making small circles on the top of my hand.

"No. Listening to the W.A.S.P. sickens me, but it must be done. With Drake Doyle living at the manor and being married to my stepsister, I have the best chance. We've discovered more about the W.A.S.P. in the last few months than the pixie government learned in a lifetime," I replied determinedly. "Perhaps one day we'll be able to stop them."

"Okay, as long as you are sure. However, if this gets too dangerous for you, I'll have to insist that you stop," Phillip said firmly.

"I want to be able to end the W.A.S.P. like they believe I can. The look on Arnold Baber's face would be worth it when he realizes the W.A.S.P. was destroyed by a half-pixie. Besides, don't you think we make a good team?" I said, trying to lighten the mood.

Phillip chuckled softly, turning the carriage onto a deserted road, his shoulder brushing mine. "I can't tell if you're the bravest woman I've ever met or the most foolish," he replied, shaking his head and pulling a *teleportation charm* from his pocket. His right hand still held mine, and he pulled the stopper from the vial with his teeth. Before I could respond, he cast the charm over us. His broad smile was the last thing I saw before everything faded to darkness.

⁊

Light shone brightly through my window on Christmas morning when Josefina came bounding into my room to wake me up.

"Merry Christmas, Jane," Josefina called, flopping down on the side of the bed.

I rubbed my eyes and squinted at her. "Good morning and Merry Christmas," I responded, struggling to sit up.

"Get up, sleepy head. The presents are waiting downstairs!" Josefina said, enthusiastically patting my leg.

I couldn't help but laugh at her childish excitement. I hadn't had a proper Christmas since my father, and I barely remembered. I tossed the covers off and swung my legs over the edge of the bed.

"Okay, give me a moment to get dressed," I said, but Josefina shook her head.

"No, just grab your robe! We can get dressed later!" Josefina insisted. "Everyone else is in their pajamas downstairs."

I stood from the bed and crossed the room to where my robe was hanging. My eyes slid to the window. The sun sparkled brilliantly on the freshly fallen snow. It looked magical, and I smiled as I slipped my arms into the robe. While Josefina leapt off the bed and headed toward the door, I quickly brushed through my hair before following her.

Josefina's family was crowded around the large Christmas tree in the sitting room. Kairi and Zachary were also there, and I felt slightly embarrassed to be the last person to wake up. As Josefina said, everyone was in their robes and pajamas. Uncle Fernando and Aunt Teresa were seated on the loveseat, and Carlos was in the big, overstuffed armchair. Ana Luisa was placing a tray of cookies on the coffee table. Miguel, Juan, and Lena were seated on the floor at the base of the tree, and Zachary was standing next to Kairi's wheelchair.

Miguel's eyes were bright as he looked at the Christmas tree.

I could tell he was just as excited as his twin. Kairi looked slightly sleepy, but she had a big smile. She had probably been roused from her bed like I had. Zachary's dark brown hair was standing up at odd angles, but it wasn't unattractive. He noticed my stare and his aqua eyes met mine. Instantly, he smiled as I crossed the room with Josefina. His gaze remained on me as I sat on the floor next to Miguel.

"Merry Christmas," Ana Luisa said, followed by a chorus of greetings from everyone else. "Jane, dear, I'm making coffee, tea, and hot cocoa. Which would you prefer, and how do you take it?" she asked me.

"Coffee, please, with lots of cream and sugar," I responded before she disappeared in the direction of the kitchen.

Uncle Fernando leaned forward and grabbed the cookie tray. He plucked one for himself and then passed the tray around the room. When Josefina passed the plate to me, I selected one of the raspberry tarts. Before I could give the cookies to Kairi, Zachary crossed the room.

"I've got it," he said with another smile. His fingers grazed mine as he took the tray from my hand.

Josefina gave me a sideways glance and raised her eyebrows. Before she could say anything embarrassing, Ana Luisa returned to the room. She went around handing out the mugs before settling down in the other armchair. For a few minutes, everyone sipped their beverages and munched on cookies.

After a few moments, Miguel stood up and cleared his throat. "Who's ready for presents? I'll pass them out!"

"Of course, you can't wait any longer! I could practically see you dying of excitement. I'm surprised you waited this long," Ana Luisa said with a sigh and a roll of her eyes.

"I've been waiting awhile since I was the first one awake. I would've done presents earlier, but you said it was inappropriate to wake our guests, Mother."

"Aren't you the first awake every year?" Aunt Teresa said with a chuckle.

"You would think the boy was five again," Uncle Fernando commented.

Miguel shook off their teasing. "The magic of Christmas dies when you lose the childish excitement," he replied, reaching for a wrapped present. "This one is for Dad." Miguel approached his father and handed him the gift.

Carlos opened the present, which ended up being a nice sweater from Josefina. After that, Miguel continued to hand out presents to each family member. I had placed the gifts I'd purchased under the tree last night, so Miguel also passed those out. Everyone seemed to like what I'd gotten them, and Miquel seemed the most excited about his magnified glass and book about Atlantis. I couldn't remember the last time I actually felt like a member of a family, and I couldn't stop smiling.

I received many wonderful presents. Kairi had gotten me a bathing suit in case I ever got to join her on her father's ships. Zachary gave me a book of poems and a gorgeous silk scarf. From Carlos and Ana Luisa, a fur coat with a matching muff and hat, and Uncle Fernando and Aunt Teresa presented all the girls with jewelry from Egypt. Juan and Lena had gotten me a saddle blanket for Thistle and a pair of riding boots. Miguel and Josefina had enormous smiles when I opened their present. One box contained a silver bangle bracelet decorated with large white stones, and the other had silver earrings with metallic stones. Both pieces of jewelry were stunning, but I didn't understand why the twins looked so excited.

"Thank you, Miguel and Josefina," I responded, touching the gems on the bracelet.

"They're for when you spy on the W.A.S.P.," Miguel began.

"The bracelet has milky quartz, an ingredient in the *invisibility charm*. Though wearing the bracelet won't make you invisible, you'll be less noticeable and able to blend into a crowd. The earrings are made with marcasite and bismuthinite, which I'm sure you know are used in the *heightened hearing charm*," Josefina explained.

"The earrings should work the same way as the charm, so you won't have to cast it," Miguel said.

"I wanted to give them to you earlier so you could use them when you went to the meeting, but Miguel insisted we wait until Christmas," Josefina added.

"Thank you both so much. These will really help, and they're beautiful too!" I said, hugging the twins.

When all the presents had been opened, everyone went to their rooms to bathe and prepare for dinner. After my relaxing bath, I dried my hair and put on my red empire gown with an off-the-shoulder neckline. Then Josefina and I headed down to Kairi's room so we could do each other's hair. Josefina wore a white gown decorated with a holly berry pattern, and Kairi was wearing emerald green to offset her sea-green eyes.

All the men were already in the sitting room when we arrived. Carlos saw us first and began applauding lightly.

"You ladies look exquisite tonight," he commented as he poured out three glasses of champagne and handed one to each of us.

I could feel a blush spreading across my cheeks, and I took a small sip of the pale liquid. Ana Luisa and Aunt Teresa bustled into the room carrying trays of light hors d'oeuvres, and I asked if there was anything I could do to help.

"No, dear, just have a seat and enjoy the evening. Teresa and I have everything handled in the kitchen," Ana Luisa insisted.

I sat on the loveseat next to Josefina, and Kairi sat alongside the armrest on Josefina's other side. Zachary offered his sister the tray of appetizers before circling the back of the couch, coming to sit on the armrest next to me.

"You look lovely tonight, Jane," he said softly.

"Thank you, Zachary. Your tie really brings out the blue of your eyes," I responded before taking another sip of my champagne.

"Did you like the scarf and book of poems?" he asked.

"Yes, the scarf is beautiful, and even though I haven't read any yet, I'm sure the poems will be captivating," I responded.

"Many of the poems reminded me of you," Zachary whispered, but the doorbell rang before I could think of what to say.

Carlos rose from his armchair and went to the front entrance. I could hear the door opening and Carlos's pleasant greeting.

"Phillip Withermyer, so nice of you to come," Carlos's voice boomed. "Let me take your coat."

"The pleasure is all mine," Phillip responded.

The men remained in the front entranceway for a few more moments, and they both entered the sitting room. Phillip looked debonair in his black suit. His facial hair was neatly trimmed, and for some reason, his green eyes looked an even more intense color. I excused myself from my previous conversation and rose to greet him.

"I'm glad to see that you could come. I hope you didn't disregard your family this Christmas," I said.

Phillip shook his head with a laugh. "No, I didn't neglect my family. I joined them for a Christmas brunch this afternoon. Lettie was a tad disappointed that I wasn't staying for dinner, but when she heard I was calling on you, she instantly forgave me. My family sends their regards and wishes you a Merry Christmas," he replied.

"You must share my sentiments and Christmas wishes the next time you see them," I said.

"I will," Phillip told me as he walked over to the empty sofa. We both took a seat, and I angled my body toward him. "I've brought a little something for you," Phillip continued, reaching into the inner pocket of his sports jacket. He pulled out a long, slim, brightly wrapped box.

"I have something for you as well," I replied, jumping up to retrieve his present from under the tree.

I handed Phillip the small box and sat down beside him again.

"Ladies first," Phillip stated, gesturing toward the present in my lap.

Slowly, I unwrapped the box and lifted the lid. On top was a small book, and when I opened the cover, I was startled to see a face very similar to my own. The book contained photographs of my mother from when she attended the Jelf Academy. There were a few subtle differences in our appearances. She had a big smile in all the pictures, and I could tell she was happy. In most of the photos, she was standing next to Irene at school dances. I flipped through, stopping when I came to a picture that included a boy with dark hair and piercing green eyes.

Phillip was taller than my mother, but he was lanky and boyish in the picture. He did not have the broad shoulders and strong jaw he had now. Nevertheless, he was still good-looking for his age, and I wondered exactly how old he had been.

"Look how young you were!" I commented, running my finger down the edge of the picture.

"Yes, I was either thirteen or fourteen," Phillip said, leaning closer to peer at the photograph. "I found these pictures and figured you should have them."

"Thank you, Phillip. This is lovely. I really appreciate this gift. It's one of the best presents I've ever received," I replied, almost leaning over to hug him. I stopped, remembering that we were seated in the Martinez sitting room. Physical contact would probably be considered inappropriate.

"There's something else in the box," Phillip responded, and I reached down to move the layer of tissue paper.

The object underneath looked like a strange belt with two straps. It was made with dark brown leather, and upon further inspection, I saw a pouch between the two straps. An intricately carved wooden handle protruded from it, and when I tugged on the handle, a knife slid free of the sheath. The blade was about five inches long and had a double edge. The steel glinted in the light, and I looked at Phillip quizzically.

"It's an ankle holster with a spear point knife. We've been doing some dangerous work for Arnold Barber. I wanted you to have something to defend yourself with in case your charm work fails you. Besides, you'll be at risk when you return to the manor. With the holster, you can always keep the knife by your side, and no one will know. I'll teach you how to use it during our lessons," Phillip answered.

"Thank you," I said, slipping the knife back into the holster. "I look forward to our next lesson."

Phillip smiled and began tearing the paper off his present. He seemed excited about the watch and immediately slipped it onto his bare left wrist. Phillip was enthusiastically examining the watch's features when I noticed Lena had finally entered the room. I hadn't realized she hadn't been present earlier.

Lena looked absolutely radiant. Her dark brown hair was piled elegantly atop her head, and little diamond pins glittered among the curled tresses. The diamonds in her hair matched the design of her gown, which was white at the bodice, cascading down to a darker blue at the bottom. Rhinestone snowflakes patterned the fabric; she also had snowflake earrings dangling from her ears. I heard a sigh of breath and turned toward the noise to see Juan gaping at Lena, his mouth hanging open. Lena gracefully crossed the room toward Juan, and he quickly rearranged his expression.

I realized the room had gone slightly silent when Lena had entered, and now Uncle Fernando was resuming a story he'd been telling about his time in Egypt. Phillip rose from the couch and retrieved two glasses of champagne. I had taken a couple of sips when Ana Luisa emerged from the kitchen and announced that dinner was ready. Everyone stood and began shuffling into the dining room. Phillip allowed me ahead of him, and I followed Zachary into the doorway.

"Oh, Jane and Zachary are both under the mistletoe," Josefina called behind me.

My eyes drifted up the door frame and came to rest on the tiny sprig of mistletoe tacked in the center. I could feel a blush coming to my cheeks, and it felt like a lead weight had dropped into my stomach. My eyes flicked to Zachary's face, and he looked just as embarrassed. The last time I stood beneath the mistletoe, Robert kissed me, told me he loved me, and gifted me his ring as a promise. The memory seared through me like a hot poker, and I struggled to catch my breath.

Zachary let out a nervous chuckle, and I found myself doing the same. Maybe we could save ourselves from the embarrassment and just move through the doorway. I was about to do that when Uncle Fernando's voice boomed throughout the room.

"What are you waiting for? Kiss the girl!"

Zachary looked down at me, an enormous smile on his face. I supposed a small peck couldn't hurt since I couldn't see any way out of this predicament. Slowly, I inclined my head to some extent and pursed my lips. Zachary leaned toward me, and I felt his hands touch my shoulders. He lowered his lips to mine for what I assumed was going to be a brief kiss. Instead, Zachary's lips moved against mine, deepening the kiss. I attempted to pull away, but his grip was firm, and to further my embarrassment, I heard whoops and cheers. When Zachary decided that I had been thoroughly kissed, he finally let me go.

I continued into the dining room in a daze. I kept my eyes on the ground, too flustered to look at anyone. I took a seat next to Josefina, and Phillip sat on my left. For some reason, I couldn't bring myself to look at him. I shook my head, trying to recover and act naturally. My heartbeat still sounded in my ears, and my breath hitched.

The food had already been laid on the table. Ana Luisa and

Carlos sat at each end of the table, and the rest of the family picked chairs. Miguel sat across from his sister, leaving Zachary to sit across from me since it was easier for Kairi to place her wheelchair at the end of the table. Zachary had a sheepish smile as he stared across the table at me, and I turned my head toward Josefina. I struggled to think of a topic of conversation when Carlos stood from his seat.

"We thank the gods for this Christmas feast. With their blessings, we will hopefully continue to prosper in the upcoming year," he recited, holding his champagne glass aloft.

Once everyone filled their plates, I began to feel normal again. The conversation flowed with ease, and I lost my feelings of awkwardness. Carlos and Uncle Fernando made everyone laugh with tales of past Christmases of their youth. It was nice to enjoy a Christmas dinner for once, surrounded by a loving family. I had never laughed so hard or felt so included. The Martinez family had a special way of making their guests feel at home, and once again, I realized how lucky I was to be acquainted with them.

Dinner was winding down when Juan stood abruptly from his seat. He grasped his champagne flute and cleared his throat.

"If you all don't mind, I wanted to make a toast," he said, glancing around the table.

We grabbed our glasses and gave him our full attention.

"I just wanted to say I'm so grateful for my family and the wonderful friends joining us this evening. The Christmas season is the time to be thankful for everything you have. I've been extremely lucky. It doesn't seem possible for me to be any luckier, but I hope to be wrong on that account. It's why I couldn't think of a better time than Christmas, surrounded by friends and family, to press my good fortune. Lena, I know you can't remember our past together, but I want to believe these last two years have shown you what kind of man I am. I have loved you all my life, and I'm hoping it was possible for you to fall in love with me again." Juan put his glass down, reached into his pocket, and fell to one knee.

"Helena Rodriguez, would you make me the happiest man and marry me?"

The entire table waited with bated breath to see how Lena would respond. Lena's brown eyes filled with tears, a few escaping down her tan cheeks. Her lower lip wobbled a bit, but then she nodded her head.

"Yes, Juan Martinez, I will marry you."

Juan appeared momentarily stunned before Lena flung herself into his arms. He almost fell to the floor from the unexpected force. Everyone broke out into applause as Juan kissed Lena and slipped the ring on her finger. Lena's face was radiant as they both stood. Carlos rose from his seat with his glass of champagne.

"Congratulations to Juan and Lena. Lena, the Martinez family is proud and honored that you will join our family."

"She's already a part of our family!" Ana Luisa exclaimed, raising her glass.

We toasted to Juan and Lena's happiness, and afterward, the family began to meander into the sitting room.

"Leave the dishes, and I'll clean them up later. We have some celebrating to do! My son just got engaged!" Ana Luisa announced, gesturing for everyone to follow her.

I was about to follow when a hand landed on my arm.

"Jane, could I please talk to you for a moment?" Zachary asked.

Caught off guard, I nodded and allowed him to lead me through the other door. Maybe he was going to apologize for the kiss. He stopped in the deserted hallway and clasped my hand. His aqua eyes scanned my face, and I noticed a light sheen of sweat across his brows. He took a deep breath before speaking.

"Jane, I just want you to know how much I appreciate your acceptance of Kairi and keeping her secret. We've never had a friend like you before. I think you are beautiful inside and out. Juan and Lena's love for each other has also emboldened me to share my feelings. I've fallen in love with you, Jane. I thought you were beautiful the first time I saw you, and getting to know you confirmed that your beauty is not only skin-deep. How you care for my sister makes my feelings for you even stronger. I know you've been through so much, and I wanted to give you some time before confessing my feelings, but life is too short, especially with all the recent W.A.S.P. activity. So, after kissing you tonight, I would like to ask your permission to court you," Zachary finished, his face alight with excitement.

I took a deep breath, and my heart clenched. "Zachary, I really like you…." I began but paused when I heard the floor creak in the other room. Zachary obviously wanted this conversation to be private, and I didn't want to publicly break his heart. I waited a few moments until I was sure no one would burst through the door. When I determined it was safe, I continued speaking.

"I'm so sorry. I really like you, but I don't have the same feelings. I genuinely don't want to hurt you, but I never thought of you in that way. You've always been a friend to me. I'm sorry because I don't want to ruin our relationship or make things awkward between us," I said sadly.

Zachary was a wonderful man, and I felt so terrible, but I didn't love him like that.

Zachary hung his head and let go of my hand. "Did I ask you too soon? Is it something I did?" he asked.

"No, you've always been a gentleman. You are a wonderful person. I'm honestly sorry that I don't have romantic feelings. I think you're handsome and smart and so kind, but you're my friend," I said softly.

"I appreciate your honesty even though it hurts," he replied. "I don't want to jeopardize our friendship because I stupidly decided to tell you how I felt."

"It wasn't stupid. It was a very brave thing to do. I really do wish I could feel the same way. You're an amazing man, and how you care for Kairi really says a lot. I don't want our relationship to change, and I promise I won't make things odd between us," I answered.

Zachary nodded and let out a shuttering breath. "I'm glad you aren't repulsed by me and still want to be my friend. I was so hopeful, but I understand."

I patted his shoulder. "I could never be repulsed by you. I'm sure the right person is out there," I replied, my mind going to Taylor. I was pretty sure she had feelings for Zachary, and even if I had any romantic feelings for him, I wouldn't act on them because of her.

"Let's get back to the party before they realize we're gone," Zachary suggested, holding the dining room door open for me.

We entered the sitting room to find everyone still celebrating Juan and Lena's engagement. I glanced around the room and was surprised when I didn't see Phillip. Confused, I approached Josefina.

"Where did Mr. Withermyer go?" I asked her.

"It was very abrupt. Not long after we moved into the sitting room, he thanked us for dinner and announced he had to leave. He apologized for cutting the evening so short and congratulated Juan and Lena before taking his leave. He must've had another obligation," Josefina said with a shrug.

I nodded but couldn't help feeling disappointed by his hasty departure. I found my champagne glass and tried to keep a smile on my face as we toasted the happy couple again. However, I was confused and, if I had to admit to myself, a little sad. Why hadn't he sought me out to say goodbye?

31

A MESSAGE FROM
THE OTHER SIDE

THE CHRISTMAS HOLIDAY breezed by, and soon, we were back at the Jelf Academy. Thankfully, things between Zachary and me weren't awkward after his confession. I told Josefina what had happened, and she admitted that she and Kairi sensed his feelings for me. Kairi seemed slightly disappointed that Zachary and I would never have a romantic connection, but she understood my feelings.

The month of January passed by quickly. I was so consumed with my classes and assignments. My lessons with Phillip had also resumed, but he seemed aloof. I didn't understand why. He was still polite to me, but he didn't talk as much as he used to. I wondered what had happened on Christmas, but I was too afraid to ask. I hoped I hadn't done anything to offend him, but I couldn't think of why he would be upset. We attended the January W.A.S.P. meeting, and he behaved normally but seemed distant. Perhaps I was just paranoid, and it had nothing to do with me. I just wished he would return to being the person I had gotten to know over the past year.

At the January W.A.S.P. meeting, we hadn't learned anything new. With Drake away on vacation, Seth O'Doherty was struggling to keep his control of the leadership role. Some members, especially Lieutenant Marchberg, questioned all his commands and ideas. As far as I could tell, Lieutenant Davis hadn't gotten any farther with the young woman he was courting, and the group had no further discussions about the advanced weapon. I wished there was a way I could infiltrate the room during the meeting so I could make a note of who was who. Needless to say, Mr. Barber wasn't thrilled about our progress.

February brought a heaping amount of snow and the excitement for the annual Valentine's Day dance. Since my stepfamily would be away until March, Josefina and I were glad I could attend. It would be nice to have a break from the ever-increasing workload. It seemed like every teacher was determined to cram in as much information as they could before the end of the year.

The first half of my day was consumed with a series of complex charms, but the second half was less stressful. History of Pixies had been slightly more interesting than usual because Mr. Collyworth lectured about the French Revolution. Apparently, Marie Antoinette had been one of the last pixie queens. During the revolution, the W.A.S.P. members of the Jacobin club petitioned for Marie Antoinette to be executed by the guillotine, two of those members being Robespierre and Hebert. Unfortunately, she couldn't escape her sentence and was guillotined on October 16, 1793. After Marie Antoinette's death, more pixies went into hiding, increasing the number of secret pixie locations. The interactions with humans became more limited since even queens weren't safe from the W.A.S.P.

As we made our way through the falling snow back to the main building after Magical Creatures, Miguel used a *deicing charm* to keep snow off the path for Kairi. We easily made our way up to the

Predicting the Future classroom. Ms. Crescent was sitting cross-legged on her pillow when we entered. She had a strange-looking board displaying all the letters of the alphabet and the numbers zero through nine. In each corner were the words yes and no. At our seats, we discovered similar boards stationed between the pillows, with an odd triangle-shaped object.

"Everyone, come in and take a seat," Ms. Crescent said in her wispy voice. "We have an important lesson today." She picked up the board in front of her. "As you know, we've been focusing on the spirit realm. Today, we are going to attempt to contact someone who has passed on. We will be able to do that with this object. For those who have read ahead, you should know this is an Ouija board. Using letters and numbers, spirits can spell out messages and answer questions. A yes and no is written on the board for simple questions.

"Our questions will be answered by using this triangle called a planchette. The spirit can move the triangle over the letters and pause on the ones needed to spell the message. You'll see them appear in the circle located in the middle of the triangle," Ms. Crescent said, holding up the planchette.

"You'll work with your partner to attempt contact with someone from the spirit realm. There are also candles at each workstation, which you should use so the spirit can gain enough energy to communicate. Remember to keep your mind open and focused. Contacting the spirits is difficult, and not every spirit that reaches out is benevolent. Keep a strong mind and focus in case you attract something sinister. You'll need good energy to banish a spirit whose intentions are evil. Even though a spirit might reach out, it doesn't mean they're someone you know. Some spirits are tricksters, especially the ones from Ifrinn. Read the spirit's energy and aura to determine if they convey the truth. If you need help, I will be here, but you can find the instructions on page 326 of your books. When you have cleared your mind, you may begin."

Josefina and I both turned to the page. After reading the first few steps, we placed the Ouija board between us and put the planchette in the middle. According to the book, both our hands had to be on the planchette the entire time. However, we weren't supposed to push down on it. The spirit needed to be able to move it to communicate. Josefina insisted that I ask the questions.

"I'm too nervous, and you have the best focus of anyone in our class," she insisted.

I was worried about Ms. Crescent's warning about summoning an evil entity, but I agreed to be what the book called the medium. I took a deep breath to focus my mind, and we lit a few candles. The book suggested moving the planchette in several circles to warm up the board before we began. It also recommended that our first few questions have yes or no answers. When Josefina and I were ready, we placed our fingertips lightly on the planchette and pushed it clockwise in the middle of the board. I felt a heaviness rest on my shoulders when we stopped the rotation.

"Is anyone here and willing to communicate with us?" I asked quietly, not wanting to disrupt the other Ouija board sessions around us.

The planchette began to slowly slide away from the middle of the board. Josefina's brown eyes widened.

"You're not doing that, are you?" she whispered as the circle slid over the word yes.

I shook my head no, not wanting to lose focus. Besides, in the role of medium, I didn't want to confuse the entity.

"Do you wish to communicate?" I asked.

The planchette shifted off the word yes and smoothly slid back over it.

"Do you wish to harm us?" I questioned, holding my breath. The planchette quickly raced across the board to the opposite corner onto the word no.

I was about to ask another question when the triangle began

moving toward the center. It paused on the letter J and continued moving to the left. The triangle stopped on A, and Josefina said both letters out loud. Then it moved to the N next, followed by the letter E.

"Jane," Josefina whispered, continuing to say letters out loud as the Triangle skirted around the board.

"I-H-A-V-E-A-M-E-S-S-A-G-E-F-O-R-Y-O-U."

The planchette stopped moving while Josefina and I figured out what the spirit had just spelled.

"Who is this?" I asked with a shaky breath.

The planchette jumped into action again, and I gasped when the letters spelled out Robert. Was it even possible for Robert to communicate? Could human spirits have the ability to contact pixies? After discovering Robert's family, my dreams of him ceased. Was it possible that he was trying to contact me again, or was this a trick? Ms. Crescent had said the spirit might not be someone we'd know. What would be the chances it was actually Robert? The Predicting the Future book warned about evil spirits whose purpose was to trick and deceive. What if this was one of those occasions?

"How do I know this is Robert?" I asked firmly.

The planchette moved with a frenzy. I-A-M-R-O-B-E-R-T, it spelled. J-A-N-E-B-E-L-I-E-V-E-M-E. Y-O-U-F-O-U-N-D-M-Y-F-A-M-I-L-Y.

Josefina and I took a moment to decipher everything. I wanted to believe Robert was really coming through from the other side. If he was, maybe it would be possible for me to see him in the afterlife, even though he was human. Then, with a deep sigh, I asked another question.

"If this is truly Robert, where were we the first time we kissed?" I asked, my heart pounding. I had to think of something only the real Robert would know.

M-I-S-T-L-E-T-O-E, the planchette wrote.

I began shaking my head. We didn't have our very first kiss under the mistletoe. We had been in the barn when Robert kissed me on the lips. This couldn't be Robert. I glanced toward my book, looking for ways to banish the summoned spirit. Suddenly, the planchette began moving again.

N-O-T-L-I-P-S-H-A-N-D

It took us another moment to decipher the letters, and I didn't understand what the spirit was trying to say. What did 'not lips, hand' mean? However, the planchette didn't wait long before it began coasting over the board again. We watched as it spelled out the words, indicating it had a message for me.

"What message?" I asked in frustration. None of this made sense. I needed to gain control of the situation and dispel the spirit. The planchette began spelling out the answer.

B-E-C-A-R-E-F-U-L. W-A-S-P-IS-D-A-N-G-E-R-O-U-S.

My heart was beating quickly. If this spirit wasn't Robert, why was it claiming to be, and what did it know about the W.A.S.P.? Josefina was glancing at me with concern. I needed to focus on ending the session, but it was difficult when the planchette continued to move.

I-J-U-S-T-W-A-N-T-Y-O-U-H-A-P-P-Y, the planchette spelled before the bell rang to signal the end of the class. I was so startled by the noise my concentration broke, and my hands flew off the planchette. It felt like a weight had lifted from my shoulders, and I could tell the connection with the spirit had broken. It had been spelling something else right before I lost concentration. I wasn't sure, but I thought the last words were, "Move on." Whether anything followed, I would never know. I didn't understand the message. Was it only a warning? Did the spirit know something about the W.A.S.P.? If it wasn't Robert, why did it wish for my happiness, and what did the last part mean about moving on? A chill moved up my spine as I collected my belongings and blew out the candles. Was something terrible going to happen, or was this meant to confuse and worry me? How could I ever move on after such a bizarre message?

32

CONFESSION

THE RESULTS FROM the Ouija board bothered me throughout dinner and even as I headed toward Phillip's office. Josefina and I discussed the possibility that the spirit wasn't Robert. Some things had made sense, and others hadn't at all.

Again, when Phillip answered his door, he acted briskly. "Let's go up to the gym," he said, brushing by me and heading for the stairs.

I sighed quietly, slowly climbing the staircase. I hoped Phillip's attitude would fade over time, but a month had passed. I couldn't help but feel angry. I hadn't done anything and didn't deserve to be treated so coldly. Perhaps I could channel my anger into whatever defensive maneuver we would be practicing today.

When we reached the gym, I dropped my bag in a corner and paused to attach the knife holder to my ankle. We hadn't practiced much with my Christmas present, but I always brought it to lessons. I straightened my skirt and turned to face Phillip.

"Are you going to tell me what we'll be practicing today, or are you just going to let me figure it out on my own again?" I said sharply, narrowing my eyes at him.

Our lessons mainly consisted of charm making, where he silently watched me, or physical lessons, where he would stage attacks without warning me. Both types were carried out with minimal talking. When I would attempt conversation, Phillip would have one-word answers.

"I was going to start with basic defense to warm up, and maybe I'll teach you more techniques with the knife strapped to your ankle," Phillip replied.

"Are you actually going to teach me during this lesson, or are you going to remain silent again?" I questioned, my temper coming to the surface. After the confusing message from the spirit this afternoon, I was tired of being in the dark.

"What do you mean?" he asked.

I took a breath and plunged ahead. "You've been acting strangely this last month. You seem so distant, and you're not talkative during these lessons. Have I done something to offend you?"

"No, you didn't do anything. I haven't been any different," Phillip insisted.

"Yes, you have. You barely speak to me. Also, you were unnaturally quiet when we went to the January W.A.S.P. meeting. Never mind, it's probably not any of my business," I said with a shake of my head. "Let's just get on with our lesson." I turned away from him and went to the middle of the room.

Phillip cast a *shield charm* over himself and approached me, but I went on the offensive before he could even attack. His green eyes widened in surprise, but it didn't take him long to recover. Soon, we were entangled in a sparring match. I was attacking with all my energy, feeding my anger into each movement. I didn't understand why he was lying. That much was evident, and I wasn't an idiot.

Phillip approached again, and I centered my magic before thrusting it directly at his chest. He flew backward and landed with a hard thud on the other side of the room. I paused to catch my breath and waited for him to get up. Phillip didn't rise to his feet, and after a moment, he let out a groan. Cautiously, I approached him. Was he really injured, or was this another deception?

Phillip had his eyes closed as I moved closer.

"That knocked the wind out of me," Phillip muttered, sensing my proximity.

"Did it really, or are you just being dishonest about this, too?" I asked, crossing my arms over my chest.

Phillip's green eyes slid open. He groaned again as he struggled to sit up. "No, I'm winded. Thankfully, my shield charm lessened the blow," he replied with a rough chuckle.

While Phillip caught his breath, I summoned glasses of water and handed him one. He took a long gulp and wiped the sweat from his brow. His dark hair glistened with perspiration, and he slicked it back with his right hand.

"I'm sorry if I have been distant lately. I have a lot on my mind, and I didn't mean to hurt you," he said, glancing at the floor.

"Ever since Christmas, I feel like you've been brushing me off," I replied, sitting beside him. "I thought I'd done something to upset you. You left without saying goodbye."

"I apologize. I didn't think it would bother you so much. You seemed occupied, and I didn't want to take up any more of your time."

"How could you possibly think I wouldn't be concerned and confused by your abrupt departure? I was glad you'd come to visit. I was excited to give you my Christmas gift. All this time we've spent together, I felt like I've gotten to know you. You've been so supportive, and I've come to consider you one of my friends. If you needed to leave, I would've liked to say goodbye," I said.

"I'm sorry, Jane. I've been inconsiderate. I didn't mean to hurt you. Can you forgive me for my foolish behavior?"

"Yes, as long as you're honest with me. Maybe you don't want to discuss everything on your mind lately, but I knew you were acting differently," I said.

Phillip nodded. "I've been so concerned about these W.A.S.P. meetings and collecting enough information. If anything happened to you, it would be my fault. We need to find a way to get closer, but you're already in so much danger. I couldn't live with myself if we were discovered."

"I'm worried too, but I think I'm doing the right thing to help the pixie world. I need your support now more than ever. Please don't pull away from me," I replied.

"I'm sorry. I should've told you how I was feeling sooner," Phillip answered.

"It's okay. I thought I had done something to make you mad or for you to hate me again," I stated.

"I couldn't hate you," he responded.

"You used to," I said with a laugh to break the seriousness of the moment.

"Well, I've always been a foolish person. I guess I need to be knocked out every once in a while so I can see the light," Phillip said, massaging his temples.

"I hope I didn't hurt you too badly," I said with concern.

"No, but I can't say I didn't deserve it. My head might be pounding for a while, and dizziness may be a side effect, but I think I'll be able to manage," Phillip replied with a slight chuckle.

"I certainly hope so. The dance is next weekend, and if you're out of commission, I'll lose several dances on my card," I joked, a blush rising to my cheeks.

Phillip's green eyes glanced at me. "I'm sure you won't have a problem filling your dance card. I can't imagine Mr. Walsh allowing you to miss any."

"Mr. Walsh?" I replied questioningly. "Whatever makes you think I'm attending the dance with Zachary?"

"You're not?" Phillip asked with raised eyebrows. I shook my head. "I just assumed after Christmas..." he trailed off.

"No. I'm not attending the dance with Zachary Walsh. I'm not attending with anybody."

"He seemed quite smitten with you after that peck beneath the mistletoe. I just expected him to be courting you by now," Phillip replied teasingly.

I shook my head. "No, Zachary is a friend of mine, and he knows that now. I don't feel that way about him. Do you think I want all my male friends to court me? You thought Miguel was a potential suitor when I said the Martinezes felt like family."

"Well, it would only be natural for an attractive female such as yourself to be courted by men who were originally friends," Phillip continued.

"I don't have any natural romantic feelings for them," I said as I shoved his arm. "Now, can we stop discussing potential suitors and get on with our lesson before it becomes too late?" I asked, rising to my feet.

"You're right. It's none of my business," he laughed, accepting my outstretched hand.

"I gave you the knife to use as a last resort when you see no chance of escape. If you're not careful, any weapon in your possession can be used against you. If your attacker is aware of the knife, he could wrestle it from your grasp and use it on you. So, you must keep the weapon a secret. Only use it when it would be most effective," Phillip lectured while he began pacing.

It didn't occur to me what Phillip was up to until it was too late. He effectively wrestled me to the floor, and I hadn't seen it coming this time. Angry with myself, I struggled under his grasp, trying to get the upper hand. He chuckled at his success, pinning my arms to the floor. I attempted to throw him off but was unable to focus. I was aware of his body pushing down on mine. His knees were on both sides of my rib cage, and I could feel his leg muscles on each side of my body.

My breath was coming in fast pants, and I stopped struggling to slow my heart rate. In my moment of stillness, Phillip pushed my wrists together and attempted to hold them both with one hand while his other hand slid to my neck. I began fighting again to free one of my wrists. Finally, I managed to free my right hand, and I reached up to grab the collar of his shirt. If I could shift his center of balance, I would be able to throw him off.

As I pulled him toward me, the world seemed to stand still. His green eyes connected with mine, neither of us looking away. My body relaxed as I tugged downward on his shirt. Phillip's face was inches from mine; our breaths mingled as we breathed heavily. I wasn't sure if it was my action or his, but suddenly, his lips pressed against mine. Fire raced through my veins, and I wasn't aware of anything besides the feel of his mouth. Somehow, my hands were in his soft, dark hair, and his hand was caressing my cheek and neck. Phillip kissed me with wild abandon, and I lost myself in his touch.

Just as suddenly, Phillip broke the kiss. He leapt away from me, scuttling a few feet away. I was too stunned to move.

"Jane, I'm so sorry. I didn't mean.... No, well, I did, but..." he stammered.

With a shaky breath, I pulled myself into a seated position. "Phillip, I…"

"No. I shouldn't have taken advantage of you. I don't know what I was thinking!" Phillip exclaimed, smacking his forehead with his hand. "I wasn't thinking."

I swallowed the lump in my throat. "Well, I'm not sorry," I said, struggling to keep my voice from wavering.

Phillip's eyes darted to me; his expression glazed with confusion.

"I'm not sorry at all. If I'm completely honest, I've secretly been hoping you would do that for some time," I said bravely. My heart raced in my chest, and my cheeks were hot.

"You have?" he asked, startled.

I nodded, slowly creeping toward him. "It took a long time to admit it to myself, but now I'm sure."

Slowly, I reached out my hand and placed it on his arm, hoping he wouldn't shrug me off. After his passionate kiss, his rejection would shatter me. After all the months we spent together, my heart had opened to him. My excitement whenever I was around him and my jealous thoughts toward Lette when I didn't know she was his sister could only mean one thing. His fingers touched mine, and he stood, pulling me along. He smiled down at me and lightly brushed my hair from my face.

"I would've never imagined you had any feelings at all," he murmured, bringing my right hand to his lips. A pleasant sensation flowed through my body as his lips brushed my knuckles. His eyes floated back up to my face, and at that moment, I didn't think I would ever tire of gazing into their vibrant green depths.

"I'm not too young for you?" I asked, my voice shaking with emotion.

Phillip shook his head. "No, I've never felt so completely connected to anyone. The difference in our ages means nothing to me." He caressed my hands, and I interlocked my fingers with his.

"You've never felt this way before?" I questioned.

Phillip shook his head again. "I thought I had a long time ago, but not like this," he responded. "I know I shouldn't have these feelings for you. Everything about our relationship is probably unethical; you are my student, but I don't care."

"I never thought this would be possible, but I can't imagine being without your touch," I whispered. "I don't care if this is unethical."

Phillip pulled me into his embrace, and my hands roamed across his back and into his hair. I couldn't stop touching him, and I didn't want him to stop touching me. I knew this was scandalous, but I couldn't help myself. He bent his head toward me, and his forehead touched mine. We stared into each other's eyes for the longest time.

"This is the happiest I've ever been. I've dreamed of holding you so many times. I'm afraid I'll blink, and this will have been a dream," Phillip murmured.

I closed my eyes and tilted my chin up. Phillip's lips caressed mine, the kiss starting off soft. I pushed my lips into his, electricity shooting through my body at the feel of him. I had never experienced anything so passionate, and I wanted to melt into him. My heart felt like it was going to pound out of my chest. If I died at this moment, I would die feeling the happiest I'd ever been in my entire life.

33

PLANS AND CHARM PRACTICE

I FELT LIKE I was walking on air. I was afraid of feeling so happy and excited. Every time I allowed myself happiness, something always came along to ruin it. The last time I felt this way, my dreams had literally gone up in smoke, and I had been devastated, almost beyond repair. Phillip had somehow managed to put me back together, and I was frightened that it would only be a matter of time before something would rob me of my joy. I told myself I could only live for one day at a time.

Though I had come to look forward to my lessons with Phillip, I now craved them. Whether in the gym or Phillip's office, I never felt so relaxed and content in his company. However, just because we were aware of each other's feelings didn't mean we ignored our lessons. There was still so much to learn, and Phillip was concerned about my returning to the manor. We practiced with my knife, Phillip showing me the vital areas I should aim for if I became trapped in a situation where I would have to use the weapon.

We also spent our lessons pondering a better way to access the W.A.S.P. meetings. The next one was at the end of February, and we hoped we would attain more valuable information.

"Besides disguising ourselves and going to the *Dew Drop Inn*, I don't know what else we can do," Phillip said, running his hands through my hair.

We had just finished one of our lessons. I was lying on the floor with my head in his lap.

"I wish there was a subtle way to gain access to the room," I said, frustrated.

We discovered several of the W.A.S.P. members' names, but we hadn't gotten any further than that. Perhaps if we could identify the members, we would come upon another significant discovery. My mind was turning in circles while Phillip continued massaging my scalp.

"Phillip, can the *transfiguration charm* be used to change yourself into someone? Would I be able to make myself look like you if I imagined it when I cast the charm?" I asked.

Phillip froze, his hands lightly resting on my head. "Yes… it's possible, but it's complicated magic," he replied with hesitation.

Quickly, I sat up from his lap. "That's it! This would be our way into the meeting!" I exclaimed.

"No, it's too dangerous. You can't disguise yourself as one of the members!" Phillip burst out.

"Not one of the members," I said with a sigh. "I could disguise myself as Mary, the waitress."

Phillip was still shaking his head. "That would still be too dangerous. As I said, that type of transfiguration is complicated magic. It's difficult because you couldn't possibly know everything about a person, and we all see each other differently. For example, what if Mary has a small mole on her cheek that you've never noticed, but Mr. O'Doherty has? It's almost impossible to recall every feature of someone who already exists. That's why we make up our disguises instead of trying to be someone else," Phillip said.

"But that kind of transfiguration has the potential to be possible?" I asked insistently.

"Well, I suppose so. Anything could theoretically be possible...." Phillip began, but I cut him off.

"So, if I studied Mary's appearance and movements, I could transform myself into her?" I said.

"Jane, it's much too dangerous. Even if you managed the transformation, going into that room by yourself is out of the question."

I leaned toward him and kissed him passionately. "You worry too much. I think I'd be able to pull it off. If I study Mary at the next meeting and commit her image to memory, I could practice the transfiguration during our lessons," I replied.

"What makes you so sure and smug that you'd even be successful?" Phillip questioned.

"Because darling, weren't you the one to say I was among the most talented pixies you've ever seen?" I replied, kissing him again.

Phillip chuckled, then grabbed me, pulling me close. "You, my dear, can be so insufferable. When will you ever accept my rejection of your crazy ideas?"

"When I have proof, my crazy ideas won't work. I will not insanely rush into the middle of a W.A.S.P. meeting, which is why I suggested studying Mary during the next meeting. Then, I'll practice the charm. If I'm not able to create a convincing likeness, then we won't follow through with the plan. I have to try, though," I said determinedly.

"When did you become so fearless?" Phillip asked, nuzzling my neck and sending chills down my entire body.

"I wouldn't say I'm fearless. I'm terrified of the W.A.S.P. I've seen what they are capable of, but I think I'm more afraid of what will happen if the W.A.S.P. gets enough information about the pixie society. So if I can do anything to prevent it, I have to try," I responded.

"My brave woman," he murmured, placing delicate kisses on my neck.

"I couldn't be brave without you," I replied, sweeping my

hand through his hair, around his ear, and stopping at his jaw. My thumb brushed over the short stubble. Phillip closed his eyes and sighed deeply.

"I can't get enough of your touch," he whispered. "It's going to drive me mad not to be able to hold you like this at the Valentine's Day dance."

"Will you still put your name down on my dance card? I don't want to dance with anyone else," I replied.

"Of course, but I can't request more than what would be appropriate. We can't act as if anything has changed between us, though if I could, I would take every one of your dances. I would be by your side every second if I could. I wish our relationship didn't have to be a secret. I would tell the world what you mean to me," Phillip responded, holding me tightly.

"I know. We both agreed it would be better if we didn't tell anyone. We're both adults, but I know our relationship would be viewed as a conflict of interest. Strangely, I'm glad because it's our secret, something just between us," I said, kissing his temple.

"I promise one day everyone will know you are by my side. Our secret is not because I'm ashamed to be with you."

"I know that, Phillip," I said, breaking away from his embrace. "It's getting late. We should call it a night, as much as I don't want to." I stood up and stretched my arms above my head.

Phillip nodded in agreement and rose to his feet. After several good night kisses, we left the gym, both heading toward our rooms. I smiled, knowing I couldn't wait for our next moment alone together.

The Friday before the Valentine's Day dance was going to be busy. Phillip mentioned that the beginning of the section in our books deals with medical charms. He told me he wanted the class to attempt the *blood clotting charm*. It was a bit complicated, but he planned on walking us through it. I also had a test in Transfiguration and a paper due in Teleportation, so the first half of my day was overloaded with activities.

As soon as I entered the Charms classroom, I organized my materials and flipped to the medical section in the textbook. While waiting for the bell to ring, I read the instructions for the *blood clotting charm* and pulled out the materials. Josefina leaned over to see what I was doing.

"How do you know what we'll be working on?" Josefina whispered.

"Mr. Withermyer mentioned it during our lesson last night," I replied as Josefina opened her book to the same page.

When the bell rang, Phillip got up from his desk chair and paced to the dark board. He projected the words *blood clotting charm* in big white letters. When he turned to face the class, his green eyes landed on me for several seconds before he spoke.

"I know it's the Friday before the Valentine's Day dance, but I thought we should get started on the medical charms section. You will learn a few basic medical charms between this year and your fifth year. Things like the *blood clotting charm*, the *pain relief charm*, and the *fever-reducing charm* are simple home remedies every pixie should know. Granted, they aren't that simple to make, but to learn more complicated healing methods, you would need to go to a special school after the Jelf Academy. I want you all to attempt the blood clotting charm today, and I'll be here to assist you. Don't worry. I won't assign work outside of class this weekend. Just focus on doing your best during today's lesson," Phillip said as he listed the ingredients to the *blood clotting charm* on the board.

I already had my ingredients organized, so I glanced at the first step. I needed two cups of crushed carnelian, an orange-red stone. Slowly, I broke up the mineral while Phillip explained the first step to the class.

"The *blood clotting charm* can be used in two ways. One: You can apply it directly to a wound. Two: If the wound isn't visible, it can be ingested with water," Phillip explained.

The second ingredient in the *blood clotting charm* was, fittingly, bloodstone, a black and red gemstone. I needed a cup of it and noticed it was slightly softer than the carnelian. Soon, I became absorbed in the intricate measuring and mixing that the charm required, following along with Phillip as he explained each step in detail. By the end of class, everyone turned in their vial to be tested and graded.

I was packing my belongings when the bell sounded, and I paused as Phillip approached my desk.

"Miss Fitzgerald, may I have a brief word with you before you leave for your next class?" he asked.

I nodded, continuing to collect my things. Josefina paused in the doorway, but I motioned for her to go on without me. I was sure by Phillip's tone he intended for us to be alone. He beckoned me over to his desk, and as the last student exited the classroom, he used his mind to close the door.

I leaned slightly across the desk. "What did you need to discuss?" I murmured.

Phillip paused for a moment, listening to noises in the hallway before cupping my head in his hands and bringing his lips to mine. The kiss wasn't very long, but it contained all the passion I felt for him.

"I've wanted to do that since the moment you walked into this room," he said with a smile.

"Is that really the word you needed to have with me?" I asked with a laugh.

"No, I have something for you," he replied, reaching into his desk drawer. He placed a box with a red ribbon in the middle of his desk.

"Phillip, what is this?" I whispered.

"Just a little Valentine's Day present," he replied.

"Phillip! You didn't have to! I didn't have a chance to get you anything," I exclaimed.

"You don't have to get me anything. I thought you could wear this since I can't officially escort you to the dance tomorrow. It would be a secret symbol of our relationship. Go ahead and open it," he said eagerly.

I slipped the ribbon from the box and slowly opened the lid, savoring the anticipation. I gasped at the beautiful heart-shaped setting with diamonds. In the center of the hollow heart hung a smaller diamond that was also cut into the shape of a heart.

"Phillip, it's beautiful," I sighed, touching the gems. "Thank you."

"Diamonds are for happiness, which is what I always wish to make you feel," Phillip said, grasping my hand.

"Just being near you makes me happy," I admitted, rolling my thumb in a circle on the top of his hand.

Phillip pulled me toward him to place another kiss on my lips when the bell rang.

"Oh no, I'm late for Transfiguration!" I yelped.

"Don't worry. I'll write you a note," Phillip replied, grabbing a piece of paper on his desk. He quickly jotted out a memo while I placed his gift in my bag.

He handed it to me, and with another quick peck, I hurried from his classroom. My heart raced as I rushed toward the Transfiguration classroom. Ms. Pregmon wouldn't be happy with my tardiness, but I hoped Phillip's note would help. When I reached the classroom, the door was closed. I pulled on the handle, but the door wouldn't budge. Through the window in the door, I could see Ms. Pregmon handing out the tests. She must've heard the door rattling because she turned to look at me. Her evil brown eyes lit with amusement.

After she finished passing out the exams, Ms. Pregmon sauntered toward the door. "You're late. I cannot let you in, Miss Fitzgerald," Ms. Pregmon said nastily through the door.

"I have an excuse from Mr. Withermyer," I replied, plastering the note to the window so she could see it. Her eyes darted back and forth before she flicked her gaze to me.

"I don't care, Miss Fitzgerald. Mr. Withermyer should be aware of the time between classes and should've discussed your extra lessons at another time," she hissed. "I'm not letting you in!"

"But there's a test today," I protested. Ms. Pregmon's exams counted for a large part of our grade.

"Late is late, Miss Fitzgerald. That is my policy. You'll be receiving a zero today on the test for your tardiness. Now, please remove yourself from outside my door. You're distracting the students who were decent enough to come on time," Ms. Pregmon said with a nasty look, and she waved her hand in a shooing motion.

Fuming, I turned away and stalked back down the hallway. Not knowing what else to do, I headed toward Phillip's office. I was sure he had a free period since no students had been waiting to enter his classroom. I knocked on his office door and waited to see if he was available. Within a few moments, the door opened. Phillip looked surprised to see me.

"Jane, what are you doing here? Shouldn't you be in Transfiguration?" he asked, stepping back to allow me entrance.

"I tried, but Ms. Pregmon charmed the door closed, and she wouldn't let me in," I huffed as I sat in the chair across from his desk.

"Didn't she see my note?" Phillip asked.

"Yes, through the window in the door, but she said she didn't care. She said being late was unacceptable and that you should know by now how much time is between classes."

"She said that?" Phillip questioned, and I nodded.

"So now I'm going to receive a zero on today's exam, which will greatly affect my class score," I said with a sigh.

"I'm sorry, Jane. That's not fair. Let's go talk to Dr. Tweedle. Maybe he can convince Blair to let you take the test," Phillip insisted, tugging on my hand.

I got to my feet and followed him. We crossed the hallway, and Phillip knocked on the door.

"Mr. Withermyer and Miss Fitzgerald, please enter," Dr. Tweedle called. "To what do I owe this pleasure?"

Dr. Tweedle had a quizzical expression when we entered and sat on the comfortable sofa.

"I accidentally made Jane, ah, Miss Fitzgerald," Phillip said, catching himself. "late to her Transfiguration class today," Phillip began. If Dr. Tweedle noticed Phillip's familiar use of my first name, he made no indication of surprise. "I wrote her a note to excuse her tardiness, but Ms. Pregmon refused to accept it and allow Miss Fitzgerald into her classroom."

"Hmm… is that so, Miss Fitzgerald?" Dr. Tweedle asked.

"Yes, sir, her classroom door was charmed closed, and even after seeing the note, she refused to let me in. Therefore, I will receive a zero on today's exam," I answered.

"I don't want Miss Fitzgerald to be penalized. It was my fault she was late today. We were discussing our private lessons," Phillip said.

"I'll have a word with Ms. Pregmon. It does seem a bit harsh for her to keep you out of the classroom when you had an excuse. As for discussing lesson schedules, perhaps you could speak to Miss Fitzgerald during lunch or when classes are over for the day," Dr. Tweedle replied.

"I'm sorry, sir. I lost track of time. I won't make Miss Fitzgerald late again," Phillip replied.

"Good. Since I have you both in my office, Mr. Barber was inquiring whether you would be attending the February W.A.S.P. meeting. I just received a letter from him, which is why it's strange both of you showed up at my office door just now," Dr. Tweedle stated.

"Yes, we'll be spying at the February W.A.S.P. meeting," I responded quickly.

"I'll let him know, even though I don't agree with this internship," Dr. Tweedle said, shaking his head. "It's much too dangerous."

"I will protect Miss Fitzgerald with my life," Phillip stated.

"We have always been cautious," I added.

"Please continue to be. I don't like this type of work, but I'll send my response to Mr. Barber so he knows to expect a report," Dr. Tweedle answered.

"I've gained so much information about the W.A.S.P., and if we can prevent an attack like we did at Coillewood, my being in danger is worth it," I insisted.

"Not to me if both your lives are at stake. I care about both of you, Jane. I don't like putting any of my students, or staff for that matter, in jeopardy," Dr. Tweedle said with concern. "Your mother was very special to me, and if something were to happen to you, I would be devastated."

"I appreciate your concern, Dr. Tweedle. You've been so good to me, and it means a lot. I'm only doing this job to stop the W.A.S.P. Maybe if we succeed, no child will have to lose a parent, a sibling, or a family member to this evil organization," I replied.

"Your heart is in the right place, dear. I understand why you're working with Mr. Barber. As you are both adults and not children, I cannot stop you. I can only stress my concerns. Please don't do anything risky. Let the trained government officials take on the precarious plans."

"I promise to make the right decisions while on the assignment," I said. "Thank you again for your concerns about my safety," I said with a slight smile.

As I left Dr. Tweedle's office, I wondered if he would think my transfiguration idea would be too risky.

34

Secret Love

Ms. Pregmon agreed to let me take my exam after all my classes were over, but she didn't seem happy about it. I tried to complete the exam as fast as possible to escape her nasty stare. When I approached her desk to give her my test, she barely acknowledged me, but as I was about to leave her classroom, I heard her clear her throat.

"Miss Fitzgerald, don't be late for my class again. Just because you are a favorite of Dr. Tweedle's doesn't mean you can get away with whatever you want. I know he's the headmaster of this institution, but Transfiguration is my class, and I will find a way to penalize your behavior. So consider this the last warning," Ms. Pregmon said nastily.

I thought better of responding and left the classroom, eager to begin the weekend with the Valentine's Day dance.

⁓

Josefina and I spent the evening organizing our accessories for the dance and speculating who would fill up the spaces on our dance cards. I pulled out the necklace from Phillip and placed it with everything else I planned to wear.

"What a beautiful necklace," Josefina exclaimed when she saw it. "Where did you get that from?"

My stomach flipped, and I swallowed the lump in my throat. I hated to lie to Josefina, but I couldn't tell her Phillip had given it to me. I paused for a moment as I turned toward my closet.

"I found it with my mother's things in the attic a while ago. I thought it would be appropriate for Valentine's Day since it's a heart shape," I said, feeling incredibly guilty.

"It goes well with your dress. What a lucky find!" Josefina said.

I nodded as I smoothed out the skirt of the dress I'd chosen. The dress was made of a shimmery pink fabric, a semi-sweetheart neckline, and an A-line skirt. It was one of the dresses Dr. Tweedle purchased for me in my second year. The dress wasn't extravagant, but I thought it was perfect. I hoped Phillip would like it.

∼

As usual, the excitement permeated throughout the building in the morning. The other students were buzzing during breakfast, and the evening festivities were all anyone could talk about. Josefina and I spent the afternoon preparing, and Josefina was slightly disappointed no one had asked to escort her.

"Why do you need a man to escort you when we have each other?" I teased her, trying to brighten her mood. "Who did you have your eye on anyway?"

Josefina blushed and glanced away from my gaze through the mirror as I pinned her hair. "No one in particular. I'm just saying it would be nice to be escorted by someone other than Miguel for a change."

"You must be thinking of someone, or else your cheeks wouldn't look so pink right now," I replied.

Josefina sighed and made eye contact with me. "Okay, you caught me. I was hoping Evan Foster would've asked me."

Evan Foster was a brown-haired boy I'd only spoken to once during a Zodiac Signs lesson.

"Have you ever talked to him?" I asked.

"A few times. I asked him to pass me a scale once in Charms and another time when I accidentally bumped into him in the hallway. He took a few of my dances last year, and I hoped he would notice me. I think he's very handsome," Josefina commented as she twirled a loose strand of her hair.

"Maybe he'll notice you again tonight and ask for several dances," I said as I finished pinning her dark brown tresses.

"Who are you hoping to get dances from?" Josefina asked, and I could feel heat moving up my neck. I tried to keep my face neutral and not give anything away.

"No one in particular. I'll be lucky to get dances from my male friends," I responded, switching places with Josefina so she could style my hair.

"It's too bad you didn't have feelings for Zachary. He seemed to adore you," Josefina said with a slight frown.

I shrugged slightly. "Zachary's a charming man, but I can't force how I feel. Besides, the last time I was escorted to a dance, it didn't turn out so great," I joked.

"Thomas Whitmore was an idiot, and you'll never have to deal with him again," Josefina huffed, twisting my hair into a braid. "Anyway, I'm sure Zachary will take a few dances. Miguel will, too, of course. Oh, how could I forget? Mr. Withermyer will probably want a few."

I tried to keep my cheeks from turning red. "Yes, I suppose he will," I said nonchalantly.

"You seemed very close at Christmas, visiting his family before the W.A.S.P. meeting. I forgot to ask you because of Zachary's confession," Josefina said.

"Oh, it was nothing important. We ran into his sister while we were in the Jewel Caverns, and she invited us to lunch," I said with a shrug.

Josefina was silent for a moment as she continued braiding my hair. "Well, I sensed some kind of connection between you. Strangely enough, it's always been there, but I sense it stronger than before. I've been practicing auras, but what do I know?" Josefina said with a laugh. "Every time I think I finally understand Predicting the Future, something happens to make me unsure."

"If it makes you feel any better, I do spend a lot of time with Mr. Withermyer. So, it would be difficult not to get to know him," I replied evasively.

"That's true," Josefina replied, and I caught her reflection in the mirror as she cradled her chin in thought. "Maybe I should stop trying to read people. Miguel would say Predicting the Future is a hoax, anyway. I just thought I was getting good at it." Her mouth turned down in a frown.

"What do you mean?" I asked curiously.

"Sometimes I get these extreme feelings about certain things. Never mind, you'll think I'm crazy."

"Josefina, you know I would never think that," I insisted.

"Okay, I'll tell you, but you must promise not to judge me or laugh," Josefina began, and she didn't continue until I promised. "There are times I'll catch myself staring off, and then a random thought will enter my head about someone. It comes on so strongly that I'm convinced it's true. For example, when I first met Taylor, I could've sworn she wasn't an only child, but that can't be right because Taylor has never mentioned any siblings. So why would I even think that?" she asked.

I swallowed the lump in my throat. Josefina's instincts about Taylor were correct; she wasn't an only child. She had told me about her twin sister who was murdered by the W.A.S.P. She'd asked me not to tell anyone about Tammy because she wasn't ready to share her grief with anyone else nor the pain she had gone through since she was mentally connected to her sister. Taylor had felt all the torture her twin had.

"I don't know," I managed to say.

"Do you remember last year when that mysterious stranger showed up at the Masquerade dance? I could've sworn her aura matched Kairi's, but that's impossible. The mystery woman was dancing. We both know that Kairi's not able to. She doesn't have the ability to stand, let alone dance. See, I told you my visions, or whatever they are, don't make sense. Maybe I just have a good imagination," Josefina sighed.

My face felt hot, and I hoped Josefina didn't notice. I couldn't tell my best friend that her premonitions were correct, and I realized at that moment how many secrets my friends had shared with me.

"Though, I somehow knew Lena would say yes to Juan's proposal. Maybe I'm just imagining things, and only a few of them turn out true. I know, for example, that Miguel is sweet on Kairi, but it's probably due to the fact that we are mentally connected."

"Miguel is interested in Kairi?" I asked. "I thought you told me that even though twins were connected, you still had to 'knock on the door' to gain access to each other's minds," I added, trying to make Josefina feel better.

"Yes, we do, but it's possible for thoughts to slip through when emotions are involved. So, I really don't have an advanced psychic ability at all. I can read my brother's mind, and I knew Lena would because I'm in her company often. Those other visions are impossible, so I must be doing something wrong."

A knock sounded on the door of our room, saving me from having to answer. Josefina paused to answer the door. As if we had conjured them, Kairi and Taylor entered the room. At least their appearance ended my discussion with Josefina. Josefina finished with my hair, and I examined my reflection. I pinched my cheeks, even though they were already pink.

Taylor and Kairi both looked stunning. Taylor wore a light pink gown, her wavy hair pulled into a fluffy bun. Kairi was wearing an aqua-blue A-line that concealed her tail, and her reddish-brown locks were stylishly braided and pinned in an elegant design. Instead of using the main staircase, Kairi insisted we join her in the device Dr. Tweedle installed for her wheelchair. The space was tight, but we all managed to cram onto the lift, and using our magic, we helped work the pulley system.

"I've never entered a dance this way," Josefina exclaimed.

"We can escape the crowded hallways and staircases," Taylor observed. "The lift is a great way to navigate, so I don't mind helping Kairi at all." A giggle escaped Taylor's lips.

"Oh, this is why you're such a good friend?" Kairi joked, laughing too.

Taylor lightly pushed Kairi's shoulder as the lift lowered to the first floor. Josefina pushed the door to the side, and we stepped into the noisy hallway, the sound of music coming from the dining hall.

This year, the hall was decorated like the night sky with an under-the-stars theme. The ceiling was charmed to look like constellations, and the lighting was muted. Large trees decorated with lights and dangling crystals stood around the room's perimeter. On the food tables were large ice sculptures shaped like swans. It looked absolutely magical and romantic. My heart beat wildly as I scanned the room for Phillip.

My friends and I chose a table and collected our dance cards. It wasn't long before our gentleman friends arrived. Miguel, Zachary, and Andrew took two dances each. I thanked them and excused myself to get a drink.

As I approached the food tables, I saw the punch in a fountain with two swan ice sculptures. The liquid flowed through the sculptures somehow, the display reminding me of an elegant garden fountain. I held a glass beneath one of the swans' beaks to fill it. When I looked up, I noticed a dark shape behind one of the taller sculptures. I craned my neck to see what was causing the dark shadow. Suddenly, a hand darted from behind the ice and caught my hand.

Before I could cry out, I was pulled around the table so fast I almost spilled my drink as I collided with Phillip. He levitated the cup from my hands and lightly kissed my fingers.

"What are you doing?" I whispered. "We could be seen."

Phillip shook his head. We were standing between the table and the far wall, the ice sculpture obscuring us from view. "No one can see us, and I've been longing to touch you."

My face flushed at his words, and I could feel my heart beating double time. I swallowed. "I've also wanted to, but isn't this too risky?" I asked.

Phillip sighed. "I guess you're right. Here, take your glass and go around the table. I'll come around in a minute so I can choose some dances on your card," he replied, releasing my hand.

Slowly, I backed away from him. The dining hall filled with students, and I didn't think anyone noticed I'd been behind the sculpture. I moved away from the table and waited patiently for Phillip. What was he thinking? It was only a moment before Phillip came to stand beside me.

"Miss Fitzgerald, would you honor me by allowing a few dances on your card?" he asked, formal as ever.

"Yes, you may," I replied, handing my card to him.

I waited patiently as Phillip wrote down his name. When he returned the card, I could see he had claimed three. It was more than anyone else, but not too many to appear suspicious. I thanked him and headed back to my table. Though I preferred spending most of my evening with Phillip, I knew it would be unwise.

I sat next to Josefina and waited for the first dance to begin. Now that Josefina had told me about Miguel's feelings for Kairi, it was quite obvious. He sat next to her and was very attentive to everything she said. I wondered if he'd be surprised to learn that the mysterious girl he'd been so taken with at last year's Valentine's Day dance was the same girl he was sitting beside now. Had Miguel subconsciously known?

The band began playing the first song, and Andrew swept me onto the dance floor. The tempo was quick, not giving us a moment to talk since our concentration was on the dance steps. I barely had time to catch my breath before I was swept back onto the floor by Zachary for the next waltz. I was grateful this dance was slower, but it also allowed for conversation.

"You look lovely this evening," Zachary commented, and he twirled me under his arm.

"Thank you," I replied, looking down at his chest instead of his aqua eyes.

"I'm not trying to make you uncomfortable. I'm only trying to give you a compliment," he replied.

"I appreciate that," I answered, forcing myself to meet his gaze.

"I told you I didn't want things to be awkward between us. I understand and respect your feelings," Zachary said as we flowed around the dance floor.

"I know, and I don't feel like you've acted differently toward me. I've been trying to do the same."

Zachary chuckled. "I'm sorry. It's probably tactless of me to even mention it now. I just wanted to assure you my compliment was only that."

I laughed, too, releasing the slight tension. "Yes, you could say bringing it up is embarrassing, but I understand what you mean."

We finished the rest of the dance, and before I could take a drink, Phillip swooped in to claim the third one. I couldn't keep the smile off my face as he pulled me into his arms. My body buzzed like I had been shocked. I was very aware of his fingertips near my spine and the feel of his hand in mine.

"That necklace is very becoming on you," Phillip whispered before the music began.

"It's very kind of you to notice. Thank you," I replied.

"You look dazzling tonight. I was speechless when I saw you enter the dining hall," he added as the music started.

Phillip led me into the dance effortlessly, and I was reminded of the first time I'd ever danced with him. He was an excellent dancer, and I could follow his lead easily. I'd never danced with anyone else who matched his caliber. This time, though, surpassed all the other dances we'd shared. I was aware of his every move, the subtle adjustments, and the feel of his body beneath my fingers. Somehow, I knew exactly how he wanted me to move as if our minds were connected. It was almost as if we had choreographed the dance beforehand.

I was breathless when the music stopped. I loathed to remove my hand from his. Phillip escorted me off the dance floor, and I felt his fingers give my arm an extra squeeze before he released me from his grasp.

"Until our next dance," he murmured before disappearing into the crowd.

Feeling weak-kneed, I returned to my table, glad no one had taken my fourth dance. Kairi applauded as I approached my seat, and I could feel my body flush all over.

"I didn't know you could dance like that," she exclaimed. "Are you really having dance lessons instead of charm lessons with Mr. Withermyer?"

My cheeks felt extremely hot, and I reached for my glass. "No," I replied with a chuckle, hoping everyone would assume my cheeks were red from exertion.

"You both looked like professionals. If you didn't practice, that was certainly impressive," Kairi responded.

"Well, thank you, but I can assure you we did not," I laughed.

"Now I'm nervous to have my dance with you. I can't dance like that," Miguel added.

"Nonsense, you're a wonderful dancer," Kairi said, and then catching herself, added, "at least from what I've observed."

Miguel didn't seem to notice Kairi's blunder, and he beamed at the compliment.

I enjoyed my drink while I waited for my next dance, and as the night went on, I continued to have a good time. All my dance partners were admirable, but I longed for the touch of Phillip's hand and couldn't wait for the next time he would be my partner. When he claimed my arm for our second dance, I felt like a light had been turned on inside me. Though I felt anxious about drawing attention to us, I couldn't turn off the feeling of pure joy I felt when I was in his arms.

The evening was winding down as I placed my hand in Phillip's for the last dance he'd taken.

"I've had such a delightful evening," I said softly. "Though I wish I could have more time with you."

Phillip nodded as he began the waltz. "Yes. I've yearned for that, too."

"The night doesn't have to be over," I began, my heart rising into my throat. A crazy thought entered my mind.

"What do you mean?" he asked with a slight smirk.

"I should check on Thistle tonight. I should make sure she isn't too cold," I replied with a grin.

"Oh, that's an excellent idea. It's a frigid night," Phillip replied with a nod.

"This is my last dance of the evening, so I think I'll slip out to the barn," I stated, leaning toward Phillip's ear.

We finished our waltz. The entire time, I could feel his energy vibrating around me. My hand slipped from his, and I moved through the crowded dance floor toward the great hall. My heart pounded hard as I glanced around before sliding through the front doors.

The cold air hit me, but I couldn't tell if the shivers were from the cold or anticipation. I used my magic to warm myself as I crossed the grounds. Thankfully, the path was cleared of snow, but the moon's light glistened on the ice crystals clinging to the grass and tree branches. Despite the beauty of the night, it was a relief when I finally entered the shelter of the barn.

Warm air and the quiet breathing of animals greeted me, and I walked toward Thistle's stall. My dragon was curled up, her nose tucked under her tail. She was sleeping soundly, and I slowly backed away from the gate, not wanting to wake her. Instead, I sat on a haybale across the aisle from her pen.

It wasn't long before I heard the creak of the barn door and the sound of Phillip approaching. I rose, and Phillip stopped within inches of me.

"This is insane," he whispered, reaching up to tuck a loose strand of my hair behind my ear.

"I know. Perhaps we shouldn't…" I began but was silenced as Phillip's lips claimed mine.

All thoughts immediately vanished from my head as I lost myself in the feel of his mouth. For as cold as I'd been outside, I was instantly hot. My heart fluttered in my chest. As strange as it would seem, I'd never felt more content or sure of myself. Being in Phillip's arms was where I belonged, and my connection to him was genuine. How could anything that felt like this be reprehensible?

When our kiss finally ended, I was breathless again. Grasping Phillip's hand, we both sat on the haybale.

"We are completely crazy," I sighed.

"I agree," Phillip grinned. "and I don't care." He raised my fingers to his lips and kissed them.

A pleasant shudder went down my body, and I slid closer to him. Phillip wrapped his arm around me, and I rested my head on his shoulder. His right hand continued to caress my numb fingers, and I sighed at the satisfying feeling of his warmth.

"I don't think I've ever danced like that before," I whispered.

"You moved so beautifully," Phillip responded.

"We should've been more cautious. People probably noticed. Josefina commented about my aura, and Kairi observed how we interacted."

Phillip sighed. "Yes. Perhaps I was a bit careless this evening. You're right. We need to be more cautious, but I lose all logic when I'm near you. I've never felt so compelled, and I can't fight this magnetic pull I feel whenever you're around."

"Is this normal?" I exhaled, running my finger along the curve of his cheek.

A soft growl escaped his lips. "I'm not sure," he replied, pressing his mouth to my temple.

I knew exactly what he was talking about. Every time I was around Phillip, it felt like an invisible string was between us, pulling us toward each other. I hadn't noticed it before, but in one way or another, it felt like it had always been there, like some deep-seated connection had finally surfaced. I couldn't explain it. I'd loved before, but never this fiercely. I had loved Robert with all my heart, but it didn't compare to what I felt now. The thought made me feel guilty. I pushed thoughts of Robert out of my mind, clinging to Phillip while he brought his lips to mine again.

I allowed myself to be lost in the kiss once more, my heart rejoicing that I could even feel this way again. Phillip's pulse beat against my fingertips as my hand rested against his neck. It seemed to be moving as quickly as mine, and it spiked even higher when we both heard the barn door creak. We instantly leapt apart, my heart feeling like it was going to come out of my chest. My eyes flew to the entrance, but I didn't see anyone. Phillip's green eyes scanned the dark, too, and after a moment, he nervously chuckled.

"It must've been the wind," he stated with a shake of his head, but I could tell he was just as spooked as I was. "It's getting later. Perhaps it was a sign that we'd pressed our luck enough for the evening. I should return to the academy. I wouldn't want my presence to be missed while cleaning up from the dance," he sighed.

I nodded in agreement, my entire body on edge from the sound of the door. "Go on ahead, and I'll wait a few minutes before I leave," I suggested.

Phillip gave me a good night kiss before standing to leave. I remained seated, trying to get my breathing under control. My heart was racing, and I attempted to slow it down. A good five to ten minutes passed before I stood from the haybale. On shaky legs, I exited the barn. The night closed in around me, and immediately, I felt apprehensive. I tried to shake off the feeling, but it was one I was very familiar with. I was reminded of my nightmares, and I glanced in both directions, knowing in my gut I was being watched. I debated sprinting for the academy when suddenly, a hand clamped down on my shoulder.

35

EXAMINE AND OBSERVE

I ACTED ON INSTINCT alone. Grabbing my attacker's hand, I used my body and magic to propel the offender over my left shoulder. With a loud thud, he landed in front of me in the snow.

"Zachary!" I shouted in shock once my eyes adjusted to the light of the moon, and I could see my assailant clearly.

Zachary groaned and rolled on the fresh snow, obviously in pain. "My gods, Jane! What in the world did you do that for?" he finally gasped.

"I'm sorry, I didn't know it was you. I thought you intended to harm me," I cried, crouching in the snow beside him.

"I never expected you to almost knock the lights out of me," he said, struggling to sit up.

"Well, that's what you deserve, sneaking up on a lady like that. You frightened me half to death," I said.

"I don't think I was the one sneaking," he replied with a scowl.

"What do you mean?" I asked. I could feel the color draining from my face.

"I think you know damn well what I mean," he replied, brushing the snow from his jacket. I looked away from him as he stood. "I guess you have nothing to say?" he questioned harshly.

"What do you want me to say?" I asked, finally glancing at him.

"How long have you been sneaking around with Mr. Withermyer?"

"Not long, and I wouldn't say we were sneaking," I began, but Zachary huffed.

"I guess that's why you rejected me at Christmas," he said.

"No, that's not why I rejected you. Though I suppose I didn't realize my feelings for Phillip then," I replied.

"Phillip," Zachary said with a shake of his head. "After what I saw, of course, you're on a first-name basis. What are you doing, Jane?"

"Zachary, I'm sorry I don't feel that way about you. I thought you understood," I said, crossing my arms over my chest. I wasn't sure if I was shielding myself from the cold night or Zachary's icy stare.

"I did understand until I saw you with him. He's an instructor at the academy! What are you thinking?" Zachary asked.

"I don't know, and I can't change how I feel. I'm not a child. I'll be twenty in a few days. So, it's not like I'm being taken advantage of," I said, adopting his tone of voice.

Zachary shook his head. "I can't even believe this."

"Are you going to tell someone?" I asked.

My heart pounded due to Zachary's anger. Would he expose my feelings for Phillip?

"I probably should tell someone," Zachary sighed in expiration. "Come on, I'll escort you back to the academy. It's too cold to stay out here,"

We continued on the path, my heart in my stomach. I wasn't sure what else to say. I shivered and pulled my arms tighter around myself. Using magic, I attempted to heat my skin, but it was hard to maintain concentration. Another shiver pulsed through me, and Zachary offered his arm. Hesitantly, I accepted, and we walked toward the school.

After a few steps, Zachary finally spoke. "You've kept my sister's secret, so I feel obligated to keep yours. My sister would be destroyed if she was exposed for being a half-pixie." His voice sounded resigned.

"I would never reveal your sister's secret, no matter what you decide to do about me," I replied.

"I know, which is why I've decided not to tell. I'll keep your secret, Jane, because you're a kind and caring person. Just promise me you'll think about what you're doing. I wouldn't want you to get hurt," Zachary responded.

Zachary knew about Phillip now, and I had to trust he would keep my secret. A large part of me believed he would. Zachary knew how painful exposed secrets could be after what happened to Kairi at the Capra Academy of Magic. I just hoped he wouldn't become vindictive since I had rejected his affections.

"I didn't plan on this, nor did I want to hurt your feelings," I whispered.

"I know, Jane. I didn't mean to be harsh with you. I'd just hate to see you get your heart broken because I do care," was all he said as we approached the front doors.

I nodded but didn't understand what he wanted me to think about. My feelings for Phillip weren't going to change, and I believed that Phillip truly felt the same way about me. I just had to rely upon Zachary to keep his word and my secret.

The night of the February W.A.S.P. meeting arrived swiftly, and before I knew it, Phillip and I had transfigured into our new disguises. I hadn't told Phillip about Zachary and decided to focus on my mission for the W.A.S.P. meeting instead. Tonight, not only would I pay attention to the meeting's proceedings, but I'd also study the waitress, Mary, so I could execute my plan for accessing the back room.

Nervous anxiety pulsed through me as Phillip held the door

of the *Dew Drop Inn*. This evening, we were disguised as an elderly couple again. Phillip came in behind me, and I clung to his arm while he leaned some of his weight on a wooden cane. We hobbled to a table, and once I was seated, Phillip reached up to remove his bowler hat. It wasn't long before Mary approached our table with menus.

I observed her brunette hair, pinned up in a messy, curly bun. She also had a ribbon around her head, which helped to hold her hair out of her face. She had a sweet smile with full lips and a small petit nose. When she handed us the menus, I noticed her light blue eyes framed by long lashes. I tried not to openly stare, but I needed to memorize everything. Thankfully, she didn't seem to notice my gaze through my thick glasses.

"What can I get you to drink?" Mary asked sweetly.

"Excuse me, I didn't hear you. I have a hard time hearing anymore, dear," Phillip said, pointing to his ear. I knew he was trying to keep Mary at our table so I could continue to study her.

Mary patiently repeated the question, and Phillip requested a list of all the available beverages. I continued to take a mental picture while Mary repeated the list twice. Finally, Phillip ordered, and I took pity on the girl and quickly ordered a coffee with plenty of cream and sugar.

"You're going to annoy her," I whispered once she'd left.

"I'll do whatever it takes since you won't give up on this crazy plan of yours," Phillip answered.

After a few moments, Mary returned and asked if we had decided on our meals. This time, I pretended it was hard to read the menu. I had to commend Mary's patience. She read multiple entrée choices in a loud voice. This gave me even more time to notice the curve of her cheeks, the beauty marks on her arms, and her slim figure. I also paid close attention to her movements and expressions. I wouldn't be able to get by on appearance alone, especially if the W.A.S.P. members came here once a month.

It wasn't long before the W.A.S.P. arrived, and we added our *heightened hearing charms* to our drinks. As they filed in at different intervals, I counted each group while they walked back to the room. I had reached seventeen when Seth O'Doherty entered. He looked as cocky as ever, his eyes raking over Mary while he strolled toward the back room.

"I don't like how he looks at her," Phillip whispered.

"Is this another way of trying to talk me out of my ideas?" I asked.

"Partially," Phillip responded with a shrug. "It's risky, but who knows what that man is capable of. We don't know how he feels about Mary, but his stare says a lot."

"He looks at all women that way. I'm not particularly worried," I commented before sipping my coffee.

Phillip's mouth fell open, and he stared at me in shock.

"The man is a friend of Drake's. He's been at the manor a few times," I replied in a hushed tone.

"I knew that, but I wasn't aware you directly interacted with him."

"Yes, I've been under his stare before," I said.

Phillip leaned across the table. "Jane, you have to stay away from him. All the W.A.S.P. members are dangerous, but something about that man seems worse than the others."

"I understand what you mean. I've always gotten a terrible vibe from him. Even before I knew about his involvement, I would've avoided being in a room alone with him."

"Well, don't ever be alone with him, and if you can keep away from him, please do," Phillip said.

Seth's voice interrupted our discussion as he began the meeting.

"Good evening, comrades, and welcome to our February meeting." The room quieted down, and I knew he had their attention. "As you all know, Major Doyle will return for next month's meeting, but I'll be in his company in the next two weeks. So I hope you have something good for me to report."

No one said a word at first. Then, after a moment, I heard someone clear their throat.

"Yes, Lieutenant Davis?" Seth asked.

"I've made my conclusion on the status of the girl I'm court-ing. I've determined she is indeed a pixie," Lieutenant Davis said. "Would you be willing to accompany me on my next visit? Perhaps it would be the perfect time to test that weapon you discussed at the last meeting."

"That sounds like an excellent idea. Talk to me after the meet-ing, and we'll select the day," Seth replied.

"You're just going to take his word that the girl is a pixie? What proof do you have, Lieutenant Davis?" said a man who I believed to be Lieutenant Marchberg.

There was a pause, and I heard Lieutenant Davis stuttering.

"Please, Lieutenant Marchberg. Do you always have to insert yourself with something negative?" Seth said, sounding annoyed.

"Lieutenant Davis hasn't given us any reason for how he knows the girl is a pixie. Were you even going to ask before potentially com-mitting a crime against another human?" Marchberg asked haughtily.

"Of course, I would confirm the girl was a pixie before using the weapon. This wouldn't be my first pixie capture. I also happen to trust Lieutenant Davis's judgement," Seth replied.

"Well, because of your judgement, we lost men at Coillewood, but you'll be thrilled to know I have recruited twenty-five new members. I'm in the process of training them. That's one thing I'm sure Major Doyle will be happy to hear," Marchberg bragged.

"Good. I'm glad to hear about it. I suppose you have a roster of the new recruits since I shouldn't take anyone's word," Seth said sarcastically.

I heard the rustle of paper. "I do have a roster. I hand-wrote the copy myself!" Marchberg replied.

"I'll make sure Major Doyle receives this," Seth commented with a sigh. "Does anyone else have good news?"

A man whose voice I hadn't heard before spoke. "I have intel on a new pixie town."

"Okay, Captain Gordon. Tell us what you've found," Seth said, and the entire room sounded like they were holding their breaths.

"It's called Pyske Isle," Captain Gordon said.

"Pyske Isle?" Seth asked, sounding doubtful. "That seems a little obvious."

"I swear it's an island hidden by magic in the North Atlantic Ocean," Captain Gordon insisted.

"Aren't they all?" Marchberg sneered. "The devils hide everything with magic."

"Where is this island supposed to be hidden?" Seth asked.

"It's off the coast of Maine, Captain. I received this information from a pixie I captured two weeks ago. You can find it if you sail out from the mainland toward Nova Scotia. Just like Coillewood, there's a special way to access the location. It involves some alignment of the North Star or the sun. I took very detailed notes from my captive," Captain Gordon said.

"I would enjoy speaking to your prisoner," Seth said wickedly. "I love obtaining information from already broken pixies."

"Unfortunately, he expired after my round of questioning, but I'm confident I could find the location from my notes. My captive also hinted at other magical creatures native to the area, like mermaids," Captain Gordon announced proudly.

"Mermaids? Hmm… I've heard of a few rumors about other creatures, but I haven't seen proof of them myself. I'll look into this location, and if I may read your notes, Captain Gordon. I'm sure Major Doyle will be most interested," Seth responded.

"I knew you would," Captain Gordon said with an evil laugh. "I'm hoping we'll be able to organize an expedition and potential attack soon."

"When I speak to Major Doyle, I'll inform him of this. I'm

sure we can get something together soon, maybe even before the next meeting," Seth said, and the room erupted with applause.

"This is exactly what we needed," Lieutenant Davis cried enthusiastically.

Phillip tapped me on the arm as the men continued to cheer, bringing my attention back to our table. His expression was full of worry.

"We need to warn Arnold Barber immediately," Phillip whispered, leaning toward me. "Pyske Isle is indeed an all-pixie island, located exactly where they discussed. We have to stop them as we did for Coillewood."

I nodded my head and kept my eye on Mary. It was even more critical to gain access to the meeting. I said as much to Phillip.

I'm afraid they won't wait until the next meeting. You heard they want to plan the attack right away. So we have to figure out how we can discover their plans before it's too late," Phillip murmured. He had a puzzled expression on his disguised face.

My mind began to turn, looking for a solution, a way I would be able to discover when an attack on Pyske Isle would occur. Suddenly, Seth's words from earlier in the meeting began to sink in. Mr. Doyle would be returning, and with him, my stepfamily. My freedom from them was almost over, but with their homecoming, I would have to return to the manor. Once again, I'd have access to Drake's correspondence.

"We won't have to wait until the next meeting to discover what the W.A.S.P. is up to. My stepfamily returns soon, so leave all the spying to me," I whispered. Phillip's head bobbed, but I could tell from his expression that he was apprehensive. "It will be fine. You trained me well," I said, continuing to keep my voice low. I was hoping that by keeping a confident attitude, I would reassure him, and maybe I could also convince myself, too.

36

HEINOUS PLOTS

THE CARRIAGE PULLED up the driveway. I let out a sigh, but it didn't relieve my tension. The day I'd been dreading was here. Marie and her progeny were returning. I removed myself from the window and headed toward the front entryway. Closing my eyes, I centered myself, knowing a headache would come on once I opened the front door. I gripped the handle and turned the knob.

The horses had stopped at the end of the front steps, and I stepped onto the porch. With a flourish, the coachman opened the carriage door, and Marie extended her hand to be helped down. Her gray-tinged hair was pinned up and half hidden beneath a dark green traveling hat. As soon as she climbed from the carriage, her steel gray eyes found me.

"Jane, get down here at once and help unload our bags," Marie shrieked.

Without a word, I descended the stairs and walked toward the back of the carriage. Since Marie had been handed out of the carriage, the footman climbed up to unstrap the trunks. He began handing them down, and I placed them along the drive.

Next, Preston came bounding out of the carriage, his flaming red hair shining in the sunlight. He had grown another inch or two, his trousers riding up from the ankles of his gangly legs.

"Mother, when will the other carriage be arriving? I need my new things," Preston whined.

"The carriage with our possessions will arrive in a week or so," Marie replied, monitoring the unloading of the trunks.

"I must pick the perfect location for my alligator trophy!" Preston exclaimed, rushing into the house.

Drake was next to step out; his black hair was slicked back beneath his gray derby hat. He wore his gray ulster coat, and I noticed the W.A.S.P. pin attached to the lapel. He immediately turned around and extended his hand. Emily took a while to emerge. She placed a foot on the carriage step, and I could see how swollen it was in her patent leather colt shoe. Her inflated stomach was the next thing to come forth, and finally, her bloated face. The pregnancy had not been kind to her despite the trip to warmer weather. I knew she was almost seven months pregnant, but she looked so different from when she'd left.

"Drake, please help me upstairs to my bed. I'm exhausted from the traveling," Emily sighed, placing the back of her hand across her forehead.

Slowly, they made their way up the front steps and into the house while I continued to help with the bags. Marie stood on the porch until the carriage was emptied. Then she immediately turned to me.

"Jane, get these bags upstairs and begin unpacking. Then I will need you to assist me out of my traveling clothes and into a warm bath," Marie demanded.

I bowed to her and acknowledged her request. Quickly, I scooped up two suitcases and headed upstairs. Marie stalked off toward the kitchen, probably to discuss dinner plans with Ellen. I lugged the bags into Marie's room and hurried to carry the rest.

When I entered Emily's room, I found her sprawled across her bed. Her large, pregnant stomach looked like a pumpkin beneath her dress. She groaned dramatically as I made my way to her closet.

"I'm so hot, and my feet hurt," Emily moaned, and I heard the sound of her shoes hitting the floor as she kicked them off.

I ignored her as I proceeded to hang up her dresses. Compared to the other clothes in her closet, I could tell Emily had alterations done to accommodate the weight she gained from the pregnancy. I had almost emptied the first suitcase when I heard Emily screaming my name.

"Jane! Jane, get out here right away!"

Expecting an emergency, I bolted from the closet. "Is it the baby?" I asked, panicked.

"I guess you could say it's the baby's fault. I can't get up. Pull me up and prop me on my pillows," Emily complained, looking very much like a turtle turned onto its back.

"I thought you were in pain," I replied.

"I am in pain, you fool! This baby hurts my back, I'm always nauseous, and my ankles are swollen! Now help me prop my feet up with some pillows!" Emily screamed at me.

I grasped her hands and attempted to pull her into a seated position. Emily was no help in the matter. Her body was dead weight and very heavy. I subtly used some of my magic to get her situated on her pillows. She complained the entire time until I slipped the last pillow beneath her knees.

By the time I had Emily's suitcases unpacked, she had fallen asleep on the bed. I quietly left the room and crossed the hall to Marie's room since she demanded I help her with a bath. Marie wasn't in the room when I entered, but I headed to the bathroom and began running the tub. As the hot water ran, I started unpacking Marie's luggage. It wasn't long before Marie came in.

"Oh, good. I'm glad you're already hard at work here. Help

me out of my traveling dress," Marie snapped when she saw me emerge from her closet.

She spun around so I could undo the silver buttons down her back. My fingers worked nimbly, and Marie soon stepped out of the dark green dress. The hem was stained with mud, so I carried it to the laundry shoot. Marie walked to the bathroom wearing her shift, and I gave her a private moment to undress.

"Jane, have you unpacked everyone's luggage?" Marie questioned as I massaged soap into her increasingly graying hair.

"No, ma'am, I still have Mr. Doyle's and Preston's to attend to. Emily needed my assistance," I responded. I held my breath, waiting for the reprimand.

"Good, Emily should be your main focus. Do whatever she asks. The well-being of my grandchild is the most important," Marie huffed, examining her nails. "Once you rinse my hair, leave me to soak while you continue your tasks. I need to wash the red dirt of Georgia from my skin."

As I ran water through Marie's sudsy hair, I wondered how the trip had been for her to comment on washing the filth away. It probably didn't matter since Marie found fault with everything. They could've had the loveliest holiday, and Marie would have something negative to say.

Preston didn't answer when I knocked, and I cautiously let myself into the room. With a wary eye, I checked behind the door, expecting him to jump out and surprise me. I began to relax when I didn't find him behind the door or in the bathroom. Maybe he wasn't in the room at all. I started to walk toward his closet when a hand darted out from beneath the bed and grabbed my ankle. I almost tripped but managed to maintain my balance. An evil chuckle came from under the bed, and Preston's hand released my leg.

"I almost tripped you," he laughed joyously, poking his head out from under the bed skirt.

"Don't you think you are a little too old for childish games? You could've seriously hurt me! Get out from under the bed," I cried.

It didn't take him long to pull his lanky limbs from beneath the bed, and soon, he stood before me. He was definitely taller than when he left, and now he towered over me. His mischievous green eyes narrowed.

"The point was to seriously injure you, and you shouldn't talk to me that way. Mother wouldn't approve, and I'm the man of this house," Preston said with a sniff as he crossed his freckled arms.

"When you start acting like a man instead of a child, maybe I'll address you differently," I said boldly, turning toward his closet.

Preston grabbed my arm tightly with a very tight grip, and it took everything in me not to retaliate with what I'd learned in my lessons. His strength surprised me, but I willed my face not to show how nervous I was. Preston squeezed my bicep with more force, but I refused to give him the satisfaction of crying out. Instead, I returned his gaze with a steel look of my own.

"I'll act however I damn well please, and you'll obey my commands. Someday, I'm going to run this manor. Drake believes I'm a man. When I killed my first gator, he told me that," Preston snarled. He finally released my arm, and I stumbled away from him. "Don't tell me how I'm acting ever again, or I'll tell my mother how you talk to me."

I turned away from him and began emptying his suitcases, but I kept an eye on him in case he decided to attack me. Apparently, his idea of acting like a man was running to his mother and reporting my behavior. Obviously, spending time with Drake Doyle was only helping to hone his psychopathic tendencies. I wondered what else he was being taught.

The only good thing was Preston had been a baby when my magic slammed every door in this house. I didn't think he remembered; I had hidden my abilities since that day. I doubted Preston was aware that I was a pixie. Marie and Emily knew about my magic, though I didn't think Drake would share the activities of his little gentlemen's club. I just couldn't become complacent at the manor and needed to make an escape plan if I ever found myself in danger.

Pushing those thoughts away, I finished with Preston's things and moved on to Drake's suitcases. Thankfully, he wasn't in his room, and I accomplished the task fairly quickly. After checking on Marie, I went to the kitchen to help prepare dinner. Emily requested the meal in her room, so I took a tray to her once I served the other family members. Dinner was uneventful, and just as everyone was finishing up, the doorbell chimed throughout the house.

"Who could be calling on us? We've only returned today. Jane, go see who is at the door," Marie demanded, laying her napkin beside her plate.

Hurriedly, I approached the front door. My fingers tingled as I placed them on the doorknob. All I could make out through the frosted glass was a dark figure. Yet, somehow, I wasn't at all surprised when I opened the door to find Seth O'Doherty on the step. He wore the same gray ulster coat I'd seen at the W.A.S.P. meeting, the hexagon-shaped pin on his left lapel. He removed his bowler hat and gave me a wide smile.

"Good evening, my dear," Seth began as his eyes traveled up and down my body. "I've come to see Major, I mean, Mr. Drake Doyle. Could you please announce that Mr. Seth O'Doherty is here?" he said with a slight cough to cover his use of the word major.

"Yes, sir," I replied as Seth stepped into the foyer.

Leaving him, I headed back to the dining room. I was sure he'd come to update Drake on what he missed during the W.A.S.P. meetings. He was probably brimming with excitement about the news of a new pixie location. I had to find a way to listen in on their discussion.

As I entered the dining room, Marie glanced up at me. "Well, girl, who was at the door?" she snapped.

"It's a Mr. Seth O'Doherty to see Mr. Doyle," I replied as sweetly as possible.

"What's he doing here?" Drake growled while he scooped up another spoonful of pie. "Ah, I guess the man can't wait a day to discuss business. Jane, see him to the office, and I shall be there in a moment."

I curtsied before returning to the foyer. Seth was walking around, examining the décor and the crystal sconces on the walls. He paused when he noticed I'd returned.

"Mr. Doyle requested that I escort you back to the office," I said.

Seth's eyes trailed over my body again, and I fought the urge to flinch. "Lead the way," he replied with a raise of his eyebrows and a wink.

I began walking back the hallway, and Seth followed close behind. The hair on the back of my neck stood up just from knowing that he was trailing me. I tried to calm my racing heart. I needed to keep acting as natural as possible, though every nerve in my body tingled at the thought of being in a dimly lit hallway with a member of the W.A.S.P. My brain was on edge, anticipating an attack, though I knew it would be urological for him to attack me.

I clenched the brass doorknob to my father's office and slowly turned it. I allowed Seth to enter the room and went about turning on the sconces. The room had a chill, and I tried not to focus on how imposing he was in the smaller space. I watched as he paced around the office, taking in every detail.

"Would you like me to take your coat?" I asked, my voice sounding small as it cut through the silence.

"Yes, I suppose you may, though it does feel a bit drafty in here," Seth responded as he began removing it.

"I can light a fire in the hearth," I replied, taking his coat and bowler hat. My thumb brushed the pin on the lapel, and I shivered.

"That would be lovely, sweetheart," Seth said with a smirk.

Before moving to the fireplace, I hung his coat and hat on the small coat rack in the corner. Every cell in my body loathed to be in the room alone with him, but I needed to hear the discussion. I had to do everything I could to stay in the room. I reached for the logs stacked in the basket beside the fireplace when the office door creaked, and Drake entered.

His gaze passed over me and then settled on Seth. "What was so important it couldn't wait for me to settle in after my vacation?" Drake huffed.

Seth glanced a wary eye in my direction. "Drake, perhaps we should wait one moment to discuss...." Seth began, but Drake raised a hand, cutting him off.

"Now, Captain O'Doherty, don't pay Jane any heed and allow her to continue her task. The room has a bit of a chill, wouldn't you agree? You've rushed over here with some news, and I shan't hear it while I freeze to death, nor will I wait for Jane to finish. Jane's a smart girl who won't repeat anything," Drake commented, giving me a hard stare. "Besides, don't you think we need something beautiful to admire and brighten this room?"

Seth nodded his head. "Fine, if you believe you can trust her."

"Who does she have to tell?" Drake said with a chuckle. "Furthermore, who would believe her anyway, even if she did tell another servant? In my experience, gossip among household maids tends to get back to me, so I would know if she was wagging her tongue." He glared at me in a threatening way, and I understood his insinuation.

I pretended I hadn't heard a word and continued working on the fire. It would be in my best interest to pretend to be stupid since I had a few people to tell unbeknownst to Drake. I noticed Seth giving me one final look before he began speaking again.

"I'm here to tell you about what we've been working on in your absence these past few months," Seth began.

"I figured as much. I'm hoping it was something good since

you rushed over here. Did you happen to find the McCalski heir?" Drake asked.

I could feel a sweat breaking out under my collar.

"Well, no, Major, but we could be headed in the right direction. Just the other day, Lieutenant Davis and I captured an entire pixie family. They might have information on the McCalski heir. The daughter is probably of age with the McCalski girl. Perhaps they know where we can find her."

"Congratulations on the successful operation. However, it's not a definite," Drake said with a scowl.

"I know, Major, but at least we have someone to question," Seth answered.

"Are you keeping them, or is Lieutenant Davis?"

"Lieutenant Davis handed them over to me. I haven't trusted him with captives since he let that one girl escape."

"Good, that's what I would have done. I hope this isn't the only news you have for me."

"No, Major. Captain Gordon has discovered information about another pixie town," Seth said excitedly.

"Wonderful, I would love to hear about it. Jane, fetch us a tray with coffee. Also, why don't you bring some of those tea cookies Ellen made? I'm in need of refreshment," Drake demanded as he turned to me.

I dusted my hands off as I rose from the burning fire. "Right away, sir," I replied with a curtsy.

I abhorred the idea of leaving the room. They were about to talk about Pyske Isle, and I needed to hear whatever plans they were concocting. I hurried to the kitchen and began brewing the coffee. While I waited, I loaded a tray with cookies, cream, and sugar. I knew Drake liked his coffee black, but I wasn't sure how Seth liked the drink. It was torture waiting. This was my best chance to learn what the W.A.S.P. was going to plan.

Finally, when the coffee was made, I carried it back to the office. I paused outside the door so I could listen before entering.

"We need to be smart about this. We shouldn't rush into this attack," Drake was saying. "We don't even know if we can find the place using Captain Gordon's notes."

"I've seen Captain Gordon's notes, and they're very detailed," Seth responded.

"I trust your judgement if you've read them, but this place won't be easy to travel to even if Gordon's instructions are correct. It's a damn island. The travel will cost us more than usual," Drake intoned.

"I understand, Major. I just thought you would be more excited about the prospects," Seth said, sounding annoyed.

"I'm thrilled by this news! The thought of decimating another pixie location excites me more than you can imagine, but after Coillewood, we must be cautious," Drake intoned with a sigh. "The higher-ups won't be too pleased if we fail again."

"I've been working very hard to make up for the mistake at Coillewood. I've found new recruits, and I have a few rosters that other Captains and Lieutenants have secured." I heard the rustling sound of papers.

"Where is that damn coffee? Discussing this is making me parched," Drake complained.

I waited a few moments before entering the room so it wouldn't seem suspicious.

"There we are. I was just wondering if you'd gotten lost," Drake commented while I whisked the tray over to the oak desk.

"I'm sorry, sir. The coffee took longer than I expected," I replied. I poured out a cup for him and then turned toward Seth. "How do you take your coffee, Mr. O'Doherty?"

"I'll have some cream and sugar. I can't stand the stuff if it's too dark. One-fourth of the cup must be cream and three teaspoons of sugar," he stated, smiling at me. The scar on his cheek danced in the light of the fire, and if I didn't know how evil he was, it would be easy to assume he was charming.

"I'll be sure to remember that," I said sweetly as I prepared his cup.

"I like this one," Seth said with a laugh. "Where did you find her again?"

"Jane is part of my mother-in-law's household. I dare say Marie has trained her well," Drake said with an amused expression. He leaned forward to grab a cookie from the tray.

"Such stunning eyes. I've never seen such captivating eyes before and so obedient," Seth commented.

"Thank you, sir," I replied, though his words disgusted me.

"Yes, I agree. Jane is one of the most dutiful maids here. She completes anything asked of her," Drake added.

"Is that so?" Seth sniggered, his eyes saying more than his words. I tried not to shudder.

"Seth, don't allow my maid to distract you," Drake stated, picking up the documents on the desk. "This looks like a decent number of new recruits, but we'll need more. I've been working on those details myself."

Seth watched every move I made while adding his cream and sugar. When I handed him the cup, he made a point of grazing his fingers along mine. I kept the revulsion off my face as I turned toward Drake.

"Will you be needing anything else, Mr. Doyle?"

"Why don't you stoke the fire for a bit? The flames aren't giving off enough warmth," he demanded before redirecting his attention. "New recruits aside, it's going to take a while before we make a move on this Pyske Isle. First, we need to gain more information. I don't want us going in blind again."

"I understand, Major. What would you like us to do to set up the attack?"

"We're going to need funds for ships, the new recruits need

more training, and we need to research the location. Even though Captain Gordon's notes are detailed, I'm not going to risk this on one captive's instructions. We should start by raising money and working on training. I'll be over this week to interrogate your prisoner. Maybe they'll know something about Pyske Isle," Drake said, ticking off each instruction on his fingers.

"Hopefully, it won't be long before we get something underway. It's been a while since we've made some progress, and I'm itching to rid the world of more pixie scum," Seth said, his eyes glowing in the firelight.

"Patience, my good man! We'll get the opportunity soon enough, and when we do, I promise it will be satisfying."

37

PROTECTION FOR PYSKE ISLE?

ARNOLD BARBER PACED the floor of Dr. Tweedle's office. "You're sure the W.A.S.P. is planning an attack on Pyske Isle?"

"Yes, sir. We heard it discussed at the W.A.S.P. meeting, and the information was confirmed by Mr. Doyle and Mr. O'Doherty when I was at the manor," I replied, leaning forward to the edge of Dr. Tweedle's sofa.

"When are they going to attack?" Mr. Barber asked.

"I'm not sure. They haven't picked a date, but I'll bet it will be discussed soon," I answered. I hated that I didn't know, but I was confident I would find out between my spying at the manor and the W.A.S.P. meetings. Drake Doyle trusted me, after all.

"So, what you're telling me is we know nothing! You don't have a name for the family this Lieutenant Davis supposedly captured, we don't have a date for an attack, and we know nothing about the weapons the W.A.S.P. have. This meeting is a waste of my time," Mr. Barber spat.

"I don't believe it was a waste of time, Arnold," Phillip protested. "We know where the W.A.S.P. is going to strike next, and it will only be a matter of time before we find out when."

"Pyske Isle is a tiny community; half the population isn't even pixies. Am I supposed to squander my staff and permanently install a crew on the island? To be honest, we have more important things to worry about than an island full of half-bloods, especially when the island is the most difficult place to access," Mr. Barber exclaimed.

"Why, Arnold, I'm disappointed you would ignore this warning just because the population is not all full-blooded pixies!" Dr. Tweedle said in shock.

"That's not my only argument. Pyske Isle is minuscule in terms of the pixie population. I don't have the resources to keep a unit there. What I'm trying to say is that our government is not responsible for the mermaids, which is why I cannot justify it, especially since Miss Fitzgerald has no further information. Also, Pyske Isle is one of our best-hidden cities. I highly doubt the W.A.S.P. really knows how to access it," Mr. Barber said pretentiously.

"Captain Gordon claims he has detailed notes, which he acquired from torturing a captive. They probably have more information than you think," I objected.

"Have you laid eyes on these notes?" Mr. Barber asked with a smirk.

"Well, no…"

"Then how do you know?" Mr. Barber questioned, cutting me off. "You have one job, Miss Fitzgerald, and that is collecting information I can use. I can't work with maybes and probably," Mr. Barber sighed.

"If you don't want to place a defensive unit on Pyske Isle, couldn't you at least figure out which family Lieutenant Davis captured? The daughter should be about my age," I said desperately.

"Miss Fitzgerald, do you realize how many pixies go missing? We have a hard enough time keeping our reports up to date. If no one reports a missing family, then how would we know? I can check our files for persons about your age, but I'll have no way to know for sure. They must've been the type to consort with humans if Lieutenant Davis claimed he was courting the girl. Our society frowns upon those types. We should only interact with humans when necessary. We shouldn't become their friends," Mr. Barber sniffed.

I couldn't keep the glare off my face. It didn't appear Mr. Barber cared about Pyske Isle or the missing family. What good was reporting to him if he didn't do anything with the information? Granted, I didn't have a clue when the W.A.S.P. planned to attack, nor did I know the name of the family, but it was better than knowing nothing at all.

"Well, if that's all you have for me today, I'll be on my way," Mr. Barber said in a clipped voice, grabbing his coat and hat.

Dr. Tweedle said goodbye to Mr. Barber, but Phillip and I remained silent. Once Mr. Barber had departed, Dr. Tweedle turned to us.

"You both better head down to dinner. Especially you, Jane dear. I wouldn't want you to miss it. Don't feel discouraged. I'm sure Mr. Barber won't let anything happen to the pixies and mermaids on Pyske Isle. I know he said other magical species aren't under his jurisdiction, but Pyske Isle is a pixie town despite other races sharing it. It's still his job to protect our kind," Dr. Tweedle said.

"He didn't sound very convincing," I replied, rising from the sofa.

"Jane, I know Arnold Barber can be crass, but he's one of the best government operatives. Let him handle how he uses the information you give him," Dr. Tweedle said. "Now go and enjoy the rest of your evening. Don't get caught up in Arnold Barber's decisions. He'll do the right thing."

Phillip held the door for me, and I exited the office. Though Dr. Tweedle had known Mr. Barber longer than I had, I didn't believe Mr. Barber would do the right thing. He seemed prejudiced about half-blooded pixies and other magical races. I said as much to Phillip once we were further down the hallway.

"I agree. The Barbers have always made their feelings known about other magical species. Not only do they think pixies are superior, but they also believe their own family is," Phillip replied.

"I'm afraid he isn't going to protect Pyske Isle, even if I do discover more. He made it clear to me he doesn't care about that place," I said, feeling anxious.

"The only bit of truth is that Pyske Isle is difficult to access. It's unlike Jewel Caverns, where you find a lever in the rocks, or Coillewood, where a special tree marks the entrance. Since it's an island, there is a complicated way to access it by boat. Most pixies I know just teleport directly onto the island," Phillip said, and I knew he was only trying to reassure me.

We walked down the main staircase, and Phillip headed toward the staff's dining room.

"I'll see you later tonight for our lessons," I stated, glancing toward the dining hall to see Zachary watching us.

Phillip nodded, and we went our separate ways. I tried to keep a smile on my face as I approached Zachary.

"I can tell nothing has changed between you two," Zachary commented as soon as I got closer.

"No, it hasn't," I replied. I couldn't see how it was any of his business, but I didn't want to anger him. He was keeping my secret, after all.

Zachary nodded but didn't make any further comments. Instead, he stepped to the side to let me enter the dining room first. I collected a tray and cup, then got in line for dinner. Zachery followed behind.

"Jane, I didn't mean to sound condescending," Zachary continued. "I just thought you might've thought about what I said."

"I did think about it, Zachary, and I understand all the points you made, but I cannot turn my feelings off like a water tap," I replied. "Your comments make me feel like you're badgering me."

"I'm sorry. I just care about you. I won't ask again," he replied.

"Ask what?" Kairi's musical voice sounded behind us, and I hadn't realized she'd gotten in line with Taylor.

"Nothing," Zachary and I said simultaneously, then chuckled nervously.

"Okay," Kairi responded with a laugh. "I guess it's not for Taylor and me to know."

"Jane, I saw Mr. Barber leaving the school. Did you have a meeting with him?" Taylor asked.

"Yes," I replied, happy for the change of subject. "He's the most egotistical ass I've ever met besides his daughter."

"What happened?" Kairi asked, her focus shifting away from her brother.

"I discovered some information about where the W.A.S.P. plans to attack next. It's a small island off the coast of Maine called Pyske Isle, and Mr. Barber refuses to place a unit at that location. I don't know if it's because I haven't discovered when the attack will occur or because the island is inhabited by more than pixies," I answered.

"Wait, did you say Pyske Isle?" Zachary asked, looking alarmed.

"Yes, why?' I inquired.

"Our father lives on Pyske Isle when he isn't aboard one of his cruise ships," Kairi answered, her face turning pale.

"You don't know when this attack is supposed to happen?" Zachary asked, and I shook my head.

"The W.A.S.P. hasn't picked a date, but it seemed like they didn't want to rush into an attack. They want to collect more information," I replied, dread filling my stomach.

"We'll have to warn him!" Kairi gasped.

"Jane just said the W.A.S.P. hasn't discussed when. What are we warning him of if we don't know the day? Dad is at sea most of the time anyway, and Pyske Isle is even difficult for pixies to get to unless they teleport to the island. I don't even know if humans have the capabilities to find the place," Zachary responded.

"I'm at least going to send a letter so he knows what's going on," Kairi exclaimed.

"Jane might get in trouble if you send the letter. I'm sure Mr. Barber wouldn't be happy if there was mass panic over something that might not even happen," Zachary told his sister.

"I think you should send the letter. Your father and other pixies on Pyske Isle deserve to know. I don't care what Mr. Barber thinks. He didn't seem like he cared too much about Pyske Isle. Like I said, he doesn't even want to place a unit on the island," I replied.

Zachary swore loudly, and a few people, including Kairi, gave him a look. "He probably doesn't want to because mermaids live on the island and in the surrounding ocean. The Barbers don't seem like the type that would be sympathetic to other magical beings or half-pixies," he said after lowering his voice a bit.

Kairi's expression dropped; I knew it was because her brother had never mentioned mermaids and half-pixies in public before.

"I believe that's the exact reason Mr. Barber doesn't want to send protection. He claimed he wasn't responsible for other magical races, but that doesn't change the fact that pixies live on the island," I said with a frown.

Zachary helped his sister fill her tray, and I picked up a hot turkey sandwich.

"That's typical," Zachary sighed. "So many pixies are like Mr. Barber, and they believe they're the primary magical race."

"Isn't there something that can be done?"' Taylor asked.

"No, Mr. Barber isn't going to change his mind. The only thing I can do is keep spying on the W.A.S.P. until I discover their plans. Hopefully, once I discover something more substantial, Mr. Barber will take the threat more seriously," I said as we walked to our regular table.

Josefina, Miguel, and Andrew were already seated, and I filled them in on my meeting.

"I'm not surprised," Miguel said, shaking his head.

"Jane, if you learn more about Pyske Isle, will you let me know immediately?" Kairi asked.

"Of course! I'll do anything I can to protect pixies and other magical races, no matter what Mr. Barber wants me to do," I said defiantly.

⌘

After dinner, I climbed the stairs to the ninth floor to meet Phillip. Tonight, I'd be practicing my transfiguring charm to become Mary. Mary's face floated in my memory, and I hoped I remembered enough details about her to make the transformation convincing. Now more than ever, I needed close access to the W.A.S.P. meetings.

As I crossed the pool area, my thoughts returned to Kairi and Zachary. Stopping the W.A.S.P. had always been important to me, but the fact the W.A.S.P. planned on attacking a town where the Walshes' father lived made it seem personal. I couldn't allow them to succeed. Feeling determined, I entered the fitness room. I pulled up short when I almost ran into Ms. Pregmon.

"What are you doing in here? This is a staff-restricted area!" she snapped at me.

"I'm meeting Ph... Mr. Withermyer for our lessons," I said, catching myself. I could feel my cheeks going red. Ms. Pregmon was the wrong person to catch me using Phillip's first name.

"Lessons?" Ms. Pregmon sniffed.

"Yes, Mr. Withermyer has been tutoring me for over a year," I responded.

"Oh, well, I wasn't aware you were struggling with Charms," she replied snidely.

"Not struggling," I responded with a shake of my head. "Dr. Tweedle requested advanced lessons since I've excelled with my regular classwork."

Ms. Pregmon's expression fell for a moment, but then her sarcastic smile returned. "I'm surprised Phillip agreed to tutor you. Though I suppose with Dr. Tweedle's influence, he didn't have much choice in the matter, you being the star pupil and all."

"Even though it was Dr. Tweedle's idea, Mr. Withermyer has never complained," I said.

"Well, of course not! I doubt he'd want to lose his job. I never would've suspected him of tolerating it, especially with his animosity toward humans. He absolutely hates them. Ever since we attended the Jelf Academy, he had nothing good to say about them, or half-breeds for that matter. Oh, I probably shouldn't have told you that," Ms. Pregmon said, raising a hand to cover her tight-lipped smile.

"We knew each other fairly well back then and even stayed in touch after we left the Jelf Academy," she answered with a strange smile. "It was so nice when I was offered the job here. I was glad to become acquainted again."

I wondered why she was telling me this, and I was relieved when Phillip walked through the door.

"Blair, I didn't realize you were using the room," Phillip said, addressing Ms. Pregmon.

"Oh, hello, Phillip," Ms. Pregmon said sweetly. She flipped her wavy dark hair over one shoulder. "I was just leaving. So, you can have the room. It's so nice of you to spend time tutoring Miss Fitzgerald."

"Miss Fitzgerald is excellent at charm casting. Sometimes, I'm not sure who is teaching whom," Phillip replied with a chuckle.

Ms. Pregmon scowled. "Well, in that case, I'll leave you to it. Oh, Phillip, would you be so kind as to stop by my room when you're finished? I could use your help with something."

"It depends on how long my lesson goes," Phillip responded.

Finally, Ms. Pregmon turned and left the room.

"Stop by her room?" I asked with a raised eyebrow when I was sure she was gone.

Phillip chuckled and then shrugged. "Blair's always been like that, claiming she needs assistance with the most mundane things. Sometimes, I think she asks for help because she wants attention."

"I almost forgot you attended the Jelf Academy with her. She was just informing me of how much you hated humans back then," I said, crossing my arms over my chest.

"Honestly, I wasn't fond of humans at the time, but really no pixies were. You know the pixie laws and the only one I know who broke them was your mother," Phillip replied. "What made her mention it?"

"She was surprised you were tutoring me since you hate humans and half-breeds."

Phillip shook his head. "Don't pay attention to her. You know that isn't true." He crossed the room and finally encircled me in his arms.

"I know. I think Ms. Pregmon was trying to make me feel insignificant. I'm more disturbed at the thought of you stopping by her room. It seemed she was insinuating that she knew you too well," I breathed, my stomach fluttering.

"Is that jealousy I detect?" Phillip murmured, brushing his lips across my fingers.

"She seemed rather envious of our time together," I said nonchalantly, not wanting to reveal my feelings. However, I couldn't ignore the sickening sensation when Ms. Pregmon hinted at a past that included Phillip.

"Well, my darling, you have nothing to fear. I only have eyes for you," he responded, his eyes piercing into mine before his lips covered my mouth.

I lost myself in his kiss, all thoughts and insecurities leaving my mind. It felt good to be in his arms, and I could've stayed that way all evening. However, my sensible side got the better of me. Reluctantly, I stepped out of his embrace.

"We'll never accomplish my transfiguration practice this way," I scolded lightly.

Phillip chortled and then sighed deeply. "This is exactly what I meant when I said I don't know who is teaching whom."

I pulled my pixie dust case from my pocket and expanded it to look for the *transfiguration charm* I had created earlier. Once again, I conjured Mary's image to the forefront of my mind. I could see her round face framed by her brunette hair, her light blue eyes rimmed by long lashes, and her petite nose perfectly centered in the middle of her face. I pictured her slim figure wearing the clothes she wore the last time I saw her. Taking a deep breath, I grabbed the vial. With every cell of my body focused on my memory, I cast the pixie dust over my head.

Like any other transformation, I felt my body morphing to become what I envisioned. My legs became longer, my hips thinner, and my hair transformed into dark waves that brushed my shoulders. I waited for all the pixie dust to settle before looking at Phillip's startled expression.

"What do you think?" I asked nervously in Mary's sing-song voice.

Phillip continued to gape at me, his mouth hanging open. Finally, he cleared his throat.

"I think this might be crazy enough to actually work!"

38

Becoming Mary

MY HEART WAS pounding so loudly I swore Phillip could hear it. We were on our way to the W.A.S.P. meeting. I prayed everything would go according to plan. Phillip was supposed to enter the *Dew Drop Inn* and somehow confuse Mary into leaving. Once she was out of the way, I would enter in disguise. So much depended on Phillip's ability to distract the waitress and my convincing performance.

Phillip parked the carriage down the street on the opposite side of the *Dew Drop Inn*. My hands were shaking slightly, and I tried to hide them from him as he turned to face me.

"Jane, you don't have to do this if you don't feel comfortable. We can disguise ourselves like usual if you've changed your mind. However, I'm not saying this because I doubt your ability. Every time you've practiced this transformation, you've been so convincing. I just don't want you to feel pressured," Phillip said.

I felt my heart calm a bit at his words. "No, I want to do this. This is our best chance of getting more information. I really believe I can," I answered.

Philip nodded his head. "I thought you would say something like that."

He took a charm vial from his coat pocket and cast the charm over himself. Before my eyes, he transformed into a blonde man with dark blue eyes. Even though the form he'd chosen was very attractive, I missed his green eyes.

"Once I distract Mary, I plan on being around in case anything happens. I hope to use a *confusing charm* and then a *sleeping draught* once I lure her out here." Phillip stated.

I nodded. We had run through a few options, but I wasn't entirely sure what Phillip would decide.

"When I get Mary out here, be ready," Phillip instructed, climbing from the carriage.

I held my breath as I watched him cross the street and head toward the *Dew Drop Inn*. Slowly, I released the air from my lungs when he entered the establishment. I needed to focus on the task ahead of me and be ready to move if Phillip was successful.

Minutes seemed like hours. I had the vial filed with my *transfiguration charm* in my hand and kept my eyes locked on the *Dew Drop Inn*. Suddenly, I caught movement from the alley beside the inn. I blinked rapidly, noticing two figures emerging from the darkness. One was wrapped in a cloak. In the light of the street lamp, I recognized a glint of blonde hair on the larger figure. My hands shook a little as I cast the charm I was holding and began the transformation.

The man led the cloaked figure to the carriage, and I hurried to get out.

"Help me get her inside," Phillip said, guiding Mary toward the carriage door.

Quickly, I assisted the confused Mary into the carriage, and Phillip pulled another vial from his pocket. I laid Mary across the seat while Phillip cast the *sleeping draught* over her. In seconds, Mary was snoring, and Phillip draped the cloak over her like a blanket.

"She should sleep for a few hours," Phillip said, closing the carriage door. "Let's get you back over there before anyone realizes Mary is missing."

I linked my arm with Phillip's as we rushed toward the inn. I followed Phillip down the alleyway, grateful for his steady arm since it was so dark. Finally, we reached a back door, and he held it open for me. A light from inside washed over my body, and Phillip smiled.

"You look perfect, by the way," he whispered, quickly kissing me on the cheek.

I tried to suppress my smile as I followed the hallway back into the main dining area. Surveying the occupied tables, I began Mary's role of taking orders and reporting back to the kitchen. The work wasn't hard, and it was similar to waiting on Marie. Soon, I'd worked myself into an easy rhythm and almost started to relax.

My relaxed state didn't last long when Seth O'Doherty walked in the door, followed by a few other men. his hazel eyes lit up when he saw me, and I pushed down my urge to cringe as I walked toward him.

"Good evening, Mr. O'Doherty. It's so nice to see you again," I stated in Mary's voice.

Seth grinned wickedly at me, and I forced myself to smile back.

"Hello, Mary. Is our regular room ready?" Seth asked, removing his bowler hat.

"I believe so, sir. You can follow me back. Would you like anything to drink?"

I began walking toward their usual room, and I could feel Seth following me at a close distance. I caught Phillip's stare from across the room, and it wasn't hard to make out the grimace on his face. Ignoring the look, I walked into the back room.

"Scotch the way I like it," Seth responded as he sat at the table.

My heart pounded as I headed back toward the bar. I wasn't sure how Seth liked his scotch. Did he want it neat or on the rocks? Sweat began sliding down my back, and I focused on keeping hold of my transfiguration. My knees wobbled when I stopped at the bar, and the bartender looked at me. I was debating on which option to choose when the bartender spoke.

"Scotch on the rocks for Mr. O'Doherty?" he asked.

I was too relieved to do anything besides nod my head. I hoped Mary wouldn't be expected to know every member of the W.A.S.P.'s regular drinks. As I took the scotch back to the room, I noticed the front door open, and more members of the W.A.S.P. entered. They all filed into the room as I placed the scotch in front of Seth and began taking orders.

Thankfully, Mary had not been expected to know everyone's usual. Now that I was in the same room as the W.A.S.P., I took a better look at each of them. There was a man who appeared slightly younger than Seth. His expression looked eager to please, and he sat on the edge of his seat. He had short caramel-colored hair, cobalt blue eyes, and a freshly shaved face. Opposite him sat a surly-looking man who appeared to be in his late thirties. He had thick black eyebrows framing dark hooded eyes. His hooked nose was slightly crooked over the sneer of his mouth. This man glared at Seth, and I wondered if he was Lieutenant Marchberg.

I moved around the table, taking note of drinks before exiting the bar with my list. The bartender quickly filled a tray, and I returned as more men arrived.

"Hello, Marchberg, my good man. How have you been?" one of the newcomers asked the man with thick eyebrows, confirming my suspicions.

"I'm doing better, Captain Gordon, now that Major Doyle has returned," Marchberg replied.

I glanced at the man who addressed Marchberg. I remembered Captain Gordon was the man who had the notes regarding Pyske

Isle. He appeared to be in his late forties or early fifties and had a lean body with slicked-back salt-and-pepper hair. I could tell from his mannerisms that he seemed sure of himself, and I shuddered to think of how many pixies he had captured.

"It will be good to see Major Doyle again," was all he replied.

Marchberg's lip curled. "Yes, I'm sure Major Doyle will correct these farce meetings. I'll bet he actually has a plan."

Captain Gordon took a seat next to Marchberg and glanced across the table at the caramel-haired man. "What are you drinking, Davis?"

"Whiskey," grinned the young Davis as he held up his glass.

"Miss, I'll have the same," Gordon demanded in my direction, and I quickly took requests from the newly arriving members.

The room was filling up, and at least twenty men had taken a seat when I returned with another tray full of drinks. As I passed them out, a cheer erupted from the men as Drake Doyle entered the room. I stopped myself from flinching as I beheld the same dark smile and sharp eyes that followed me around the manor.

"Have you all missed me that much?" he commented, striding fully into the room. He swaggered to the head of the table.

"It's good to see you, Major Doyle," Davis stammered.

"Hasn't Captain O'Doherty done a good enough job in my absence?" Drake questioned.

No one responded as Seth glared around the room, but Marchberg did release a snort.

"Well, regardless of what you think, I put Captain O'Doherty in charge for a reason. I don't appreciate reports questioning my authority," Drake scowled.

Marchberg was smart enough not to respond.

"No matter. I've returned, and we have much to discuss. I've recently promoted a new Lieutenant, who will join us later this evening. We can begin, and I can fill him in when he arrives," Drake announced.

Drake made eye contact with me and motioned for me to come toward him. My heart almost stopped before I remembered I was disguised as Mary.

"Good evening. What can I get for you?" I asked Drake in Mary's sweet voice.

"Bring me a scotch, neat," he said, barely looking at me.

I was about to return to the bar when Seth grabbed my arm. He pulled me close, and I felt his hand graze my thigh through my dress. Not sure how Mary would react, I froze.

"Mary dear, how about another scotch on the rocks while you're at it?" Seth purred in my ear.

"Yes sir," I managed and was glad when he let me go.

I tried to remain steady as I made my way out of the room. I'd never observed Mary looking disturbed during a W.A.S.P. meeting, so I forced myself to act naturally. Before returning, I checked on the other patrons, taking longer at Phillip's table. I hurriedly filled him in on what I'd discovered so far, and he slipped me a heightened hearing charm so I could still hear the meeting when I wasn't in the room.

Drake Doyle was on the topic of Pyske Isle when I stopped for the drinks.

"I've sailed my ship to the exact location in the notes. I've followed every set of instructions exactly, and I've yet to discover an island," said a voice I was unfamiliar with.

"Are you sure? Those notes were very specific," Gordon said harshly.

"Are you questioning my sailing skills or my ability to read?" the man demanded.

"Maybe both," Gordon replied hotly.

"Gentlemen, that's enough," Drake's voice sounded. "Lieutenant Edison, you claim to have found nothing?"

"As you asked, I took my small boat and the instructions you gave me and sailed to the location. I followed each note, and before you ask, I know the constellations like the back of my hand. Don't assume that's why I failed. I'm telling you, no island appeared."

"The pixie filth was very detailed with what he gave me. How could you not find it?" Gordon hissed.

"I'm telling you the damn pixie lied. There is no island," Edison snarled, pounding his fist on the table.

The room fell silent when I entered. Some of the men eyed me suspiciously. I delivered the drinks, asked if anyone needed anything, and managed to escape Seth's clutches. As soon as I exited the room, their discussion began again. I figured they wouldn't discuss pixies in front of a civilian, but I already felt I had gotten more insight from having access to the room. I could observe the men and potentially get a glimpse of those notes if they'd brought them tonight.

"The pixie you received this information from, is he still around to be questioned again?" Drake asked.

"No, I informed Captain O'Doherty of his demise last month."

Drake huffed and then growled. "So you're telling me our only lead to this island is dead?"

"Unfortunately, sir, I killed the beast just to get this information," Gordon answered.

"So this pixie island was dangled in front of me, and now we have no way of knowing if it even exists?" Drake growled.

"Pyske Isle exists," Davis said, his voice barely audible.

"Excuse me?" Drake yelled. "If you have something to say, Lieutenant Davis, you better speak up!"

"Pyske Isle exists, sir. The family I captured claimed they've heard of it," Davis stuttered.

"I know I haven't had the time to question your prisoners myself, but have they shared news about the island?" Drake asked.

"No, sir, but I haven't asked them much. I assumed we had everything we needed from Captain Gordon's notes. Instead, I've been focusing on the McCalski heir. Miss Stevenson claims she doesn't know anything, but I could tell she was lying," Davis said.

I paused at the name. Stevenson was a common enough name, but a girl in my year had that sir name. I'd been so preoccupied with my classwork and extra lessons that I didn't know if Lacey was missing. Was it possible the W.A.S.P. had captured Lacey and her family, or was it just a coincidence?

My legs were shaking as I made my way to Phillip's table to report a few other things I observed. I didn't stay long and continued to listen as I stopped at the other tables.

"I hope you're a better judge of when someone is lying than Captain Gordon is," Drake was saying.

Some of the men in the room chuckled.

"I can tell she's lying. I'm sure of it, sir," Davis stammered.

"You really need to push harder to get the truth from her. This could be the closest we've come to finding the McCalski heir. Captain O'Doherty is an expert at extracting information. O'Doherty, you need to assist Lieutenant Davis with his investigation. You're our most skilled at procuring intelligence," Drake insisted.

"I'll do whatever you need of me," Seth purred, and I could hear the anticipation in his voice.

My stomach roiled, and I took deep breaths so I wouldn't lose my glamor. I didn't even want to imagine what the W.A.S.P. did to extract information.

"Good, I'll leave you two to work on that. While you're at it, see if anyone in the family knows anything about Pyske Isle. If the location is complicated to access, maybe the pixie Gordon questioned didn't share all the information. These are the best leads we've had in a while, and I don't want to jeopardize them. Do whatever it takes to sniff out the McCalski heir and the directions to Pyske Isle. There's no need to rush the questioning and kill any captives too soon. These pixies are too valuable to waste. Do not lose your control, O'Doherty," Drake exclaimed.

"I won't, Major Doyle. I promise to take my time. Then, we'll be sure the information is true. I'm a man who enjoys the hunt," Seth said wickedly.

The men in the room cheered, and I heard the clinking of glasses. The room went silent as the men drank deeply, and I headed to the bar when I heard someone call for more. Drake resumed speaking while I waited for the bartender to fill my tray.

"I'm happy with what you men have accomplished in my absence. I'm sure the General will be pleased when he receives my next report. Continue the good work! I expect the rest of you to continue recruiting. Now seems like a critical time for more men to join our cause. If Pyske Isle proves to be real, we'll need a strong force for our attack. I want everyone focused on training. If you've managed to add to your units, they need to be taught our methods. Those men have to be prepared for these pixies and their magic."

Some of the men mumbled in agreement.

"I will not stand for another mistake like Coillewood, and the General won't tolerate another mistake. I want these new boys in the best possible condition. To ensure you follow these instructions, I'll be checking up on each of you. Your progress will be reported to the General, and we all know how he feels about laziness and weakness," Drake continued.

Drake paused in his speech, and I entered the room with the beverages. The other men fell silent as I went around the table collecting empty glasses and replacing them with fresh ones. I made sure to maintain my distance from Seth. Drake Doyle checked his wristwatch, and even though I was still in the room, he resumed speaking.

"My new lieutenant should be here at any moment. Before he arrives, I'll tell you a bit about him. This young man was a big help to me when I was in Georgia. We ran into a bit of trouble while we were down there, and he really had my back. He's fearless and willing to follow every order I give. He's young to be promoted to lieutenant, which I'm sure upsets some of you older members, but he has the experience and is loyal. Those are the reasons I promoted him right away. Just trust my judgement when I tell you this young man will go far in this organization. In fact, I would even go so far as to say he was born to be one of our members." Footsteps sounded outside the room.

"Oh, speak of the devil! Here he is now! Gentlemen, I would like to introduce you to Lieutenant Draven."

My head snapped up at the last name, and it took everything in me not to lose my glamor as Preston walked into the room.

39

A GHOSTLY MESSAGE

MY HEAD FELT like it was going to explode because the blood in my veins was pumping so fast. Somehow, I'd escaped the *Dew Drop Inn* without losing my glamour. Thankfully, Phillip and I had managed to make the switch again without getting caught. Phillip cast several charms over Mary before she woke up so she wouldn't remember us. Everything we planned had worked out perfectly, but I still couldn't breathe.

It felt like the world was closing in around me. Preston was now a member of the W.A.S.P. My safety at the manor was slipping away. Did Preston even remember when I slammed all the doors? He couldn't have because I would probably have been captured by now. My only worry was Preston would share the details about his new club with his mother.

When we were far enough away from the *Dew Drop Inn*, Phillip finally spoke.

"Jane, are you alright?"

I nodded as I gazed into his green eyes, our transfigurations slipping away.

"Yes, I'll be okay," I replied.

"Do you know what this means?" Phillip asked.

"Drake recruited Preston, and now he knows about the pixie world or everything the W.A.S.P. thinks they know," I said.

"No, it means you shouldn't return to the manor. It's too dangerous now."

I stared at Phillip with wide eyes. "I can't just leave! We have so much to do. I need to find out when they're planning the attack," I protested.

"I can't let you risk your life. Doesn't Preston know you're different? I'm sure he'll make that connection now."

"No, I don't think he remembers. He was only two when I used my powers. I haven't done anything like that since, and Marie never mentions my 'abnormality,'" I said.

"It doesn't matter. They're closing in on you now. You're living with two W.A.S.P. members!" Phillip burst out.

"Neither have any idea about me. Drake said Preston helped him when they were in Georgia. They've been back from that trip for almost a month. Don't you think they would've captured me by now?"

"How long do you think this is going to last now that they've captured Miss Stevenson?"

I stared at him with a shocked expression. It took me a moment to catch my breath before responding.

"Are you telling me you know they captured Lacey?"

Phillip lowered his head. "Yes, I made the connection when you told me the family's name. Miss Stevenson wasn't in class. I didn't tell you when we were in there because I didn't want to lose focus."

"When did you realize Lacey was missing?" I asked.

"I didn't notice right away, and it isn't uncommon for families to take their children on holiday during the school year. I mentioned it to Dr. Tweedle a week ago, and he said he'd look into it. So I just connected the dots tonight," Phillip replied.

I felt like my lungs were constricting. The W.A.S.P. had

Lacey Stevenson. Not only was I worried for her, but she was someone who actually knew me. It wouldn't be long before they discovered who I was if she broke under their torture. Every logical voice in my head said I should do what Phillip suggested, but we'd come so far.

"Her capture is even more of a reason for me to stay. I have to find out where Davis is keeping them. If I knew, they could be rescued," I said after a moment.

"Jane," Phillip sighed. He shook his head. "Don't be so self-sacrificing."

"You don't understand, Phillip. This is all my fault. Lacey was captured because they were looking for me. So, I have to try and save her," I almost screamed.

"Jane, please. Even if we discover the location, we don't know if they can be saved. We don't know how long it will take to discover it or if you even will."

"I have to try," I responded firmly.

"If anything happened to you…" Phillip began, and then he paused to look into my eyes. "I can't lose you."

He pulled me to him and kissed me fiercely. I melted into him, and he held onto me as if he would lose me if he let go. I could feel all his emotions through his passionate kiss, but I knew I had to do what I thought was right.

"You're not going to lose me," I finally whispered as his lips left mine. "I have to go back there, Phillip. It's the right thing to do. Besides, you trained me well. You have nothing to worry about."

A defeated chuckle escaped his mouth. "Oh, Jane, I knew you would say something like that. As much as I'd like to stop you from going back there, I knew you would defy me anyway. You're a strong woman, and I can see you made up your mind," Phillip said with a shake of his head.

"I am afraid, but this is something only I can do," I replied.

"Just promise me you won't be foolish. Promise me you'll get yourself out of there before anything goes wrong. I know discovering the information is important, but not more important than your life."

I nodded, looking into his pained eyes. "I'll prepare myself to leave the manor if I have to."

"If you have anything you'd like to take, you can use a *vanishing charm* to send it to my family's house near the beach. I'll store it for you in case you need to leave the manor quickly," Phillip said.

"Thank you," I replied as we let go of each other.

Despite my convictions about returning to the manor, I felt a chill pass through my body. I couldn't help but feel like the world I knew was crashing down around me. With Preston joining the W.A.S.P., they had gained a psychopath who already enjoyed torturing innocent animals. Of course, it would be a trait Drake would value. If he could do such things to animals, what would he do to pixies?"

For the rest of the week, I tried to keep my mind on my lessons, but it was almost impossible. Phillip and I reported our findings to Dr. Tweedle and Mr. Barber, but I left out the fact that my stepbrother had joined the W.A.S.P. I already knew what Dr. Tweedle would say, and he probably wouldn't give me a choice about returning. It really didn't make much of a difference if Mr. Barber knew about Preston anyway.

The following weekend, I took Phillip's advice, and during the middle of the night, I went through the attic, picking out objects I wanted to keep. I used the *vanishing charm*, concentrating on the beach house. There wasn't much I wanted to keep, but I picked the chest with my mother and father's things, my mother's vanity box with her combs, and a few mementos from my childhood. My eyes scanned the space I had lived in for fifteen years. There was nothing that signified my existence except for the mattress on the floor. With a deep breath, I settled down and tried to get some sleep.

❧

Sunlight broke through the leaves of the trees as I walked through the woods. My feet easily glided through the underbrush, and I headed toward the break I saw in the trees. My heart began pounding, and I knew I'd been here before. When I reached the tree line, my breath hitched as I recognized the clearing. My eyes flashed to where I expected to see Robert, but his body wasn't there. The meadow looked peaceful, and I glanced around, anticipating the dark figure. When I didn't see anything sinister, I stepped into the sun. My skin instantly felt warm, and my body began to relax.

As I was about to let my guard down, I noticed movement across the meadow. Alert again, I watched a fawn enter the clearing, followed by the figure of a woman. She was so far away I couldn't make out her features. Feeling compelled, I took several steps toward her. When she noticed me, I saw her mouth curve up in a smile. Slowly, we both began walking toward each other. As we got closer, a slight chill worked its way down my body when I took in her appearance. It was almost like looking in the mirror except for a few subtle differences.

"Momma?" I asked when we were only a few feet away.

The woman smiled and nodded her head, but she didn't say anything. She had blonde hair, the same shade as mine, braided elegantly down her back, and her violet eyes sparkled in the sun.

"How are you here?" I asked. "I've longed to see you my whole life."

Her smile dropped for a moment. "I've been watching over you, my baby, but it's difficult to make contact with the living," she finally said.

"Where are we? What do you mean?" I asked.

"I've finally broken into your subconscious while you sleep. It takes so much energy to make contact, and I probably only have a few moments," my mother said, glancing nervously over her shoulder.

When she turned back to me, she had a worried expression. "I've been so proud of how you've grown. You've become a beautiful woman and such a talented pixie. I always knew you would be strong, but something terrible is on the horizon. I can sense it all the way from Spuera. The W.A.S.P. have grown stronger these last few years, and I fear for your safety."

"I'm afraid, too, but I must continue what I'm doing. The pixies could finally have the ability to stop the W.A.S.P. if I get enough information," I replied.

"I admire your courage, daughter. I had the same hopes when I worked with Waldrick the Great. I just want you to be careful, Jane. I can sense a great danger and am concerned for your life."

"I'll be okay, momma. I know what the dangers are," I insisted, but suddenly, she took a step toward me.

"No, you must listen. I'm coming to warn you," she said forcefully. "The future is not clear, even for those of us in the afterlife, but spirits are able to sense things even the most gifted seer can't see. That's why it takes so much energy to contact the living; fate has a way of playing itself out, and it doesn't like to be stopped. I get the sense that your well-being could be in jeopardy."

A clap of thunder interrupted my mother's words, and I noticed the sky darkening. A jagged bolt of lightning pierced the dark gray clouds, carrying a gust of cold wind. The hair on my arms and neck stood on end, and a bad feeling settled in the pit of my stomach. My mother started to reach for me, and I watched, horrified, as she began to disappear.

"No, come back. Don't leave me!" I cried, trying to grab her slowly dissolving body. My hands grasped at empty air, and in the blink of an eye, she was gone.

I sank to my knees as the storm began to rage around me. I felt a wetness on my cheeks, and I didn't know if it was rain or my tears. Another sound of thunder startled me, and I climbed to my feet.

Despite the darkness of the storm, my eyes were drawn to a darker shape across the meadow. A dread worse than the storm gripped me. It was the same figure I'd seen many times before. My mother said this was a dream, but I didn't know how to wake myself up.

Quicker than I anticipated, the cloaked figure came at me. Two gloved hands tried to grab me, but I swatted them away. I kicked at the figure, hoping to harm it enough to make my escape, but it managed to snare my foot. Painfully, my leg was tugged out from under me, and I fell to the ground. Before I could react, the figure was on top of me, their gloved hands at my throat. I struggled against his fingers, and as the lightning flashed, I almost got a glimpse of my attacker's face. I thought I'd seen the outline of a scar in the brief flare of light, but with the pressure on my windpipe, I could tell I was close to blacking out. I thrust my hips again in a last attempt to throw my attacker off, but my vision went black.

I awoke gasping for breath, my hands clutching at my throat. My body trembled as I sat on my mattress, trying to calm my racing heart. The dream felt so real, like the many others I had before. Except this time, I'd seen my mother. I shivered as I tried to recall every detail, but terror clouded my mind.

Shakily, I stood up and began pacing in an attempt to warm my chilled limbs and focus my mind. What did these reoccurring dreams mean? I thought it was because Robert wanted me to find his family. I hadn't dreamt of the meadow or the dark figure since I had discovered Robert's family were members of the W.A.S.P. Robert hadn't been a part of this dream. Why would I start having these nightmares again?

As I walked past the window that looked out into the woods, the hairs on my arm began to rise. I thought I'd seen a movement along the tree line. I blinked and moved closer to the glass. My eyes swept back and forth, searching for the figure that haunted my dreams. Was something lurking out there, or was it all my imagination?

40

UNDERCOVER ERROR

S ETH'S EYES FOLLOWED me around the table as I placed the drinks in front of the other W.A.S.P. members. I was disguised as Mary again. Phillip and I had come to the April W.A.S.P. meeting. I'd been trying to find information for the past month on what the W.A.S.P. was planning. Every weekend, I searched through Drake's room and the office, hoping to find anything that would let me know where they were keeping the Stevenson family.

I'd discovered several letters between Seth and Drake, but none mentioned Lieutenant Davis's captives. I feared Lacey might already be dead or that she would reveal my identity. However, at the end of each weekend, I safely returned to the Jelf Academy. Nevertheless, I considered myself a failure and knew I was running out of time. I needed to find out something tonight.

"Good evening, men," Drake Doyle said, entering the room, Preston on his coattails. "Oh, and lady," he added, inclining his head to me.

The members murmured their greeting, and Drake took his place at the head of the table.

Preston snapped his fingers in my direction. "Get me a brandy and soda," he demanded.

I rushed to the bar to retrieve Preston's order and Drake's scotch, not wanting to miss the discussion. I caught Phillip's eye as I waited for the drinks. He was disguised as a young man with light brown hair and bluish-gray eyes. This time, he was seated at the bar, so I wouldn't have to go to a table to pass information. Phillip gave me a comforting wink while I loaded the drinks onto my tray, and I smiled before heading back.

"We received some updated information on Pyske Isle," Lieutenant Davis was saying when I entered the room.

When he stopped speaking, Drake urged him to continue. "Out with the information. I've been waiting for this report and refuse to wait any longer. Mary has been serving our meetings for over a year, and I doubt she cares about our business. You have no desire to be concerned with our manly discussion, right, Miss Mary? You probably don't even listen to what we're saying."

It took me a moment to realize Drake was talking to me.

"I'm sorry, sir. I didn't realize you were speaking to me," I answered, pitching my voice higher. "My only job is making sure you have your food and drinks. Your business is not a concern of mine. Again, I apologize for interrupting."

"No, Mary, you're fine. See Davis, Miss Mary isn't even paying attention. So please continue," Drake insisted.

I tried to keep a bored expression as I continued around the table.

"Apparently, Pyske Isle is going to be harder to access than we originally thought, but it's not impossible. Most of Captain Gordon's notes were correct, and the longitude and latitude were spot on. However, the island is obviously hidden, and a few revealing steps were omitted," Davis continued.

I could tell he was reluctant to speak of magic in my presence, so I collected the empty glasses and stepped out.

"I knew that filthy pixie lied!" Lieutenant Edison cried. "I wasn't able to find that damn island, and I was following the instructions to the letter."

"Supposedly, you have to wait until a certain time of night. The moon has to be at a certain position and phase. The tide also has to be low enough to expose a rock formation. This is how the island can be accessed," Davis continued. "I've just managed to extract this information."

I could hear grumbling around the room, and the snooty voice of Marchberg rose above the din.

"How can you be sure these animals are telling the truth now? They could be withholding information just like the last one."

"I can vouch for what Davis is saying. I helped with the extraction of the information," Seth answered.

"Your reputation is renowned when it comes to the torture of our enemies, Mr. O'Doherty, but why should we believe you are successful one hundred percent of the time?" Marchberg questioned.

"Because pixies are animals, and they have a soft spot for their young. We were able to extort this information when we threatened to harm their two youngest children. Both were under the age of ten, and the parents were willing to do anything to spare them," Seth said evilly, and my stomach roiled.

It took everything I had to re-enter the room, and I fought to keep the tray steady.

"Davis, I want you to look into the moon phase and the specific time. If this information is correct, we can choose a date soon. We have enough men to participate; they're anxious to see action. Keep pressuring your honored guests for the information we need," Drake said, drumming his knuckles on the table.

"Yes, sir, I will triple-check this new report," Davis said eagerly.

"O'Doherty, how is it coming with the eldest daughter?" Drake asked.

Seth's expression turned grim. "I've been working on her. It seems she's not as fragile as her name suggests. You would think lace would be easier to break."

Suddenly, a loud crash echoed in the room, and I realized with horror that the glasses had spilled from my tray and shattered on the floor. I struggled to maintain my glamour as I bent down to collect the more significant shards.

"I'm so sorry. I didn't mean…" I stuttered. I managed to get my focus under control, but my mind was still reeling. Hearing the comment about Lacey's name made the situation more intense. I thought I was going to be sick.

"Just a bit of glass," Drake was saying. "Get the broom and clean it up. No harm done."

I nodded slowly and left the room to search for cleaning supplies. I could've sworn I saw a closet by the bathrooms when I slipped in the back door. Hurriedly, I walked in that direction. I could feel Phillip's eyes on me, but I refused to meet his gaze.

The mops and brooms were in the closet, and I pulled out the largest one. I closed my eyes and took a minute to steady my breathing. There was no question now that the W.A.S.P. had Lacey, and the gods only knew what Seth was doing to her. I had to get back to the room, even though I felt like I was going to vomit. The best thing I could do for Lacey would be to find out where the W.A.S.P. was keeping her.

I'd just built up enough resolve to return to the meeting when I felt a hand brush my shoulder. I opened my eyes, expecting to see Phillip, but Seth stood before me instead.

"Sweetheart, are you feeling okay today? You don't seem like yourself," Seth said, his hazel eyes pinning me to the floor.

"Yes, I'm fine," I responded, though my heart felt like it was coming out of my chest.

"If you're upset about that girl, she doesn't mean anything to me. You have to know you're one of my special girls," Seth went on, coming closer.

I took a slight step away. My back was soon pinned against the wall, and I had nothing besides the broomstick between us.

He thinks you're Mary, my brain rationalized, but I wanted to jump out of my skin. I had to play this right, or my cover would be blown. I wasn't aware of Mary's relationship with him, but apparently, he thought so.

"Of course, I know that." I tried not to stammer.

Seth placed both hands on the wall, one on each side of my head, making me feel even more trapped. His hazel eyes bored into mine, and I told myself not to look away.

"Good, I'm glad. I wouldn't like it if you were jealous," he answered, his hot breath brushing my face.

I had a sense of what he was going to do before his lips covered mine, and I fought down my revulsion. Mary probably wouldn't push him away, and as much as I wanted to gag, I had to maintain my disguise. His lips lingered on mine, and I tried to pretend that Seth wasn't the one kissing me.

Thankfully, the kiss didn't last long, and I was relieved when he pulled away. I didn't want to look at him, but I forced my eyes back to his face. Seth's wicked grin curled around the edges of his mouth, and as he opened that mouth to say something, the sound of someone clearing their throat caught his attention.

"Excuse me, Miss, but is this gentleman bothering you?"

Phillip stood at the end of the hallway, and his eyes glowed like a fire behind them. I could feel my face growing red, and I wondered if he'd seen Seth kiss me.

"The lady and I were just talking," Seth growled. "I don't see how it is any of your business."

"Pardon me, but I was asking the lady," Phillip replied. "If you want to have a talk, you should probably do it somewhere respectable instead of down a dark hallway. You wouldn't want to ruin the lady's reputation, now, would you?"

"You need to mind your damn business," Seth snarled as he backed away from me and stepped toward Phillip.

"I'm fine. We were just talking," I finally managed, and Seth smirked. "I do need to clean up the mess I caused," I added, gripping the broom and side-stepping around Seth. I held Phillip's gaze as I walked toward him, hoping he would understand I was okay now.

Quickly, I returned to the meeting room and began cleaning up the broken glass. I didn't make eye contact with anyone and tried to act naturally when Seth returned to the room.

"My apologies, gentleman. What was I saying?" Seth asked as he took his seat.

"You were telling us about Miss Stevenson," Drake reminded him.

"Yes. Miss Stevenson is very elusive, but I can tell she knows the McCalski girl. She's fighting my persuasive techniques very valiantly."

I brushed up the rest of the broken glass and hurried to the door, unsure if I wanted to be in the room for this discussion.

Seth's rough voice stopped me. "Mary dear, why don't you bring me a cup of coffee? I'd like to keep my head together tonight," he said with a wink.

"Of course," I replied quickly and hurried from the room.

Phillip stared at me intently as I headed toward the bar. He was on the edge of his seat when I came around to address him.

"Can I get you anything else?" I asked, keeping up the façade.

"What happened?" Phillip urgently whispered.

"Nothing. I'm fine," I replied, brushing him off.

"Jane," he said so low I wouldn't have been able to hear him without the *heightened hearing charm.*

"They definitely have Lacey and her family. I was hoping they were away, but Seth just confirmed it," I replied.

"I know. I've been listening. I'm talking about what happened in the hallway," Phillip insisted.

I didn't want to talk about it. If I talked about it, I would have to accept that it had happened.

I shook my head. "I'm fine," I repeated. "Can we talk later? I appreciate your concern, but I have to make coffee now."

Phillip stared at me for a few moments but then nodded his head. I disappeared into the kitchen. The chef didn't pay me any mind, which was fine with me. I didn't need another opportunity to bring suspicion to Mary. While I waited, I tried to compose myself. I needed to discover what I could and get out of this meeting alive.

My hands shook slightly as I poured the coffee into a cup and prepared it the way Seth liked. Hopefully, this coffee would be the last personal interaction I had with him this evening. I prayed the real Mary would return to her place before Seth tried anything else.

Feigning confidence, I entered the meeting room with the coffee and placed it in front of Seth.

"Here's your coffee, sir. One-fourth cup of cream and three teaspoons of sugar, just as you like," I told him.

Seth gave me a quizzical expression, but he didn't respond as he picked up the cup. When no one else demanded a refill, I left the room and took care of a few tables. I continued to listen, holding my breath as Seth explained his questioning of Lacey.

"I can tell she's close to cracking. If I could have your permission to use a tougher form or questioning…."

"No," Drake said, cutting Seth off. "Don't do anything that could permanently harm the girl. We need to check the information her parents gave us. They might not be so willing to share if something life-threatening happened to their eldest daughter. What we want is almost in our grasp. I don't want anything to jeopardize this. If the family can lead us to a pixie-inhabited island and the McCalski heir, I would like to keep them alive a little longer."

"As you wish, Major," Seth responded, but he sounded disappointed.

"When do I get to be involved in the questioning?" said a voice that sent a chill through me.

"Be patient, Lieutenant Draven. You'll have your chance soon enough," Drake said with a chuckle. "See how eager my protege is! He can't wait to get his hands on a disgusting pixie."

"Perhaps when Captain O'Doherty and I are done with the Stevenson family, you may have a turn. I wasn't much older than you when I got my first. Everyone has to learn sometime," Lieutenant Davis suggested.

Another wave of nausea hit me, and I had to take a deep breath. I could almost picture Preston's twisted expression. Many times, I'd seen the result of his delight in torture. How many animals did I discover over the years? Now, he wanted to get his hands on a person. It always blew my mind how the W.A.S.P. talked about hunting and torturing as if it were a game.

Drake must have agreed to Lieutenant Davis's proposition for Preston because Preston spoke again.

"I would be delighted to be included. Drake, I'm sorry, Major Doyle has told me so much. I can't wait to witness it for myself."

I could feel bile rising in my throat, and I paced around the tables, trying not to let my illness overtake me. I didn't want to go back into the room, but I hadn't heard anything new. How would I be able to find out where Seth and Davis were keeping the Stevenson family? Would I be able to seduce Seth into telling me? Just as I contemplated how to do that, Phillip grabbed my hand and pulled me behind the bar. He crouched, pulling me with him.

"What are you…" I began, but Phillip raised a finger to his lips.

I was confused until I heard the real Mary's sing-song voice. "I feel so foggy tonight," she said.

Panic and fear raced through my veins. What was I supposed to do now? Phillip met my eyes, and I could see the same fear reflected. I couldn't very well keep my glamour, and I could hardly become myself again. Also, performing a transfiguration charm behind the bar was entirely too risky.

My heartbeat increased when I heard one of the chefs tell Mary that Mr. Doyle's meeting could probably use another round of drinks. I needed to make a decision now.

"I'm going to drop my glamour and run to the bathroom. Hopefully, anyone who knows me won't notice as I pass by the door. I'll see you at the carriage," I whispered to Phillip.

He began to shake his head, but before he could object, my glamour faded. I quickly sprung to my feet and hurried toward the hallway. As I passed the meeting room, I raised a hand to block my face and quickened my pace. I held my breath, expecting to hear a commotion from the room, but the *Dew Drop Inn* remained relatively silent. Darting down the hallway, I exited out the back door to the alleyway.

Finally, I allowed myself to breathe. Doubling over, I placed my hands on my knees and gasped for air. How had Mary woken up so soon? The *sleeping draught* should have lasted longer. I could only imagine what would have happened if I'd been in the meeting room when she came in.

My adrenaline was still pumping as I hurried to the parked carriage across the street. I huddled inside, waiting for Phillip. I hoped he would come soon. Everything had gone wrong at this meeting, and I prayed no one noticed. Would Mary remember what had happened to her?

As panicked thoughts raced through my head, I finally saw Phillip's disguised form leaving the inn. When he wasn't followed, I allowed myself to breathe a sigh of relief. I waved from the window, and he climbed into the driver's seat. Quickly, he snapped the horse into motion. When we reached the edge of town, he steered the carriage off the path and pulled the horse to a stop. I threw myself from the carriage and into his arms.

"I don't know what happened," I sobbed. "The *sleeping draught* I gave her should have lasted much longer."

"It's okay," Phillip said in a soothing voice as he patted my hair. "We're safe now."

"What if she remembers? What if someone realizes she wasn't there the entire time?" I cried; my emotions felt heightened from the adrenaline still coursing through my body.

"I managed to slip her a *confusion charm,* so she shouldn't remember us," Phillip said, running his fingers through my hair.

We stood silently, holding each other while I tried to rein in my emotions. I was comforted by Philip's touch and grateful we were both alive.

"That was a close call tonight, Jane," Phillip murmured, echoing my thoughts.

I shuttered as I recalled Seth's breath on my face, his lips on mine. Becoming Mary had turned out to be more dangerous than I initially thought, and I prayed I had done enough to go unnoticed.

41

INTO THE WOODS

ANXIETY CLAWED MY chest because I knew I was running out of time. Lacey's life and mine were on the line, and I needed to find out where they were keeping her. I cocked my ear toward the door and listened for movement. When I heard nothing, I continued to rifle through papers in the desk drawer. Drake had to have some kind of correspondence about the new captives.

Drake and Preston were out for a ride, Marie was out to tea at an acquaintance's house, and Emily was confined to her bed. With her ninth month approaching, her doctor demanded bed rest. Her belly was enormous; she was having difficulty getting around as it was. Emily was more irritable than ever, but at least she couldn't leave her room to check on me.

After the disaster at the last W.A.S.P. meeting, I agreed I would no longer disguise myself as Mary. It was too risky, and I'd already taken a detailed account of names and appearances. We could still hear with the *heightened hearing charm*, so I agreed to Phillip's ultimatum. The May meeting at the end of the month could possibly be our last opportunity to spy. With my upcoming finals and the summer months, I wasn't sure if we could continue to attend. I could if I left the manor for good, but I wasn't ready to make that decision. I needed to find something in Drake's papers today.

Carefully, I went through the letters. I remembered Seth had helped Davis capture the Stevenson family, but he was keeping them. Would he hold them at his home address or another location? I needed to find his address so somebody in Mr. Barber's division could investigate.

I glanced through letter after letter, searching for anything that might be important. Most of the letters pertained to events I already knew about. Every once in a while, I would pause to read more, but I didn't come across anything new or important.

Just when I'd almost gone through the whole stack in front of me, I heard Ellen calling my name. I hurried to replace the papers just as Ellen walked into the office.

"Jane, what are you doing? Mrs. Emily has been ringing her bell."

"I was just straightening up the office," I answered, and Ellen raised her eyebrow. "I'll head up to attend to Emily right away."

I tried to keep the guilty expression off my face as I glided past Ellen. From the hallway, I could hear Emily hollering and repeatedly ringing the little brass bell Drake had purchased for her. Swallowing the lump in my throat, I pushed her bedroom door open.

"Finally! What took you so long?" Emily pouted, slamming down the bell on the bedside table.

"Your mother does demand other things from me besides waiting on you," I answered.

Emily's nightgown was pulled tightly over the bulge of her stomach, and sweat glistened on her forehead. Her ankles were incredibly swollen, and she hardly resembled the petit girl she'd been before the pregnancy. Dark circles stood out below her eyes since her skin was so pale, and it looked like she was having trouble sleeping. Her gray eyes glared at me.

"My mother should've stressed that my needs are more important than all others! I shouldn't have to call so many times. Do you want me to lose my voice?" Emily shrieked.

I decided it was best not to answer, so instead, I asked a question of my own.

"What do you need, Emily?"

"I'm hot and swollen, so bring me ice, and I'd also like something refreshing to drink after you made me yell like that. Don't think my mother won't hear about it."

Without another word, I left Emily's bedroom and headed to the kitchen to collect her requests. I wrapped ice in a towel for Emily's ankles and poured a cold lemonade before returning to her room. Emily sighed with relief while I situated the ice, and she sipped the drink.

"I just want this baby out," she moaned, leaning back against her pillow. "I hate being trapped in this room."

"The baby will be here soon," I commented.

"Not soon enough. I've hated everything about this pregnancy. I've been sick and tired. My body is bloated like a balloon. Since this confinement, I've been so alone. Where is everyone?" she whined.

"Your mother was invited to tea, and Preston is with Mr. Doyle riding," I answered as she motioned for me to prop up her pillows.

"Out riding again!" Emily sighed. "Probably on their way to visit Mr. O'Doherty again."

"Mr. O'Doherty?" I asked, my breath hitching.

"Yes, his property isn't far. It's only through the woods. Drake and Preston have been spending most of their time with him lately," Emily groaned.

She was quiet for a moment. Then suddenly, she pierced me with her flinty eyes.

"Why do you suddenly seem so interested in Mr. O'Doherty?"

"I'm not," I replied quickly, but Emily started to laugh.

"Do you honestly think a man like Seth O'Doherty would be

interested in you?" Emily cackled. "Is that a fantasy of yours? Do you think he'll come and rescue you from being our servant for the rest of your life?"

"No," I said, but Emily kept laughing.

"Mr. O'Doherty was a potential suitor of mine, but Mother didn't think he had enough money. His estate isn't extensive, and I don't believe he's the marrying kind. Perhaps he would take you on as a mistress. I've heard he has lots of those."

I turned away from her and began heading toward the door. Emily continued to laugh.

"Are you jealous, Jane? I'm surprised. I thought you were still pinning away over that horse boy. What was his name again?" Emily sneered.

Her words caused me to stop in my tracks. Robert and I had kept our relationship a secret. How did Emily know? I refused to give her the satisfaction of knowing that talking about him still hurt me.

"I don't know who you're talking about," I replied, leaving the room.

Emily's chuckles followed me into the hallway, and I continued to ignore her. As much as I hated her, she unknowingly gave me a piece of valuable information. I was one step closer to finding the Stevenson family. I knew I had to find out tonight.

Night fell faster than I anticipated. Drake and Preston had returned in a jovial mood. Had they visited Seth and helped him torture the Stevensons? My stomach felt sick as I assisted Ellen with dinner. I was grateful no one demanded anything extra, and the family retreated to their rooms after dinner.

My hands shook as I climbed the stairs to the attic. I wasn't sure if I'd find anything even if I did make it to the O'Doherty property, but I wanted to be prepared. I made sure Phillip's Christmas present was fastened to my ankle and tucked into my boot. Securing my hair in a tight bun atop my head, I took a deep breath and crept back down the stairs.

The night was dark, but I could see in the faint light of the crescent moon. When I reached the tree line, I turned to take another look at the manor. It was strange to consider it a safe place at this moment. Mentally, I built up my courage and entered the trees. If Lacey was trapped at Seth O'Doherty's, I needed to do something.

The woods were darker because of the foliage, and I regretted not bringing a light. However, I had the comforting knowledge of being in this forest many times before. Carefully, I made my way along, watching my footing so I wouldn't fall. When I reached the lake, I stopped to catch my breath. I hadn't gone much further than the lake before, so I really had to pay attention to the path. I glanced at the stars to check my direction and continued toward my destination.

The cool night air chilled my skin, and I pulled my sweater tightly around me. I didn't have much of a plan for when I reached the house. I was hoping I would see some evidence through a window. I prayed entering would be easy if I had to. My palm patted my dress pocket, making sure my pixie dust case was still inside. I could always use a *transfiguration charm* to disguise myself.

As I walked, I began getting a strange sense of déjà vu. The woods looked familiar, but I knew I'd never been this far. My mind didn't connect all the dots until I broke through the trees into a meadow. I blinked rapidly and stared across the field. My pulse pounded hard, and blood rushed to my head. It was the meadow from my dream, but I knew I wasn't dreaming.

I paused beside a large oak tree, unsure of what to do. Should I return to the manor or keep moving forward? I remembered my mother's warning, and even though it had been a dream, I knew it was a premonition. Deciding to turn around, I took a few steps back the way I'd come, but a deep voice to my right made my breath hitch.

It's a little late for a walk, isn't it?" Seth asked, stepping out from behind a tree.

A fear I'd never known flooded my body, and I wasn't sure what to do. Should I run or attack? Both would seem suspicious. Perhaps I could talk myself out of this.

"I just needed some fresh air," I replied, trying so hard not to let my voice shake.

"It's a strange time to get air, especially so far from the house," Seth commented, his scar glinting in the dim light.

"I didn't realize how far I'd come. If you'll excuse me, sir. I should be on my way."

"Oh, Jane, you must know I can't let you do that," he said with a wicked grin.

Dread settled in my stomach, but I kept a confused expression. "I don't understand," I said.

Seth chuckled and took a step closer. "You've been playing a very convincing game, but I won't be fooled any longer."

"I don't know what you are talking about," I replied, deciding to play stupid. What did Seth think he knew?

"I know what you are. Of course, it took me a moment to put it all together. You were at the *Dew Drop Inn*. You're a filthy pixie, and somehow, you used your evil ways to look like Mary," Seth growled.

I couldn't think of anything to say. I just gaped at him, wondering how he could know.

"Speechless? At first, I wasn't sure, but I knew Mary wasn't acting like herself. You see, Mary has never once dropped a tray before. I thought maybe my talking about another woman had made her jealous, but I was certain when I kissed her, or you as it were. Though your lips were sweet, Mary has never hesitated to kiss me back.

"I could sense something was wrong, which is why I ordered the coffee on a hunch. You see, I've never ordered coffee at the *Dew*

Drop Inn. I rarely drink the stuff, so I was very suspicious when you brought back the cup prepared just the way I like it. There was also a brief moment when I could've sworn someone who looked like you rushed past the door, but I thought my mind was imagining it," Seth grinned.

I shook my head, bewildered.

"Don't try to deny it. I know it was you. I know that none of my staff members are disgusting animals, and I remembered it wasn't long ago that I had coffee with Major Doyle. If I wasn't convinced before, your friend Lacey confirmed my suspicions. When she told me the McCalski heir went by the last name of Fitzgerald, I thought it was too much of a coincidence that Drake's mother-in-law went by that last name."

"What did you do to Lacey?" I asked angrily.

"I must admit, that girl was hard to break," Seth laughed. "She was stronger than I anticipated and almost didn't give me what I needed to know. She was relatively loyal to you until the end, but nevertheless, she gave me your name. Don't worry. I put her out of her misery for her efforts."

I felt tears spring to my eyes. Lacey was dead. I'd failed to save her. Seth continued speaking.

"Her family probably won't cooperate now, and I'm sure Drake won't be pleased, but when I deliver the McCalski heir's body, I'm sure he won't be too hard on me."

He began stalking toward me, and his last words registered. Suddenly, he lunged at me, and I dodged his attack. I managed to land a kick to his knee, causing him to fall, but he just chuckled.

"Think you can fight me?" he asked as he started to rise to his feet.

Before he was fully standing, I connected a blow to his head combined with magic. He flew sideways, and I ran. Pumping my legs as fast as possible, I dodged branches and tree trunks. I needed to find somewhere to hide so I could use a *calling charm* to contact

Phillip. I hadn't practiced the *teleportation charm* on my own yet, so I couldn't disappear without help. Trying not to let panic take over, I kept moving. I could hear footsteps behind me, but I didn't look.

Suddenly, a large form collided, and I connected hard with the ground. I struggled, but Seth was too strong. He clawed his way up my body until he straddled my hips. I beat him with my fists, but none of the blows distracted him. Seth grabbed my hands and slammed them into the ground. Pain exploded in my wrists from his tight grasp.

"I forgot how I enjoy the thrill of the hunt and capture," Seth sneered.

I wriggled beneath him, trying to break his grasp, but he just laughed.

"Don't worry. We're going to have some fun," Seth whispered, pinning both my hands with his one. His fingers trailed down my body, and I froze when I felt his hand pulling up my skirt. I tried to force my body to remain calm despite every nerve being on edge.

"What did you have in mind?" I asked, trying to sound seductive.

Seth paused, and a wicked smile spread across his mouth.

"Oh, I think you can guess. I've tasted your lips, and I'm wondering if anything else is as sweet."

"Kiss me again," I breathed.

Seth leaned forward and brought his lips to mine, but in doing so, his body became unbalanced. I thrust up with my hips, throwing the unsuspecting Seth off me. I quickly climbed to my feet and aimed a kick at his jaw. Faster than I could've imagined, he grabbed my foot and pulled me down. My head slammed into the ground, and stars crossed my vision.

"You bitch!" Seth growled, crawling over me again.

This time, his hands went straight for my throat. It was exactly like my dream, except this time, I knew I wouldn't wake up. My fingers scratched at his hands, but it didn't make a difference. He had such a tight grip on my neck, and I knew I didn't have much time. Spots popped in front of my eyes, and I knew it would be a matter of time before I lost consciousness. Seth was going to kill me.

All of a sudden, I remembered the knife tucked into my boot. I tried to reach it, but it was too far away. Closing my eyes, I stretched my fingers as far as I could. Using my last bit of strength, I imagined the dagger flying up to my fingers. Within seconds, my hand closed around the cold, metal hilt.

I didn't hesitate as I brought the dagger up and stabbed Seth repeatedly. He gasped in surprise, his grip loosening on my neck. Warm blood gushed over my hand and onto my body, but I kept stabbing. I didn't stop until he went limp. Finally, I shoved him off.

My throat burned as I crawled away from him and gasped for air. When I got a few feet away, I stopped and wrapped my arms around my knees. My entire body was shaking, and sobs rose in my bruised windpipe. My eyes didn't leave Seth for the longest time, but he didn't move. My dagger was still embedded in his neck, and I knew I'd killed him. My nerves buzzed with anxiety, adrenaline, and fear. I couldn't stop shaking.

I sat stunned for the longest time before realizing I was covered with dirt and blood. Shakily, I got to my feet and cautiously approached Seth, even though I knew he was dead. Quickly, I pulled my dagger out, and nausea overcame me. Turning away, I lost all the contents of my stomach. I retched until nothing else came up. Every muscle in my body hurt, and my throat was on fire.

What should I do? What should I do? My mind raced. Seth said Lacey was dead, but he mentioned her family. Did that mean they were at his home? I had to figure out a way to free them, but I had to handle my current situation. I was exhausted, but something had to be done about Seth's body. I needed assistance to rescue the Stevensons, and it wouldn't help if Drake or Preston came across Seth.

Using my magic, I began to move dirt. I managed to dig a

shallow grave, and with my last ounce of energy, I pushed Seth's body into it. His scar stood out in the moonlight, and I tried to keep my composure as I covered his body. Tears welled in my eyes. I felt so overwhelmed. I'd almost died, and I'd taken a life.

Once Seth was buried, I limped back toward the manor. When I reached the lake, I leapt into the water, eager to remove the grime from my skin. The water was cold, but I didn't care. It numbed my bruises and cleared my mind. I scrubbed my body and my clothes while I formed a plan. First, I needed rest. I was so tired, and it felt like I would collapse at any moment. Maybe I could sneak away to contact Phillip. How long would I have before Drake realized Seth was missing? How long would I have before I was discovered? After tonight, I decided Phillip was right. I needed to leave the manor.

Chills raced up my body as I climbed from the lake, but at least I felt alert enough to make it back. It was a relief to reach the lawn and leave the woods behind. I lumbered up the front steps and quietly snuck into the house. Without a sound, I made it up to the attic. I was in the middle of changing my clothes when the screams began.

42

WASP'S NEST

THE SOUND OF loud footsteps coming up the attic stairs made my heart jump. Marie burst into the attic, her hair askew. Her gray eyes scrutinized me as she stood in the doorway.

"Good, you're awake. Emily's going into labor. You need to get downstairs and be of assistance," Marie barked.

I stared at her in confusion. "What?" I asked, not sure if I had heard correctly.

"Don't ask questions, and go to Emily's room now. She's in labor, you stupid girl! Get moving!" Marie screamed at me.

In a daze, I followed her to Emily's bedroom. Emily's screams were horrendous. When I entered the room, I saw she was curled up in bed, her arms wrapped around her abdomen.

"Mother, it hurts," she cried when she saw Marie.

"It's called labor, Emily. Did you expect it to be easy?" Marie asked curtly. "Jane, bring me a chair so I can sit by my daughter's side."

I grabbed one from Emily's sitting room and pulled it next to the bed while Emily continued to scream.

"Where's the doctor?" she wailed.

"Your husband has gone to fetch him," Marie replied.

"Help me," Emily cried, rolling back and forth on the bed. Marie turned on me.

"Jane, get Emily some warm wet towels. You'll have to prepare her for the birth."

In my tired state, it didn't even cross my mind to object. I did as Marie instructed and washed Emily's stomach and thighs while she groaned and continued rolling back and forth on the bed.

"Jane, I'll need you to get a spare sheet. Tie it to Emily's bedpost. That way, she can grip it during the pain," Marie yelled at me after I'd finished cleaning Emily.

I could feel myself beginning to sway on my feet as I left the room. My mind felt foggy, and I tried to focus on my task. Emily's screams continued to rip through the house, putting my nerves on edge. I was so tired from my ordeal with Seth. I just wanted some rest.

When I returned to the room, Marie tried to help Emily focus on breathing. I took the sheet and tied it to the bedpost as Marie instructed. Once it was secured, Emily gripped it for dear life. Unsure of what to do next, I backed into a corner while Emily cried out over the next contraction. I was about to lean against the wall when Marie barked my name again.

"Jane, hurry up and grab some old towels. You need to place them under her so she doesn't mess up the bed. I thought you'd done that already!" Marie shrieked, and I hurried to the bathroom.

Searching in the back of the closet, I finally found a few frayed towels. I was on my back to the bedroom when I heard Emily hollering again.

"Why is everything so wet? What's happening to me?" Emily wailed.

"Your water just broke," Marie snapped. "Jane, you didn't retrieve the towels in time. Get out here and change the sheets!"

I allowed myself one moment before I jumped into action. Pulling the soiled sheets off with Emily still on the bed was difficult since she refused to be of any help.

"Everything feels worse now," Emily cried, grabbing her stomach again.

"It should. Once your water breaks, your contractions should become more powerful. That means the baby will be here soon," Marie commented.

Emily pulled on the bedpost again. Her face looked green. I moved to fix the pillow under her head before Marie could bark at me. Emily glared at me. Her hair was plastered to her head for how much she was sweating.

"Where is the doctor?" Emily bellowed.

Marie paced the room and went to the window. As if conjured, I could hear the sound of approaching hoof beats.

"It looks like Drake has returned. Hopefully, the doctor will be with him. I'll go down to greet them," Marie commented, leaving the room.

Emily screamed and pulled on the sheet again.

"Jane, help me," she managed to get out through clenched teeth.

"I don't know what I can do," I replied.

"You're a witch, aren't you? Do some magic and help me," Emily said, and panic gripped me.

"I'm not a witch," I hissed, hoping she would keep quiet.

"You have magic. I remember what you did to the doors all those years ago," Emily breathed.

"I didn't do anything. The pain is muddling your memory. You sound crazy," I cried, listening intently for footsteps.

"I'm not crazy. You have magic. Help me, and I won't tell my mother. Help me with the pain, and I'll never mention it again," Emily begged. "If you don't help me, I'll tell everyone what a freak you are."

I paused at her words. I wasn't as worried about Marie anymore, but would she tell her husband? Would she scream out my secret while racked with pain?

"I don't know what you mean, but let me get you a glass of water," I answered, heading toward the bathroom.

I grabbed the cup from the sink and filled it. My hands were shaking as I pulled my pixie dust case from my pocket. Quickly, I searched through it for the *pain-relieving charm*. It was a fifth-year charm Phillip had taught me in case I ever needed it. I hoped it would work on a human and Emily would forget her threat. I sprinkled the charm into the water and watched it dissolve before I returned to Emily's side.

"Here, let me help you drink the water," I said, holding out the glass.

Emily kept one hand on the bed sheet and used the other hand to guide the cup to her mouth. I held the glass steady as she gulped down the entire cup.

"Would you like more?" I asked.

Emily shook her head as she relaxed on the pillow. Suddenly, Marie stormed into the room, followed by the elder Mrs. Doyle.

"What is she doing here? Where's the doctor?" Emily whined, but I noticed she was no longer clutching the sheet.

"Drake told me my grandson was being born tonight, so I demanded to be here," Mrs. Doyle said, coming to the foot of Emily's bed.

"We won't know the sex of the baby until Emily has delivered," Marie sighed. "Dr. Bradley will get here as soon as he can. Apparently, he's assisting another woman at the moment."

Emily screamed in frustration this time. "He promised I was a top priority!" she howled.

"See, I knew we should have spoken with a midwife. We shouldn't have listened to you," Marie said to Mrs. Doyle.

"Dr. Bradley is one of the best physicians. Midwives are becoming a thing of the past. Doctors know best. I'm sure he'll be here soon. I can't help that you didn't go into labor sooner," Mrs. Doyle said with a sniff. "Somebody, bring me a chair."

I grabbed the other chair from the sitting room and put it on the other side of the bed. To Emily's dismay, Mrs. Doyle took a seat.

"Are you going to stay there?" Emily asked Mrs. Doyle rudely.

"Where else would I be? I've said I've come to see my grandson being born. You think you would be grateful to have another woman in the room who has given birth. If I were you, I'd pull my knees up higher. The baby isn't going to come out in that position," Mrs. Doyle said crudely.

Marie gave Mrs. Doyle a disgusted look but helped her daughter get into the suggested position.

"Emily, you're going to have to start pushing soon. When you feel the contraction come, you need to try. I don't think we can wait for the doctor," Marie commented, holding her daughter's hand.

Emily nodded, and though she didn't appear to be in pain anymore, she still looked uncomfortable. I wanted to flee the room, but Marie and Mrs. Doyle put me to work changing towels, getting Emily water, and applying a cool towel to Emily's forehead. Emily labored for hours, and still, the doctor did not arrive. Just when I thought I would collapse from exhaustion, Marie began to scream.

"Emily, keep going. The baby's almost here! I believe I can see the head."

A strangled cry escaped Emily's lips, and suddenly, Marie was scooping up a baby from the towels at the bottom of the bed. After a few moments, the baby erupted with loud wailing.

"What is it?" Mrs. Doyle asked, springing up from her chair.

"It's a boy!" Marie cried. "Jane, get me a bowl of water."

I hurried to get the water as Mrs. Doyle shouted with glee.

"I knew it would be a boy. The Doyle name will continue," Mrs. Doyle exclaimed.

Marie began cleaning the new baby boy when I returned with the water. He was crying so loudly, and Emily was getting irritated.

"Let me see my baby!" she screamed.

"One moment," Marie said. "Once I have cleaned him off, I'll let you see him. He's beautiful."

"I'm going to tell my son that he has a son," Mrs. Doyle announced, leaving the room.

Emily sighed in relief as Mrs. Doyle disappeared down the hallway.

"I thought she would never leave. I swear if she had demanded to hold my baby before I did, I would have strangled her," Emily said as Marie approached her with the baby.

"Here is your son," Marie said, handing the swaddled baby to Emily.

Emily smiled as she took him. She looked so tired, but she didn't seem to care. As I watched her look at her baby, I almost smiled. Maybe Emily would finally learn to love something. Then, suddenly, Emily's expression changed to one of concern.

"Mom, you missed a spot," Emily exclaimed, rubbing at the small red mark under the baby's left eye.

When she moved the towel away, the teardrop mark remained. Emily looked up from the baby, and her eyes locked on me. An awful feeling wormed its way into my stomach.

"What did you do?" Emily asked, her voice a low growl.

Marie glanced at her daughter aghast. "What do you mean? I haven't done anything besides help you with this delivery since that no-good doctor never showed up. Don't talk to me like that!" Marie responded.

"Not you, mother. Her," Emily said through gritted teeth, pointing at me.

"Jane?" Marie asked with a bewildered expression on her face.

"What did you do to my son?" Emily shrieked. "What did you give me?"

"I didn't do anything to your son," I said as I began backing toward the door.

"Did you give her something?" Marie demanded, taking a step toward me.

"I gave her water," I answered. "The red spot is a birthmark."

"Do you think this is funny? You took away my pain, but you cursed my son! You put this mark on his cheek. You marred his beautiful face with your evil."

"I didn't do anything to your baby," I repeated, continuing toward the door.

"What's going on? What did you do to my daughter?" Marie questioned.

"She's a witch! She used her magic on me! She placed a curse on my son! Witch! Witch!" Emily screamed at the top of her lungs. The baby's cries joined his mother's.

I didn't wait for Marie to react. Instead, I raced out of Emily's room and down the hallway. I needed to escape this house and get somewhere safe to call for help. Fear tore through me, and I almost fell down the stairs.

"Stop her!" Marie cried from the top of the staircase. "She is a witch, and she did something to my daughter and my grandson!"

I almost made it to the front door when Preston appeared. Mustering as much of my magic as possible, I sent my power in his direction and threw him across the entrance hall. With a cry, I grabbed the front door and pulled it open. My heart was in my throat when I heard heavy footfalls behind me, and I sprinted out the door.

Jumping a few steps off the front porch, I landed on the gravel driveway and just managed to keep my balance. My body felt so worn down, but I couldn't stop. Fear pushed me forward, and I raced down the driveway. The loud sound of gravel crunched under my feet, and I prayed I wouldn't slip. If I could make it to the woods, perhaps I could hide. Then I'd have enough time to use a charm. The trees didn't seem much further, and I let out a terrified cry as I ran toward them.

Suddenly, an excruciating pain exploded through my body. I crashed onto the ground, my limbs twitching as a current passed through me. I couldn't move and could barely think of anything besides the pain. I heard laughter in the distance and then the sound of heavier footsteps on the gravel. Just as I thought the pain was subsiding, I felt another jolt race through my body. I screamed, writhing as the pain shot through my limbs.

"I got her," Drake's voice panted while the pain continued.

The agony was too much, and I lost consciousness.

ᥬ

I awoke in a cold, damp place, barely able to see the hand in front of my face. It hurt to move, and I lay there panting with my cheek against the rocky floor. What had happened to me? I could barely remember. Closing my eyes, I tried to recall something, anything, but all that lingered was pain.

My body felt broken, and one of my cheeks felt like it had been scrapped raw. My skull felt like it was going to explode, and I didn't move off the cool, wet floor. Instead, I counted my breaths, each one reminding me that I was still alive.

After a few moments, I tried to move and discovered the heavy metal chains covering the floor. Thick metal bands wrapped around my ankles, and two smaller ones encircled my wrists. Besides the pain, Drake's laughter circled around in my head. Finally, my thoughts began to clear, and everything came rushing back to me.

Seth's attack in the woods, fighting back and ending his life, Emily going into labor, the baby boy born with a birthmark on his cheek, Emily accusing me of being a witch, and my failed escape. Drake had captured me, and now I was being kept wherever he imprisoned pixies. Before I could begin to wonder what would happen to me, a bright light rounded the corner.

The light burned my eyes, sending a sharp pain to my brain, and it took me a minute to adjust. I could now see the bars of a cage in front of me. The place looked like a basement. Drake and Preston stood before me, both with evil looks on their faces.

"Good, she's awake," Drake sneered, setting down the lantern. "I didn't think she'd come to so quickly."

I glared back at them while I tried to sit up. Preston laughed at my attempt. His face was bruised on the left side, probably from being tossed across the room. He stopped laughing when he saw me examining his face.

"You're going to pay for that little stunt you pulled while trying to escape," Preston sneered.

"What are you going to do? Kill me?" I spat, refusing to show any fear.

"Eventually," Drake said. "but don't worry. We're going to have so much fun first."

Preston laughed again. "My mother always called you a freak, and now I know why."

"I can't believe you've been under my nose this entire time. What a coincidence. I've had the McCalski heir in my back pocket for years," Drake said.

"I wouldn't brag that it took you years to figure it out," I commented as they scowled at me.

"Watch your mouth when talking to Major Doyle," Preston spat. He stuck a long-handled weapon through the bars and touched me with it.

Electricity coursed through my body, and I felt pain all over. I writhed around on the floor as my nerves turned to jelly. Stars exploded behind my eyes. I yelled in agony, wanting it all to stop.

Finally, Drake spoke. "That's enough, Preston. We want her to be conscious when our guest arrives." A bell chimed somewhere in the distance, and he smiled. "It looks like he has arrived."

The light dimmed as I quivered on the floor of my cell. What was Drake talking about? Electricity had all my nerves jumping, and it was hard to focus on what he meant. Laying in the dark,

I waited for the twitching to stop and tried not to imagine what they had planned for me.

Sooner than I expected, the lantern returned, revealing Drake, but he was not alone. When the second man stepped from the shadows, my heart stopped beating. Mr. Lyons, Robert's father, stared down at me. His brown eyes looked so much like Robert's, except they had an evil glint.

"Jane, this is General Lyons, the head of the American North East W.A.S.P. division. He has waited a long time to meet you," Drake announced.

Mr. Lyon's smirked. "I believe we've already met. Haven't we Miss? What name are you going by today-Withermyer-McCalski-Fitzgerald? You're lucky I didn't realize the McCalski heir paid me a visit all those months ago. By the time I knew you and your companion were pixies, you had already eluded me. I should've realized you looked familiar."

Thankfully, I was able to gain more control of my body, and I propped myself up, meeting his cold stare. Gathering my courage, I managed to spit through the bars, my saliva landing on his shoe.

Mr. Lyons scowled down at me, then laughed as he flicked his foot.

"Don't you worry… You'll be singing a different tune soon. I can't understand how I didn't notice the amazing similarities when we previously met. You look exactly like your mother did right before I killed her. Let's see if you can last longer than she did," Mr. Lyons growled, coming closer. I tried to keep my brave expression as his body blocked the light.

ACKNOWLEDGEMENTS

Thank you to all the readers who've supported the Jelf Academy Series and been fans of the books. This series has been such a big part of my life, and it touches my heart to hear that some people have been dying for this book to come out. Nothing can describe that feeling because it still feels so unreal! Are there really readers out there who want the continuation of my story? So, thank you again because, without you, the dream of being an author wouldn't be a reality.

I give a humongous thanks to God because, through you, all things are truly possible. I am so blessed by the wonderful and supportive family you gave me and the handful of friends who are as close as family.

As always, thank you to my supportive parents! You both have been in my corner from the beginning, and I know how proud you are! None of my dreams would've been possible without your loving encouragement. Everything I am, I owe to both of you.

Thank you to my other phenomenal family members who have supported this series, especially Aunt Val, who accompanies me on my crazy book-signing adventures. Spending the weekends with you has been my favorite time of the week, and I appreciate all the early mornings and long days. Without a doubt, I have the best godmother in the world!

I am also grateful for my best friend, Kayla (though at the risk of sounding cliché), who truly is my sister from another mister. You've always been there for me and have been cheering me on since we were twelve. I am blessed to have you in my life. You always know how to put a smile on my face and are always there for me at my lowest points. You always say I am the calm to your crazy, but I love the crazy fun whenever we do something together. Honesty, my life would be dull without you.

A round of applause for Damonza for another fantastic cover and internal formatting. I'm so glad I decided to work with you for my series. Every single cover is gorgeous and eye-catching! I've received so many compliments on my books due to you! Working with you again has been a pleasure, and I look forward to what you create for the cover of book five, *Unicorn Blessed*.

About the Author

Jenna E. Faas is the author of the *Jelf Academy Series*. She lives in Pittsburgh, Pennsylvania, with her husband, son, and two Australian shepherds. From the very first time Jenna turned the pages of a book, she was obsessed. As a young girl, she always made up stories, which she jotted down in school notebooks. An avid reader, she would get lost in fantasy and wish magic existed. Jenna began the concept of *The Jelf Academy Series* when she was seventeen and expanded her creation of the world through her college years. Her bachelor's degree in Geology helped inspire pixie magic since gemstones and minerals are the ingredients to create pixie charms.

When Jenna isn't writing or reading, she enjoys spending time with her family, working on arts and crafts, and singing her favorite songs. She is currently working on the final installment of the *Jelf Academy Series- Unicorn Blessed*.

Find Jenna on the web at *http://www.jennaefaasauthor-sparksandcinderspublishing.com*.

Printed in the USA
CPSIA information can be obtained
at www.ICGtesting.com
LVHW040159221124
797337LV00018B/55